# NO WAY BACK

Before turning to full-time writing, Andrew Gross was an executive in the sportswear business. Andrew has written seven novels, five of which were Top Ten bestsellers in the UK. He has also co-authored five *New York Times* Number One bestsellers with James Patterson. He currently lives in New York with his wife Lynn and their three children.

Novels by Andrew Gross

*15 Seconds*
*Killing Hour*
*Reckless*
*Don't Look Twice*
*The Dark Tide*
*The Blue Zone*

By Andrew Gross and James Patterson

*Judge and Jury*
*Lifeguard*
*3rd Degree*
*The Jester*
*2nd Chance*

# ANDREW GROSS

# *No Way Back*

HARPER

*Harper*
An imprint of HarperCollins*Publishers*
77–85 Fulham Palace Road,
Hammersmith, London W6 8JB

www.harpercollins.co.uk

This paperback edition 2013
8

First published in Great Britain by
HarperCollins*Publishers* 2013

A catalogue record for this book is
available from the British Library

ISBN: 978 0 00 748957 2

Set in Meridien by Palimpsest Book Production Limited,
Falkirk, Stirlingshire

Printed and bound in Great Britain by
Clays Ltd, St Ives plc

*If a body is just a body, who will step forward to ask why someone is killed and who killed them? If a body has no name or no history, then who will demand justice?*

—A grieving mother of a victim of Mexico's drug wars

# *Prologue*

The trip had been Sam's idea.

A five-day R and R down in Mexico over spring break. Only a twenty-hour-drive away. Ned's dad had brought up all the trouble they were having down there, but then things seemed to have quieted down recently. Anyway, where they were going, Aguazula, was just a sleepy town along the coast with not much more than a beach, a thatched-roof cantina, and maybe a little blow-away weed. Sam's buddy George lived there, teaching English. He said it was paradise.

*Aguazula.*

Blue waters.

At the last minute, Ned's girlfriend, Ana, decided to come along, lured by the promise of some first-rate photo ops for her photography project. The three of them were seniors at the University of Denver. And it would probably be the last real fun they'd have, at least for a long time, since they were all graduating in a couple of months and then it was out into the world. The only things he'd have on his résumé; two years of lacrosse, a 3.2 GPA, and a business degree. If there would even be a job out there by the time he graduated. The last two summers Sam had interned back east at this boutique fixed-income shop. But now even Wall Street wasn't hiring anymore, and in truth, Sam wasn't even sure finance was his thing. He really didn't know what he wanted to do. Other than, right now, a swan dive off a rocky ledge into a grotto of warm, blue water.

Ned was sleeping in the passenger seat of the Acura SUV, having driven most of the night once they hit New Mexico, all the way to the Mexican border. Culiacán was only ten minutes ahead, according to the AAA map they had. Aguazula was still a three-hour-drive away.

*Paradise.*

In the hazy light, Sam saw a car coming up from behind him. Once dawn had broken, Sunday morning, he had begun to enjoy the drive, drinking in the amazing countryside. He'd never been in rural Mexico before. Flat stone houses hugging the hills; farmers with goats and chickens along the side of the road. Spindly jacaranda trees. He'd been to Cabo once, with the family. But that was just about fancy resorts with PGA golf courses and deep-sea fishing. And he'd also been to Cancún once, on spring break, but that was such a party freak show, they hardly left the hotel. This was the real thing. An old woman sat behind a stand on the roadside selling melons and dried chiles. Sam waved to her as they passed by.

On the outskirts of town, the car caught up and went by them on the two-lane highway. A white Jeep with Texas plates. A man and a woman inside. In Culiacán they'd have to fill up. Maybe grab some breakfast. The road seemed to bring them right into the center of town. They passed a school, Escuela Autonomous de Centro Sinaloa. Just a flat-topped, one-level building with a droopy flag and what looked like a rutted soccer field.

There was a backup of some kind, as the road wound down into the center of town. It all seemed pretty quiet this time of the morning. Everyone must be getting ready for church. He was struck by all the crosses. A virtual sea of them—white, shimmering—atop the roofs. It was one of the most beautiful sights he'd even seen.

Next to him, Ned finally stirred. "Where are we?"

"Culiacán. Couple of more hours. Dude, check it out."

Ned sat up and gazed around. "Whoa!" His eyes growing

startlingly wide. "What is this, like a spawning ground for churches?"

Sam nodded. "The mother ship."

The narrow street that led into Culiacán's central square was momentarily backed up. Some old farmer seemed to be stuck, trying to drag his cart across the cobblestone road. Sam pulled up behind the same white Jeep that had passed them a few minutes ago.

In the back, Ana sat up, rubbing her eyes. "Hey, where are we, guys?"

"*Paradise,*" Sam declared, looking at the sea of white crosses. "At least, only a couple of more hours away."

Ana groaned. "Right now, my idea of paradise is a place we can grab some coffee and take a pee."

"I can go for that myself," Ned chimed in approvingly.

"Okay." Sam feathered the clutch. "Soon as this dude goes by, let's see what we can do."

Lupe stood on the roof, with its view of the town square, his AR-15 ready. It was quiet on a Sunday morning. A few food stalls were setting up to do business after Mass. A handful of unemployed men were already drinking in the cantina. A church bell rang. *La ciudad de cruzes.* The City of Crosses, it was called. Lupe knew the names and could count ten of them from right here.

He was nineteen, the son of a baker. He had dropped

4

out of school in the fifth grade and come under the influence of his uncle, Oscar, who took out a wad of American hundred-dollar bills and asked Lupe if this was what he wanted in life. And he answered, yes, it was. He'd seen the American movies. It was always the rich men who got the girls, who knew how to enjoy life. He started by doing simple things, like being a lookout and delivering packages. He knew exactly what the packages contained. Then, a few months back, they needed a local policeman to disappear. It was easy to do these jobs; these *magistrados* were fat and bought and sold themselves to the highest bidder. They lined their own pockets and did nothing for the poor. The man Lupe worked for had built schools and soccer fields. He had provided food for those who needed it. The policeman disappeared; only his hands and feet were ever found. And his badge. Which sent the message *You do not fuck with the Z's. Or we'll paste you*. Now, nervously, Lupe manned his own crew for the first time.

The white SUV would come down the road into town at a little after 10:00 A.M., he was told. Two Anglos would be inside. A man and a woman. *Do it in the open*, he was instructed. *Let the whole world see*.

Lupe didn't like killing people. He would rather play football and impress the girls. With his sandy-colored hair and bright blue eyes, he was always popular. Except he knew this was the way to climb up the ladder. And

5

they were all part of the same corrupt game, no matter which side they were on. *Govermentales*, politicians, the police. Even the priests. No one was innocent. Even he knew that much.

Someone shouted, one of the lookouts from the roof-tops up ahead. *"They are coming!"* Then: "Hay dos!" he heard. There are two.

"Dos persones?" Lupe called. Just as told.

"No. Dos coches." Two cars.

No one had told Lupe that.

He quickly radioed back. His uncle, who was having coffee at his hacienda, asked him, "Are you sure?'

*"Sí.* Two white wagons. Anglos. They are passing the school now."

That meant they would be in the square in a matter of seconds. Lupe gave the signal to the old man, who brought the cart across the narrow stone street, instructing the burro to stop. Coming down the hill, Lupe did see two white vehicles making their way down Calle Lachrimas, named for the Holy Mother's tears.

"There are two!" he radioed Oscar, and looked up to the verandah across the square. "Both Anglos. Which one is it? Do you know the plate number?"

His uncle's voice came back. "No. Let me check."

The front car honked at the cart. The old man appeared to do his best, moving as slowly as possible, but he couldn't block the road all day. The joke was, he'd probably had a hand in more killings than all of them!

"What do you want me to do?" Lupe asked again, as the old man cleared the road. "It must be done now?"

"Kill them all," his uncle's voice came back. "Let God decide."

The old man gave the burro a whack, and the cart seemed to magically clear the road.

By that time, Ned was going over the map. Ana had pulled out her Nikon and was snapping away at a little girl who waved back at her, going. "Oh, man, this is great!"

Sam put the car back in gear. "We're rolling!"

All of a sudden several men in jeans with white kerchiefs around their faces stepped out from the buildings. From the square itself. Some were even on the rooftops.

The one in front of Sam seemed no older than himself, maybe even younger, looking at him with a dull indifference in his eyes.

They were all aiming automatic weapons.

*No!* Sam wanted to tell them, *No, wait . . . You've made some mistake!* but the next thing he heard was a scream—Ana's, he was sure—as the car's front and side windows exploded virtually at once, ironlike fists slugging him all over like the hardest lacrosse balls he had ever felt, and then the explosions seem to just go on and on, no matter how much he begged them to stop. On and on, until the boy pulling the trigger in front of him was no longer in his sight.

# WENDY

# CHAPTER ONE

He *was* handsome.

Not that I was really checking anyone out, or that I even looked at guys in that way anymore—married going on ten years now, and Neil, my youngest, my stepson actually, just off to college. I glanced away, pretending I hadn't even noticed him. Especially in a bar by myself, no matter how stylish this one was. But in truth I guess I had. Noticed him. Just a little. Out of the corner of my eye . . .

Longish black hair and kind of dark, smoky eyes. A white V-neck T-shirt under a stylish blazer. Late thirties maybe, around my age, but seemed younger. I would've chalked him up as being just a shade too cool—too cool for my type anyway—if it wasn't that something about him just seemed, I don't know . . . natural. He sat down a few seats from me at the bar and ordered a Belvedere on the rocks, never looking my way. His watch was a rose-gold chronometer and looked expensive. When he finally did turn my way, shifting his stool to listen to the jazz pianist, his smile was pleasant, not too forward, just enough to acknowledge that there were three empty seats between us, and seemed to say nothing more than *How are you tonight?*

Actually the guy was pretty damn hot!

Truth was, it had been years since I'd been at a bar by myself at night, other than maybe waiting for a girlfriend to come back from the ladies' room as part of a gals' night out. And the only reason I even happened to be here was that I'd been in the city all day at this self-publishing seminar, a day after Dave and I had about the biggest fight of our married lives. Which had started out as nothing, of course, as these things usually did: whether or not you had to salt the steaks so heavily— *twice*, in fact—before putting them on the grill—he having read about it in *Food & Wine* magazine or something—which somehow managed to morph into how I felt he was always spoiling the kids, who were from Dave's first marriage: Amy, who was in Barcelona on her junior year abroad, and Neil, who had taken his car with him as a freshman up at Bates. Which was actually all just a kind of code, I now realized, for some issues I had with his ex-wife, Joanie. How I felt she was always belittling me; always putting out there that she

12

was the kids' mother, even though I'd pretty much raised them since they were in grade school, and how I always felt Dave never fully supported me on this.

"She *is* their mother!" Dave said, pushing away from the table. "Maybe you should just butt out on this, Wendy. Maybe you just should."

Then we both said some things I'm sure we regretted.

The rest of the night we barely exchanged a word—Dave shutting himself in the TV room with a hockey game, and me hiding out in the bedroom with my book. In the morning he was in his car at the crack of dawn, and I had my seminar in New York. We hadn't spoken a word all day, which was rare, so I asked my buddy Pam to meet me for a drink and maybe something to eat, just to talk it all through before heading home.

Home was about the *last* place I wanted to be right now.

And here it was, ten after seven, and Pam was texting me that she was running *twenty min late*: the usual kid crisis—meaning Steve, her hedge-fund-honcho husband, still hadn't left the office as promised, and her nanny was with April at dance practice . . .

And me, at the Hotel Kitano bar, a couple of blocks from Grand Central. Taking in the last, relaxing sips of a Patrón Gold margarita—another thing I rarely did!— one eye on the TV screen above me, which had a muted baseball game or something on, the other doing its best to avoid the eye of Mr. Cutie at the end of the bar.

Maybe not looking my 100 percent, knockout *best*—I mean, it was just a self-publishing seminar and all—but still not exactly half-bad in an orange cashmere sweater, a black leather skirt, my Prada boots, and my wavy, dark brown hair pulled back in a ponytail. Looking decently toned from the hot-yoga classes I'd been taking, texting back to Pam with a mischievous smile: BETTER HURRY. V. SEXY GUY @ BAR AND THINK HE'S ABT TO MAKE CONTACT. *GRIN*

And giggling inside when she wrote me back: HANDS OFF, HON! ORDERED HIM ESP FOR ME!

THEN BETTER GET YOUR ASS HERE PRONTO :-) I texted back.

"Yanks or Red Sox?" I heard someone say.

"Sorry?" I looked up and it was you know who, who definitely had to be Bradley Cooper's dreamy first cousin or something. Or at least that's what the sudden acceleration in my heart rate was telling me.

"Yanks or Red Sox? I see you're keeping tabs on the game."

"Oh. Yanks, of course," I said, a glance to the screen. "Born and bred. South Shore."

"Sox." He shrugged apologetically. "South *Boston*. Okay, Brookline," he said with a smile, "if you force it out of me."

I smiled back. He was pretty cute. "Actually I wasn't even watching. Just waiting for a friend." I figured I might as well cut this off now. No point in leading him on.

"No worries." He smiled politely. *Like he's even interested, right?*

14

"Who happens to be twenty minutes late!" I blurted, thinking I might have sounded just a bit harsh a moment ago.

"Well, traffic's nuts out there tonight. Someone must be in town. Is he coming in from anywhere?"

"Yeah." I laughed. "Park and Sixty-Third!" Then I heard myself add, not sure exactly why, "And it's a *she*. Old college friend. Girls' night out."

He lifted his drink to me, and his dark eyes smiled gently. "Well, here's to gridlock, then."

Mr. Cutie and I shifted around and listened to the pianist. The bar was apparently known for its jazz. It was like the famous lounge at the Carlyle, only in midtown, which was why Pam had chosen it—close to both her place and Grand Central, for me to catch my train.

"She's actually pretty good!" I said, suddenly not minding the thought of Pam stuck in a cab somewhere, at least for a while. Not to mention forgetting my husband, who, for a moment, was a million miles away.

"Donna St. James. She's one of the best. She used to sing with George Benson and the Marsalis brothers."

"Oh," I said. Everyone in the lounge seemed to be clued in to this.

"It's why I stay here when I'm in town. Some of the top names in the business just drop in unannounced. Last time I was here, Sarah Jewel got up and sang."

"Sarah Jewel?"

"She used to record with Basie back in the day." He

15

pointed to a stylishly dressed black woman and an older white man at one of the round tables. "That's Rosie Miller. She used to record with Miles Davis. Maybe she'll get up later."

"You're in the business?" I asked. I mean, he did kind of look the part.

"No. Play a little though. Just for fun. My dad was actually an arranger back in the seventies and eighties. He . . . anyway, I don't want to bore you with all that," he said, shrugging and stirring his drink.

I took a sip of mine and caught his gaze. "You're not boring me at all."

A couple came in and went to take the two seats that were in between us, so Mr. Cutie picked up his drink and slid deftly around them, and asked, motioning to the seat next to me, "Do you mind?"

Truth was, I didn't. I was actually kind of enjoying it. And I did have a rescue plan, if necessary. I checked the time: 7:25. *Wherever the hell Pam was!*

"So this friend of yours," he asked with a coy half smile, "is she real or imaginary? Because if she's imaginary, not to worry. I have several imaginary friends of my own back in Boston. We could set them up."

"Oh, that would be nice." I laughed. "But I'm afraid she's quite real. At least she was this summer. She and her husband were in Spain with me and my . . ."

I was about to say *my husband*, of course, but something held me back. Though by this time I assumed he

16

had taken note of the ring on my finger. Still, I couldn't deny this was fun, sitting there with an attractive man who was paying me a little attention, still reeling from my argument with Dave.

Then he said, "I suspect there's probably an imaginary husband back at home as well . . ."

"Right now"—I rolled my eyes and replied in a tone that was just a little digging—"I'm kind of wishing he was imaginary!" Then I shook my head. "That wasn't nice. Tequila talking. We just had a little row last night. Subject for tonight with friend."

"Ah. Sorry to hear. Just a newlywed spat, I'm sure," he said, teasing. This time I was sure he was flirting.

"Yeah, right." I chortled at the flattery. "Going on ten years."

"Wow!" His eyes brightened in a way that I could only call admiring. "Well, I hope it's okay if I say you surely don't look it! I'm Curtis, by the way."

I hesitated, thinking maybe I'd let things advance just a bit too far. Though I had to admit I wasn't exactly minding it. And maybe in a way I was saying to my husband, *So see, David, there are consequences to being a big, fat jerk!*

"Wendy," I said back. We shook hands. "But it sure would be nice to know where the hell Pam is. She was supposed to be here twenty minutes ago." I checked the time on my phone.

"Would it be all right if I order up another of whatever

you're drinking?" He raised his palms defensively. "Purely for the imaginary friend, of course . . ."

"Of course," I said, playing along. "But no. One more of these and I'll be up at that piano myself! And trust me, I wasn't playing with anyone in the eighties . . . Anyway"—I shrugged, deadpan—"she only drinks *imaginary* vodka."

Curtis grinned. "I'm acquainted with the bartender. Let me see what I can do."

My iPhone vibrated. Pam, I was sure, announcing she was pulling up to the hotel now and for me to get a dirty martini going for her. But instead it read:

> Wend, I'm so sorry. Just can't make it tonite. What can I say . . . ? I know u need to talk. Tomorrow work?

*Tomorrow?* Tomorrow didn't work. I was here. Now. And she was right, I did need to talk. And the last place I wanted to be right now was home. *Will call*, I wrote back, a little annoyed. I put down the phone. My eyes inevitably fell on Curtis's. I'd already missed the 7:39.

"Sure, why don't we do just that?" I nodded about that drink.

I'm not sure exactly what made me stay.

Maybe I was still feeling vulnerable from my fight with Dave. Or even a little annoyed at Pam, who had a habit of bagging out when I needed her most. I suppose

18

you could toss in just a bit of undeniable interest in the present company.

Whatever it was, I did.

Knowing Dave was out for the night on business and that it was all just harmless anyway helped as well. And that there was a train every half hour. I could leave anytime I wanted.

We chatted some more, and Curtis said he was a freelance journalist here in town on a story. And I chuckled and told him that I was kind of in the same game too. That I'd actually worked for the Nassau County police in my twenties before going to law school for a year—having signed up after 9/11, after my brother, a NYPD cop himself, was killed—though I was forced to resign after a twelve-year-old boy was killed in a wrongful-death judgment. And that I'd written this novel about my experience, which was actually why I'd been in the city today at a self-publishing conference. That I'd been having a tough time getting it looked at by anyone, and that it likely wasn't very good anyway.

"Care to read it?" I asked. I tapped the tote bag from my publishing conference. "Been lugging it around all day."

"I would," Curtis said, "but I'm afraid it's not exactly my field."

"Just joking," I said. "So what is your field?"

He shrugged. "I'm a bit more into current events."

I was about to follow up on that when the pianist

finished her set. The crowded room gave her a warm round of applause. She got up and came over to the end of the bar, ordered a Perrier, and to my surprise, when it arrived, lifted it toward Curtis. "All warmed up, sugar."

Curtis stood up. I looked at him wide-eyed. He shot me a slightly apologetic grin. "I did mention that I played . . ."

"You said a bit, *for fun*," I replied.

"Well, you'll be the judge. Look, I know you have a train to catch, and I don't know if you'll be around when I'm done"—he put out his hand—"but it was fun to chat with you, if you have to leave."

"I probably should," I said, glancing at the time. "It was nice to talk to you as well."

"And best of luck," he said, pointing as he backed away, "with that imaginary friend of yours."

"Right! I'll be sure to tell her!" I laughed.

He sat down at the piano, and I swiveled around, figuring I'd stick around a couple of minutes to hear how he played. But from the opening chords that rose magically from his fingers, just warming up, it was clear it was *me* he was playing when he coyly said he only played "a little."

I was dumbstruck, completely wowed. The guy was a ten! He wasn't just a dream to look at, and charming too—he played like he was totally at one with the instrument. He had the ease and polish of someone who clearly had been doing this from an early age. His fingers danced across the keyboard and the sounds rose as if on a cloud, then drifted back to earth as something beautiful. It had been a long time since goose bumps went down my arms over a guy.

Donna St. James leaned over. "You ever hear him before, honey?"

I shook my head. "No."

"His father arranged a bunch of us back in the day. Sit back. You're in for a treat."

I did.

The first thing he played was this sumptuous, bluesy rendition of Elton John's "Goodbye Yellow Brick Road," and the handful of customers who were paying their checks, preparing to leave, started listening. Even the bartender was listening. I couldn't take my eyes off him. Whatever my definition of *sexy* had been an hour ago, forget it—he was definitely rewriting it for me now.

I didn't leave.

I just sat there, slowly nursing my margarita, growing more and more intoxicated, but not by the drink. By the time he segued into a sultry version of the Beatles' "Hey Jude," it was as if his soul had risen from that keyboard and knotted itself with mine.

Our eyes came together a couple of times, my smile communicating, *Okay, so I'm impressed* . . . The twinkle in his eye simply saying he was happy I was still there.

By the time he finished up with Billy Joel's "New York State of Mind," goose bumps were dancing up and down my arms with the rise and fall of his fingers along the keys. With a couple of margaritas in me—and fifteen years from the last time anyone looked at me quite that way—the little, cautioning voice that only a few minutes back was going, *Wendy, this is crazy, you don't do this kind of thing*, had gone completely silent.

And when our eyes seemed to touch after his final note and didn't separate, not for a while, I knew, sure as I knew my own name, that I was about to do something I could never have imagined when I walked into the place an hour before. Something I'd never, ever done before.

# CHAPTER TWO

Ten minutes later we were up in his room, my coat and bag strewn on the floor, one meaningless comment about the view before my breath seemed to jump out of my skin the second he touched me and backed me against the wall.

I was waiting for that voice inside to go, *Hold it, just a second, Wendy. You know this isn't right.*

But what I seemed to want even more was for his hands to be all over me. Under my top. Beneath my skirt. Electrical shocks dancing all over my body. Places I hadn't let another man touch me in years.

In a second his mouth was on mine, and I kissed him back just as eagerly. I felt the feel of his tongue dance against mine, just as I had watched his fingers dance along the keys. Then he traced a meandering path

23

with his lips along my neck, my breaths leaping. His hand slid inside my skirt and down my rear, and I felt a shiver travel down my thighs and my heartbeat go out of control. My mind was like a dark vault, shutting out any thoughts of whether this was right or wrong.

I lifted my arms and let him pull me out of my sweater. I undid my thick, dark hair, letting it drape all over him, every cell inside me bursting with desire. He lifted me up against the blue, Japanese-wallpapered wall, my arms around his neck, and we knocked into the bamboo desk, sending the hotel directory onto the floor, not even stopping to go "Oops" or acknowledge it. Every time his lips brushed along my skin, my body seemed to explode, as if a live electrical cord was jumping around in it, amazed at what I was letting him do. Eyes locked on each other, he pulled my bra straps off my shoulders, my heart speeding up and getting stronger.

"There's a perfectly good bed over there," he said, his own breaths growing short and rapid.

"I know. There is." Then I kissed him again and almost smothered him in my hair, feeling the zipper on the back of my skirt being drawn down, the leather wiggling down my thighs, the click and tug of his belt becoming undone . . .

A part of me was going, *Yes, yes, take me over. The bed.*

24

Another part went, *The hell with the bed . . . I'm ready . . . here. Now . . .*

*Now.*

And then something stopped.

Inside me. Like the emergency brake pulled on a train.

It was as if that one shuddering sound, the *click* of his belt buckle being undone, shot through me like cold water reviving an unconscious man, rocketing me back to earth.

Instantly awakening me to the reality of what I was doing.

It suddenly shot through me just how incredibly wrong this was. Wrong what I was letting him do. Wrong to even be here, in this room.

Wrong to betray a marriage I had worked so hard to make successful. To do this to someone who I knew I loved. And who loved me! How maybe I was only doing this to get back at him.

Just wrong.

And then this overwhelming feeling of dread wormed through me. Of how, when trust is broken, like that first crack in a dam about to give way, it only leads to more and more pressure against it until it can no longer hold. And then it bursts. Not just your marriage, but your whole life. Whatever was truthful in it. It all just starts to crumble and wash away. Everything. And how this was that first crack, what

I was doing now. *And how you couldn't do it, Wendy . . . You just couldn't unless you were willing to take that risk. That everything will go.*

Which I wasn't willing to take.

No matter how it may have felt downstairs. Or even a moment ago.

*No, I didn't want it all to burst.*

Something came out of my mouth that a minute earlier would have been the farthest thing from my mind. From my desires.

*"Stop,"* I said.

Maybe a little under my breath at first; it could have been mistaken for a shudder or a sigh. I wasn't even sure Curtis actually heard me. He was slowly weaving his tongue along my belly, getting lower, eliciting electric waves.

But then I said it again. Louder. "Please . . . stop. I can't." My hands went to his shoulders and I eased him slightly away.

This time he looked up.

"Curtis, I'm sorry. I just can't."

My skin was on fire and slick with sweat, and part of me was begging to just say, *Fuck it*, and let him carry me over to that bed. But the better part of me drew in the deepest, most determined breath I'd ever drawn.

*"I can't."*

"You're kidding, right?" Curtis gave me an uncomprehending smile, slowly rising.

26

"No. I'm not. I know how this must seem. But I just can't. I'm sorry. It's just not right." I blew out a breath. "Curtis, you're a totally irresistible guy, and I know there's a part of me that is going to one hundred percent regret this in an hour on the train . . ." I shook my head. "But I can't do this with you. I thought it was okay. Even a minute ago it seemed so. But it's not." I let my hand fall to his face, and I looked into his confused, almost incredulous eyes. I didn't know how he was going to react. Clearly, I'd played as much a part as he had in getting us up here.

The fire in my eyes was suddenly replaced by tears. "I'm so sorry. I just can't."

He blinked.

I wasn't sure exactly what was going through him. Confusion. Frustration. Disbelief.

Absolutely disbelief.

And there was a moment when I admit it crossed my mind, *Shit, Wendy, you're up here with a guy you don't know. No telling what he might do now.*

But all he did was take a step back and nod, slowly, resignation seeming to drown the ardor. He glanced down, his jeans undone, my skirt down around my thighs, my black panties drawn. My hand now covering my breasts; breasts that only a moment ago I was willingly offering up to him.

"I'm totally embarrassed," I said, putting my other hand in front of my face.

27

My face that was now flushed with shame.

He nodded. Thankfully, not the nod of someone who was about to do something crazy, which I guess, in another situation, could have been the case. More like the nod of someone caught by the total absurdity of what had just happened. Clothes strewn all over the floor. Pants down. Sweat covering both of us. Breathing heavily.

"No chance this is simply your particular spin on foreplay?" He smiled hopefully. A last-ditch plea.

"I wish it was." I shrugged, pushing the hair out of my face. "It would probably make the whole situation a lot easier. Sorry."

His nod seemed almost dazed. "Figured it was worth a check."

He took the waist of my skirt and shimmied it back up, letting out a deep sigh, as if to say, *I can't believe I'm actually doing this.*

"Thank you," I said. "You're really a saint for not making me feel like a total shit."

"I'm not sure the word *saint* exactly applies right now."

"You're right." I just stood there covering myself, bursting with embarrassment. I shrugged. "I think I need to straighten up."

He nodded resignedly. "Bathroom's over there."

About as awkwardly as I'd felt since maybe back in college, I scurried around, covering myself up with my bra, and picked up my sweater off the floor, my bag that had spilled over on the floor, my boots. "I can assure you, I haven't been in this position in about twenty years."

Curtis just looked on and picked up his own shirt. "You can trust me, neither have I!"

With my bra and my sweater covering me, my handbag dangling from my arm, I turned at the bathroom door, grinning. "I suppose this isn't a particularly good time to ask you again to take a look at my novel?"

"No," Curtis said, unable to hold back his laugh. "Definitely not."

"Thought as much." I forced a rueful smile. "I'll be out in a while."

I closed the door behind me and took a deep, releasing breath as I looked in the mirror. My face was profusely blushing with shame. How had I let it get this far? I knew I could never tell anyone. Surely not Dave. Never. Not even Pam. No, this one was mine to deal with and try to rationalize. In a way I felt lucky. Lucky I had come to my senses when I did. Lucky Curtis was actually a decent guy. It could have been a whole lot worse.

Lucky I hadn't done something that I'd look at with shame for the rest of my life.

I ran the cold water, wet a washcloth and pressed it to my flushed face. I put my arms back through my bra and started to brush out my hair, until I began to resemble a manageably put-together version of the person who had come up here a few minutes before— though still far too ashamed to even look at myself fully. I threw on my sweater and straightened myself out. Even dabbed on a little makeup and lip gloss. Then I took a breath. *Okay, Wendy, now, you have to face him one more time and make your way home. And then go on with your life and pretend like this never even happened. And when Pam asks you about that cute guy at the bar you were texting about, it's "What guy?" I merely finished my drink and caught the 7:39 and was home by* Law & Order *. . . right?*

I blew out a final, steadying breath and steeled myself, when suddenly, over the running water, I heard something coming from the bedroom.

Voices. At first I just thought it was Curtis on the phone.

Then I realized I was hearing someone else's voice as well. Another man. I turned the water down slightly and listened. This was already embarrassing enough. The last thing I needed was to face anyone else.

I cracked the bathroom door open and peeked out.

My heart came up my throat at what I saw.

There was another man in the room. Gray suit, white shirt open. Salt-and-pepper hair. The second I saw him I realized I'd seen him before. Downstairs in the lounge.

He and another man, a black man, had been sitting around a table.

Except now he had a gun pointed at Curtis, who was on the bed.

I instantly froze, then drew back inside. I didn't know what to do. I was worried he would hear the running water. He'd see my jacket and shoes. He'd have to know I was here. Years before, I'd been on the Nassau County police force, but that was basically as a cadet, a lifetime ago. Eleven years. God forbid he did something terrible to Curtis. His next move would be to come in here for me!

"Pick it up!" I heard the man order him.

Holding my heart together, I peered back out.

He'd tossed a second gun onto the bed. It landed next to Curtis, who stared at it with growing terror.

"I said fucking pick it up!" the intruder said again, leveling his own gun menacingly.

"No, I'm not going to pick it up," Curtis said, his voice in between panic and defiance. "I know what you're going to do. You just want to make it look like I drew on you . . ." He pushed the gun away and it rolled to the edge of the bed and onto the floor. "You're going to shoot me, no matter what I do?"

The intruder just looked at the gun and shook his head. "Doesn't matter anyway . . . This is for Gillian, asshole."

He pulled the trigger. My eyes bolted wide.

31

There was a loud, muffled *pop*, and Curtis's body jumped off the bed with the impact. He tried to scream "No!" Then there was a second *pop*, and to my horror, Curtis jerked and then went limp.

I drew back inside, muffling a terrified scream. I couldn't believe what I'd just seen.

As I stared through the slit in the doorway, it was clear—a hundred percent clear, in that horrifying split second—that he had to know I was in there. His next move would be to come for me. My heart started to race uncontrollably. What the hell could I do? The bathroom door seemed to open on its own. My eyes locked on the gun on the floor, only a few feet from me. Old instincts kicked in, instincts I hadn't felt in years. I stepped out of the bathroom and picked it up. The intruder had gone over to check on Curtis's body.

I raised the gun at him, two-handed, shouting, *"I'm an ex-cop!* Put the gun down. Put your hands in the air!"

I hadn't even held a gun in years, and never to someone's face. In this kind of situation. My hands were visibly shaking.

The man just looked at me and put up his palms defensively, as if to say, *Slow down, okay, honey . . .*

But inwardly, I saw him sizing up the situation: My nerves. His chances. How quickly he could raise his gun. I'd just watched him commit a cold-blooded killing. I

32

knew then he wasn't about to let me call the cops on him.

"Lady, you have no idea what you stepped into . . ."

I leveled the gun at his chest. "I said lay the gun down and put your hands in the air!"

That's when I saw it. A realization etched into his face. Something he knew and I didn't. Like the situation had suddenly shifted, his way and not mine. And then in horror I realized just what it was. The gun I was holding had been a plant. To make it look like Curtis had drawn on him first. He would never have risked Curtis taking it and using it on him.

The safety was still on!

Frantically I turned the gun on its side and found the lever. I thumbed it forward, just as the killer took a step to the side and leveled his gun at me.

I screamed and pulled the trigger, the recoil knocking me backward.

He staggered back, continuing to hold out the gun.

I pulled it again.

The first shot struck him squarely in the chest. I saw a burst of crimson on his shirt, hurtling him back against the wall. The next shot hit him in the throat, his hand darting there as he slowly slid, blood smearing against the wallpaper, his gun clattering against the floor.

He was scarily still.

There was this awful, heart-stopping silence. I just

stood there, an acrid, all-too-familiar smell filling up the room. My heart pounding like a boom box turned all the way up. *Wendy, what have you done?* Frozen, I stared at him in disbelief. The guy didn't move a muscle, the flower of blood widening on his white shirt.

*Oh my God, Wendy, what have you just fucking done?*

Dazed, I put the gun back on the bed and rushed over to Curtis, who was clearly dead, the smoky, dark eyes that had so intrigued me at the bar just minutes before now glassy and fixed. *You have no idea what you stepped into*, the intruder had said. *Okay, so what . . . what have I stepped into? What* have *you done, Curtis, to deserve this?* I tried to think, but my mind was jumbled and confused.

My heart still racing, I ran over and checked the man on the floor. You didn't have to be an MD to see he was dead as well, his cold, gray eyes glazed over and inert; the pool of blood on his chest continuing to spread. *You killed him, Wendy . . .* I'd pulled a trigger once before on the job, and it had changed my life. But not like this. Not at point-blank range. Not with my life on the line. I thought, *What the hell do I do now?* Call security? The police? *You just killed someone, Wendy . . .* I knew I didn't have any choice. I'd just watched the son of a bitch kill Curtis in cold blood. He was about to shoot me too. I was lucky to even be alive.

Anyone would see it was clearly self-defense.

But then the reality of where I was swelled up inside me.

No. I couldn't do that at all! Call the police. That was the last thing I could do. I was in the hotel room of a complete stranger. A place I absolutely shouldn't have been. How would I possibly explain that? Not just to the police, even if I could convince them of what had happened.

But to my husband. To Dave. To our kids!

That I was up here to have sex with a guy I'd just met at the bar when the whole thing happened.

My whole life would be torn apart.

My eyes fell on the intruder. *Who are you? Why were you following Curtis? What were you up here to do?* Leaning over him, I saw he had an earphone in his ear. Which suddenly unnerved me even more, realizing that there was likely an accomplice somewhere. Probably in the hotel at that moment!

Possibly even right outside.

*If he has any idea what had just happened in here . . .*

Terrified, I took the earphone out and held it to my ear. I heard a voice on the other end.

"*Ray?* Ray, what's going on up there? Answer me, Ray, are you all right?"

His jacket had fallen open, and I saw an ID folder in the breast pocket. I started thinking, What if he *was* security? Or maybe even the police? What then?

I was suddenly encased in sweat.

. I opened the ID folder and stared. And whatever panic or fear I had felt up to that moment became just a dry run for what was rippling through me now.

I was staring at a badge. But not from hotel security. It read:

UNITED STATES OF AMERICA. DEPARTMENT OF HOMELAND SECURITY.

# CHAPTER THREE

My heart, which to that point had been acting as if a live wire were loose in my chest, went instantly still, as if the power had been cut. The agent's ID fell out of my hand.

I'd just killed a government agent.

Not just an agent—Raymond Hruseff. *From the Department of fucking Homeland Security!*

Who only seconds before I had watched commit a cold-blooded murder and then try to frame someone else. And who would have surely done the same to me had that gun not happened to be close by.

My throat went completely dry.

*You have no idea what you stepped into,* Hruseff had said to me. I turned to Curtis and wanted to shake him from the dead. *Tell me . . . tell me, damn it,* what *did I stumble into? What the hell did you do?*

I knew I had only seconds to decide what to do. But, clearly, staying here wasn't an option.

I found a duplicate room key in the agent's jacket pocket, which was no doubt how he'd gotten in. He had icily put two bullets into Curtis right in front of my eyes. He was in the process of trying to make it seem as if Curtis was the one about to shoot. Even more troubling, when I identified myself as an ex-cop, instead of laying down his weapon and putting his hands in the air—and identifying *himself*, standard operating procedure—he'd made a move to shoot *me*. Clearly, he wasn't up here on official business.

What I'd stumbled into was an execution.

And I knew if the person on the other end of that earphone happened to find me in this room, I'd be as good as Curtis.

*Wendy, you have to get the hell out of here now!*

I hurried over to the bed, wiped down the gun I'd used to shoot Hruseff, and placed it back on the bed. I did the same with the bathroom doorknob and everything else I'd touched. I took my coat. Only a minute and a half or so had passed since the actual shooting. The shots might have attracted people's attention. There might already be a crowd gathered outside the room.

The guy's partner could be on his way up!

I grabbed my bag and my leather jacket, which had fallen off the desk chair and onto the floor, and saw Curtis's cell phone next to his laptop. I threw his phone into my bag, thinking that down the line I might well need something to prove my innocence, and I had no idea in hell who the guy even was.

I didn't even know if Curtis was his real name!

I hurried over to the door. It was 8:41. It seemed like an eternity had passed since the shooting, but it had only been about two minutes. I prayed that people hadn't been inside their rooms. That they would be out to dinner somewhere, or at a play, or at the fucking Knicks game for all I cared. Just somewhere! I put on my floppy cap and covered my face with my scarf as best I could, my blood pulsing with adrenaline. Collecting myself, I opened the door a notch and looked out. Thank God, the only people I saw in the hallway were an elderly couple heading to the elevators at the far end. Still, I didn't think I could risk it. I needed another way out of the hotel. There had to be an emergency stairwell somewhere.

I stepped out, averting my face from any possible cameras, but just as I headed down the hall in the opposite direction from the elevators, someone bolted around the corner, behind me.

I spun.

It was the black guy who I had seen with the dead agent down in the lounge. Who had to be the person I'd just heard on the radio.

Our eyes locked and he seemed to recognize me. Then he reached inside his jacket for his gun.

*Oh my God, Wendy . . .*

*"Federal agent!"* he yelled. "Stop and put your hands in the air!"

I stood, frozen. A voice inside me shouted that a federal agent had just ordered me to stop.

But another, far more convincing, told me, *If you do, this guy might kill you, Wendy! You just watched his partner murder a man. They were clearly here for something dirty. You can't chance it. You have to get out of here now!*

"He's in there!" Backing down the hall, I pointed toward the hotel room door. "Your partner. He's been shot."

Then I started to run.

*"Stop. Now!"* I heard him shout again from behind me.

I didn't. Ten feet away, the hallway turned to the right and I flung myself around the corner just as a bullet whizzed by my head and slammed into the wall.

I screamed.

I prayed that he wouldn't come right after me but instead would check on his partner. Who could be bleeding out. Or even dead. Which hopefully would buy me a few seconds.

Or maybe he'd radio a third person. Down in the lobby. I had no idea how many were even involved.

I sprinted down the long hallway, not sure what he was doing behind me. I knew that even if I screamed bloody murder and pounded frantically on the doors; even if people came out of their rooms to see what was

40

going on and I was somehow spared; even if the police believed my story of what actually had happened in there, I would still have to face my husband and tell him what I'd done. Either way, my life would come crashing down.

I raced around another corner, no idea if there was even a stairwell there. Up ahead, I saw a dimly lit sign that read Emergency. *Thank God!* I barreled through the door without looking behind, flew down the fire stairs as fast as my boots would take me—seven floors, my heart racing almost as frenetically as my feet. I had no idea what awaited me at the bottom. Hotel security? The police? With guns drawn?

*Maybe a third agent?*

I made it down the seven floors in what seemed like seconds. Above me, I heard the echo of the door opening and someone shouting down the stairwell. Loud footsteps coming after me.

*Oh, God, Wendy, hurry . . .*

Almost out of breath, I pushed through the security door on the ground floor. It opened to an unfamiliar part of the lobby, and I let out a gasp of relief that no one was around. Composing myself, I got my bearings and hurried toward the main entrance. An hour ago, I had come through it, a marital spat with my husband the most pressing thing on my mind.

Now I was a witness to a murder. Now I had killed someone myself.

Now I was just hoping to stay alive.

I buried my face in my jacket and scarf and hurried through the revolving doors, the brown-uniformed doorman pushing me through with an accommodating wave. "Have a nice night."

I gave him a quick wave in return, not knowing what else to do.

Outside, I didn't know which way to turn. I wasn't sure how close behind me the agent was. Park Avenue is a two-way street, bisected by a divider in the middle. The closest cross street was Thirty-Eighth, but the block to Madison Avenue was straight and long, and if the guy came out and saw me turn, there would be no place for me to hide.

Grand Central station was four blocks north. Even at this hour, it would be busy with commuter traffic and offer plenty of places to hide. I knew I'd be safe there.

I buried my head in my down coat and ran across to the other side of the street, heading north. I clung to the dark cover of the high-rise buildings.

A block away I glanced back and saw the agent who'd been chasing me come out of the hotel. He looked up and down. I pressed myself against a large, bronze sculpture in the courtyard of an office building on Fortieth Street. My heart was ricocheting off my ribs, and I was praying he hadn't seen me. He looked in all directions, gesturing in frustration, and spoke into a radio. I didn't move a muscle. He looked around again; he seemed to be staring directly at me.

42

I went rigid.

Then finally he went back in.

I think I exhaled so loudly in relief that a person a block away would have turned at the sound. I was in tears, tears from the thought of what I had just witnessed. At what I'd just done. Not knowing if I was safe, or about to be implicated in a double murder? Or if my family was about to fall apart? I knew I had to bring this to the police. But I also knew that then everything would spill out. *Everything!* And they would likely just bring me back to the hotel and hand me over to the very people who had just tried to kill me.

All I could think of was to just get home. To the person I trusted most in the world. If this was going to come out, he was damn well going to hear it from my lips, and not from the police. I had no idea what I would say to him. Or how he would react. I only knew that together, we'd figure out the right thing to do. How could I possibly hold it inside? A dark, shameful secret that would haunt me the rest of my life? Every time I looked at my husband.

Every time I looked at myself in the mirror.

Not just what I'd done to a federal agent . . .

But having that second drink. Going up to that room. Everything!

# CHAPTER FOUR

It only took about five minutes to make it the couple of blocks to Grand Central.

There were a couple of policemen stationed at the entrance. I thought about stopping them and telling them what happened. But I just ran past.

I saw on the large schedule screen in the Grand Concourse that there was a 9:11 train back to Pelham. That was only five minutes from now.

I headed down to Track 24. Before going underground, I called the house. It didn't surprise me that there was no answer. Dave had a business dinner with some prospective new partners. When our voice mail came on, I hung up and tried his cell. No answer again. This time I left a harried message, trying to calm my voice as best I could: "Honey, I'm sorry about what happened last night. I'm on the nine-eleven. I'm looking forward to seeing you at home. Please, I need to talk to you about something. I love you."

What else mattered now?

The ride home was the most nerve-racking half hour of my life. As soon as we got out of the tunnel, I checked Google News on my iPhone to see if the story had hit. So far it hadn't. I looked in the faces of the people sitting across from me. Just regular commuters. A black woman with her young daughter who was playing a handheld electronic game. A businessman heading home from a late night at the office. A couple of loud twenty-somethings. Could they see it on me? Was it all over my face? Could they hear it in the pounding of my heart? What I'd done!

Pelham is the second stop in Westchester County. It was a quiet, upper-middle-class town tucked in between Mount Vernon and New Rochelle. I'd left my Audi SUV at the station. We live in Pelham Manor, an upscale neighborhood only a couple of minutes from the town, in an old Tudor on a wooded half acre with a carriage-house garage, just two blocks from the Long Island Sound. Dave was a partner in a small advertising company that was looking to merge with a larger one. That's what his meeting tonight was about. It would be a huge moment for him, for us both, if it all went through. And it could mean a little money for us, which we surely could use. We lived well: We had a ski house in Vermont; we belonged to a nice country club, ate out pretty much whenever we wanted. But not so well that it wasn't a struggle to pay full tuition for the kids in college and go out west, skiing in Snowmass with friends once a year.

All of a sudden, everything seemed threatened.

I drove home, my mind a daze, and went in through the garage. Once in my kitchen, surrounded by all our familiar things, I actually felt myself start to feel safe, for the first time since the incident. Dave wasn't back yet. I threw off my coat, pulled off my boots, and heaved myself into a chair in the den. I had to decide what to do.

It all seemed like a dream to me—a haunting, night-marish one. Had it all actually happened? I'd witnessed the execution of a defenseless man. I'd killed a government agent in self-defense. A rogue agent maybe. One who was about to kill me. But if I came forward, I'd probably destroy my life. A woman in the hotel room of a man she had met at the bar only an hour before? Who guiltily fled the scene? Over and over I replayed the seconds leading up to my firing that gun: the intruder shooting Curtis without even blinking. The second gun pushed off the edge of the bed within my reach. Screaming at Hruseff that I was an ex-cop and to put down his gun. Then the calculating expression that came over his face and the panic in my chest as he raised his gun toward me.

I'd had no choice. I knew I would have been dead if I hadn't pulled that trigger.

But how could I ever explain it? To the police? Or to my husband?

He could walk through that door at any time. That this horrible thing had happened . . . that I was in a hotel room to screw some guy. Would he even believe that I had stopped it? That I had come to my senses? Would it even matter? Everything would fall apart. My marriage. My relationship with the kids, whom I'd basically raised and whom I adored.

Our trust.

*My whole fucking life.*

*Sorry, honey, hope dinner went well with the prospective new partners and all, but while you were having salmon tartare at the Gotham Bar and Grill, your pretty little wife just killed a government agent after she was about to fuck a . . .*

Hot flashes running all over me suddenly made it feel like it was a hundred degrees.

I got up, went into the bedroom, pulled off my clothes, and hopped into the shower, trying to wash off the oily film of guilt and complicity. It felt good, almost freeing, to be clean again. I was in my robe, in the kitchen having a cup of tea, when I heard the automatic garage door go up and then the back door open as Dave came in.

"How did it go?" I asked, my heart beating nervously. The first words we'd said to each other all day.

"Good. It went well." He nodded. At first a bit stiffly. He'd worn his Zegna cashmere blazer and the green striped tie I'd bought for him last Christmas. He looked a little bit like Woody Harrelson, only handsomer, in my view. Then he grinned. "Actually, it went really, really well. I'm starting to think this might work out."

I ran over and buried myself in his arms.

Did I say that this was my second marriage? For both of us. Dave's first was with a magazine editor who developed a serious prescription pill problem, and he got custody of the kids. Mine was just a youthful mistake at twenty-one that lasted a year. We'd both put in a lot to make this one work. And for the most part it had.

"It's okay. It's okay," he said, patting my shoulders. He could feel me shuddering against him, and I couldn't stop crying. "Jeez, Pam must've been one hell of a support system . . ."

I couldn't let go of him.

"Hey, what's going on? This isn't like you, Wend. Look . . ." He stroked my hair. "I know we have to talk. I know I said some things last night. Maybe this meeting was on my mind, I don't know . . ."

"No, that's not it. That doesn't matter." I looked at him and wiped my eyes. "Dave, something happened in the city tonight. You have to listen to me. I've stepped into a nightmare."

48

# CHAPTER FIVE

I didn't know where to begin, so I just blurted it out.

"Dave, I shot someone tonight. I killed him."

"*What?* What do you mean you shot someone, Wendy? What are you talking about?"

"Dave, please just listen to me!"

It was jumbled and rambling, and it felt like knives were stabbing me when I got to the part I dreaded most. Which was going up to that room.

"I don't know why I did it, David." I sat on a stool at the kitchen island holding a tissue, shaking my head. "I was just so angry from the things you said to me last night. Then Pam didn't show up. This guy came up to the bar . . ."

It took everything I had to get the words out. I

watched Dave's face twitch in surprise at first, as he realized what I was telling him, then go blank, maybe waiting for the part when I said I was joking, which never came. Then it simply slackened with the most confused, heartbreaking look.

"Dave, I swear to you, nothing really happened between us up there." I reached out and took his hand. "I give you my word. I stopped it before it really got anywhere. I was just so angry, David—"

"You went up to this guy's room?" He stared at me shell-shocked, and pulled his hand away. "To do what? To screw someone, Wendy?"

"Sweetheart, I never meant to hurt you." I latched back onto him, my heart almost falling off a cliff. "My relationship with you means more to me than anything in the world, and I realize what I've done. But that's not it! That's not all I'm trying to tell you, David. Something else happened up there. Something even more important."

"You shot someone?" His face screwed up in confusion. "What the hell did he do to you, Wendy?" His concern was mixed with anger and accusation. He searched my face and arms as if looking for signs of a struggle.

"Nothing. He didn't do anything to me, Dave. The guy's dead. He was shot. By someone else. Someone else came into the room—as I was in the bathroom. Freshening up."

*"Freshening up?"* This time the edge of accusation in his voice was clear.

"Dave, just listen to me! The guy was killed. Thank God I was in there, or I'd be dead too." I took him through what happened. Hearing the killer's voice. Curtis pushing the gun off the bed. Watching him be killed.

Picking up the gun and having no other choice than to do what I did.

My tears cleared and now there was only the deepest urgency in my eyes. "The guy was going to shoot me, David. I identified myself. I told him I was an ex-cop. I gave him every chance to put his weapon down. He didn't. What he did do was raise it up to me. I shot him, David. I had no choice. He would have shot me!"

I drew myself close to him. I needed to feel his support so badly. Stiffly, he put his arm around me as my heart pattered against him. Then I finally felt him draw me close. Hesitantly. His arms seemed remote and strange.

"I don't even know how to react to this, Wendy. What did the police say?"

I shook my head against him. "I never went to the police, Dave. I couldn't."

"You shot a murderer in self-defense. You'd just watched him kill someone, right? No one would question it."

51

"That's not all that happened, Dave. I was scared. I realized my life was about to fall apart. Because of where I was. I just wanted to get home to you." I lifted my face. "But that's not all . . . The guy I shot wasn't just a murderer. I checked him out and saw his ID after. He was a government agent, Dave. He was from Homeland Security."

The rest I told him as if in one long, rambling sentence. How I ran from the hotel room, straight into the killer's partner. How he shot at me, and I had to run. "I fled down the fire stairs, David. I'm lucky to be alive."

"Oh God, Wendy . . ." I sensed both sympathy and disbelief in his voice. I didn't know if *I* would believe it if he was telling it to me.

"I don't know what I stumbled into, Dave. But whatever it was, it was a murder. And something these people wanted to cover up. If I went to the police, they would have brought me back to the hotel, to the very people who were trying to kill me. I've never been so afraid in my life. All I could think of was getting back here to you." I cupped his face. "I knew whatever we had to do, we could do it together. Honey, I'm so sorry for what I did. I never meant for this to happen."

"But it did. It did happen." I could see he didn't know how to react.

"Yes, it did." I nodded guiltily.

"Does anyone know who you are?"

"I don't think so. But it's going to come out. There may be security cameras. And Pam knows I was there. I texted her about this guy. Besides, I killed someone . . ."

He blew out his cheeks and nodded somberly. "We don't have any choice but to go to the police."

"I know." Though the thought of it filled me with dread. A married woman up in a strange hotel room— to screw some guy she'd only met an hour earlier. Then shooting a government agent and fleeing . . . Would it be seen as just trying to cover up what I had done? I thought of my family and stepkids. It was all going to come out. "I'm scared, Dave." I kind of fell against him.

Again he wrapped his arms around me with a lukewarm squeeze. "I know you're scared. We can let someone intercede. A lawyer. There's Harvey Baum from the club." He'd handled Dave's divorce. "Or Hal . . ."

"Who the hell is Hal?"

"Hal Pritchard. He's been advising us on the deal."

My mind suddenly flashed to it. Given the sordid publicity, who the hell would want to merge with them now? "Dave, I'm so sorry I got you into this. I know how important everything was tonight." I hugged him. "I can't believe this has happened."

"We'll get through this," he said. "They'll have to understand. *The rest . . .* " He looked at me measuredly. It was clear what he meant. "The rest we'll have to deal with later. There are gonna be some things we have to talk over. Okay . . ."

"Okay." I nodded against his chest. I shut my eyes, as if I could wish this whole nightmare away.

"This other guy," Dave said. He pulled himself away from me. "The one who you . . ."

I knew perfectly who he meant. The one I went up there with. "Curtis."

He shrugged. "What do you know about him? Who is he? What did he do?"

"I don't know anything about him, Dave. I just met him at the bar." I winced, hearing just how that sounded. "He just sat down, while I was waiting for Pam. I don't even know if Curtis is his real name. Wait a second, I took his phone . . ."

"You took his phone?"

"From the room. I thought I might need it. To help me prove what happened."

I ran up to the bedroom and came back with my bag. Dave had turned on the television. It was almost 11:00 P.M. "This had to have made the news . . ."

I dug around in my bag, searching for his BlackBerry, and found it, at the bottom next to my iPhone.

I put the bag down and a weird feeling came over me. Something didn't seem right.

Like something was missing.

I sifted through my purse, finding my makeup kit,

my e-reader, trying to figure out what it was. Then it hit me.

My tote bag. With my program and some materials from the conference. It wasn't with my bag or on the kitchen island, where I put things down when I come in.

A feeling of dread came over me.

"What's wrong?" Dave asked.

"Something's not here." I went out the kitchen door to the garage and searched around my Audi. It wasn't there either. I recalled I'd had it at the bar. I'd even joked to Curtis about it. And I remembered taking it up to the room. I'd thrown it on the floor along with my bag and coat. We weren't exactly focused on that then. But in my haste, I must've left it.

For the third time that night my insides turned to a block of ice.

I came back in, my face no doubt white. Dave looked at me. "What's missing?"

"My program. From the conference I went to today. It was in a tote bag. Along with some other stuff. It's not here . . ."

"Our life is falling apart. Who gives a shit about the fucking tote bag, Wendy?"

"You don't understand . . . it's not the program." I could have cared less about my goddamn program.

It was that it said *Wendy Gould. Pelham, New York* on the printed label on the cover.

*It could identify me.*

My heart clutched in horror. The people looking for me, who had tried to kill me twice to keep what I had seen quiet . . .

They probably had my name right now!

# CHAPTER SIX

"Dave, we have to leave," I said, urgency crackling in my voice.

"We will. I just want to see if it's public yet. Then I'll call Harvey—"

"Dave, you don't understand. I think they know who I am. We have to get out of here now!"

That was the moment the news came on. The lead-in sent a shiver down me: "A shooting in a room at a posh midtown hotel, and two people are dead."

I watched in horror.

The reporter came on and described how an unspecified victim had been shot in his room at the "posh" Hotel Kitano, along with a second victim—details still unclear—"who was rumored to be a possible government agent."

She said that a third person was being sought. *A woman*, who might have been in that room when it all happened, and who had fled the scene.

My stomach wound into a knot. *I* was that third person.

The person they were looking for was me!

The newscast went on. By this time they'd have found the tote bag. So they had to know who that third person was. More than three hours had passed. If the police knew, *why weren't they already here?*

The only possible answer hit me. And it didn't make me feel any better. If the NYPD had it, they'd have been here by now. The neighborhood would be lit up with flashing lights. They wouldn't have even mentioned a third person on the news . . .

*They would already have me in custody.*

But if the people who had killed Curtis had found it first, *they'd* want to keep the whole thing quiet. They might not hand it over so quickly. They'd be just as scared that I'd be in the hands of the police and divulge what I had seen, which they'd want to cover up. *Which meant . . .*

I felt my throat go dry.

Which meant they might be heading here themselves, at that very second. To finish the job.

Their role in all this could remain secret as long as I stayed away from the police.

*Or was dead.*

Suddenly I became encased in sweat. We weren't safe here. We had to get out of here now.

"Dave, I'm going to get dressed. It's not safe to be here. You wanted to go to the police. So let's go! Let's just get out of here now!"

I ran to the bedroom and threw on some jeans and a fleece pullover. Back in the kitchen I grabbed my bag and Curtis's phone. We headed into the garage and climbed into Dave's Range Rover, me behind the wheel.

I opened the garage door and turned on the ignition.

Dave put his hand on my arm. "We'll make this all work out, Wendy . . ."

"I know," I said. "Thanks." I started to back out.

Suddenly a bright light enveloped us from behind. Headlights from a vehicle at the end of our driveway.

"Hands in the air!" someone yelled. "Out of the car! Now!"

I spun around in fear.

It was over. The police were here. I let out a deep breath, ready to comply. Thinking what I was going to say.

Then I saw that the light was from a black SUV. A single SUV.

"It's them," I said. I grabbed my husband's arm, terror running through me. "Oh, Jesus, Dave, they're here."

# CHAPTER SEVEN

Someone stepped out of the passenger's side of the SUV and cautiously approached us along the circular drive, his gun extended from the top of the semicircular drive.

Dave turned to me. "Wendy, you said these people were from the government. I'll talk to them."

That's when I looked out the window and saw the same black agent who had shot at me at the hotel perched behind the SUV's open driver's door.

My heart almost exploded in fear.

"David, we can't go out there!" I seized his arm. "These aren't the police. You heard what I told you. They're here to kill us!"

*"Kill us?"* His tone was as skeptical as it was uncomprehending. "Wendy, we have to go out there. I'll call Harvey. I promise, I'm not gonna let them take you

without knowing where—" He started to open the door.

*"No! Don't!"* I screamed, reaching over to him. "You're not going out there, Dave!"

There was no time to convince him. I threw the car into reverse and floored it. With a roar, the Range Rover lurched out of the garage and shot right at the oncoming agent, who dove out of the way.

I gunned it toward the SUV.

"Close the door!" I screamed at Dave, twisting around to see behind me. "Close the fucking door!"

He couldn't. We smashed full force into the grill of the government SUV, Dave's door flying open. I was jolted out of my seat, my head hitting against the sun roof. The black agent disappeared. I didn't know if I had hit him or not. I didn't care! I had to remind myself that these weren't the good guys—they were covering up a cold-blooded murder. That I was the one trying to save our lives.

Two shots rang out. Not loud cracks. More like muted thuds. Suddenly the rear windshield splintered and my heart almost clawed up my throat. Dave looked at me, his gaze bewildered as mine was fearful and panicked.

If there had been any doubt what these people were here for, it was clear now.

I jammed the car into drive and floored it again, this time forward. Dave's door was still open, the car's wheels screeching.

*"Wendy!"* he shouted. I hit the gas and steered toward the far entrance of our driveway.

By then, the first agent had risen to his feet. He ran ahead to block our way out, his weapon trained on us.

I bore down on him, prepared to run him over.

This time he leaped out of the way on Dave's side, firing as we sped by. *"No!"* Another shot thudded into us from behind, the rear windshield shattering. Another hit the side as I turned.

"Dave, close the fucking door!"

He reached for it in desperation, bullets flying into the car. The agent was emptying his gun. I heard a horrifying *"Oooof"* over the rain of glass and the engine roar. I looked at my husband. His head pitched slightly forward and he had a glazed look in his eye, and I realized in panic what had happened before I saw the blood flower on his chest and his hand drop limply to his side.

*"Oh my God, David!"* I screamed in horror.

Even as I rambled over our front circle, our eyes met for an instant. Our last instant. I'm not sure if there was anything in them anymore, just a kind of blankness and futility, as if he was somehow letting me down. It was a look I'll carry with me the rest of my life.

Frantically, I lunged for him, as we bounced over the Belgian block, the force of the turn pitching him to the side. And then Dave slid, fell out of my grasp, and onto the pavement like some lifeless sack of grain, as I turned the corner of the driveway onto our street.

I slammed on the brakes and stared at him in horror. *"David!"*

I knew he was dead. The glassy eyes staring blankly up at me. And dead only because of what I'd done. Staring up at me, like some disturbing image I'd seen on a news clip, someone else's husband, twisted, inert, two dark blotches on his chest.

Another shot pinged through the car from behind me, and I saw Agent Number One running toward me. I knew if I stayed even a moment longer, I'd be dead as well. I looked one last time at Dave.

My heart was crumbling.

I hit the gas, the Range Rover lunging forward. I sped away, tears flooding my eyes. I drove down my dark, sleeping street, anguish tearing at me. Disbelief. I told myself that this was only some horrifying, nightmarish dream and screamed at myself to wake up from it. Now. *Wake up!*

*Please.*

But as I sped through the darkened town, cutting down side streets and weaving through a parking lot only a resident would know to make certain I wasn't being followed, not knowing where I was driving, only that I had to get away, as far away from this as I could; I knew with certainty it was no dream.

*Oh, Dave . . .*

And I saw clearly how it was all going to look once it became public. That I'd killed a government agent in a panic after being caught in a stranger's hotel room, and now, having escaped the law enforcement agents who had come for me, I'd gotten my husband killed too. How, after an argument the night before, I'd betrayed him. I could just hear Pam on some news clip tomorrow reinforcing the whole thing. How down I had sounded. How desperate I'd been to meet her at the hotel.

And even if the police did somehow believe me about how the shootings there went down, how would the people who did this ever let me be, having witnessed what I had? How would I ever feel safe again, knowing they had to cover this up too?

They would never let me be free.

# CHAPTER EIGHT

I drove.

I'm not sure for how long or how far. Until I felt far enough away that I was certain no one was following me. Every set of headlights that flashed in my mirror sent a shiver of dread rattling through me. Several times I was sure I'd been found. Several times I froze, rigid with fear, waiting for the inevitable siren or flashing light.

But it didn't come.

I came to my senses on the Hutchinson River Parkway, heading north. A few miles up, I merged onto 684, just getting as far away as I could. Then Route 22 into Dutchess County. I finally stopped, from sheer exhaustion and the throes of grief taking over me. That time of night, I was practically the only car on the dark road.

I pulled into a dark, closed-up gas station and cut my lights. It was going on 1:00 A.M. My heart had barely slowed a beat since the shooting.

I started to sob. Deep, shame-filled sobs, everything starting to come up all over again, my forehead slumped on the wheel. My body convulsing. Over and over, I pictured Dave's empty face staring up at me. That final, befuddled look in his eye, how he didn't understand. How could he? His final word to me simply a helpless plea. "Wendy!"

And I knew he was dead only because of me. Because of what I'd done. How I'd betrayed him.

I screamed to no one, *"Why did I ever go up to that room?"* And no one answered. Tears cascaded down my cheeks.

I reached across the seat for my bag, fumbling for something I could use to dry my eyes.

Instead I found Curtis's phone.

An unstoppable urge came over me to hurl it as far away as I possibly could. Since I'd set eyes on him, it had only brought me hell. I opened the door, took the phone in my hand, and went to fling it into the darkness.

Then I stopped. Suddenly it occurred to me this might be the one thing that could help me.

There had to be something in it that would show what Curtis was into. Why he was being targeted. Who his killers were, and why they wanted him dead. What had Hruseff said? *"This is for Gillian . . ."*

66

It might well be my only chance to find out. I knew in the morning I'd be a hunted woman, sought for a connection to one murder and complicity in another. And that even I, if I looked at the situation through impartial eyes, would likely be convinced I was guilty. Until I knew why they wanted Curtis dead, I'd be a wanted woman. I'd never see my children again. I'd be running for the rest of my life.

I turned the phone on, the BlackBerry powering to life. I scrolled through his recent e-mails and texts, scanning for something from Hruseff or from someone named Gillian. I didn't find either. What I did find out was Curtis's last name—Kitchner. CBKitchner@gmail. com being his e-mail account. I looked over his messages. From friends. His family. His Facebook account. I looked under his contacts for a Gillian. Nothing. I didn't know where to begin.

I was about to put it aside when something made me look through his photos. Maybe it was simply the worry that once I put aside his phone I had no idea what my next move would be. I didn't know in which direction to drive. Maybe I was just so desperate to find out anything I could about him and what he might have done.

I saw his life: with friends at bars, a team photo of what looked like a rugby match. Then some in rugged terrain—Curtis with some soldiers in combat gear. It looked like Iraq or Afghanistan to me. He and a woman

I took to be his sister at a table with what I took to be his parents. They were all smiling and happy. They probably had no idea yet they had lost a son.

Then something caught my eye. A woman. The last picture he had taken. She was pretty and small, dark-featured, with full, dark hair pulled back. I noticed what appeared to be cuts and bruises on her face, and as I enlarged the shot, I saw that she was in a bed, wearing a green hospital gown. There was a date—five days ago. The only identification was simply an initial, L.

A shiver traveled down my spine.

The dark complexion. The oval shape of the face. Anyone might have easily made the mistake. Anyone who had been watching us . . . perhaps from the hotel bar.

I was staring at someone who looked a lot like me.

# LAURITZIA

# CHAPTER NINE

"Jamie, Taylor. Can you move forward, please?"

Lauritzia Velez got the kids' attention as they waited for the elevator on the third floor of the Westchester Mall.

Not her kids, actually. The Bachmans'. Lauritzia had only taken care of them these past two years. Taylor was nine, and was texting her friend Cameron, all excited about running into Michael Goldberg at the Apple store in the mall, and Jamie, eleven, was already completely obsessed with the new PlayStation 3 game he had just bought with a birthday gift certificate.

"You know, when we get back home, that game is on the shelf until you finish your homework."

"But it's Peyton Manning," Jamie muttered, his eyes still glued to the box.

"And you too, Miss Fancy Fingers." She pushed Taylor forward, the girl's fingers continuing to text at warp speed.

A heavyset woman carrying two shopping bags next to Lauritzia smiled at her sympathetically, as if to say, *It's no use. I've got my own.*

Lauritzia was twenty-four, dark-haired, with pretty dark-brown eyes that were the color of the hills at dusk where she was from, and she had worked for Harold and Roxanne Bachman since she had moved here from Mexico two years earlier. For the first time, she'd been able to put the hardships of the past few years behind her. She loved Mr. and Mrs. B; they'd been so good to her. They treated her like part of their family. They took her on vacations, encouraged her to call them by their first names, which she still wasn't comfortable with. They even paid her tuition at the community college where she was taking classes. Maybe one day she would have a degree. In retail merchandising. Perhaps she'd even open her own store. In the meantime, she looked at Taylor and Jamie as if they were her own. Like her younger cousins, whom she had always taken care of back home. With what had happened to her own family, they were practically all she had now. For the first time since everything started, she actually felt she had a new life. A life she trusted. Not to mention a home.

The elevator door had opened, but the kids just stood there.

"Let's go, Jamie, please." Lauritzia pushed them forward. Out of the corner of her eye she noticed a Hispanic-looking man in sunglasses leaning against a railing. She thought he seemed to be watching them. Things like that always gave her a shudder. "Taylor, take my hand."

They stepped inside, along with the woman with the shopping bags and two or three others. The doors closed and the elevator stopped at the second floor. A young couple got on, along with two black guys in the usual team sweatshirts and baggy pants.

"Kids," Lauritzia said, pulling them to the rear, "let everyone in."

"Lauritzia, can we stop at Five Guys?" Jamie asked. His favorite burger place.

"We'll see."

The doors closed and the elevator went down to the first retail floor, then on to Level 1, where they had left the car. Lauritzia let her mind drift to what she would make them for dinner. The Bachmans said they were going out. She had some chicken she could thaw. And there was leftover macaroni.

Maybe Five Guys wasn't the worst idea . . .

The doors opened on the ground level. "C'mon, guys." Lauritzia placed her hands on their shoulders and started to push them forward.

That was the moment when her life was rocketed back to her own private hell.

A man stood in the doorway. A man who looked like a thousand men she had seen in her past: dark skin, black hair knotted into a roll, sunglasses; the all-too-familiar tattoo running down his neck.

She saw him reach inside his jacket.

Lauritzia knew. Even before she watched him search through the elevator for her eyes, scanning through the other people getting off.

Before she saw him pull out his weapon.

*She knew.*

And in the horror of what she knew was about to happen, her thoughts ran to the one thing she knew she could not lose.

*"Taylor, Jamie!"* As they stepped forward, she lunged for them, pulling them behind her as the first deadly *pops* rang out.

People began to scream.

The chilling sputter of the gun was a sound that had riddled through Lauritzia a thousand times back in her own town, as common as church bells. A sound she knew all too well, and that had cost her everyone she once held dear.

*If this is my time, let it be so,* she said to herself. *But Jesus, Mary, please, not the kids.*

The familiar sounds of panic rang all around her. The gunman was quick on the trigger and did not wait. Jamie and Taylor screamed, not fully realizing what was happening. Lauritzia forced them to the floor, pressing herself on top of them, praying that whatever evil was being done, it would leave and not take them.

*Just spare the kids,* she begged God. *Please, do not take these kids!*

She pressed her face against Taylor's, saying her own prayers, and tried to stifle the girl's cowering sobs. Someone fell in front of her, and she waited for the bullets to hit, for the end to come.

But suddenly there was a different sound. Not the ear-splitting sputter of a machine pistol. But two loud *pops*.

Then there was only silence where a moment before there had been mayhem. Silence and that awful, smoke-filled smell that always came before the wails.

She looked up. The tattooed young killer was on his back, dead, his semiautomatic pistol at his side. A young policeman came up with his arms still extended. What happened next was the aftermath she knew all too well: the awful smell of lead rising like smoke. The anguished screams and moans. The hushed murmurs of shock and disbelief.

The woman with the shopping bags who had smiled at her was dead, her once kindly eyes frozen and wide. One of the black guys was moaning, his T-shirt soaked in blood. The young man who got on with his girlfriend on Level 2 was holding on to her body, moaning in disbelief. *"Kelly . . . Kelly . . ."*

Beneath her, Jamie and Taylor were sobbing.

The policeman finally took his gun away from the shooter. "Is everyone all right?" Then, shouting into a radio, *"Emergency. Emergency!* Shooting at the Westchester Mall. Level One. We need EMS immediately—everything you've got. Suspect down."

Other people wandered up and began to help the shell-shocked people out of the elevator. Lauritzia lifted herself up, and then the kids, who were whimpering in shock. *I have to get them out of here*, she knew. *Before anyone comes.*

*Before they ask her questions that she did not want to answer.*

"Is it over? Is it over, Lauritzia?" Jamie kept muttering.

"Yes, yes," Lauritzia reassured him. She hugged them with all her might. "You are safe." But she knew it wasn't over.

Only then did she feel the burning on her face and put her hand there and notice the blood. Her blood.

"Lauritzia, you're hurt!" Taylor yelled.

"We have to go!"

She pressed their faces close to her as they stepped over the bodies to shield them from the horrible sight.

"Everyone wait over there," the policeman instructed them. "EMS is on the way. You too," he said, guiding Lauritzia.

But she could not wait.

*"Come!"* she told them, lifting them off the ground and carrying them past the swarm of bodies. They were

76

trembling and whimpering—who would not be?—but there was no time to delay. She took a last, quick look at the shooter. She had seen his face a thousand times. The tattoo. Only by the grace of God had they been spared.

But these others . . . She glanced back sadly at the heavyset woman's frozen eyes. *Dios toma ellos almas.*

God take their souls.

But by the time the police came she had to be long gone.

*"Children, quick!"* she said, dragging them toward the garage. "We must get out of here now!"

# CHAPTER TEN

Thirty minutes later, the tears ran freely in the Bachmans' kitchen. Tears mixed with horror and elation.

"You saved their lives," Roxanne said as she dabbed Lauritzia's cheek with a cloth and hugged her. Held her as warmly and gratefully as if Lauritzia was one of her own. "There's nothing we can do that can ever thank you enough."

Mr. B rushed home. They told Lauritzia over and over that she was a hero. But she knew she wasn't a hero. She knew she was anything but that.

Still shaking and in tears, Jamie and Taylor sat in their parents' arms and told them how Lauritzia had pulled them to the elevator floor before they even realized what was happening, and how she had covered them with her body as the shooting broke out, shielding them from harm, and then got them out of there.

"It must have been so horrible," Roxanne said over and over, tears in her own eyes, unable to let them out of her arms.

"*It was*. It was," Taylor said, her face buried in the crook of her mother's arm. "Mommy, I saw this woman and she was—"

"Don't talk about it. Don't talk about it, honey." Roxanne pressed her daughter to her cheek, stroking her hair.

Jamie, still white as a ghost, could barely speak at all.

"Maybe we should contact the police," Mr. Bachman said. He had rushed home from his law office in Stamford as soon as his wife called. "You got a look at him, didn't you?"

"Not a good one," Lauritzia said. "I was on the ground. No, please, no police. That is not a good idea."

"Maybe later, Harold," Roxanne said. "You can see how they're all still rattled."

"Yes." Lauritzia nodded. "Maybe later. If they need me."

"Anyway, there were witnesses all over," Roxanne Bachman said. "We don't have to involve the kids."

Mrs. B was tall and pretty, and usually wore her shoulder-length blonde hair in a short ponytail. And she was very smart; Lauritzia knew she had once been in the financial investment business. That was how she

79

and Mr. B first met. Now she did a lot of charity work for the school. And did yoga and ran marathons. And was the president of the neighborhood in Old Greenwich, where they lived.

"It's just all so horrible." Roxanne couldn't stop squeezing her kids.

"They're saying it was some kind of drug thing," Harold said. His prematurely gray hair always gave him an air of importance, and Lauritzia knew he was important; he was a senior partner in a big law firm. "There was no immediate connection to any of the victims, but one of the people who was wounded has a record for selling drugs or something . . ."

"*Sí*, it was horrible," Lauritzia agreed. They would never know how horrible. *Yes, those poor people*, Lauritzia knew, feeling ashamed.

"You ought to get that looked at," Roxanne said of her wound. "I can take you to the emergency room—"

"No, the blood has stopped. It's nothing."

"Anyway, you should lie down. You're still in shock. I'll look in my medicine cabinet. I might have something."

"Yes, I think that would be good." Lauritzia nodded.

Roxanne put her hand to Lauritzia's cheek. "Look how close this came . . . We can never make up to you what you did for us today."

Soon the phones began to ring.

Mrs. B's parents. Judy and Arn. Roxanne had called

them, having told them the kids were heading to the mall, and knowing they would hear about it on the news. And then their friends. Then Jamie and Taylor's friends. Soon it would be chatter on Facebook. After that, maybe local reporters. They'd want to hear their story.

And maybe hers too—the one who saved the kids!

Next it would be the police.

In her room, Lauritzia lay on her bed. She was growing more sad than she was afraid. Sad that it had come to this. That she had never been completely truthful with them. Or told them anything of her past. Except a made-up story, about how her father was a cook in the village where she came from. That had once been true. And how she had come here to visit her sister. That was partially true as well.

Before the nightmare began.

Now she knew she could no longer stay. They knew. They knew where she was. She could not put the family in any more danger than she already had. She could not do that to them. People she had grown to love. Anyway, once the truth came out, they would lose all trust in her. They would ask her to leave.

A drug thing. That's what Mr. B claimed that it was . . .

It is always a drug thing, Lauritzia knew.

*La cuota.* That which is owed. To the *familia*, the cartel. A tax to the grave.

For her, what she owed was clear.

She had seen them. Through the maze of people.

Before dragging Jamie and Taylor to the ground and burying her face in their trembling bodies. She had seen the shooter's face and the dull, businesslike indifference in his eyes. The tattoo that ran down his neck. There was no attempt to hide it. The skeleton's head that brought back all the terror and fear she had prayed she had forever left behind.

She knew who they were and where they were from.

And worse, Lauritzia thought, pressing the photo of her dead brothers and sisters to her pained heart, she knew exactly why they were here.

# CHAPTER ELEVEN

Lauritzia knew she had to leave. Leave now. She could not put them in danger another time.

There was just nowhere in the world for her to go.

Only back home, she realized, though that would be a fate of certain death for her. The day she left, she knew she could never return. She no longer had a home. Except here, while it had lasted. The Bachmans had given so much to her. She would miss Taylor and Jamie as if they were her own. But she could not put them at risk. She had lived two years in the fantasy that she had somehow escaped her fate. Part of a new family. Going to school. Pretending there was an outcome for her except that which she knew would ultimately find her.

Maybe that was someone else's dream. Like the one

of her own store. And surrounding herself with happy things. She perfectly understood this, as she took her bags from the closet.

*La cuota.*

It had found her. And it would have to be paid.

Two mornings later she made breakfast for the kids, as she did most every weekday. She had waited for them to feel fit and ready to go back to school. Mrs. B had met with the principal the day before and decided it was okay for them to return. The two were strangely quiet and withdrawn on their ride there, as if they somehow suspected something. Maybe they were just nervous to face the many questions about what had happened and have to recount their frightening tale. Maybe it was something deeper—the violence always did that to children. Why would they understand? As she drove up to the school and they were about to run out, Lauritzia reached over and held them.

"Wait a minute," she said. "I want a hug. An extra-special hug this morning. For friends forever."

They looked at her as if it seemed a bit peculiar.

"I think I've earned it," Lauritzia said, flashing them her happiest smile, trying not to show her sadness, which was killing her inside.

"Okay," Jamie mumbled, and tilted his head against her arm. Taylor gave her a real hug, which Lauritzia put her whole soul into in return.

"I'll see you soon," she called after them. Then quietly to herself: *"Quizá un día."*

Perhaps one day.

Back at the house, she hastily packed her belongings into her bags. Her clothes, many of them the fine things Mrs. B had given her. The pictures she had kept of her family. And ones with her new family too. A wooden carving of Santa Bessette that her sister Maria had given her, which now meant more to her than anything in the world. Sadly, Lauritzia put her textbooks aside on the night table.

She would not need them anymore.

When she was done, she dragged her bags out to the foyer and called for a taxi. Roxanne was at exercise class, and that gave her about half an hour. She sat at the kitchen island and tried to put her thoughts down in a note. To all of them. She told them how much she loved them all and how they were like family to her now, her only family, and always would be. But that she had to go back home.

"Lives here are not like where I come from" was all she said. The words were hard to get out. "There, they are not fully your own. I wish you all the love of God. You will always be in my heart. Each of you. Every day. You treated me with love and made me part of your life and for that it is *I* who can never repay you enough, not you me."

She felt herself starting to cry.

Mercifully, she was saved by the sound of the cab honking outside. She brought her bags to the step and asked the driver to wait. Just a few moments more. She ran upstairs one last time, to the kids' rooms, and placed a flower from the kitchen on each of their beds.

Where she was from it meant someone would always watch over you, no matter where in life you went.

As she finally went out the front door, carrying her bags to the taxi, she took a final look at the house that had given her a home for a second time.

Then she went down the stairs, wishing someone had put a flower on her pillow too.

# CHAPTER TWELVE

Roxanne parked the Range Rover SUV in front of the three-car garage and went in through the kitchen. The bar method had been a real killer today. Jan was the instructor, and she always made her do things she didn't think she could. Things no body was meant to do!

She had a crazy day ahead of her. There was the spring fund-raising lunch for the kids' school, then a 2:00 P.M. meeting with a prospective new landscaper for the home owners' association where they lived. She had a session planned with a trauma psychologist for the kids, so she had to pick them up herself; Harold said he would join. She had just put in a call to the school to check on how they were doing, and the principal said, while it was still early, so far everything seemed fine.

They'd been through hell, and Roxanne didn't want to rush getting them back to normal.

"Lauritzia!" Roxanne called out as she came in, opening the fridge and grabbing a coconut water container. She took out her vitamins, magnesium pills, and fish oil. *"Lauritzia, are you here?"*

No answer. Maybe she was at the store. She took her iPad and sat down at the counter, thinking about her day.

That's when she saw the note.

*"Mr. and Mrs. B . . ."*

As soon as she read the first sentence, which took her by surprise, her heart began to crumble.

*"This is so difficult for me to write . . . ,"* the letter began. *"I have to go back home."*

*Back home.* Roxanne was dumbstruck. She was certain Lauritzia didn't have any family there anymore. She had never completely spelled out the details, but she always said there was nothing for her back home anymore.

*"You and your kids, you have been like a true family to me . . . You spoke of this after the terrible thing we witnessed the other day. But it is I who can never repay you, not . . ."*

"Oh, no, no, no, Lauritzia . . ." Roxanne felt herself almost start to cry.

She didn't know what could have caused Lauritzia to panic so. Obviously it was connected to what had happened at the mall. That had triggered something. She and Harold had noticed that Lauritzia hadn't seemed herself since. But to leave like this. Out of nowhere. Without even saying good-bye. *And to go where?* Back home . . . back to a place where she had nothing. Running away as if she was in fear. *Running from what?* The kids would be brokenhearted.

The note made it seem as if she felt she had no options. But she did. She did have options.

Roxanne ran into Lauritzia's room. The bed had been made, her textbooks piled neatly on the night table. How proud she had been the day she came back with them! The closet was cleaned out. Roxanne checked the bathroom. Empty. She sat sadly on the bed.

*Oh, God, Lauritzia. Why?*

It was clear she could only have left just a few minutes earlier. She had driven the kids to school. And the Ford Escape, the car she always used, was still in the driveway, so she must've called a cab.

Roxanne punched in the number, already sure where Lauritzia would head. She glanced at her watch. She knew she only had minutes.

"Riverside Cab."

"Hi, this is Mrs. Bachman, at 230 Brookside. I think our nanny just left in one of your cars?"

"Yes, Mrs. Bachman." The dispatcher paused, checking. "She should be just arriving at the station now."

"Can you raise the driver? Can you tell him to tell her to wait for me? Tell her not to get on that train. I'll be right there!"

89

She ran back into the kitchen and pulled off the Metro-North schedule that was pinned to the bulletin board. It was 9:32. The next train to New York was 9:45. Thirteen minutes. That didn't give her much time.

Grabbing her bag, Roxanne jumped back into the Ranger Rover and backed out of the driveway. It was ten minutes to the station. If she didn't get there, Lauritzia might well be gone, out of their lives forever.

She couldn't let that happen. Not without letting her know, whatever it was, whatever had suddenly scared her, that she did have options.

She drove on Riverside, heading toward the station, and punched in Lauritzia's cell on the Bluetooth.

No answer. She wasn't picking up. Roxanne wasn't surprised. The voice mail came on. *"This is Lauritzia . . ."*

"Lauritzia, this is Roxanne. Hon, I know you're at the station. I'm headed there right now. I read your note. I know you feel you have to go, but whatever it is, I want you to wait for me. Just to talk, before you go. Will you wait for me, please! I'm on my way."

She drove a little crazily, barely stopping at the signs on Riverside Avenue and Lake, then wound around the traffic circle into the station.

She drove up to the southbound tracks, just as a city-bound train was pulling in. She threw the car into park and ran up onto the platform. She looked in both directions, saw about a dozen people moving toward the opening doors. She didn't see Lauritzia anywhere.

Where the hell was she? Could she possibly have made it there ahead of time and gotten on a delayed, earlier train?

She threw her arms in the air and blew out a breath in dismay.

Then she saw her. At the far end of the platform, lugging her bags, just as the train came to a stop.

"*Lauritzia!*"

The nanny turned. There was something anxious and unhappy in her reaction, being spotted. Whatever it was, it wasn't joy.

Roxanne sprinted down the platform, begging the doors not to close. "*Lauritzia, please!*"

Passengers got on. A conductor stepped out. "Nine forty-five to Grand Central! In or out, ma'am," he said to Lauritzia.

She steadied her suitcases. Roxanne could see the conflicting emotions in her eyes. Hesitating . . .

Roxanne stopped about ten feet away. She just stood there. "Lauritzia, please . . . there'll be another train. *Please!*"

The girl was tough as nails and 100 percent determined, but standing there, unsure what to do, she had the appearance of a frightened child. She took a step back onto the platform.

The train doors closed.

"I don't want you to go," Roxanne said, the train pulling away beside them. "I don't know what happened.

I don't know why you feel you have to leave. But whatever it is, Harold and I want you to stay. The kids want you to stay."

"I can't . . ." Lauritzia shook her head. "I have to go."

"We can help. You're like family to us. You're not alone, Lauritzia. Whatever it is, we'll be there for you."

"You can't help." Lauritzia's eyes flashed defiantly. "You may think you can, but you can't. And I didn't save their lives. I didn't. It was I who put them at risk."

"What are you talking about?" Roxanne asked her.

Lauritzia grabbed her bags. She attempted to move away. But then one fell out of her grasp. She stopped. They were the only ones left on the platform.

"Tell me what it is. The kids love you. They'll be heartbroken. *We'll* be heartbroken."

"And I love you all too. Don't you understand?" Lauritzia put her bags down. "It is precisely because of that that I have to go."

Roxanne went up and grabbed her. She put her arms around her and hugged her, feeling the tremor of the girl's conflicted emotions. Until Lauritzia's resistance began to wane, and her cheek fell wearily onto Roxanne's chest, and she began to weep, her words falling off her lips like tears, tears of hopelessness and futility. "It will only bring bullets and tragedy. Please, Mrs. B, let me go."

"Why?" Roxanne looked into her eyes. "Why do you have to run?"

"Don't you understand, I didn't save your children at the mall. I am the one who put them at risk. Those bullets weren't meant for those other people who were killed." Her eyes filled with terror. "They were meant for me!"

# CHAPTER THIRTEEN

An hour later they were back at the house. Harold had rushed home at Roxanne's urging. He and Roxanne went into Lauritzia's bedroom. Sitting on her bed, clutching one of Taylor's bears, her eyes red from weeping, Lauritzia told them what had happened.

"I know I told you I was from the south of Mexico," Lauritzia began, "but I'm not. I'm from a region called Sinaloa. A town called Navolato. It is a village under the control of the Juarte cartel. Their *plaza*, it is called. It means the territory they control. Juarte, you may have heard of the name?" she asked, looking at Harold.

He just looked back at her and shrugged.

"Where I come from it is famous. Famous for the wrong things. The man who runs it, Vicente Juarte, he is known as 'El Oso.' The Bear. El Oso's cartel is one of the biggest in Mexico, and he took over for his father when he was killed by a rival group. Killing and not knowing who will be killed next are a way of life in my home. The victims, they pile up in the streets. Six, seven a day. It is part of everyone's life there. *Do you know what happened to Ernesto Ayala? Did your cousin not come home from work on time?* A part of everyone's family. *My* family . . ."

She put down the bear, and Roxanne saw the wall of resistance and buried emotions Lauritzia was trying to break through. It was clear she did not tell this story to anyone.

"Three years ago, my father became a material witness against one of Juarte's enforcers, a very brutal man named Eduardo Cano. 'El Pirate.' Cano was part of a group that is known as Los Zetas, the Z's . . . maybe you've heard of them? They were once a part of the Mexican armed forces—I think trained by your own country's military to go up against the cartels. But money lures, especially in Mexico, and so they formed their own cartel killing and protecting the drug sellers, and El Pirate, he worked closely for Vicente Juarte's cartel."

"How was your father involved?" Roxanne asked, her leg curled on the edge of the bed. "You always said he was a cook."

"He was." Lauritzia nodded. "Maybe a long time ago. When I was young. Three years ago, El Pirate conducted a hit in the town of Culiacán, near where I am from.

My father, who worked for him now, was charged with carrying it out. He had his own nephew, my cousin, who was just a boy, take charge of it, in which two American citizens, a husband and wife, were murdered in their car, and by accident—though there is no such thing as an accident in Sinaloa—three other Americans, college kids, who were caught in the crossfire. It was his big step up for my cousin Lupe. His first real charge. Maybe you heard of the case here. I think it was on the news for a while . . ."

"I remember," Harold said, leaning forward on the chair at Lauritzia's desk. "I think they were there on spring break. One of them was even from Greenwich. Wasn't someone charged in the crime?"

"Sí." Lauritzia nodded. "Cano. Cano was charged. Months later he was apprehended in the United States. But somehow the case against him was dropped. You tell me, how does that happen? An attack against your own citizens. He was simply deported and never put on trial. He went back to Mexico, where he still works as a killer for Vicente Juarte.

"The government convinced my father that they would protect him. And us, his family. But when the trial was dropped, they blamed it on his testimony and did not follow through. They did not grant us asylum. Clearly he could no longer go back home. But Cano took revenge against him for his betrayal. One by one, he killed his children and nieces and nephews."

Roxanne felt a weight fall inside her as it grew clear exactly who Lauritzia meant. Her own brother and sisters. She looked anxiously to Harold.

"First, they killed my brother, Eustavio," Lauritzia said, "who was just a postal clerk in my village. They came and took him away as he was on his way to work, and they found him in a ditch a day later with burns all over his body and his genitals cut off."

"Oh, God . . ." Roxanne looked at her, a wave of sympathy rushing into her eyes.

"Then my older sister. She worked in a beauty salon. She was beautiful and she was engaged to be married. They weren't satisfied just with her. They came in and killed everyone in the salon. Twelve people. Innocent people. People who just worked there. Customers. They found Nina's body with sixty bullet holes in it. No one was ever charged with the murder. No one, though they came in in the middle of the day and shot off over two hundred rounds."

"Lauritzia," Roxanne said, reaching for her hand.

"Then they killed my sister Maria, who was living with my cousins in Juárez. She'd been raped and all cut up—"

"Lauritzia, you don't have to go on," Harold said, exhaling a grim breath.

"Yes, yes, I have to go on. You should hear. This is the life we lead. This is what it is like for us there. My brother and sisters and I tried to come with my father when he was granted asylum in the States. But by that time, the trial against Cano had fallen apart and your government no longer had a need to accommodate him, so we were all denied. They said we had not proven that a threat existed directly against us, only against my father. Now they are all dead. All of them. My father could not even come back home to bury them."

"Oh, baby, I'm so sorry," Roxanne said, and leaned forward to hug her. Lauritzia pulled back and shook her head.

"Do you think it stopped there? No, it did not. It still goes on. These men, they are more vicious than animals. Animals would never stoop to do such things. They even killed my cousin, the one who conducted their own hit, that started this. Lupe. He was just a boy, nineteen. Yes, he was on the wrong side of things, but in Mexico there are two sides to life: those who are victims, who are poor and scared and cannot afford even the smallest luxury in life; and the ones who say yes and get involved. Who see the others driving big cars and carrying wads of bills and carrying on with the women. *Plata o plomo,* as we say. Silver or lead. That is their choice. He chose silver. Doing what they tell you to do is just the way. Do you think he knew any better? He was just nineteen . . .

"Then just before I started to work for you, they found my sister Rosa . . ." Lauritzia's eyes started to fill up with tears. *"Mi gemela.* My twin."

Now she had to stop. Roxanne moved over and finally took hold of her hand, squeezing it tightly. But Lauritzia just shook her head and wiped her eyes with the back of her hand, saying, "You wanted to know why I have to leave? So you should hear. You remember I had her picture here by my bed."

"I remember," Roxanne said, tears building in her eyes now as well.

"She was older. Six minutes. We used to laugh. She always insisted how she was that much wiser than me, six minutes, and no matter how much older I became she would always have that over me. She met a man. They were married. She was living in Texas. Dallas. She had a job, as an administrator for an insurance company. And she was pregnant. Five months pregnant. With my little nephew. They found her in the elevator of her building. I won't even tell you what they did . . ." Tears shone in her eyes, tears of anger now. "He would have been named Eustavio. After our older brother, who they . . ."

She stopped and turned to Roxanne, her dark eyes glistening with rage. "This is why I told you to let me go! Do I need to finish the story? Do you understand now? What happened at the mall? That the only reason I am alive and the others are dead is because the killer began shooting and a policeman happened to be there.

"Yes, I saw them!" Lauritzia said. She turned to face Harold. "Of course I saw them! Los Zetas. I saw the look

99

of the devil on the killer's face and the dead man's tattoo on his neck, and when I dragged your children to the ground, I prayed, *Please, God, whatever you have for me, do not take them too!* I swore that I would leave, so that is why I must. That is what I meant, that bullets and tragedy, they will never let up. These men, they carry their vengeance to the grave. Now you see why I have to go. It is my fate. I cannot put you or your children at risk. You should not have come after me. I've already said my good-byes. I should have gotten on that train!"

# CHAPTER FOURTEEN

Harold asked where Lauritzia's father was now. She merely shrugged and said she didn't know.

Only that he was in this country somewhere. But that even the U.S. government no longer knew for sure. "He grew afraid. Cano was trained in this country, by your own agents. Why did the trial against him just fall apart? Influence is something that can be bought on both sides of the border, is it not? My father thought it best for me not to know his whereabouts. In order to protect *me*. I haven't spoken to him since my sister was killed. More than two years now. We both protect our whereabouts."

He shot Roxanne a look that suggested maybe they could try to locate him.

"No. *No!*" Lauritzia shook her head, reading his

101

intention. "Do you really think I'd be safer with him? I would only draw him to them. Which is what they want."

Roxanne asked her where she was heading to when she stopped her at the station.

"I have a cousin. In New Mexico. On my mother's side." Lauritzia shrugged. "I was going to see if she would let me stay there for a while."

"And if she wouldn't?"

"If she wouldn't, then I do not know what I would do. I am in violation of a court order to return home. I have no job, and without a job I can no longer remain. I would go home."

*"Home?"* Roxanne looked at her in shock. "Home is a death sentence for you, Lauritzia."

"My life is a death sentence, Mrs. Bachman, don't you see? Tell me what other choice I have! Live on the streets here and beg? Sell myself?"

Roxanne reached out and clasped her hand. "That's why you never allowed us to sponsor you for your green card, isn't it? Because you were afraid?"

"Yes. I was in violation of a court order to leave the country. They would have found out who I am and sent me back. And even if they didn't, look what happened to Cano. He is Zetas. He is very connected with the United States. He would have found out where I was. I am sorry that I never told you these things." She took Roxanne's hand in hers. "I never wanted to place my worries on you. I never wanted to put your family at risk. You must believe that. But now that you know, the children will be coming home soon. I should leave . . ." She started to get up.

"No," Roxanne said.

"No, Missus, it is not right." Lauritzia stood up, but her eyes welled with tears. "It will be very hard for me to see them again and have to—"

"No." Roxanne held her back by the arm. "This isn't just a place of work for you. This is your home. No one forces you to leave."

Lauritzia smiled, a smile that was both pleased yet skeptical, and went to pick up her coat and scarf. "I'm sorry, but I do not have a home anymore."

"Yes, you do." Roxanne took Lauritzia in her arms, the girl attempting to pull herself away, to grab her coat, to break free, until she just surrendered, not knowing whether to resist or go, the torrent building in her eyes, until she just gave up and put her head on Roxanne's shoulder and began to cry.

Roxanne looked at her husband over Lauritzia's shoulder as she stroked her hair. "You poor child. God only knows what you've been through. Well, you damn well have one now."

"I know what you're going to say," Roxanne argued to Harold outside, his lawyerly, gray-templed look of reason and restraint. "I know what's happened. But we can't just let her leave. That girl's been through hell. If we let her walk out that door, we'll be sending her to her grave. She'll be dead in a week!"

"Rox, you heard her story . . ." Harold leaned against the wall. "We've got the kids. These people could try again anytime."

"And speaking of the kids, look what she did for ours at the mall. She put them before herself. You saw how close that shot came. That could have been Jamie or Taylor. We can't just abandon her, Harold. What kind of a thing would that be?"

"There's a lot involved here, Rox. It's not just a question of good intentions. She's in violation of a court order to return home. She's been illegally hiding here. For all we know her father may be at odds with the U.S. government. Not to mention the little matter that if these people actually now know where she is—"

"I realize they know where she is, Harold! But we can't just walk away from her. This girl saved our children."

"I was talking about our children, Roxanne." Harold looked at her sternly.

"I know. *I know* . . . But if she goes back and something happens to her, I couldn't live with that. We don't do those kinds of things, Harold. If what she says is true, the U.S. government has treated her every bit as cruelly as this Cano. They've got blood on their hands as well. She saved Jamie and Taylor. We can't turn around and say, 'Thank you very much, but you have to be on your way. It's just too much of a risk. Here's a little money.' Not after what she's been through. You're a lawyer. The case can be reopened. We can represent her in some way. Or we can set her up somewhere. We can afford it. What the hell is it all for, anyway? We don't just call her part of the family, and take her on vacations and trust our children in her care, and then when something comes out that interferes with our neat, orderly lives, give her fifty bucks and a train ticket and tell her we don't have the heart!"

"Mexican drug enforcers aren't exactly a minor interference in our neat, orderly lives, Rox. Not to mention taking on the U.S. government. Anyway, she's not even asking for our help. She's seen these people. She understands. She knows firsthand."

"I realize she knows, Harold. But that doesn't mean that we just back down. We owe her something. When those bullets were flying, her first thoughts weren't for herself. They were for our kids. That's my *cuota*, Harold. And I damn well intend to pay it back. You're as smart a lawyer as I know, and you've got an office full of even smarter ones back there. So think of something."

He had that look, that look when he knew he was worn down. Or at least strategically outflanked. He picked up his suit jacket. "I'll ask around. In the meantime, I don't want her leaving the house. And God knows, not with the kids. I'm going to hire a private security outfit, just to keep an eye over the house. The first sign of anything, Roxanne, and she's got to go. Is that clear? This isn't some stray dog you've picked up on the street. You heard her story. You know what these people are capable of—"

"Jesus, Harold, we live in a goddamned gated community in Greenwich. They can't just barge in here . . ." She leaned against him and hugged him. "But I'm not abandoning her. As long as that's clear too."

He squeezed her on the shoulder and, when she looked up, took a long, admiring look into his wife's glistening eyes. "You know somewhere in all of this is precisely the reason why I love you. You know that, don't you?"

"You don't need to look very far, Harold. It's what's right. And you know *that*, don't you?"

"Yes." He nodded begrudgingly, putting on his jacket.

"Just find something. Something that gives this girl a chance. But, yes . . ." She centered his jacket on his shoulders and straightened his tie. "I know that, Harold. About why you love me." Roxanne smiled at him. "I do."

# CHAPTER FIFTEEN

When Harold came home the following night, he spoke with Roxanne privately, and after a few minutes with the kids, helping Jamie do his fractions and Taylor download photos on Apple TV, he and Roxanne asked to speak with Lauritzia in their study.

It was his office at the house, littered with briefs and law books. She hardly ever went in there.

Harold sat in the high-backed chair at his desk, and Lauritzia on the green leather couch. Roxanne sat next to her. It was clear they had something important to tell her.

"Your family has a case file with an immigration court in their attempt for asylum?" Harold asked her.

"Yes." Lauritzia nodded. "My sister filed it. In Texas, when we tried to move here. She wanted her son to be born in America."

"Do you remember the name of the judge who presided on it?"

Lauritzia thought back. She hadn't come here yet, and she was a minor back then. Her older sister and father had handled it. "It was Esposito, I think."

"We'll need to find it."

Lauritzia stared, confused.

"We can represent you, Lauritzia." Mr. B leaned closer to her, a serious but somehow hopeful look on his face. "We can file an appeal, to the Immigration Appeals Court. We can go for what's called a 'motion to re-open,' which basically means you could stay here, if we win. And judging by what happened the other day, I can't imagine a court in the country not agreeing that the clear threat against your father extends as well to you. You wouldn't have to go back home."

"Represent me?" Lauritzia asked, looking at them both. "This will cost a lot of money."

"Let's just say we won't spend our time worrying about that right now. The firm can pick up the majority of the costs. And if there's more, well . . ." He nodded toward Roxanne. "The first thing we have to do is familiarize ourselves with your case. You're the one remaining plaintiff of record now. Then we have to find someplace for you to stay. Someplace that's safe. You understand that, don't you, that you can't remain here?"

"Yes, I understand," Lauritzia said, her insides warming to what she thought she understood they were saying. The darkness that had weighed her down like a leaden overcast sky began to clear. This was more than she could ever have hoped for. No one had ever been there for her before.

"We'll win this for you." Harold reached across and squeezed her hand. A faint smile broke through. "I promise we'll win."

"No one's going to walk away from you, Lauritzia." Roxanne took her hand. "When we said you were like a part of this family, we meant it. Like it or not, you're stuck with us!"

Mrs. B's confident eyes and warm, determined smile infused Lauritzia with a strength she had never felt before. "So I don't have to go?"

"Not unless you want to," Harold said, grinning. "And even then, I believe it'll be over my wife's dead body."

Lauritzia looked at him and laughed. She didn't know what to say. Suddenly she felt joy come out of her. As if out of every pore. A joy she hadn't felt for years, since when they were all children, back at home, before everything happened. It was a joy she felt she could trust, not a fake one, like a *governmentale* kneeling over a body telling her they would look into it. Which everyone there knew was just a *pantalla*, a sham.

"Thank you!" she exclaimed.

"Not me," Mr. B said. "I'm just the hired hand. Her." He pointed to Roxanne. "This is all her doing."

"Thank you both!" Lauritzia said, unable to hold herself

in. She leaped up and hurled her arms around Harold and hugged him, taking him totally by surprise. And then Roxanne. A warm, deep, penetrating hug, as deeply as if Roxanne had brought Rosa back to life and her sister stood with her arms open in front of her.

Never before had anyone stood up for her. Stood up against them. She had only seen the pall bearers and those who grieved. Tragedy and death. Now she had something she'd had only a few times in her life: a feeling of hope. The last time was when Rosa had told her that she was pregnant. She was in the United States and would have a boy, and there was hope for a new life for them. Away from all the bloodshed.

That hope did not live long, but this one was real. One she could touch and count on.

Roxanne said, "I don't know if you'll be able to remain with us when it's over. Purely for your own safety."

"I understand."

"But we'll set you up in a place where you'll be safe. You can visit. You can get a job, or go back to school somewhere. Don't be so quick to leave those books behind . . . you still might get that store."

Lauritzia couldn't hold back from laughing.

Roxanne squeezed her hand. "Maybe you'll even find your father . . ."

Lauritzia's eyes filled up with tears. "A day ago I felt there was no light anywhere in my life . . . just terror, and I had to face it alone. Now, when I look at you, at

you both, there is nothing for me but light. Excuse me
. . ." She felt the tide of emotion rushing up inside her.
"I'll be right back," Lauritzia said, rushing to the door.

"Where are you going?" Roxanne asked.

She was going to cry. But she didn't want to show
that to them. "I want to tell the kids!"

# WENDY

WENDY

# CHAPTER SIXTEEN

I woke up, hearing the *whoosh* of rushing water outside. For a moment it filled me with peace, a sound I had awakened to a hundred times, one that always made me feel like everything was calm and right in my life. And that usually meant my family was around me.

Then I realized where I was, and the reality of the night before came crashing back to me. Not like the peaceful brook outside a country home. But like a raging flood of dread. A tsunami of darkness and nightmare I never saw coming, taking with it every plank and brick I had built my life on, sweeping it all away in an instant like a dark torrent of debris.

I blinked my eyes open. I sat up and looked around the familiar living room of our ski house in Vermont. The truth knifed into me, like a punch in the solar plexus.

I had driven here in the dead of the night. Arrived here at four in the morning. Exhausted. Not knowing where else to go. I just needed a place to collapse and think. Think what to do. Who I could contact. I opened the door and hurled myself onto the living room couch and just passed out. I slept like a corpse, hiding from my haunting dreams. The sun cut through the room. My watch read 9:30 A.M. The truth dug into me that if I were here, and not back in my own home, then what I'd been praying was just an awful dream was real. Exactly the way my mind was rebelling against remembering it.

*Please, please, don't let me really be here . . .*

I looked around and saw the antique signs we collected. CHEAP CORN, 5C. HOOF IT TO DIAMOND GRAIN AND CATTLE. The vintage board games Dave scoured flea markets for displayed on the wooden shelves.

The vintage pinball machine in the corner.

I recalled how I had pulled over to the side of the highway, somewhere in Massachusetts, and called the kids. I woke Neil in the middle of the night at school.

"Jeez, Wendy, what's going on?"

"Neil, something terrible has happened. To your father . . ." I did my best to tell him; the words fell from my lips like stones off a ledge. "Dave's dead. He's been killed, Neil. I'm so sorry . . ." Then in the vaguest, clumsiest way I tried to tell him what happened. I knew it wouldn't make any sense. Only make me appear guilty and all mixed up. Agents coming to our house in the night. *"What agents?"* he asked, becoming clearheaded. Shots as I tried to escape.

*"Escape from what, Wendy?* What the hell are you talking about? What do you mean, Dad's dead? He just called me earlier today. You're sounding crazy . . ." He was an eighteen-year-old kid, and I was telling him his father had been killed, and I couldn't bring myself to tell him why.

*"What are you saying, Wendy?"*

"Neil, honey, I need you to trust me and do something for me," I said, urgency coming through the desperation. "I want you to go to your aunt Ruth's and uncle Rob's in Boston. First thing tomorrow morning. Just go! Don't ask me why. This is important. You're going to hear some crazy things . . . about what happened to your father. About *me* . . . Sweetheart, all I can tell you is they're not true. I loved your dad very much, and now I've done something, I don't know how, that's gotten him killed. I just don't want you to believe what they may be saying—"

*"Saying?"* His sleep-strained voice grew elevated in exasperation. "What are you talking about, Wendy? *What's* happened? *What* can't you tell me?"

Tears rushed into my eyes. *I only wish I knew.*

"Neil, you've always trusted me like your own mother. And I think you know that's exactly how I've always felt about you. Like you're my own! And now

117

you just have to trust me, honey. I can't be with you just now. It won't be safe. For *you*. Something's happened and I need to sort it out. I know I'm sounding crazy. I know I'm not telling you what you want to hear. Just get to your uncle Rob's. It'll be safe there. And please, I beg you, Neil, don't tell a soul where you're heading. Not even your roommates." I knew the people who were looking for me could find him. Could do to him what they had done to Dave. "Just go, first thing in the morning, okay? Promise me that, honey—"

"This isn't a joke, is it, Wendy?" he said, fighting back tears.

"No, honey, it's not a joke. I wish it was. Just promise me you'll go, okay?"

Now he was weeping. "Okay . . ."

"And I give you my word, baby, whatever you may hear, it's not the truth. I swear to you on that! Now go, I have to call Amy. I'll be in touch as soon as I can." I heard him sniffling, trying to sort through the shock and confusion and grief. "I love you, baby."

"I know. I love you too, Wendy."

I hung up, the bass drum inside me beating through my brain. Then I did it all over again, with Dave's daughter, Amy, six hours ahead in Spain. She was just heading off to class. Amy, who had always had issues with me. She was nine when Dave started seeing me, a year after separating from her mother. Old enough to feel like I had stolen him away from her, and kept him

118

from ever going back. I understood. It just took her a while to learn to truly trust me. But eventually we worked it out. Neil was always my baby. I'd lived with him since he was eight. How I wanted to put my arms around them both. I needed to. I'd just lost *my* partner in life as well.

My world was crumbling too . . .

I knew I couldn't stay here for very long. It was no secret we owned the house. Once word got out—maybe it already had!—someone would surely come by and check. The West Dover police. Or one of the neighbors. I got up and flicked on the TV, hoping to hear something about what was going on. I went into the kitchen and put on some coffee, then trudged over to the computer we kept there and punched in Google News.

I wasn't sure what I was hoping for. To find nothing—like none of it had ever happened. Which would still mean my husband was dead, and that a government kill squad hadn't even informed the police and were trying to silence me.

Or what I saw, the third article down.

Which stopped my heart as quickly as if a syringe of paralyzing fluid had been injected into it.

PERSON OF INTEREST IN NEW YORK TRIPLE MURDER NAMED.

# CHAPTER SEVENTEEN

Numb, I focused on the headline and knew what everyone must be thinking. My kids. My family. Pam.

Anyone who knew me.

My eyes riveted on my name. *Wendy Stansi Gould.*

I almost retched, my name juxtaposed with such horrible crimes. But there it was, hitting me squarely in the eyes. Taking away my breath. I could barely move the cursor, my hands were shaking so noticeably.

The article was from the AP, and posted only eight minutes earlier.

"A person of interest has been named in the string of Metro New York shooting deaths that began Wednesday night in a posh midtown hotel room and ended in an affluent suburb where the husband of the person police are seeking was found dead."

*Found dead?* Dave wasn't "found dead." He was killed. Something already didn't seem right to me.

"Wendy Stansi Gould, 39, whose husband, David Michael Gould, was found shot to death at his Pelham, N.Y., home, is being sought in connection with his and two other shooting deaths: a man identified as Curtis Kitchner, a freelance journalist, and a person yet to be identified, said to be a federal law enforcement agent. Both were shot in Mr. Kitchner's room at the Kitano Hotel. Ms. Gould is suspected to have been present at both crime scenes."

I felt the blood rush out of my face.

"Police report that Ms. Stansi Gould was seen with Mr. Kitchner at the hotel bar only minutes before he was found dead in his hotel room, the result of an apparent shooting incident with the unidentified law enforcement agent. Soon after, Ms. Gould was spotted fleeing the hotel."

"Of course I was fleeing!" I said out loud. *I was scared for my fucking life that they were trying to kill me!*

"Later, when investigators arrived at her house in Westchester," I read on, "they found the body of Ms. Gould's husband in the kitchen of their tony Pelham Manor home."

*What!* My stomach started to come up. Dave wasn't shot in the kitchen. He was shot in my car. As we tried to escape. A numbness began to take hold of me as I started to see exactly what was going on.

121

"A 9mm handgun was also found at the house, which is now being tested to determine if it matches the weapon used in the shooting of the law enforcement agent in Mr. Kitchner's hotel room. An unnamed police source suggested the make and caliber could prove to be a match."

*The same gun.* That was impossible. I'd left the gun on the bed in Curtis's room. I tried to think back to the gun Agent Number Two had used to shoot Dave in my car.

I never saw it, of course. I was speeding by.

I read the section again as my stomach turned upside down.

*"No, no, no!"* I shouted. "That's a complete lie! It didn't happen that way at all!"

They shot Dave in the car, not inside the house. And the gun from the hotel couldn't be there. Unless . . . I began to see the script.

Unless they took it.

Unless they had taken it directly from Curtis's room and used it on Dave. I didn't have to even finish reading to see how incredibly incriminating this looked. They were framing me for Dave's death, just as they were trying to frame Curtis at the hotel, make it seem like he was the one who had drawn on Hruseff.

*"No!"* I shouted again. "No. That's not how it was at all!"

"Ms. Gould was seen drinking in the company of Mr.

Kitchner at the hotel bar shortly before they moved upstairs. A police spokesman speculated she may have panicked and grabbed a gun when some confrontation between Mr. Kitchner and the second victim took place in Mr. Kitchner's room."

*Panicked? Of course, I panicked! The bastard murdered a man right in front of my eyes. He was about to turn his gun on me!*

I clicked to the next page. "After fleeing the hotel, it is presumed Ms. Gould made her way back to her home, where after a possible altercation with her husband, she shot him as well, and fled. Her Range Rover SUV was reported missing from the garage."

Gripped by nausea, I scrolled through the rest of the article, numbly coming to accept how this would all look to the world. To my kids! The whole thing had been twisted. Twisted to make it look like I had killed that agent in a panic and fled. Then made it home and killed Dave.

In horror, I saw how every detail about the entire evening would only back up this very scenario. Even Pam, who would attest to how upset I'd been about my argument with Dave the night before. How I'd mentioned this cute stranger at the bar. As if I'd scoped him out.

It was all, *all* going to back up exactly how they wanted it to look. I read on, until I crashed headfirst into the one moment I regretted from my own past that now was twisted to fit in too:

Ms. Gould worked in financial sales and studied law at Fordham University. She was a Nassau County police detective assigned to the Street Crime Unit, who resigned in 2003 after she and two other members of the unit were involved in the shooting death of an unarmed twelve-year-old boy in Hempstead. Ms. Gould, then 26, and two other detectives were brought up on charges of reckless discharge of a deadly weapon after Jamal Wilkes was shot five times while being chased through an abandoned building. Sergeant Joseph Esterhaus, the team leader, discharged his weapon eight times believing he had seen a weapon in Mr. Wilkes's hand. He and fellow detective Thomas Swayze were charged but ultimately cleared in a departmental review. Ms. Gould, Wendy Stansi then, who fired her weapon twice, neither shot striking the victim, was not criminally charged and left the force. Ultimately, no weapons were found on him, only a plastic water bottle, prompting outcries of the reckless use of firearms and racial profiling.

Senior Homeland Security agent Alton Dokes announced that "as one of the victims was an agent of the Federal government, federal authorities would be taking the lead in this case."

I stared at the screen, my body encased in sweat. I could only imagine what anyone reading this would now think of me. What my own children would think.

That I was a loose cannon. Of questionable moral character. That I had done this kind of thing before. That I had killed their father. With the same gun I had taken after panicking and killing a federal agent.

After sleeping with someone I had met at a bar just an hour before!

*You have to believe me*, I had begged them last night on the phone. *You're going to hear some things . . .*

Not to mention that the very people now in charge of trying to apprehend me were the ones who had set it all in motion. Who had the most to gain by keeping me silent.

The most nerve-racking, sickening feeling knotted up in me. If I ended up in their hands, I didn't know what would happen. These agents had already tried to kill me. Twice. And here I was at our house in Vermont, which was easily traceable. The news report had been posted only ten minutes ago.

I had to get out of here now!

I threw on some new clothes, a T-shirt and a blue Patagonia pullover over my jeans. I bundled a few other things together—clothes, toiletries, the laptop—and hurled them into a duffel bag from the ski room, grabbed a parka, and ran downstairs. I was about to toss them into the Range Rover when I realized my car was no longer safe to be driving now. An idea hit me. Our neighbor across the street, Jim Toby, was a New Yorker who kept an Expedition in his garage up here. It was a Thursday. He and Cindy wouldn't be up. I knew the security code. We'd been watching over each other's ski houses for years.

I started up the Range Rover and drove it around the back of the house, under the deck, so it was out of sight. Anyone who searched the house would easily find it, but at least someone just passing by wouldn't realize I'd been there.

I lugged the duffel and my jacket across the street to Jim's, a modernized A-frame from back in the sixties. I punched the security code—his and Cindy's wedding anniversary, 7385—into his garage panel. The door slid up, and the familiar navy SUV was parked there just as I'd hoped. I tossed the duffel into the backseat and hopped behind the wheel. The keys were in the well; I drove out, closing the garage door behind me. I headed straight down the hill, my heart pounding insanely inside me, not a clue in the world where I would head. Suddenly I saw flashing lights appear ahead of me; two state police cars sped up the hill. I held my breath. My rational side told me I was safe in this car; no one would stop me. But my nerves jumped out of control. I closed my eyes and averted my face as they shot by.

I blew out a relieved but anxious breath. It was clear where they were heading.

If I'd only left five minutes later, I would have been caught.

I knew I couldn't do this forever. I had one chance,

and that was to turn myself in to someone who would hear my story first. I drove down the hill toward West Dover, the realization beating through me that I was a fugitive in three murders now.

# CHAPTER EIGHTEEN

It's funny, how you might not speak to a person for years, someone who was once a key part of your life. But then, when you need someone in a moment of crisis, theirs is the one name that comes to mind.

In my case, that was Joe Esterhaus.

Joe took me under his wing when I was a rookie on the Nassau County police force, and I guess he caused me to leave it too. I come from a family of cops. My father was one. He and Joe came up together. My older brother too, out of the One Hundred and Fifth Precinct in Queens, and he happened to be on assignment in lower Manhattan and rushed into the South Tower on his twenty-eighth birthday when it was hit by a plane the morning of September 11. It was why I signed up, as a twenty-four-year-old bond salesperson on Wall

Street, trying to give some honor to his life. I never really wanted to be a cop. I wanted to be a soccer player. I'd played left wing on the soccer team at Boston College. My junior year, we even made it to the Big East championship game.

Joe was one of those people in your life that you would always want in your foxhole, no matter how hard he pushed you or even yelled at you in public. He ran the respected Nassau County Street Crime Unit, and it wasn't just that he'd known me since I could first kick a ball, or went to my First Communion, even my high school graduation. Or just because of my brother Michael, whose death made them all weep like babies. For them all.

It was that his best friend, my dad, Timothy Edward Stansi, was a first responder. He'd lost a son that day, and took a leave, and spent that last good year of his life picking through the ruins, never finding a sign of him. By 2003 he was dead from congestive lung disease.

That was why I was fast-tracked out of cadet school and put straight onto the Street Crime Unit. It was a way for Joe to keep a promised eye on me. He kept me under his wing. Though it didn't take long for me to realize it wasn't for me.

When Dad got sick, Joe became kind of a second father to me. Before the incident at the Haverston Projects, he was the first person I would have called, and if I told him I wasn't guilty, no matter how it looked, I wouldn't have had to say another word.

But soon after, things just fell apart. It was an angry time back then, after Amadou Diallo and Abner Louima in the city; everyone pointing fingers, shouting about racial profiling and trigger-happy cops. We ended up cleared by a department review, but he was forced to resign. He started drinking, and his wife, Grace, died from breast cancer. I went to law school for a year. Then I met Dave, at an advertising cocktail party. Our lives just moved in different directions. I suppose we both kind of reminded ourselves of a different past. Mine moved forward; Joe's, well, his was never the same.

Truth was, I hadn't spoken to him in a couple of years.

Still, he knew half the people of any importance on the forces in New York and on the Island, and the other half would probably say they knew him.

I pulled the car over on Route 100, not knowing where to go or who to call, my name out there in connection with three murders. I wished that my dad was around, but he wasn't.

The only other person I could think of was Joe.


"Wendy!"

"Joe, thank God, I didn't know who else I could call," I said, the nerves clearly audible in my voice. "I wasn't even sure this number was still good."

"It's all right. I'm glad you did. Wendy, before you say another word, you have to be careful about the phone."

"I think it's safe, Joe. I stopped at a market on the way. I bought a disposable one."

"Good. That was smart. Wendy, we've all heard the news. No one can believe a word of what they're saying. What the hell is going on?"

"Joe, listen, before I tell you anything, you need to believe me—what they're saying isn't true! I didn't kill Dave, I swear. You know that. And I damn well didn't kill that government agent the way it's being said. It was entirely self-defense. He was shooting at *me*! I'm scared, Joe. I stumbled into something, and I'm being set up. I saw something . . . and now to keep it quiet they're trying to kill me too."

"Who's trying to kill you, Wendy?"

As calmly as I could, which wasn't easy under the circumstances, I told Joe everything that had happened to me over the past twenty-four hours. How I'd met Curtis at the Hotel Kitano bar and ended up in his room.

"First, I swear, Joe, nothing really went on . . . We kissed a little, that was all. I know how all this must sound—"

"Wendy, I don't care about that stuff. But they're saying you killed a government agent . . ."

"It's true. But it was one hundred percent self-defense, Joe. I was actually in the bathroom, getting ready to leave . . ."

131

No matter how many times I went through it, I still couldn't quite believe it had actually happened.

"Joe, he was trying to make it seem like the guy had pulled a gun on him." I told how I'd identified myself as an ex-cop and how, instead of putting down his weapon, he made a move. "He was one hundred percent intending to kill me too. I'm sure of that. He might have been a government agent, but this was a murder, Joe. An execution. And I watched it happen."

"Did you happen to see what agency the guy was from? No one's saying."

"You sitting down?" I told him how, before I left the room in panic, I pulled his ID. I sucked in a breath, knowing exactly how this was going to go over. "Homeland Security."

There was a pause. I heard him blow out a breath. "Nice work, Wendy."

"I know . . . Joe, all I could think of was that my life was about to fall apart if anyone found me there. When I ran out in the hall I ran straight into the guy's partner. He took a shot at me and I panicked and ran. I went down the fire stairs. I don't even know how I managed to get away."

"You took the train home. Why didn't you go straight to the police?"

"Because the police would have brought me right back there. I'd just seen someone murdered in front of my eyes! The killer's partner had just tried to kill me too! I was scared to death. I didn't know what I'd stumbled into. Not to mention, all I could think of was that my whole life was about to fall apart. If I hadn't run, I'd be dead! I'd be dead," I said. "But Dave . . . Dave would be alive . . ." A wave of guilt mixed with shame rose up in me. I started to sob again. I couldn't hold it back.

"I know. I know, Wendy. I know exactly what you're feeling. I know this is hard. But these are only questions someone else is going to put to you. And with a lot more at stake behind them. Why did you take the gun?"

"I didn't take the gun," I said, wiping away the tears.

"They're saying Dave was shot with a weapon they're matching up against the one in the hotel."

"I'm telling you I didn't take the gun, Joe. That's all a frame-up. I left it back at the hotel."

"So how did Dave get killed?"

I took him through how I'd made my way home, and how I realized I'd left my tote bag and that they had to know who I was. "I grabbed Dave and told him we had to get out of there. We were actually heading to the police, in the car about to leave, when all of a sudden these lights flashed on from behind us. It was them!"

I went through the rest. Not the police, but the agent who had shot at me at the hotel. "I knew we couldn't just give ourselves up. That's why they were there, at the house, instead of the cops—to finish the job. And I never took that gun from the room! I left it on the bed, I swear!"

"So Dave was with you? In the car? Not inside the house?" His tone contained an edge of incredulity.

"Yes, he was in the car, trying to leave with me. They started shooting and killed him as we drove away. The door was open and he fell out. I stopped and stared at his face, Joe. I knew he was dead. Then they started shooting at me. But if someone took that gun from the hotel room, it damn well wasn't me."

Joe grew silent, probably trying to absorb what I was telling him. I knew much of it sounded like a stretch. It was one thing to say I was unjustly accused, another thing entirely to fight back against a government cover-up trying to put the blame on someone else.

"I give you my word, Joe, they're trying to frame me for Dave's murder, just like they were trying to frame Curtis in that room. To make it look like he had drawn a gun first."

"All right. I got it. Wendy, exactly what do you know about this guy Curtis?" he asked me.

"I don't know a thing about him. He claimed he was a journalist. That he was in New York on a story. I took his cell phone. I thought I might need to find out something if I ever had to prove my innocence. I didn't even know his last name. Though I do now . . ."

"Kitchner, right? I heard it on the news."

"Yeah." I heard him writing it down. "Joe, someone has to look through his computer . . ."

"Whose computer, Wendy?"

134

"Curtis's. It was on the desk in the hotel room when I left. He said he was a journalist. There has to be something in there that would show why these people wanted him dead. That would back me up."

"In the room, you say?" Now I was sure he was writing it down. "On the desk?"

"Yes. I know I should never have gone up there, Joe. I can't undo that. But I didn't intentionally kill anyone. And I damn well didn't kill my husband. I loved him. You know that." My throat was like a desert, and a clinging sweat had sprung up on my back. "You see any way out for me here?"

"The agent, the one you ran from at the hotel," Joe said. "Dokes. You probably won't want to hear this, but he's been put in charge of the case."

"I saw that," I said glumly. The very person with the motive to keep me silent. Who has already tried to kill me. Twice. "My kids probably think I'm a murderer too. That I killed their own father. After completely betraying him. I can't live with that, Joe. Either I find out what's behind this, why these people needed to kill Curtis—they had to be into something dirty—or I turn myself in. But not to them. To someone else. To someone who will hear me out. I'll go to the press and blow the whole thing open. Let the truth come out that way. I guess that's why I'm calling *you*. I need someone to help me, Joe. I don't have anyone else."

If there was one person I knew wouldn't put me on

hold and contact the police on the other line, it was him. He knew more than anyone how your life could come crashing down in just an instant. Because of one ruinous decision. And what it was like to be thought of as a killer.

"Let me think about that awhile. I'll be back with you."

"I don't really have a while, Joe. I don't have anywhere to go."

"Maybe I can help you with that. I have a summer cottage," he said. "In Waccabuc. That's in upper Westchester. It's not much. But you'll be out of sight there until we figure out what to do."

My insides lit up in gratitude. "I don't want to get you involved like that, Joe. It's bad enough that you're helping me now."

"You must be kidding, honey. I haven't felt this alive in years."

"So how do I find it? Your cabin," I said, putting the Explorer back in gear.

# CHAPTER NINETEEN

The press conference on the steps of the FBI Field Office in lower Manhattan was both electric and emotional.

A federal Homeland Security agent gunned down apprehending a suspect.

A doubting husband killed by his suspect wife—Wendy Stansi Gould. The only link between the two murder scenes, a woman who had clearly gone unhinged. And who was on the run.

The deputy director handled it. Alton Dokes was only a step away.

She couldn't get far.

Dokes settled into his makeshift office as senior team leader of the investigation. They'd set up a joint task force with the FBI. They'd track her bank and credit cards. They had her cell phone number; they'd track all activity. Sooner than later she'd have to refill the car. She wasn't a professional at this. They were tracking down her family and friends. There were only so many places she could go. She'd have to surface.

They'd get her.

If he didn't get her first.

Her bad luck, Dokes knew, to even be in that room at that time. But Hruseff was a fool. He always threw caution to the wind. From way back. He should have waited for her to leave. However long it took. Like Dokes had pushed him. But no, Ray was always impetuous. Ever the cowboy. Even if he had handled her in there, it still would have made complications.

Now it had fallen into his lap.

The poor woman had no idea, no idea of the sort of damage she could create if her story about what happened got out. No idea of the network of contacts he had to find her. *Not that anyone would ever believe her*, Dokes told himself, chuckling. A hot little number who stepped out on her husband. Then killed him when he found out what she'd done. He'd set that up well. That story of how she got dumped from the police force was only the icing on the cake.

Dokes wasn't even sure they had to silence her. She could shout it from the rooftops. Who would ever believe her now?

No, best to do what they came for. Best to end it as

soon as the opportunity came about. He'd put too much into his career, they all had, to see it end now.

Too bad. Dokes rubbed the birthmark on the side of his face. He had watched her in the bar. Hot little number.

Too bad she'd never know what she'd stepped into.

Too bad she'd likely never make it into custody alive.

# CHAPTER TWENTY

The sound of crunching gravel in Joe's driveway sent a series of shock waves through me.

I ran to the window. If it was the police, I was resigned to give myself up.

But to my relief, I saw it was Joe's old Pontiac coming down the driveway.

I'd driven here yesterday afternoon, found the key to the front door in a fake rock set under the front step, exactly where Joe described it. The place was cold; there was some canned soup in the kitchen cabinet I was delighted to heat up. And on the subject of heat, it must've been twenty degrees out there during the night. It took the better part of three hours for the cottage to churn up enough warmth to stop me from hugging myself in my parka until I finally fell asleep, searching for any news of me on the relic twelve-inch TV.

Joe stepped out of his car and came toward the landing. An older version of Joe than I was prepared for. He was in his sixties now—I hadn't seen him in three or four years—and maybe not doing so well. His once salt-and-pepper hair had now become white, and the lines on his face that used to speak of toughness and experience had now hardened into the telltale canals of age, burrowed by life's disappointments. He came up to the door and was about to knock. I thrust it open and let him in.

"Joe!"

He smiled back, warmly, happily. Mostly with his eyes. "Hey, doll."

We looked each other over, his expression shining with a kind of close uncle's affection; mine, no doubt, showing how taxing and overwhelming all of this had been.

"Let me give you a hug," he said.

"I can use one," I said, weightlessly falling into his still-strong arms.

"I'm so sorry about David," he said into my ear as he squeezed me. Not that I recalled them actually meeting more than a couple of times, and by that time Joe and I had moved apart. But I knew it meant a lot to him, who'd vowed to Dad that he'd be my protector, for me to have landed safely into a new life after how we'd left the force.

"He was a good guy, Joe," I said, unable to let go. "He didn't deserve this." For that moment, it felt as if nothing bad had happened, as if we'd been transported back in years. "I'm sorry too." I felt tears running down my cheeks.

"I'm glad you found the place okay. Sorry about the heat. It's real nice in the summer. The lake is just down the road. I know I didn't leave you much in the way of food. I haven't been up here since September—"

"Joe, it's perfect, please." I pulled away, wiping the tears from my eyes. "I can't tell you how much this means to me. I had nowhere else to turn."

"Well, I'm glad you came to me, Trey." Trey was my nickname as a cadet on the Nassau force. Third-generation cop. "We're gonna see what we can do. First," he said, rubbing his palms together, "let's crank up that burner. I don't thaw out as well as I used to anymore. Any coffee?"

There was, and I made some. He took off his jacket and sat at the wood table in a plaid, wool shirt. I noticed his hands shaking as he lifted the mug, and it became clear it wasn't from the cold. Our eyes met as he steadied it with his other hand. This time I was the one looking on with empathy.

"How long?" I asked him.

He shrugged, like a guilty child who'd been discovered. "Three years. Just after Grace passed away. It's not as bad as it looks. I can still take care of myself."

I knew that he had lost most of his medical benefits as a result of the incident. A subsequent civil suit and lawyer's fees had taken much of the rest. Parkinson's required treatment. And care. Lots of it.

"Robin and Steve are going to add something onto the house if it reaches that point," he said with a resigned sigh. Robin was his daughter, a couple of years older than me. "Though, uh, we're not exactly tooting our horns over the construction business about now, are we? Anyway, we're not here about me. I thought the plan was to figure out how we're gonna have you get out of this mess."

I nodded and put my hand warmly on his shoulder. "Ten-four, Sarge."

"This morning I went into town and grabbed a few minutes with an old buddy of mine. Jack Burns. Remember him?"

"No." I shook my head.

"He was captain of detectives at One Police Plaza back in the day. He was at Mike's funeral. Timmy's too. Anyway, ten years later he's got the gold stars on his sleeve now. Assistant chief. In charge of Borough Services."

"What did you tell him?" I swung my chair around.

"I told him what you told me. All of it. Including how you say it happened at your house. With Dave. And how you never took the gun. I told him I could get you in. But we had to do it safely. Without it getting out."

143

"I'm listening."

"Wendy, what do you know about this guy? Curtis, you said his name was, right?"

"Yeah, Curtis." I shrugged. "I told you. I don't know anything, Joe."

"What about why these particular people would be in his room?"

"The guy said something about Gillian. Before he shot him. I think that was it. I was scared. 'This is for Gillian.' I looked through Curtis's cell phone. I couldn't find anyone by that name. I'm hoping they'll find something in his computer."

"I mentioned that," Joe said, his face sagging into a frown. "To the NYPD." He leaned closer, forearms on his knees. "They didn't find any computer, Wendy."

"*What?* It was in the room, Joe. On the desk. It was a Mac. I saw it before I left."

"I know you told me it was there. But according to the evidence sheets, in the reports, there was nothing."

"There *was* something there, Joe!" Again, my stomach twisted into a knot. "The feds took it. Just like with the gun. Like how they're trying to pin Dave's murder on me. They're whitewashing the whole thing. There's something in there they don't want anyone to find."

"You said you had his phone?"

I nodded. I reached into my jacket pocket and put it out on the table.

Joe said, "Maybe they can find something in there.

144

Jack remembered right away that you and I had a history together. He never liked how it all ended up with me. He knows we did good work in that Street Crime Unit."

"You can trust him that it won't go straight to the investigation?" To Dokes.

"Look, I can't promise where any of this goes . . . only that he committed to take you in and hand you over safely to the FBI, and not the people who came after you. I told him you were scared and that the situation at your house didn't go anywhere near how the government people are saying it did. But that's a stretch, for someone like him to believe. You understand that? You have a lawyer?"

I shrugged. "Harvey Baum. He was Dave's—"

"I don't mean a divorce lawyer, Wendy. Someone who knows what the fuck he's doing in a criminal court."

"Then, no. I don't."

"This is the United States, Wendy. Whatever you stumbled into, they're not going to just take you into a cell and you won't come out. You'll get to tell your story."

"There's my car. It was shot up pretty good. I left it in Vermont. That has to count for something."

"The word coming down is that they arrived there just as you were fleeing the house, after killing Dave. And that they shot at you only as you tried to avoid capture."

"That's just not true . . ."

"Apparently their vehicle is pretty battered up, Wendy."

I nodded sullenly. "That part is." Everything fit their narrative. I sucked in a nervous breath. I knew that if I was taken into custody, I'd be arguing for my life. I knew it would be a hell of a lot more intense than this. "So when does this all happen?"

"Tomorrow. I told them I'd get back to them with a place. Somewhere public. Midtown. A hotel lobby, maybe. Bryant Park."

"What about Grand Central?" I proposed.

"That could work."

"At rush hour. It's crowded. There are multiple entrances and exits if something goes wrong."

"Nothing's gonna go wrong, Wendy . . ."

"They killed my husband, Joe. They've completely twisted things around and tried to cover up what really happened. I watched them kill an innocent man right in front of my eyes. They're the ones who have something to lose if this all comes out. They're never gonna let me tell my story. We both know that, Joe. They can't. I'm scared . . ."

I leaned over to him and he hugged me again. My heart beat nervously against him.

"I'm glad I told him," I said into his flannel shirt.

"Who?" Joe asked.

"Dave. I'm glad he knew. Before he died. What I'd

146

done. When those goddamn lights flashed on behind us. It's hard for me to accept, that he died thinking that of me. What I'd done." My eyes stung with biting tears.

"I promise." He squeezed me again. "He wasn't thinking that, Wendy. And nothing's gonna go wrong. I'll look the place over myself, when I get back into town."

"You weren't at my house, Joe. You weren't in that room. How can you be so sure?"

He cupped my face and looked at me almost the way my father used to. I felt a wave of confidence run through me.

"'Cause I'll be there."

# CHAPTER TWENTY-ONE

There are at least fifteen separate entrances to the main atrium of Grand Central Terminal.

I figure, at some point, I've probably gone in through them all.

There are the two main ones on Forty-Second Street, and the ones on Lexington and Vanderbilt Avenues. There's the Fiftieth Street and Forty-Eighth and Forty-Sixth Streets, through the North Annex that lead directly onto the tracks. Down the main escalator from the MetLife Building. Through the alleys of Park Avenue East and West that border the Helmsley Building. There's even the stairway from the Campbell Apartment, an old speakeasy situated off Vanderbilt Avenue that not many people know of and that Dave and I occasionally went to before heading home. I counted fifteen. There could be more.

But enough that the people who wanted to keep me quiet would never be able to cover them all.

I thought the best way for me to arrive was to come in directly on a train. With sixty-some-odd tracks on two different levels, at rush hour, there was no way they could watch them all. I left Jim and Cindy's Explorer in a lot near the Rye train station and took the Metro-North into New York. I wanted to be sure I turned myself over to Joe's contacts with the NYPD and not anyone else. No way the bastards who'd killed my husband would ever let me fall into the right hands.

The plan was to meet Joe at the information booth at the center of the Grand Concourse at 5:15 P.M. This was the height of the rush hour, when the crowds would be heaviest. I was told there would be three people from the NYPD waiting for me. Joe's friend Burns, the assistant chief, who'd be wearing a blue New York Rangers cap, and two other senior detectives. No one could guarantee I wouldn't ultimately be handed over to the feds—they had jurisdiction; it was their case. But the whole thing would be made public. The press would be fully aware. I'd be able to meet with a lawyer.

I had a story to tell—and I wasn't about to tell it to anyone else.

My train from Rye rolled into the station at 5:04. I stepped onto the platform and blended in with the crowd. I had on the blue Patagonia pullover I'd taken from Vermont, a hooded microfiber shirt underneath. I wore sunglasses. I told Joe I'd meet him at the ticket counter just before 5:15. He said he'd scout the place out and make sure everything looked okay. The crowd pushed me forward, and the platform slowly fed into a narrow staircase leading to the upper level. I stepped in behind a black woman and her young son who'd gotten on in New Rochelle. My heart was starting to beat heavily. I got on my disposable phone and called Joe.

"I'm here," I said when I heard him answer.

"I'm here too. Don't be nervous. Everything seems to be a go."

"'Don't be nervous.'" I chortled grimly. "Let me keep that in mind." I pulled the hoodie up over my hair.

The kid in front of me stumbled on the stairs and I steadied him from behind. I gave him a smile and he shot a quick one back to me. "Reggie, watch yourself," his mother said, tugging on his arm.

*C'mon, Wendy,* I begged my pounding heart. *Keep it together.*

I came out onto the Upper Concourse around Track 42, underneath the overhanging balcony.

The scene was just as I had hoped—a maze of commuters crisscrossing the vast Grand Concourse from all directions. Grand Central had always been one of my favorite spots, with the restored, majestic Beaux Arts ceiling, the food emporium down below, and the new Apple store on the east balcony. I just put my head down and told my heart to calm.

"Joe, I'm on my way," I said into the phone. "I'll be there in a minute."

I crossed the main concourse as far from the information booth as I could, my face tucked into my jacket. I spotted the ticket counter. There were five or six windows open and lines at each of them.

I didn't see Joe.

"Joe. I'm here," I said, stepping into one of the ticket lines. Anything was getting me worried. "Where are you?"

"Right here," he said.

I finally spotted him, hands in his pockets, the same corduroy jacket with the wool collar he had on the day before, waiting on one of the lines. I forced a brave smile and stepped in line next to him.

"How you holding up, kid?" he asked with a bolstering wink.

"I'm okay." My nerves clearly apparent. "Barely."

He squeezed my arm. "Everything's gonna go down fine." He glanced at his watch. The huge overhead clock in the station read 5:11. "I have their word."

"Okay . . ." I blew out a tight breath. I wondered if lookouts were scanning the bustling crowd for me right now.

"Wendy, you know they'll have to turn you over to the feds. But there'll be a joint news conference and

151

I've put my own attorney on notice. You're free to change, of course, at any time . . ."

I nodded, a knot of worry forming in my gut. "I appreciate this, Joe. I can't tell you how much . . ."

"Ready?"

"No. But if we don't do it now, I don't think I ever will . . ."

I was about to turn when he stopped me by the arm. "Wendy, whatever happens, I want you to know that it's been one of the deep regrets of my life to have let you down back then. To have let your father down. The only thing that made it bearable to me was that I saw how you went on and got your life together, and met Dave . . . I want to see nothing more than for you to get back with your kids as best you can . . ."

"Thank you, Joe." My eyes grew moist and started to sting. "That's all I want too."

"So let's get on with it."

Slowly, we wove our way across the concourse toward the information booth. My legs felt rubbery, and Joe held me by the arm to keep me steady. The place was mobbed, which was okay. It seemed like most of the world was rushing to make a train or just coming off one.

"Just stay to my side," he said.

The bronze-gilded information booth came into view. The three men standing around it. One was in a blue cap. Burns. That had to be him. One of the others was shorter, bearded, wearing a flat-brimmed hat and black leather jacket. The last one looked Hispanic; it was hard to make out. Someone bumped into me from behind, practically scaring the wits out of me, I was so jumpy. "Sorry," he muttered as he passed by.

"Joe, I'm scared," I said. And not just by the threat that the government people might be here. Because of what I was doing. Everything falling apart. My life. My husband dead. My kids doubting me. Whether I'd be spending the rest of my life in jail . . .

"I know. I know, Wendy. Everything's gonna be all right."

I scanned the station. It all appeared like normal, rush-hour activity. But inwardly, I figured that anyone we passed by might well be undercover NYPD or the feds. The young woman with the backpack going over the train schedule. The Hispanic guy on the cell phone turning his back to me.

"There they are," Joe said, eyeing the counter. "We're almost there. All right, stay behind me."

He took my arm as he was looking about, putting his body in front of mine. Through the crowd, I saw the three NYPDs. All that went through my mind was Dave. The people who had killed him were going to portray me as a killer. Someone completely unstable. A promiscuous thrill seeker who was cheating on her husband. They had framed me for Dave's death just as they were trying to frame Curtis at the hotel. I imagined the headlines. I just prayed people would believe me.

As we got closer, my gaze fell on the tall man in the Rangers cap. He had a trusting, ruddy face. He gave me kind of a ready, officious smile, for a moment kind of putting me at ease.

The last ease I was about to feel for a long while.

Because a second later Joe looked up at the balcony and grabbed my arm to stop me in my tracks. Then I heard him groan above the din, "Oh, shit."

# CHAPTER TWENTY-TWO

Alton Dokes scanned the floor of Grand Central Terminal from his perch on the great staircase next to Michael Jordan's Steak House.

It seemed like every fucking person in New York was rushing by, making it virtually impossible to fix on anyone in particular, even through his high-intensity field binoculars.

He quickly located the three NYPD personnel hovering near the information booth in the center. Dokes chortled. They were severely misled if they thought for a second this was going to be an NYPD operation. That would bring in press and a lawyer. They had already opened the door to way too much as it was. However the stupid bitch had managed to be up in that hotel room, she'd turned a routine operation into a raging

155

shit storm. Hruseff was dead and they could only hide what he'd been doing there so long. And what was behind it.

Now it had fallen into his lap, Dokes reflected, and it wasn't going to go any further.

He knew how to do his job. There'd be a fuss at first, maybe the press would dig in, but ultimately it would all calm down after they failed to find anything. There was only one place anyone would suspect. They had the photo image of a top Zeta operative who was already in New York ready to be sent out to the various press and investigative agencies to take the blame for this. He and Hruseff were old pros at this kind of thing, but Ray was gone.

Now it was up to him.

Dokes swept his glasses around the bustling concourse. *The trail ended here.*

He had no idea which direction the two would be coming from, only that they'd be heading for the information booth. He glanced at the image on his cell phone. Not the woman. Esterhaus. He centered on a dozen faces all moving toward the booth. Nothing yet. It was possible they would use some misdirection. He checked his watch: 5:14 P.M. The NYPD people were looking around.

*C'mon, show yourself, dollface. It's time . . .*

Then something caught his eye.

From the southwest quadrant of the concourse. A

man in a plaid jacket. Dokes looked again at the photo on his phone. The man seemed to be guiding a woman in a blue parka. He couldn't fully see her; her face was inside a hood. He couldn't get confirmation—she had on sunglasses. But he was sure. It had to be her.

*There's our gal.*

"Six o clock. Two people. Blue parka. Hood," he whispered into the radio.

His man on the balcony confirmed, just as business-like. "I've got them, sir."

The two wove through the crowd, using it for cover. Dokes checked the cops again. So far it seemed they hadn't spotted them yet.

Then there was an opening in the crowd, and he pressed the mike close to his lips and said calmly to the shooter, his eye peering through the scope of the sniper's rifle, "At your call, Wendell."

# CHAPTER TWENTY-THREE

*"Don't move!"* Joe grabbed me, forcing me to a stop.

My heart jumped out of my chest. "What's wrong?"

His gaze was fixed, but not where I expected, in the direction of the information booth. He was looking upward, at the second-floor balcony, directly in front of us.

He shifted in front of me. "Just stay behind me."

*"Joe . . ."* My heart seized with alarm. "What's going on?"

"Wendy, I want you to slowly back away," he said in a businesslike voice. His hand was on mine, his body directly in front of mine.

That's when I followed his gaze and noticed the glint. Coming through an opening in the balustrade on the second floor. And a kind of shadow behind it. The glint again. *It could be nothing. It could also be the light glancing off the lens of a sight.*

A shooter.

My alarm ratcheted up to fear.

"I'm sorry, but I think we're going to call this off," Joe said, making sure he was directly in front of me. "Wendy, I want you to just back away with me. No sudden movements. Just stay directly behind . . ."

We veered away from the information booth, Joe's arm around my shoulder, his body shielding me from the spot he'd been focused on.

He said, "I want you to find a way out of the station. Without drawing any attention to yourself. Do you have one?" His head craned back and forth. To the balcony, the information booth, the police there starting to look at him with some befuddlement.

"Yes." I nodded, shock waves shooting down my spine. I did have a Plan B. If things went wrong. "What's going on?"

"I'm not sure, but I don't think we're quite as alone as I hoped. So I want you to take that way out. I'll be in touch. We'll work something else out, when I know exactly who we can trust. Just stay in the crowd, okay? That's vital . . ." I glanced back at the balcony as he eased me forward. "Whatever you do, just—"

I never heard the shot. Just a spitting sound as Joe lurched forward with a gasp. I turned and saw a hole

159

in his coat and his face go white and blood coming from his shoulder.

I screamed. *"Joe!"* My eyes fixed on him in horror and disbelief.

"Get out of here, Wendy," he said, his eyes reflecting something between concern and helplessness. He pushed into me to get me going, just as another thud zinged in, a groan seeming to come straight from his lungs, blood seeping through his fingers. "Go! Now!"

I couldn't. My feet were paralyzed. *What have they done to Joe?*

Even though he was the only thing protecting me from being hit myself, he pushed me away. *"Wendy, now!"*

I took off.

The woman I'd noticed a moment ago studying the schedule moved toward me, but Joe staggered into her, grabbing her arm and taking her down with him as he fell to his knees. Another shot came in, hitting her.

I screamed and pushed my way into a throng, just as people began to realize what was happening and started to scream as well.

I began to run. I looked back once at Joe, helpless, blood pooling on his chest. The woman he was entangled with took out a gun and started to shout at me. *"Stop that woman! Stop!"*

I fled into the crowd, darting in and out before the NYPD people even got a sense of what was happening.

I heard the panicked murmur spread like wildfire, "Someone's shooting! Someone's shooting!"

I knew I had to get out of here now.

I hunched my face deeper into my collar and hurried away from the center of the station, praying that the next thing I felt wouldn't be a sniper's bullet tearing into me.

I moved toward the Vanderbilt Avenue staircase, to run down to the lower floor, praying that by now the guy with the rifle either had to flee himself or had lost me in the throng.

Then I caught sight of someone else standing at the bottom of the staircase. Staring directly at me.

The black agent who had chased me at the hotel. *Dokes.*

Everything in me turned to ice.

Frantic, I backed away from him, bumping into people passing by. For a second he stood as frozen as me, then he spoke into a radio. Our gazes locked on each other. I saw him reach into his jacket for a gun.

I took off across the Main Concourse.

I knew I was a sitting duck. The NYPD cops were everywhere, and a guy was peering through a sniper's scope, all searching for a woman in a blue parka, sunglasses, and hood.

I sprinted into a large group of Asian tourists moving toward Lexington Avenue and pushed my way into the middle. I tore off my parka and threw it to the floor. I pulled off my sunglasses and shook out my hair, knowing anyone looking for me would be focused on the woman they'd all seen a moment before.

I turned and saw Dokes pushing his way through the bustling crowd, trying to follow me. Maybe twenty or thirty yards behind. My thoughts went to Joe. I didn't know if he was alive or dead. I only knew what he would want me to do.

I ran.

I made it across the terminal to the east annex, where most of the shops and retail food outlets were.

But I was petrified to try to get to one of the main entrances. I was sure they would be covered.

Then it hit me. The subway entrance. It was just up the platform. A hundred yards from me.

That was my best way out.

I bolted out of the crowd and wedged myself between a businessman and a woman on her cell phone, and made it to the southeast underpass beneath the giant schedule board. I knew I was finally out of reach of the guy on the balcony. But I did spot the bearded NYPD detective I had seen at the information booth who was frantically sorting through the people passing by him. I wasn't sure if I could trust him if I just turned myself in as planned. Someone had given me away! The only thing I had going for me was that he'd be looking for someone in a blue parka and sunglasses.

I put my hand over my face as if I was talking on my cell phone and went right by him, catching sight of him jumping up and down and as he craned for a better view. From here it was only about fifty yards up the ramp to the subway entrance. There, I was pretty sure I could get lost in the myriad tunnels and trains at the Forty-Second Street station.

But then I made a mistake.

Instead of remaining huddled in the crowd, I turned around to see if the NYPD guy was coming after me.

And I found myself staring at Dokes. He had stopped to get a better vantage point and was scanning the area where he thought I'd be. His gaze locked on me. He grabbed his radio and came after me. He was around twenty yards behind.

I darted out of the cover of the crowd.

Now he had a bead on me, and I realized that my life was only as good as my being able to get to the subway. I fled up the Forty-Second Street ramp, jammed with rushing commuters who knew nothing of what had happened back in the main station, knocking into them as I darted by, frantically glancing behind me to see how close Dokes was.

He was gaining.

He knocked down a pedestrian in his way, shouting, "Federal agent!" Closing the gap on me.

I sped down the subway steps, forcing myself past the slower pedestrians, fumbling through my purse for my transit card. I looked back up the stairs and saw Dokes darting through the crowd.

My heart constricted with fear.

In the station, I had several possibilities, but there was no time to think it through. There was a tunnel that led to the crosstown shuttle, and another to the F and Q trains to Queens and Brooklyn. My thought had been to get to the uptown Lexington line and make it to 125th Street, where I could catch the Metro-North train back to Rye, where I'd left my car.

I ran my card and pushed through an empty turnstile, just as Dokes made it down the stairs.

He looked around, unable to spot me at first. There was a maze of people rushing by. I ran along the upper platform, stopping behind a jewelry kiosk. I looked back and saw him scanning in all directions, not knowing where I was. He threw up his hands in exasperation.

I couldn't wait. I was just so nervous hiding there. It was as if my breaths and the pounding of my chest were giving me away. I heard the rumble of a train coming into the station below me. I ran to one of the staircases to head down to the platform. As soon as I was in the open, Dokes caught sight of me. I ran down the stairs and saw him leap the turnstile and head after me.

*Oh, Wendy, no . . .*

I knew I had nowhere to go but onto a train, or else I'd be trapped on the platform. I figured he knew it as well. As I got to the platform, two trains arrived in the station simultaneously, an express and a local. There were dozens of people blocking my path, but I elbowed through them and hurried two or three cars down from where Dokes would be coming.

The trains hissed to a stop. The doors opened on both sides. Streams of passengers poured off. I was certain Dokes was on the platform heading toward me. I had to choose. I bolted onto the express train and pushed my way through the crowd, begging the doors to close, not knowing if Dokes had already jumped on. I stood away from his probable line of sight. If he did make it on, he could simply push his way through, car by car. Eventually, he'd find me. I didn't know if I should stay on or get off. Run to the local or go back up the stairs to the upper platform. Or if he had other people following him. I heard the conductor's announcement: "Fifty-Ninth Street, next stop."

*Close, damn it, close.* I looked at the local across the platform. I had no idea which train Dokes might be on. *Just close.*

Finally I heard the warning buzzer. I had no idea where Dokes was. Then I saw him running back on the now empty platform, scanning through the windows of both trains. The buzzer sounded again. I peered through an opening in the bodies surrounding me and, to my relief, saw him jump onto the local train, just as the doors began to close.

My heart almost imploded in relief as we began to pull away.

Somehow having second thoughts, Dokes leaped off his train and crossed the platform. He peered through the window and slammed on the door of our departing train. He took out his badge and tried desperately to flash it at a conductor as the train began to move, picking up speed.

Then he slammed the side of the train in anger and frustration.

We zoomed by.

I knew he couldn't radio to anyone ahead at the next stop, or get the NYPD involved. The police were the last people he wanted to find me.

I was safe. At least for the moment.

I dropped my head against a pole, my breaths heavy and fast. My mind flashed to Joe. I didn't know if he was dead or alive. I only knew I could no longer turn myself in. Not now.

The only way out now was to prove my innocence.

I reached into my pocket and came out with Curtis's phone.

ROXANNE

# CHAPTER TWENTY-FOUR

It took a month for Harold and an immigration lawyer to prepare Lauritzia's case. He had to familiarize himself with the records from the first trial in Texas, in which the immigration court denied the family's petition for asylum. The split ruling seemed so inexplicably flawed.

Then he got the Fifth Circuit Court of Appeals in Dallas to agree to hear them in an expedited manner.

In the meantime Lauritzia remained hidden in an apartment the firm rented for her in New Haven, Connecticut, watched over by private security. She kept up her classes on the Internet and drove back to Greenwich and Harold's office a couple of times in secrecy to go over her testimony. During all this time she saw Roxanne only once, when Roxanne drove up to New Haven for the day to visit, bringing pictures and cards from the kids. Harold found a government witness willing to talk about Cano: Sabrina Stein, who had been head of the DEA's office in El Paso as well as the government's covert action unit there, known as EPIC, the El Paso Intelligence Center. Stein knew Cano to be a ruthless and remorseless killer, whose thirst for revenge was almost as strong as his shrewdness and his instinct for survival. It was Sabrina Stein's agents who had been the targets of the hit in Culiacán, Mexico, that began this whole tragic affair.

It seemed a positive sign that the court agreed to hear the case so quickly.

The decision two years ago to deny the Velez family asylum seemed more a result of the furor at the time over lack of immigration control along the Mexican border than proper jurisprudence or fairness. The United States government no longer needed Lauritzia's father's testimony after the case against Cano broke down, and thus there was certainly no need for his children to be granted asylum in the United States, simply because of their "unsubstantiated" claim of a vendetta against them back in Mexico. Therefore they ruled that the privileges of asylum that were extended to Mr. Velez as a government witness did not extend to his children. However, now, Harold would argue, the situation had tragically changed. Lauritzia's three sisters and a brother had been killed; Cano had made no secret of his vendetta. Now Harold could show a clear pattern of "retaliation and threat" against the family, of which Lauritzia and her father were the only surviving members. He would argue that her situation was akin to any "persecuted refugee" in any political or ethnic "class." That Lauritzia legitimately feared persecution and even death should she be returned home, as was ordered by the court. A situation only worsened, in fact, by the U.S. government's decision not to pursue the prosecution of Eduardo Cano. Any test of reasonability had to find for her now.

Their court date, September 20, finally came around. Harold and his associate flew down to Dallas with Lauritzia. Roxanne came along too. It took place in the federal courthouse on Commerce Street downtown. The courtroom seemed strangely empty to Lauritzia, who had only seen trials in movies or on TV. There was no media attention; they didn't want any. And no jury. Only three judges, a woman and two middle-aged men. Harold was optimistic. The night before, they'd gone over her testimony one last time. Her story was as compelling and tragic as any the court would have ever heard.

They had to win.

In his opening, Harold began by arguing that no one could possibly be brought before this court with a stronger case for asylum in the United States. Lauritzia's father, while a criminal himself, had risked his life and freedom to testify against a notorious drug enforcer whose trail of blood included five American lives. That it was only due to the United States's questionable decision not to pursue the prosecution against Mr. Cano that he was even freed and returned to Mexico to pursue this reign of terror against Velez's family.

"Ms. Velez has faced a fate of terror and uncertainty. She has lost virtually every close member of her family due to Mr. Cano's openly declared vow of revenge. In that sense alone she belongs to a 'persecuted class,' as legitimate as any political or ethnically motivated persecution. That class," Harold argued, "being her own family."

It came time for Lauritzia to take the stand. She was sworn in wearing a dark suit they had bought her for the occasion, her hair pulled back in a ponytail, both pretty and serious-looking.

"Ms. Velez, I'd like you to tell the court the last time you spoke to your brother Eustavio," Harold said to her.

"Eustavio . . ." Lauritzia moistened her lips. "That was in 2009. Before he was found shot dead on the street in my hometown of Navolato in Mexico. His body was mutilated."

"I know this is difficult, Ms. Velez . . ." Harold approached the witness box. "But can you tell the court how the body was mutilated?"

Lauritzia glanced up at the black-robed justices and took a breath. The white-haired male judge seemed to nod for her to go on.

"His *genitales*," she hesitated. "I think it is the same

172

in English. They had been cut off and put in his mouth. Where I come from it is the sign of a traitor."

Someone in the courtroom gasped.

"And Eustavio's occupation?" Harold asked. "Your brother wasn't in the drug business, was he, Ms. Velez?"

"No." She shook her head. "He was a postal clerk, Mr. Bachman."

"And your sister Nina? When was the last time you saw her?"

"That same year. In August. She was killed in the beauty parlor where she worked. Along with twelve others who were there when the men came in. They filled her body with sixty bullets."

"And your sister Maria?"

"Two and a half years ago," Lauritzia said. "She lived in Juárez. She was shot dead in her car. My little cousin Theresa was killed too."

The female judge shifted uncomfortably in her seat and cleared her throat.

"And your sister Rosa?" Harold continued. "Your *twin*, I might add. And the person, I remind the court, who originally filed this motion for asylum."

Lauritzia nodded. She glanced at the judges and then back at Harold, who was nodding gently at her, as hard as it was to go through this. "My sister Rosa was killed too. She was here in Texas. In her home. Illegally, I know. She was five months pregnant with her first child, her son, who she intended to name Eustavio, after our brother."

"That tragically makes four—three sisters and your brother. Murdered. How many remaining siblings do you have, Ms. Velez?"

"I have none." Lauritzia shook her head.

She allowed herself a glance toward the judges. The other male judge, a heavyset black man, appeared to wince with emotion, which she assumed was a positive sign.

"And if you would tell the court what happened on July twenty-fourth of this year?" Harold changed the questioning.

"At the Westchester Mall?" Lauritzia asked, to be sure.

Harold nodded. "Yes. At the mall."

"As I was leaving, with the children I take care of . . . *your* children, Mr. Bachman . . . the elevator I was riding in was shot up by a man with a semiautomatic weapon. Three people in front of us were killed. Others were wounded. The assassin was clearly sent by Eduardo Cano, because they were Los Zetas, which he commands. It was only by the grace of God that I, or either of the kids, was not killed as well."

"And how do you know this killer was sent to harm *you*, Ms. Velez, and not one of the others?"

"I saw the shooter's neck. His tattoo. The skeleton with the dragon's tail. It is common back home, for members of the drug cartels. Especially that of Los Zetas. The length of the tail marks the time that person has spent in prison."

"But you chose not to come forward at that time, didn't you, Ms. Velez? That you suspected that what had happened there was directed at you personally?"

"No." Lauritzia nodded. "I didn't." She bowed and shook her head.

"Can you tell the court why?"

"Because I was afraid. Afraid if I did, I would be found out and sent home. I just wanted to run. To not put your family in any more danger. And I did run."

"And what fate would you face if you were deported back to Mexico?"

"The same fate my entire family has met." She looked at the judges. "Eduardo Cano has vowed to kill us all. I would be no different."

The hearing took just over three hours, including the testimony of Sabrina Stein, who stated that Eduardo Cano "was one of the two or three most ruthless killers operating in the higher echelons of the Mexican narco-sphere right now," and "what a short-sided mistake it had been for the government to have ever let him slip through our hands."

"And you know this firsthand, don't you, Agent Stein?" Harold asked her.

"Yes." She nodded, looking down.

"Can you tell us how?"

"Because I lost two of my best agents. Rita Bienvienes and her husband, Dean, who both worked under me.

They were the targets of the ambush that Ms. Velez's father was prepared to testify on."

"And you're familiar with the dragon tattoo that Ms. Velez referred to, aren't you? Which was on the body of the shooter at the Westchester Mall."

"Yes." The government witness nodded. "It's a common mark of valor and loyalty in the Los Zetas drug cartel."

The government prosecutor had his time. He argued that tragic as Ms. Velez's story was, it did not merit the "stay of removal," in that she was not a member of any accepted persecuted class, only that of her own family, and that Mr. Cano's vendetta against them did not constitute the type of "ethnic or political" persecution that merited a reversal. He also argued that Ms. Velez had not legally complied with the court's original ruling but, in fact, had secretly hidden out in the United States "in direct opposition of it."

To which Harold objected that it would have been a death sentence if she had complied. "Ms. Velez was not hiding out," he said to the court. "She had a steady job. She was enrolled in school. She has embarked on a path to better herself. Coupled with the obvious threat should she be forced to leave, there is no more compelling case of someone who deserves to remain here."

The U.S. attorney dropped this and brought up another appeals ruling—some Albanian gangster, who had gone on a similar spree of terror against a family here, who had been denied asylum—which, he claimed, acted as a precedent.

One of the male judges asked the government if Lauritzia's father was still under U.S. protection, and the lawyer answered no. The female judge asked whether, if the government had known the tragic repercussions the Velez family would face, they would have argued against a stay.

Everything seemed to be going well.

"We made the right case," Harold said in the hall outside the courtroom. "Two of the judges showed clear sensitivity to your story. That's all we need. They'll have to reverse it. It's the only reasonable thing. Even the prosecutor wasn't objecting strenuously."

"Now what do we do?" Lauritzia asked as they were transported into the basement garage and into a black SUV.

"Now we just wait."

# CHAPTER TWENTY-FIVE

She waited three weeks. Three more weeks of hiding, of not knowing her fate. Everyone seemed to think the chances were good. Certainly Mr. B felt that way. Lauritzia trusted him when he said that only a heartless person could not see what Cano had in store for her if she was denied. At least two of the judges had smiled at her and thanked her for her testimony. She deserved to be here. This was America, not Mexico. Sending her home would be sending her to her grave.

Lauritzia was reading one of her retail books when her cell phone rang. "It's Harold," said Mr. B. She got nervous. "The ruling is in. We need to talk with you."

"Do you want me to come down to your office?"

"No. Roxanne and I are on our way. We'll be there in an hour."

An hour. Her blood raced for most of it, with alternating anticipation and excitement. But when she heard the knock at the door and ran to open it, she could see immediately in the lines of their downcast faces that it had not gone her way.

*"How?"* Her hand went to her mouth.

"I'm sorry, Lauritzia. The court found two to one against our stay," Harold said, giving her a bolstering hug.

They all sat at the kitchen table as Harold read from a printed-off ruling that had been posted on the Internet. "They claimed the threat against Ms. Velez, sympathetic as it is, is nonetheless not due to her membership in 'a persecuted class,' but to no more than Mr. Cano's anger against her father for a personal transgression. Therefore it does not rise to the kind of threat that makes one eligible for protection under federal law.' They cited this Demiraj case as precedent."

She looked at him blankly. "So what does this mean?"

"It means the government is saying that whatever protection had been afforded your father for his testimony against Cano does not extend to you. The original ruling is intact. We're ordered to turn you over to a court-appointed immigration agent in the next thirty days."

A downcast silence settled over the room. For a while, no one spoke.

"Thirty days?" Lauritzia muttered. She looked at them, worry in her eyes.

Harold leaned against the kitchen counter. "Pending appeal."

"Which means it's not over," Roxanne said, taking Lauritzia's hand. "This was an appeals court, Lauritzia. It means we take this higher up, to the Supreme Court."

"If they'll agree to take it." Harold shrugged. "Their ruling is a completely narrow reading of the asylum law. It totally ignores whatever is human about it. It's like the government is somehow siding with this son of a bitch Cano. What they've come back with goes against the very spirit of the law it was designed to protect."

"Thirty days . . ." Lauritzia sat down. "This is not right." She felt numb. She had allowed herself to believe, and now once again it was clear who had won and who had lost. Harold was right, it *was* as if the government was siding with this monster. *Why?* In thirty days she could be sent back and—

"Lauritzia, we're not done yet," Roxanne said, bracing her by the shoulders. "I don't want you to give up on this fight. And I don't want you to give up on us either. Harold's already agreed to go on."

"I'm going to try to put together what they call amicus briefs from various law professors and immigration advocates—"

"Go on?" Lauritzia looked at them in confusion. "How can we go on? I can't stay here forever. With you continuing to hide me and pay for me and—"

180

"We have another plan we'd like to propose." Roxanne leaned forward, her blue eyes brimming with resolve. "We're going to fly you out to our house in Edwards, Colorado. No one will know you're there. You can stay there until we can determine the right legal move." Lauritzia's hand was trembling and Roxanne squeezed it tightly. "I know you want to give up . . . I know you don't want to burden us. But the last thing we're going to do is hand you over to the immigration department. That's not going to happen."

"You'll go against your own law?"

"If we have to," Roxanne said.

She looked at Harold. "And you agree, Mr. Bachman?"

He nodded. "We talked it over. Yes, I agree."

Roxanne took her by the shoulders. "You'll be safe out there. No one will know. I know it seems like you've lost, but we're not done yet . . ."

"Not by a long shot," Harold said.

Lauritzia pressed herself against Roxanne. *Thirty days* . . . She didn't know, maybe the right thing was just to disappear. This was her fate, not theirs. She had already cost them enough. She felt love for them, these people who treated her like their own family. Yet she'd felt the bond of love before, and it had only turned to blood and tears.

She should go.

But she heard herself mutter back, "Thank you." And felt the tears rush. Because it was a fight and she was

181

not ready to give up. To pay her *cuota*. Not without one more battle.

She hugged Roxanne and said a prayer for those who had died.

# CHAPTER TWENTY-SIX

*It would be so easy*, Roxanne thought, gazing out the window on their trip back home to Greenwich, *to simply let her go.*

They'd already done more than anyone could have asked. More than Lauritzia herself even asked. She wasn't their family, no matter how many times Roxanne declared it. She simply wasn't. They had their own lives. Their own kids. They could so easily just say that they had tried their best. A trial. Standing by her. Protecting her when others would have turned their heads.

Simply let her go.

It was night when they made the ride back home down Interstate 95. She and Harold didn't say much to each other. Most of what they wanted to say had already been said. They both felt dismal about the outcome.

Angry. They felt as if they had let her down. Their friends already thought they were crazy to have gone as far as they had. It would be easy to have treated the whole thing as if it were some kind of charity. Just write the girl a check, without ever having to have put yourself on the line. After all, it wasn't *their* fight. *Their* fate.

It was hers.

And maybe in another life, another moment, Roxanne could have done all this. *Before* what had happened at the mall.

But not now.

When those shots rang out, Lauritzia's only instinct had been to protect their kids. *She'd* put herself on the line for *them*. She'd made them *her* fight.

Now it just seemed like the right thing, the *only* thing, to do the same for her.

Roxanne asked herself, if a hundred blessed things came into their life—if Harold was named head of the firm, or got some honor, if the kids won some big recognition in school or some prestigious trophy, if she was honored by the local hospital for her charitable work there—would it offset knowing that they had cast Lauritzia away to an unknown fate? That they hadn't done all they could?

It would always haunt her.

She thought, life was safe here, seemingly protected from harm. But sometimes in that safe, predictable life, you had to risk it all. You had to go "all in." Or else the rest didn't mean anything. Love is simply love, Roxanne realized as she stared out the window. You couldn't legislate how it came into your life. Or defend yourself against it when it's inconvenient. Or divvy it up, like vegetables on a plate. When it enters, it becomes the only thing that matters. The only thing of meaning. The rest . . . the rest is not the painting, it's just the painter signing his name.

She looked at Harold at the wheel. She reached over and put her hand on his arm. "Are we doing the right thing?" Roxanne asked. "People think we're crazy."

"I don't know. I'm not sure there is a right thing." He looked back at her. "The right thing is only what you feel with a hundred percent certainty inside that you have to do."

Roxanne nodded. "Then we are." She squeezed him and looked back out the window. Whichever way it goes. Whatever happens. She was sure. Her heart never felt more at peace.

She looked back out the window.

*We are.*

# CHAPTER TWENTY-SEVEN

The following Wednesday was clear and bright. Harold had chartered a jet at Westchester County Airport to take Lauritzia out west. Everything was done in secrecy, including the flight plan. Only a handful of people who were connected with the case even knew.

Roxanne decided to go along. She'd stay a couple of nights, make the house livable for Lauritzia, then come back home. Lauritzia was pleased to have her along. She'd only been out to the house there once. And the whole thing made her a bit nervous and overwhelmed. Relax, they all tried to assure her. No one knows where you're going. It's perfectly safe. We've covered every step.

In a couple of weeks they would decide how to handle it legally.

Harold drove them to the airport before heading to work. The jet, an eight-seat Citation from Globaljet, was set to leave from a section of the airfield for private planes located at Hangar E.

Harold drove down Route 120 and through the airport gates and parked his white Mercedes in front of the private terminal. He unloaded the bags, which were taken by a Globaljet attendant. The sleek white jet was waiting on the tarmac.

"So, uh, you both take it easy out there," Harold said to Lauritzia with a smile. "No parties. Don't hit the slopes."

Lauritzia giggled back and put her nerves behind her. She hugged him. "I have no words to thank you for everything you're doing for me. You're in my heart, and I know the grace of God will look down on you."

Harold said, "We'll be in touch in a few days. Don't worry. Everything's going to be okay."

"I know."

She waved, in her jeans and black boots, her hair in a ponytail, and went inside the terminal.

"You're a good man, Harold Bachman," Roxanne said, smiling at him. "Though most people probably think we're crazy."

"We are crazy." Harold smiled back. "Actually, though, I've never been prouder of you."

"Tell me." Her eyes beamed, and she wrapped her arms around his waist.

"You remember what I said a while back. That somewhere in this is the reason that I love you. Well, it's true, Rox. You put yourself on the line for people. You live 'on purpose,' as they say; the rest of us are just bouncing around in this world randomly. You're the kind of person we would all want in our foxhole."

"Go on," she said, wrapping her arms around his waist with a wrinkle of her nose.

"I would," he said, hugging her back, "but I'm afraid the plane has a tight departure window."

"We are going to make this happen for her, aren't we, Harold?" Maybe for the first time Harold saw doubt on her, a crack in her veneer.

"We are. I believe it now more than ever."

"We're not going to send her home, no matter what the judges say."

He shrugged and smiled philosophically.

"Are we, Harold?"

He shook his head. "No. We're not."

She kissed him and strapped her bag over her shoulder. "I'll call you when we land."

"You can call me in the air from one of these things. But don't get used to it. The firm's paying."

He lingered, looking at the reflection on his wife's face, the sun off her freckles, her bangs in her blue eyes. He remembered how when he first saw her at a Merrill Lynch cocktail party he knew she was far too pretty for him. She had it all: smarts, looks, the kind of energy that attracted everyone around her. Out of his league. He had nothing to offer, other than a self-deprecating sense of humor and droopy eyes. It took him half an hour to work up the courage to go up to her.

"You look like you're dying to hear a little more about real estate bond financing," he had said, smiling coyly.

"You noticed!" she had replied.

"I love you!" Roxanne turned and waved at the terminal doors. "Make sure the kids eat at six. And no watching the Knicks game with Jamie past his bedtime."

"I love you too." He waved. And she went in.

# CHAPTER TWENTY-EIGHT

Lauritzia boarded first, while Roxanne finished up a call to the kids' school's auction committee. She wasn't sure exactly where to sit, never having been in a plane like this before. Everything looked so sleek and modern. A pretty flight attendant welcomed her aboard and told her to take any seat she wanted. She put herself in the first one she found.

Then Roxanne climbed on and took the seat across from her and a row behind. "Everything okay?" She squeezed Lauritzia on the arm.

"Sí." Lauritzia nodded. "Everything is wonderful." Though it was clear she really didn't think so. It was just that being around Roxanne made her feel that way. Thirty days out there would go by like an instant. Then what? Her whole life was now in the hands of this family.

"Would you like a glass of champagne or some orange juice?" the flight attendant asked, holding a tray of fluted glasses.

"No, thank you," Lauritzia answered.

"Soft drink?"

"Maybe a Sprite."

Then the attendant went past her to Roxanne. "You, ma'am?"

Roxanne took a champagne.

One of the pilots stepped out of the cockpit and made a quick speech about how long it would take for them to get to Denver—around four hours, as there were headwinds. Denver, they had decided, instead of Eagle Vail, in order to conceal their final destination. From there they would rent a car. He also told them that it would be a smooth flight and there were a bunch of treats to eat and drink on board, and that Kathy, the pretty flight attendant, would take excellent care of them.

"They pay him to say that." Kathy laughed. "But I'll do my best."

The copilot pulled up the outside steps and shut the cabin door.

Lauritzia started to grow nervous. She wasn't the best flyer anyway—she had only been on a couple of planes, all with the Bachmans—and the sooner she left here, the safer she would feel. Feeling the engines start to *vroom*, she put her head back and looked out the window

191

and tried to remember what it was like at the Bachmans' place in the mountains.

So pretty there. No one would know.

She rested her head against the window. That's when something unusual caught her eye.

A baggage cart had pulled up alongside the plane, two or three suitcases on it. A man in an orange jumpsuit and sunglasses behind the wheel.

She wasn't sure what exactly made her pay attention to it, other than all the bags had already been loaded on and the compartment was on the other side. She had watched them go on as she boarded.

Before the plane could leave its blocks, the vehicle came to a stop directly underneath the fuselage.

What was going on?

Lauritzia turned to Roxanne, who was sipping her champagne, leafing through a magazine. Seeing her unsettled expression, Roxanne just smiled. "Everything's okay, Lauritzia. Just sit back and relax."

Lauritzia leaned forward to locate the baggage cart.

The plane didn't taxi out. The door to the cockpit was still open, and Lauritzia could see the copilot straining his neck, peering out the side window. They seemed to be asking over the radio for the tower to tell the cart to move.

But it wasn't moving.

It just sat there, blocking them.

Something didn't seem right. Suddenly, the man in

the orange jumpsuit jumped out and began to walk away, leaving the cart directly underneath them. Lauritzia watched him; instead of heading back toward the terminal, he just kept on going, in the direction of the wire gates leading to the parking lot. Everything was so open and relaxed.

Lauritzia's heart jumped in concern.

"Missus," she said, pointing to the window. "I think something isn't right."

"Lauritzia, relax," Roxanne said in a tone she might use with one of the kids, deep in her magazine. "Everything's just fine."

"No! It isn't! *It isn't!*" She watched the man in the jumpsuit quicken his pace, her eyes growing wide. The concern that had been nagging her now heightened into outright fear. She had seen these things. *El Pirate can reach anywhere! He can know anything.* She unbuckled her seat belt. "Missus, we have to get out of here now! Something is not right."

"Lauritzia, what are you talking about?" Roxanne finally started paying attention.

"That man, *look*! He—"

The copilot climbed out of the cockpit. "Not to worry, Mrs. Bachman," he said, "but we just want to take a precaution." He pushed out the staircase door. "There's a baggage cart blocking the plane. I think we're going to have you exit. Just a precaution. Sorry for the inconvenience. But if I can get you to—"

Lauritzia pointed. *"Look!"*

The man in the orange suit was in a full run now, slipping through the wire gate to the parking lot. She was sure she saw him take out a cell phone.

"Mrs. B!" Lauritzia's eyes grew wide with terror. She grabbed Roxanne's arm and frantically started to pull her out of her seat. Unbuckle her belt. She had to get her out of there. They had to get out now!

The pilot shouted something to the flight attendant about getting everyone off the plane. Lauritzia knew the sensation—that something terrible was about to take place. And the knowledge that there was nothing she could do.

Nothing.

*Oh, Mrs. B!*

When the blast blew, Lauritzia had made it out of her seat, trying desperately to help Roxanne out. It blew her into the air and slammed her against the cockpit ceiling, and a *whoosh* of searing, suffocating, orange heat engulfed the plane.

# CHAPTER TWENTY-NINE

Harold had barely made it out the airport gate when he heard the blast. Even in his car, it almost rocked him out of his seat. He turned, seeing the plume of orange flame shooting up, followed by the spire of smoke.

*What just happened?*

He jammed on the brakes and spun the car around. The thing that truly terrified him was that it seemed to be coming from exactly where he'd just been. The private terminal at Hangar E.

*No, no!* a voice was screaming inside him. *This couldn't have happened. It can't be.*

He drove at full speed back toward the terminal. As he got close, the billow of smoke rose higher in the sky, and grew darker too. He could see it came from the tarmac he had just left. Which was scaring the shit out of him. He kept repeating to himself that it couldn't be—it couldn't be Roxanne's plane. It had to be something else. Only a handful of people knew. And all were people he trusted. Cano couldn't have found out. He sped into the terminal's parking lot. *It had to be something else.*

But the closer he got, the more he knew his hopes were futile.

He screeched to a stop in front of the terminal and bolted out of the car, leaving the door wide open. The smell of burning metal and jet fuel almost made him retch. He raced through the terminal's glass doors, the same doors his wife had just walked through as he waved good-bye to her. A woman was shouting on the phone, staring out the window at the tarmac in horror.

"My wife is on that plane!" Harold shouted, running by. *"My wife!"*

He bolted through the security gate. "Sir, you can't go out there," the woman shouted, trying to go after him.

Everyone was out on the tarmac. He pushed his way through the gate. Harold saw the same white Citation he had just been waving good-bye to—tail number CG9875. His heart sank at the sight. Only this time the fuselage was a knot of twisted, burning metal. Dense black smoke poured out of it, and orange flames whipped all around.

*Oh my God, no, no . . .*

It had only been a minute or two. A fire truck hadn't even arrived. Underneath the fuselage there was a mangled chassis of what Harold thought resembled a baggage cart. Harold looked at the plane and understood the same horrifying thought he had had years ago when he stared at the World Trade Center's North Tower in flames. *This is bad. No one's getting out of there. No one could possibly be in there and be alive.*

Except this time it was his wife in there!

*"Roxanne! Roxanne!"* he screamed, running toward the smoldering plane.

There was confusion all around. No one stopped him. The stairs were down, dark smoke billowing out from inside. His heart plummeted at the sight. *"Oh my God, baby, no, no . . ."*

Two rescuers carrying out a body. It was one of the pilots Harold had seen—dead. They put him down on the tarmac, on a yellow plastic tarp that was whipping in the fire's wind. Then they pushed their way back inside.

"My wife's in there!" Harold looked in panic at the EMT. "We were chartering the plane."

"I'm sorry, sir, you have to wait. The smoke is unbearable. They're trying to get everyone off now."

*"No!"* Harold ran toward the plane, covering his face in the intense heat.

The EMT tried to stop him. "Sir!"

He didn't care. Harold pushed him away and headed

up the stairs into the burning fuselage. The smoke was dense and black, and suffocating. His eyes instantly began to burn. He covered his face. There were two rescuers leaning over someone. Was it her? Roxanne? She was blonde. Or had been—her hair was now black. It was almost impossible to see. Harold kept his hand over his eyes, which stung like acid was burning in them.

It wasn't Roxanne. She was wearing a uniform, though it was all sheared and charred.

The flight attendant.

"Sir, you have to get out of here now!" an emergency worker yelled above the sound of sirens and whipping flames. "The fuel is burning."

"My wife is on this plane!"

He forced his way past them deeper into the fuselage. The acrid smell of fuel and burning metal. He ripped off his jacket and put it over his face, choking back the searing smoke, screaming, *"Roxanne! Roxanne!"*

He didn't hear an answer.

Though it was only an eight-seater, the smoke that pushed back at him had the force of an ocean undertow, keeping him at bay. He staggered forward. "Roxanne, are you there?"

*Why isn't she answering?* He couldn't bear to think that she was gone. Flames were leaping out of the fuselage onto the wings. Deeper back, he heard the sound of someone murmuring.

His heart soared. *"Roxanne!"* He pushed farther back, hiding his eyes, his face. "Roxanne, baby, talk to me!"

"Here . . . here . . . ," he heard. Barely muttered under breath. "It's Roxanne . . ."

He screamed to the rescuers forward in the cabin. "My wife's alive!"

He swatted his way through the clouds of smoke and flame, willing himself to the rear, where the voice had come from. *"Back here!"*

He tripped over something—a leg. He grabbed it and followed it up the body. It was so dark he couldn't see. "It's Roxanne," he heard the voice close, and he pulled it, his heart soaring in hope.

But then he saw the bracelet on her arm. It wasn't Roxanne. It was Lauritzia. Barely conscious, her blackened lips moving. Her charred eyes rolled up in her head. Harold realized in heartbreak what it was she had been murmuring: "It's Roxanne. She's here. Please, someone, someone . . . help. Roxanne!"

She had her hand on his wife's arm.

His heart sank.

"Get over here, quick!" he screamed to the workers up in front. "One of them is alive!"

Lauritzia had gotten out of her seat belt and gone behind her. It was as if she was trying to save his wife. He lifted her up and pulled her away from the person underneath. A rescuer pushed his way back and wedged her body onto a stretcher. Roxanne was slumped, her hair singed, dark burns and cuts all over her face and neck.

"Roxanne! Roxanne, honey!" he said. "It's me. Harold. *Rox?*"

She didn't say anything back to him.

Her eyes were fixed, empty, and black. Eyes that used to brim with the beauty of life. Her blonde hair was charred like burned parchment. He picked her up by the shoulders, and her head fell limply to the side.

"Oh, Roxanne. Honey, it's me, it's me, it's me . . ."

The EMS team had to pull him away from her, and only then did he come to understand that she was no longer alive.

# CHAPTER THIRTY

She blinked open her eyes. She turned and saw the maze of tubes and wires protruding from her. Her throat was blocked like it was filled with sand. She heard beeping, saw lights and monitors lighting up. There was a tube running from her mouth. And a huge compression lung she could see out of the corner of her eye.

*Estoy muerte?* Lauritzia asked herself. Am I dead?

*No*, she told herself, she was not dead. *Dios maldida.* God be cursed. She only wished she were dead. She didn't remember what happened. Only after, holding Roxanne, whose limp and lifeless body felt like a child's doll in her hands. She remembered trying to shout, *No, no . . .* But the ringing in her ears was so loud and the smoke was so thick. She thought maybe she could just go to sleep and she would die. She remembered someone

201

calling out of the haze. A voice, coming closer, merely a distant echo in her drifting mind, the flames lapping all around. A voice, maybe God's voice, angry at her for what she had done. For all the pain she had caused. So she prayed, the words barely reaching her lips. *Jesus Christos, please take the soul of Roxanne.*

Lauritzia looked around the hospital room and knew she was alive. It wasn't over. The fear would only continue. A tear came out of her eye and wound its way down her cheek.

Then she closed her eyes again.

It took a week for her to begin to recover. For the first few days, she drifted in and out of consciousness. There were burns on much of her body, miraculously mostly only first- and second-degree. She had four broken ribs, a concussion, and a crushed spleen from the impact. The doctors said she would live, that she was a very lucky woman. But she didn't feel lucky. She felt cursed. Her situation had brought only pain to so many people.

At some point Harold came into the ICU and sat by her bed. He took hold of her hand. She couldn't even look at him. All she could do was whisper, "I'm sorry. I'm so sorry . . . ," and turn away in tears.

"It's okay. Just get yourself better," he said, and through her tears she saw the hurt that covered his face. Hurt that would never go away. She wanted to tell him, *"I told you. I told you to stay out! To let me go."*

202

She looked away, too ashamed to even look him in the face.

"Just get yourself better," he said. "The kids miss you. Maybe they'll come next time."

"No, no," she whispered. "I can't."

She was too ashamed to ever see them again.

For days she just lay there, wishing she had died instead of Roxanne.

After a week they reduced her pain medication. They moved her out of the ICU. The police came and spoke with her. As well as the FBI. She was the only survivor. She tried to describe the man in the orange suit but she couldn't bring him to mind. Nothing from that horrible moment came back to her. She knew that when she was released she'd have nowhere to go. She would be deported and it would all end. More blood and tears.

She should have just gotten on that train.

The day before she was to leave, one of the nurses said she had a visitor.

"Who?" Lauritzia inquired, nervous that she was still very much a target, even in the hospital. That Cano would come and finish the job.

"A man. He's come several times."

"From the police?" Lauritzia asked, confused. "An investigator?"

"I don't think so," the nurse replied.

The only man she knew was Harold.

"Bring him in," she told the nurse. She shut her eyes and prayed. If this was it, then let it come. She would welcome it. She would not cause any more pain. She looked away, not even wanting to look in the face of the person sent to kill her. Tears fell down her cheeks and onto the bedsheet.

"Ms. Velez?"

Slowly Lauritzia turned.

The face she encountered was not one she expected. Not threatening at all. It was Anglo, with longish dark hair, and dark, friendly eyes. He was in jeans and a black leather jacket with a satchel slung over his shoulder. He stepped up to the bed.

"Are you with the police?"

"No," he said. "I'm a journalist. But I know what was behind the bombing, Ms. Velez. I know why Eduardo Cano wants you dead."

"Eduardo Cano wants my whole family dead," she muttered, surprised to hear his name. "For what my father did to him."

"No, not for what he *did*." The Anglo placed a hand on the bed railing. "For what he *knows*. For what I think you know as well. That this was never about revenge, Lauritzia, but about keeping your father from talking. About what really happened in Culiacán. That's why your brothers and sisters are dead. And why Cano was never brought to trial."

"Go away." Lauritzia turned away from him. Blood

and tears, that was all this had ever brought. She just wanted it to end.

"Who the real targets were that day. That's what they're trying to protect. You know, don't you? I think you do."

*"Who are you?"* She wanted him to leave. How did he know these things? But at the same time there was something in his handsome eyes that made her trust him.

"I'm a journalist. My name is Curtis Kitchner."

# CANO

# CHAPTER THIRTY-ONE

The sounds of a soccer ball being batted and of children laughing echoed in the courtyard of the large, white-stucco hacienda high on a hill in the Sinaloa province of Mexico.

The heavyset man with the mustache and three-day growth, his white shirt worn open against the heat, kept the ball aloft with his feet, counting, "Sixteen, seventeen, *eighteen* . . ." Keeping it at bay from his two sons, who scampered around him trying to steal it. Showing the surprising skill and agility of someone who once played at a high level.

"*Nineteen!*" the man said, pivoting away from Manuel, who was nine, then finally losing control. "No, no!" he shouted as the ball fell onto the pavement, as Tomás, who was six, ran it down near the black Mercedes

Maybach and the three Land Cruiser SUVs that were parked in the courtyard. The young boy dribbled toward the soccer goal that was painted on the fortresslike white wall.

"Pass it, Toto!" Eduardo Cano shouted to his son, who scrambled around Ernesto, one of Cano's bodyguards, whose Tec-9 semiautomatic pistol sat on the hood of the Maybach and who ran after the boy with an indifferent energy, clearly trying just to please his boss. "Pass it to Manuel. He's open!"

*"Here, Toto!"* the older brother shouted as the ball found its way to him and he approached the unmanned goal, his father hustling back into the goal mouth, announcing, "Guttierrez of Juárez coming in on goal for the win . . . Julio there to stop him . . . *Shoot!*"

Manuel swung his leg hard, but the ball weakly glanced off his ankle, the shot hugging the ground and hitting off the wall a couple of feet wide of the goal.

*"Aaargh."* The boy put his hands to his head in dismay.

"So close . . ." Cano tried to console his son, going up and messing his mop of black hair. "Next time, set yourself and strike it *here*," he said, pointing, "on the instep. But no whining now. Even the great Ronaldo went wide at point-blank range against Argentina in the America Cup. You remember?"

The boy shrugged. "Yes. But he won it with a penalty kick . . ."

"So there is still hope! But not for *you*, old lady," he

said to the bodyguard with a shake of his head. "You play like my ninety-year-old grandmother. And she had gout. Thank God you pull the trigger with better skill than you can kick."

"I didn't want to hurt the boy," the bodyguard said in his defense.

Cano heard his cell phone inside his trouser pocket. It was a number only a handful of people in the world knew, all of them important on some level. Or equally dangerous.

The call was encrypted. The screen read, KVC Consulting, which Cano knew was merely a fake address, routing through an empty office simply meant to conceal the caller.

"Who wants lemonade?" he asked.

"*I do!*" Tomás said.

"And me!" added Manuel.

"Then go upstairs. Your mama has it ready for you. I'll be up in a few minutes."

"*Papa . . . ,*" Manuel groaned with disappointment. He'd seen this happen many times before. These few minutes often grew into hours. Sometimes even days.

"Go ahead now," Cano barked, a bit sternly. "I'll be along. *Shooo* . . . it's business. Go on."

He said "Hold on" into the phone as the kids ran upstairs, and with a wave to Ernesto indicating that he should remain close by, he went up the staircase that led to one of the house's many terraces. He took a seat

211

on a chaise underneath a large white umbrella and stared out at the palm trees surrounding his house that he had brought in from the coast and the hills that reached to the sky-blue sea.

"It's a Sunday," he said in English. "Is a poor man not allowed a day of well-earned rest with his family?"

"It's because of another Sunday in Culiacán that we are even in this mess," replied the caller, who was known to him as "Grasshopper," one of Cano's highest-level contacts across the border in the U.S.

"Yes, I heard the little bitch is still alive," Cano said. "She is a hard one to kill, no? Like a centipede, you have to stamp it out with your heel or else it will follow you home. But no worry, due to the openness and accessibility of your own judicial system, it appears she has nowhere to go."

"Yes, your threats have their merit," Grasshopper said. "But Lauritzia Velez is not why I'm calling. Someone else has been asking around. He's been to the ranch. He's even been to see the girl. He seems to know about things."

"What things?" Cano lit up a cigarette.

"Gillian," the contact said.

"What does he know?" Cano asked.

"Enough," his contact said. "Why else would he be out west? Why else would he visit her in the hospital?"

"Who is this person?" Cano grunted, swatting away a mosquito that had landed on his arm. "Governmentale?"

A zealous government investigator who had stumbled onto something indeed could prove to be a pain in the ass.

"No," Grasshopper said. "A journalist."

*"Periodista!"* Cano exclaimed. "Here, a nosy journalist is like a lousy goalie in football. Or a judge. We don't like them—we just get rid of them. No trace. And I mean in a real box, my friend, not a ballot box."

"Well, here it is different," the caller replied. "Which is why you're not currently in a federal prison awaiting execution, I might add."

"Eh, well, not so different at all." Cano shrugged. He lowered his sunglasses and stared out at the blue sea. "I'm a great believer in the freedom of the press. You know that, right? Just give me the maggot's name, and we will be free of him for good."

# CHAPTER THIRTY-TWO

I slept in the Explorer that night, after making it away from Grand Central. I took the Metro-North back to Rye, my heart bouncing as bumpily as the train over the tracks, and found my way back to my car.

I had no idea where to go. All I wanted was to get away from there as fast as possible. Away from anywhere I could possibly be traced back to. I didn't know if the police had a read on my car. I didn't know if Joe was alive or dead. The news reports only said an injured bystander was rushed to Bellevue Hospital.

I drove north from Rye and pulled off I-95 in Bridgeport and drove around the city until I found a large, multistory garage downtown. I took a ticket and drove through the gate, then found an open space up on the third floor, which I assumed would be far less trafficked.

At first I just sat there. For an hour. Realizing I was finally safe. For my heart to finally calm.

I knew I had to change how I looked. And maybe switch out the license plates on the car, if I was going to continue to use it. I also knew I needed another phone. They now had Joe's in their possession, and it might well lead them to mine.

As soon as it was dark, I got out and found a Honda with Connecticut license plates in the same row as mine. I took off the front plate, using a wrench I'd found in the spare tire tool set in the back of the Explorer. It would probably take a while for the Honda owner to even notice it was gone. Then I took off the rear plate on the Explorer and replaced it with the Honda's.

I ventured out, my face hidden behind sunglasses and in an old Mount Snow baseball cap I found in the back of the Explorer. Downtown Bridgeport wasn't exactly the best neighborhood at night.

I found an open bodega on Congress Street and picked out another disposable phone, as well as a slice of pizza and a beef empanada, the first food I'd have all day. I also grabbed a box of blonde hair color and a pair of scissors.

As I stood in line to pay I found myself behind a woman who was counting out change. A cop came in and got in line right behind me. My heart almost jumped through my chest. I stood there, blood rushing, totally freaked out of my mind, sure that I was giving off this aura, like, *You know that woman who's wanted for the murder of her husband and that Homeland Security agent . . . well, hey, I'm here, buddy. Take a look. Right in front of you!*

"Next, please." The cashier looked at me. I tried to block what it was I was buying on the counter, certain it would give me away.

I paid with cash, muttering, "Thanks," and averting my face, hurried out of the store. Exhaling, I headed back to the garage. I asked the attendant there—a Middle Easterner who was more absorbed in a soccer match on the tiny TV than in me—if there was a bathroom. He pointed to the rear of the first floor.

The door was open. I didn't even need a key. I locked it immediately behind me and looked at myself in the greasy, cracked mirror: the harried uncertainty in my eyes; my face pale from nerves. I ripped the scissors out of their package and held them up to my hair—my beautiful hair that I had worn thick and below my shoulders ever since I could remember, that people always looked at with envy, and began to chop away. Fistfuls of it, sheared off. I stuffed them into the plastic bag from the bodega. I kept cutting and shearing, until I looked and my hair fell to my shoulders.

It all meant nothing to me anymore.

I opened the box of color. I had always been some kind of dark brown with occasional streaks of henna. But I bent over the sink and poured the goopy, amber-colored liquid all over my hair and massaged it in, averting my eyes from the mirror. I waited a few minutes, then rinsed it out, washing the viscous liquid down the drain. When I looked up, I saw a completely different face. One I barely even recognized. But filled with nerves and shame.

I went back to my car, unable to free my mind of what had happened to Joe. He had been so brave for me. I needed to find out how he was. I had to take the chance.

I called Bellevue Hospital and nervously asked the operator for an update on his condition. She asked if I was family, and I answered yes. I was transferred to another line; it took forever to connect, which began to get me a little edgy.

"May I help you?" a man's voice finally answered. "You're inquiring about Joseph Esterhaus?"

Suddenly it ran through me that they might be thinking I would call in and were tracing me as I spoke.

*"Hello?* Private Patient Information. May I help you? *Hello?"*

I hung up. My hands were shaking. I didn't know how to do any of this! I was ashamed to be so cowardly. Joe had put everything on the line for me. *Joe, please, just make it through.* I closed my eyes. *I'm praying for you, Joe. Please . . .*

I'd never felt so alone or isolated. I just needed to feel close to someone. Anyone. I thought of my stepson.

He'd probably be at his uncle's. I thought it was worth the risk.

I punched Neil's number into my new phone. After what had come out, I wasn't sure if he would even want to talk to me.

It rang—once, twice, three times. I anxiously waited to hear his voice. *Come on, Neil, please!*

I just wanted to hear my stepson's voice. To tell him I loved him. He'd just lost his dad. I only imagined the anguish he must be experiencing. And feeling . . . not knowing the truth. Thinking I had done it . . . By the fourth ring I was dying. *Please, Neil, pick up.*

Then I caught myself. I had no idea if he had been to the police. They might have his phone under observation too. Was it possible that they could trace incoming calls? Even a quick one, from an unregistered number?

I didn't know.

I cut off the call.

I put down the phone, my heart as aching as it had ever been. I missed Dave so much. And I was missing my dad. If he were alive, he'd be the first one I would go to. I had never felt so overwhelmed or so alone in my life.

*The hell with it,* said a voice that leapt up inside me. *They're my family! I've lost my husband too!* I rifled through my bag and took out my iPhone. I remembered reading somewhere that a text message couldn't be traced. That that was how Wall Street honchos looking to avoid a paper trail were communicating with each other these days. I scrolled under Contacts to my son's.

What would I even say?

I began to write:

I know what you must think. But don't believe it, honey. I didn't kill your dad. I swear! I miss him terribly, just like you must now.

I wish I could tell it to you myself, baby. You have to trust me.

I wish I could tell it to you all.


I closed the phone and let my head go back against my seat, the blood draining from me.

I heard a loud *beep* and a car lock go on. I jumped. A couple got into their car directly next to me, sending my heart clawing up my throat. I sank down, hiding myself in my seat.

And I began to cry.

Knowing I was so alone and in such trouble. Knowing anyone who knew me probably thought I was a murderer. Or a lunatic.

Knowing my husband was dead. Because of me. That people wanted to kill me, and I didn't even know why.

Now Joe . . .

Suddenly my phone vibrated on the car seat. My heart leaped up. I grabbed the phone and checked the screen. For a moment, I was excited, almost giddy.

It was Neil.

With a lifted heart I checked out his reply. But what I read sent a shiver down my spine.

Don't write me again.
How could you have done this, Wendy?
How?

He had it all wrong. Just like I thought he would. Like the world would. I was about to tell him to just hear me out when another text came through.

I don't want to hear from you again. Just turn yourself in, Wendy.

# CHAPTER THIRTY-THREE

I was sitting in a stolen car, on the run, inside a dank and freezing garage, but Neil's answer left me colder and more alone than ever. I found an old blanket in the back that Jim and Cindy must have used as a ski warmer and wrapped myself in it.

I was scared to be out here on my own, even more scared at the thought of turning myself in. I knew the only way to prove my innocence was to find proof that the agent who'd shot Curtis in that hotel room was engaged in some kind of nasty business that resulted in both of their deaths.

I just didn't know how.

From the car, I googled Curtis on my iPhone. What came back was that he had written articles for publications like *The Atlantic* and *The New Yorker* and some online magazines like *Mother Jones* and *The Daily Beast* on topics such as the financial meltdown and the war in Afghanistan, with titles that seemed to focus on some form of government or corporate corruption. I had to know what he was working on when he was killed. Did I dare call these publications? I knew that would be insane. What could I possibly say? That I was a reporter looking into Curtis's death? Should I try to find his agent or maybe a friend? The first call I made, I was certain the police would be all over me in minutes.

I scrolled through his phone again, through his e-mails and photographs. I stopped again at the one of the pretty Latina-looking woman in the hospital gown. There were other photos of Curtis with his friends, seemingly in party mode. Further along, I found several in a mountainous terrain, which now I figured was Afghanistan. In several of them Curtis was decked out in combat gear with soldiers and villagers. I also found a shot of him and a younger woman who looked like she might be his sister around a table with an older couple who I guessed were his mom and dad.

A shudder of emotion came over me. A mother's emotion, as I looked at Curtis's mom, surrounded by her children. Proud, happy eyes that reflected what would have been in my own, only days ago.

It suddenly occurred to me that that might be a way. She might be able to help me. If it were me, if I had lost my son, I would want to know—I'd *have* to know—the truth about what really happened up there. Not just what the news was saying.

The truth—how my son died.

At the bar, Curtis told me he hailed from Boston. I went through his contacts until I came up with a number marked Home. A 607 area code. It was after 9:00 P.M. I didn't know where his parents would be right now. In Boston, or even in New York, maybe, claiming the body? It was just a few days ago that they had lost their son.

I figured it was worth a try.

I clicked on the number and waited with trepidation until the fourth ring, when a woman finally answered. "Hello?"

I felt paralyzed. I didn't know what to say. I didn't know how she might take me. As some crazy accomplice in their son's death? Someone wanted by the FBI? Or just a panicked, promiscuous woman?

"Mrs. Kitchner?" I uttered haltingly.

The woman hesitated. "This is Elaine Kitchner. Who is this?"

"Mrs. Kitchner, I'm sorry to bother you. I know this is a difficult time. I realize you just lost your son." I heard a man's voice in the background, asking, "Who is it, Elaine?"

I sucked in a breath and said the only thing that came to my mind. "This is Wendy Gould. I don't know if you know my name. I just thought you might want to know what happened up there. In that hotel room."

I was met with silence. And who could blame her? Her son had been shot at point-blank range under mysterious circumstances. It was being portrayed in the press as if he'd shot it out with a government agent. And that I was there.

"Is this a joke?" she asked, her tone stiffening.

"It's not a joke, Mrs. Kitchner. And please, please don't hang up. I was in that room with your son when he was killed. I was there."

I waited; the silence grew stonier the longer it went on. She was probably trying to decide if this was some kind of crank, or just some freak who wanted to cause her pain. I knew she might hang up on me at any second.

"Please, Mrs. Kitchner, the last thing in the world I'm trying to do is cause you any pain. I've lost someone myself. I just need to talk with you. It's vitally important." I was almost in tears.

"How did you possibly get this number?" she finally replied.

"Please don't hang up! I know what this must seem. But I'm not some psycho. I'm a mother too, and a mother who, right now, watched her husband get killed and can't even talk to my own son. I can't even call the police. I can only imagine you would want to know what happened to Curtis. Because it's not like what anyone's saying . . . and I lost the person I loved most in the world last night too. So *my* life's been taken from me as well . . ."

I heard her husband in the background, trying to take the line from her.

"You were with him?" she asked expectantly.

"Yes, I was." The words flew out of me, jumbled and rambling. "Your son wasn't in a shoot-out, Mrs. Kitchner, like it's been portrayed. He was murdered. In cold blood. By an agent from the Department of Homeland Security. I saw it happen! I know. I was up there with him, and I know that doesn't make me look particularly good, or reliable, and for that I'm truly ashamed, though in truth, that doesn't really matter much right now. But an agent of the U.S. government found his way into his hotel room and shot your son at point-blank range. He tried to plant a gun on him, to make it appear that Curtis had a gun too, which he was about to fire. Which he did not. There wasn't any fight. Curtis barely even touched it. He was murdered. The agent went to kill me too. The only reason I got out alive was because the gun he tried to plant on Curtis fell across the bed to me, and I shot him in self-defense."

"*Self-defense?* You said this was a government agent, Ms. Gould?"

"He was, but whatever he was doing up there, he clearly wasn't up to any good."

I knew I wasn't making complete sense. I also knew

I couldn't back up a thing that I was saying. And that the accounts that were filtering out completely contradicted me. Elaine Kitchner muttered something to her husband, and then she actually pulled back the phone from him, going, "Desmond, please . . . Why are you calling us, Ms. Gould? These are things you should be telling to the FBI, not me."

"I can't tell the FBI! I tried to turn myself over to the police yesterday in New York, and I'm sure you saw what took place. I didn't try to run. People were trying to kill me. I know it seems as if I'm just some crazy woman who's out of control, but it's just not true. I need to know some things. It's the only way I can prove my innocence. I need to know what Curtis might have been working on and why a federal agent would want to kill him."

"You expect us to share this kind of information with you? All *I* know is you're implicated in my son's murder."

"If you want the truth about your son to come out, there's no other way!"

"You're wanted in connection with multiple murders, Ms. Gould. Your own husband's murder! I'm sorry, but if I were you, I would think about turning yourself in."

"*I can't!*" I said again, my voice cracking. "Don't you understand, I saw what happened up there and they don't want any witnesses." I realized how I was sounding. "I didn't kill my husband . . . They killed him. Why do you think it wasn't the police who showed up at my house? Why was it the same government agent who tried to kill me at the hotel? Please. Mrs. Kitchner, I'm not some lunatic! I don't know what Curtis was into that he had to die. The person who shot him mentioned a name, Gillian. I don't know if that name means anything to you?" She didn't say anything. "But whatever it was, my husband ended up being killed for it as well. I'm not able to see his body. I can't even touch his cheek a last time and tell him I loved him or how sorry I am. I don't even have a fucking clue where I'm going to go once I hang up this phone! But we still have one thing in common, Mrs. Kitchner, whether you like it or not. Today we're both mourning people we loved."

I was crying. Not just for Dave. From the realization that I would never see him again. And that I might have lost my family too.

But because of what I'd just said. That Dave was dead, maybe Joe as well, and I didn't know what my next step was, or where to turn. I was desperate. I was out of options, the moment she hung up.

"He was a good young man," Elaine Kitchner said. "He put himself on the line. He cared about things . . ."

I sniffed back my tears. "I could see that. This probably sounds silly, but he was a gentleman to me."

She said, "When he went up against these people . . . I told him, this time it was different. This wasn't like the war. Afghanistan . . ."

"Went up against *what* people?"

"He said he knew what he was doing. He said he was working on something important."

"Please, w*hat* people, Mrs. Kitchner?" I pressed her again.

There was a pause. I had no idea what I was expecting. She could simply say good-bye. She could just hang up on me. And then I'd be nowhere. I had nowhere to turn next.

"Do you know Boston?" Elaine Kitchner finally asked.

"A little. I went to BC."

"Do you know the island that divides Commonwealth Avenue? It's known as the Mall."

"Yeah, I know it," I replied, hopeful.

"Between Dartmouth and Clarendon. It's across from our house. I'll be on a bench that faces east. Can you be there at noon?"

"How do I know you just won't turn me in?" I asked her. "How do I know the police won't be there too?"

"I guess you don't," Elaine Kitchner said. "Other than like you said, tonight we're both mourning people we loved."

# CHAPTER THIRTY-FOUR

It may not have been the smartest thing I've ever done, going up there on a hunch. Meeting a grieving mother who thought I was connected to the murder of her son. Who reminded me I was wanted by the police.

But what choice did I have?

I guess I thought, what would Elaine Kitchner gain by seeing me in prison? I hadn't killed her son. And if she did call the police on me, maybe I thought better the Boston police or even the local FBI than the ones who were trying to kill me.

It took around three hours the next morning to drive up to Boston. I hadn't been there in years. I wound through the Back Bay and found a parking space just off Newbury, a few blocks from where she told me to meet her.

Commonwealth Avenue was upscale and residential in between Dartmouth and Clarendon, attractive brownstones lining both sides of the divided street. From a few blocks away I watched joggers running by, people out walking their dogs. By noon, mothers had come out with baby strollers. The skyscrapers from Copley Square and the Financial Center rose above the townhouses.

I suddenly saw a police car speeding up ahead. Its lights were flashing and its siren was on, and as it came closer, my heart started to grow twice its size, and I was thinking, *You're a fool, Wendy, a fool to have trusted her.* I started to climb the stairs to a brownstone, sure that the car would screech to a stop directly in front and cops with their guns drawn would jump out.

That it was over.

But it zoomed on by.

I think the breath I let out could be heard all the way in Copley Square.

I didn't see anyone else who looked like a cop or an FBI agent milling around, but of course, it wouldn't have taken much to wait until I'd made contact with her and then sweep in. Not to mention I was hardly an expert at this. I waited until precisely noon, then I circled around the block to where Elaine had said she'd be. A woman in a green down coat was sitting on a bench holding a book in her lap. As I got closer, I saw she had silver-colored hair.

The woman I saw in Curtis's phone.

I said to myself, *You can just leave, Wendy. You can just bag this.* Stock it up to intuition, but what she'd said to me the night before made me feel I could trust her.

Hopefully, she was thinking the same thing about me.

I walked up, my scarf wrapped tightly around my neck, a late-October chill coming off the bay. "Mrs. Kitchner?"

She looked up. She was a stately, attractive woman. She had warm brown eyes and sharp, defined cheekbones, though she looked peaked and gaunt from what she'd been through. I saw Curtis in her handsome face.

She said, "My husband thinks I'm a fool to even be talking with you. He said we should call the police."

I shrugged and gave her a half smile. "It crossed my mind that this isn't the smartest thing I've ever done either."

She forced a begrudging smile too.

She said, "Maybe there are mothers who loved their son as much as I did . . ." Her brown eyes lit up just a little. "But no one could have possibly loved theirs more. I need for you to tell me what happened."

I sat down next to her. At this point, whatever fears I had about walking into a trap had disappeared. "Curtis fought him." I shrugged, not sure just how much detail she was looking for. "He didn't give in."

She shook her head. "I mean it all, Ms. Gould."

So I told her. Everything. From the beginning. How I'd met him in the bar. How we talked a bit, and how I listened to him play. How magical that was. Which made her smile.

"I know I should have never gone up to that room with him. It was my doing, as much as his. Not that that matters much now."

"If you're looking for a sympathetic ear, Ms. Gould, you don't win many points from me having met my son at a bar and not an hour later you end up in bed with him."

"We never did." I shook my head. "I was about to leave when the man came in. I couldn't go through with it."

Her eyes grew wide.

"It's not how everyone is saying . . . I'm not some floozy, Mrs. Kitchner. I've been married almost ten years. I'd never done anything like this before in my life. Your son could have been angry with me, but we both . . ." I smiled. "We both kind of found the humor in it. You can't believe how much I appreciated him for that. I was in the bathroom preparing to leave when the man came in."

I told her how he'd tried to force a second gun into Curtis's hand, to make it appear like he was drawing a weapon.

"The gun fell across the bed when he and Curtis struggled. Then he shot him. Twice. Point-blank. When your son wouldn't pick it up. He said this was about Gillian. Do you know that name?"

"No, I don't know any Gillian." She shook her head.

"I knew I'd be next. While he was checking on Curtis, I came out. The gun was pretty much in arm's reach. I told the guy to put his down. He only looked back at me and said, 'You have no idea what you've stepped into.' That's when he raised his gun at me.

"I guess you know the rest . . . Except that I didn't kill my husband either, as everyone's saying." I told her how they came for me, as Dave and I were leaving. Not the NYPD, but the same people who killed Curtis. Who tried to kill me! "I'm being framed, Mrs. Kitchner. Because of what I witnessed up there. I tried to turn myself in. Now the only way I can prove what I'm saying is to find out why they wanted to kill your son."

"I'm sorry," Elaine Kitchner said with a truly sympathetic shrug.

"What was Curtis working on?" I put my hand on her knee. "What had he found out that the government needed to kill him? You told me you said that these people were dangerous. That it wasn't like in Afghanistan. What people are you talking about? Please, tell me who would have wanted him dead? *Who?*"

She stared at me. For a moment I thought we were done. That she was about to get up and leave. Then, "Please, take off your sunglasses," she said. "I want to see your eyes."

233

I did. If I could've summoned every bit of the fear and helplessness I was feeling at that moment, it would have shown right back at her.

She took out a Kleenex and handed it to me. I smiled in thanks and dabbed my eyes.

"I wish I knew what he was working on, Ms. Gould. But I don't. Curtis didn't share his work with us."

"But you do know who he was trying to expose? You said you warned him that these people were dangerous."

She looked away. I could see she was thinking about what to say. Traffic rushed by us. She waited until a man walking his terrier went by.

"Do you recall that private jet that was blown up at Westchester Airport?"

I nodded. "Of course. A month or two ago."

It had happened in the county where I lived. I'd flown out of there dozens of times. The bomber, who had posed as a tarmac worker, was never apprehended. Four passengers were killed, including the wife of the lawyer who had chartered it.

"Curtis insisted it was some sort of retribution. By Mexican drug enforcers. Against an informant, or someone who was on that plane. It was these people I told him he mustn't mess with."

*Mexican drug enforcers* . . . A tremor rippled through me. No people to mess with at all. I thought back and recalled there *was* a housekeeper or a nanny on board who had survived.

234

"I don't understand," I said. "What would all that have to do with the U.S. government? The person who shot your son worked for the Department of Homeland Security."

Elaine looked at me blankly. "All I know is what he was looking into when he went down to New York."

I felt something creepy and foreboding wrap its tentacles around my heart and squeeze. That explosion had been one of the ugliest acts of terror in recent years. The bomber had been able to infiltrate security at the private airport that was used by many hedge fund magnates and CEOs. *Drug enforcers? The United States government rubbing Curtis out?* Something between a shudder and the feeling of being completely overwhelmed passed through me. This was so far out of my league I didn't know where to begin.

That agent was right—what *had* I stepped into?

I looked back at Elaine. I knew my face had taken on a worried cast. I reached into my pocket and brought out Curtis's BlackBerry. I pushed the camera icon and scrolled to the photo of the pretty Latina-looking woman in the hospital gown.

"Do you know who this woman is?"

Elaine looked at it and shook her head. But suddenly, the hospital gown, the Latina features, combined with the story of the airport bombing, gave me the feeling I now knew.

"This was your son's," I said.

Elaine's eyes grew glassy as she took it in her palm.

"I took it. From his hotel room. I didn't even know who he was. I just thought I might need something. Was there any place Curtis might have kept his notes? Or a record of what he was working on?"

"Other than his computer?" Elaine shook her head. "Curtis's laptop was basically his office. He had an apartment over in Boylston Street. Near Fenway Park. But it's already been gone through by the police."

"The police?"

"The police were with them. My husband went. I don't know. Maybe other people too."

It wouldn't be safe to go there. Not now. Plus I knew it was also too late. There wouldn't be anything there for me to find.

"You mind if I keep this for a while?" I asked, pointing to the cell phone in her hand. "I promise, I'll make sure it gets back to you."

Elaine shrugged and handed it back. "It may be of more help to you at the moment than any comfort to me."

"Thank you." I squeezed her shoulder warmly. "I appreciate everything you've told me."

"I wish it were more."

I stood up and gave her a heartfelt smile, the kind that maybe only another woman who had lost her deepest love might fully understand. "I know you took a risk in talking with me. I'll get this back, I promise," I said, tucking her son's phone into my pocket.

"So you heard him play?" Elaine Kitchner said, her eyes lighting up.

"I did. He was brilliant."

She smiled. "I used to say he could charm the birds right out of the trees."

"He did that to me." I smiled back and started to walk away.

"Wendy," Elaine called after me. I turned. "By the way, he's alive."

*"Who?"* For a second I thought she was referring to Curtis.

"Your friend. I just heard it on the news. He was hit twice. But he's alive."

# CHAPTER THIRTY-FIVE

The private room in the trauma wing at Bellevue wasn't large, but it came with a view of the East River, which was the first thing Joe Esterhaus saw when he opened his eyes.

The next thing was a black man in a tan suit sitting in the chair across from him.

"Lucky man." Alton Dokes smiled thinly.

"And how's that?" Esterhaus stared back at him. He had seen the man on the news before he'd been shot and knew exactly who he was.

"Nothing vital hit. No infection. I hear you might be leaving as soon as tomorrow. An inch or two either way, no telling what the result would have been."

Esterhaus shifted. "The way I see it, I'm the one with a hole in my shoulder just trying to do my civic duty. We must have a different sense of the word."

"Civic duty?" Dokes smiled again. "Maybe I'm the one with a different sense of the word."

Esterhaus shifted, dragging across his IV, which an hour earlier had been delivering a morphine drip. The first shot had gone through his shoulder, a solid through-and-through. The second grazed his neck. Dokes was right—another inch in either direction, he'd be at the morgue, not in a private room. The first thing he had asked his daughter as he was coming out from under the anesthesia was if Wendy had gotten away. And finding out that she had, and that her whereabouts were still unknown, made him feel good he was still alive, and no doubt accounted for why this government agent was in front of him.

"Alton Dokes." The agent stood up and came over to the foot of the bed.

"I know who you are."

"Then let's not pretend, shall we? We're going to get her, you know. Sooner than later. You can help make that easy. On her, I mean."

Esterhaus craned his bandaged neck and gazed around. "Can't say I see her in here anywhere. You?"

"At the same time"—Dokes put his hand on the railing—"maybe there's a way to help each other out as well." He picked up Esterhaus's prescription from the bedside table. "Parkinson's, correct? You lost your pension years ago when you were canned from the force. You're going to become a burden to somebody soon. Your daughter? Her husband? Maybe we can see about getting it back."

"My *pension*?" Esterhaus chuckled. "You'd do all that for me? I'm touched."

"If you do your civic duty." Dokes kept his eyes on him.

"You mean give her up?"

"I have every belief she'll find a way to contact you. She's got no one else."

"She didn't do it." Esterhaus stared back at him. "She watched your partner shoot a man in cold blood. But I guess I'm not telling you anything you don't already know."

The agent put the medication back on the table. "That's not how it appears to me. Or anyone else who's taken a look at the evidence. I know you have protective feelings for her. We know you were tight with her dad. But the woman meets a guy at a bar and an hour later ends up in his room. She takes off from a federal agent who directly ordered her to stop. She panics and shoots her husband, likely when she told him what had happened and he called her a whore. You can't let a sense of duty to her father blind you to the facts. She's bad. She can't be trusted."

Esterhaus pushed back the urge to rip the tubes out of his arm and wrap them around this shit bag's throat and strangle him.

"There's that angle," the agent said. "Then there's the angle of making this all come out for *you*." Dokes dug through his jacket pocket. "Here. Instead of leaving a

240

card." He came out with a cell phone. Esterhaus's phone. The one they'd taken from him after he was shot. "I think we got as much off it as we can use. Especially those calls to someplace called Waccabuc. I don't have to remind you, do I, Joe, the wavy line that separates doing your civic duty, as you call it, and aiding and abetting a federal fugitive? That little shake of yours wouldn't play so well in a federal prison, would it now?"

There was a knock at the door. Esterhaus's daughter, Robin, came in, with an armful of newspapers and magazines. "Hey, Pop." She looked at Dokes. "Sorry, didn't know you had company. Good news," she said. "They're saying you're not worth keeping here past tomorrow."

"That is good news," Dokes said to Robin, smiling. "I was just trying to urge your father to rethink his civic duty . . ."

Esterhaus pushed himself up. "And I was just telling the agent here to go fuck himself with a rusty nail."

Dokes placed the phone on the bedside table next to Esterhaus's Parkinson's pills. "Tell your dad what a shame it would be for things to have worked out so luckily for him, only to end up being a burden on the taxpayers for the rest of his years.

"Have a speedy recovery," he said, heading to the door and looking at Esterhaus with an icy smile. "And let me know if you get any calls. We'll be watching too."

# CHAPTER THIRTY-SIX

I took Comm Ave. all the way out to Chestnut Hill and drove around Boston College, where twenty years ago I'd gone to school. It all seemed pretty familiar to me. Although HTM and Five Guys Burgers had replaced the Gap and Blockbuster.

On a chilly fall afternoon, people were either in class or studying. Beacon Street was pretty quiet.

I parked the Explorer near the reservoir and walked back, passing a coffeehouse with a sign on the window: INTERNET. GAMES. BEST COFFEE/CHEAPEST RATES. A high industrial ceiling and brick walls. There were only a couple of people in the place.

I took a seat at a long wooden table in front of an old recycled Dell. The waiter instructed me how to log on. I ordered a coffee and a berry tart. Between my shortened, newly blonde hair and my sunglasses, I wasn't particularly worried I'd be recognized.

I logged onto Google and typed in "Westchester Airport Bombing." More than 6,700 hits sprang up. I started with one on the first page, from the local Westchester newspaper, the *Journal News*.

FOUR DEAD IN PRIVATE JET BOMBING AT COUNTY AIRPORT.

ONE SURVIVOR. BOMBER, POSING AS TARMAC WORKER, SOUGHT

I started in, following the tragic story over several days. The eight-seat Citation 7, owned by an outfit called Globaljet, had been leased by a law office out of Stamford. Sifton, Sloan, and Rubin. The victims, all of whom were on board, included the pilot, the copilot, the one flight attendant, and a passenger, Roxanne Bachman, of Greenwich, the wife of a senior partner in the law firm. The one survivor, Lauritzia Velez, twenty-four, was a nanny traveling with Mrs. Bachman, her employer. A spokesperson at the Westchester Medical Center in Valhalla confirmed that Ms. Velez was in critical condition but was expected to survive.

I took out Curtis's cell phone and scrolled to the photo of the pretty girl in the hospital gown identified only by the initial L.

Lauritzia Velez.

The blast occurred just as the plane was preparing to

roll back from its gate. The explosives were thought to have been in a suitcase on a mobile baggage carrier that had pulled up next to the plane. The suspect, "a man with Hispanic features, and wearing the uniform and carrying the ID of a tarmac worker," managed to escape by a vehicle in the parking lot and still hadn't been found. The blue Toyota he was seen escaping in was later discovered abandoned on Route 120 in nearby West Harrison, N.Y., suggesting there had been a change of cars. A motive for the bombing was yet to be established.

I scrolled down to a follow-up article from the following day:

The Citation's final destination was Denver International Airport, where Roxanne Bachman had booked a rental car. A source at Harold Bachman's law office confirmed that the couple owned a home in the resort community of Cordillera, Colorado, near Vail. Investigators speculated that Ms. Velez, a native of Mexico, might have been the actual target of the blast, the first of its kind at any major airport in the United States, as she and her family have been targets of a bloody retaliation from a Mexican drug cartel that left several of her siblings dead. It is not known whether Ms. Velez was currently acting as an informant or in the employ of any law enforcement agency.

I wrote down Lauritzia's name, underlining "retaliation" and "drug cartel," and flashed back to what Elaine Kitchner had said about Curtis messing with the wrong kind of people. I continued past several follow-up articles. SECURITY AT PRIVATE AIRFIELD SAID TO BE LAX. HANGAR E HOME TO GLITZY A-LISTERS FROM AROUND THE REGION. Finally I opened one from the *New York Times*: REVENGE LIKELY MOTIVE OF WESTCHESTER AIRPORT BLAST. SURVIVOR HAD SUED TO REMAIN IN U.S. A WEEK BEFORE.

I read how only days before, the same Lauritzia Velez's petition for permanent U.S. asylum through the Fifth Court of Appeals in Dallas was turned down.

The logic of the ruling was difficult to follow, even with a year of law school under my belt. But what came out was that Ms. Velez and her family had previously been denied asylum, even though a Mexican drug enforcer, Eduardo Cano, had carried out what amounted to a reign of terror against her and her family, the result of Ms. Velez's father having turned government witness against Mr. Cano and his intent to testify against him at a murder trial.

The article went on to say that Ms. Velez's brother and three sisters had all been murdered, in both Mexico and the U.S., but that to date, no one had been brought to trial.

I looked again at the young woman in Curtis's photo, my stomach feeling a little hollow.

Elaine Kitchner said that her son had been looking

into the Westchester Airport bombing. He had visited Lauritzia Velez in the hospital and taken her photograph just days before he was killed. What was it he needed to find her for? Information on Eduardo Cano? The cartels? Ms. Velez's father? And how did the United States government fit into this? The agent who had killed Curtis worked for Homeland Security, not some drug cartel.

And finally, who was Gillian? The name Ray Hruseff had uttered before he shot Curtis. The name that was nowhere to be found in any of the articles related to the bombing.

Frustrated, I typed in "Lauritzia Velez." Pages of hits came back, more than 2,100 of them, but all focused on her connection to the airport bombing.

There was nothing about Eduardo Cano, or any vendetta against her family.

Nothing about her father, or what he may have testified about to incur Eduardo Cano's wrath.

Yet Curtis's interest in that bombing had been enough to attract the attention of two Homeland Security agents bent on keeping him quiet. Enough to get him killed.

I scrolled further down, filtering through the numerous articles on Lauritzia Velez's involvement in the bombing.

Something struck my eye.

It wasn't connected to the bombing, but to the appeals court's ruling on her petition for asylum, literally the week before.

*Velez vs. United States/usappealscourt.justice.gov.*

At that point, this would likely have been the only thing that came up against her name, but after the bombing, it was buried among a thousand AP wire pickups.

I skimmed the court's 2–1 decision. It mostly mirrored the article I had just read about a possible motive for the bombing.

But then I got to the summation of the one dissenting judge. Judge Marilyn Vickers wrote:

> Denying Ms. Velez's claim is a repudiation of the basis for encouraging anyone with a criminal history to testify against their co-conspirators without fear of whether the U.S. government will stand behind them. Mr. Cano, having allegedly masterminded the ambush in Culiacán, Mexico, that cost two distinguished DEA agents their lives, as well as three completely innocent U.S. college students, seems the only one the United States appears interested in protecting. Mr. Velez's decision to turn on Cano resulted in the deaths of his son and three daughters. At the very least, this government owes Ms. Velez the same rights that were extended to her father.

*The ambush in Culiacán.* Two DEA agents murdered. Lauritzia's father turning state's evidence against Cano.

I read it again. I was sure that had to be what was behind the attempt to kill her at the airport.

What Curtis had been looking into at the time he was killed.

For the first time I actually felt that I was on to something. I punched "Culiacán drug shooting" into the computer. I took another sip of coffee and a bite of my tart.

That feeling only became more real when I read over what I found.

# CHAPTER THIRTY-SEVEN

On a quiet Sunday morning in March almost four years before, two decorated DEA agents out of the agency's El Paso, Texas, office were shot dead in their car while stopped in a square in the remote town of Culiacán, in northwestern Mexico.

Up to two dozen Los Zetas gunmen under Eduardo Cano's command were said to have carried out the killing, which also resulted in the deaths of three American college students traveling on spring break, who were inadvertently caught in the rain of gunfire.

There was a picture of a handsome, athletic-looking teenager, Sam Orthwein, one of the students killed, who reminded me a lot of my stepson, Neil.

I sucked in a deep breath.

The article in *Mother Jones* online described the recent

history of violence in the Sinaloa region, one of the thriving centers of drug trafficking to the United States. It also described the group Los Zetas, known as the Z's, onetime elite Mexican special forces soldiers trained by the United States to combat the drug trade who subsequently defected and became killers for hire to the other cartels. Los Zetas had become a de facto drug cartel of its own, taking over billion-dollar supply routes, warring with the other cartels, even siphoning off supposed billions of dollars from Mexico's largest oil pipeline. Eduardo Cano, an ex–special forces captain, had built a CV of death and retaliation that included judges, reporters, politicians, and hundreds of rival cartel soldiers whose mutilated bodies could be found dumped in the streets of Juárez and Guadalajara, "jarring symbols of the cartel's unlimited reach and their willingness to resort to violence."

The article traced the lives of four individuals whose paths converged that Sunday morning: the murdered DEA agents, Dean and Rita Bienvienes, who were married. Orthwein, a lacrosse player and dean's list student at the University of Denver. And Cano.

Dean Bienvienes was an accountant assigned to the El Paso office whose job was to estimate seized contraband and follow the money trail flowing in and out of the cartels. His wife, Rita, was a decorated field agent, a former narcotics detective in Phoenix, and a veteran of two tours of combat in Iraq. At the time of her death, she was working undercover on a case involving a capo in the rival Barrio Azteca cartel—an organization currently at war with the Juarte cartel that was aligned with Los Zetas. It was thought that the killing of the U.S. agents by Cano was a kind of favor, a gesture of peace to the Barrio Azteca cartel.

But how did he know the agents would be there? And on their own, without protection?

I read on, the article going into the two murdered DEA agents, who by all rights had exemplary careers, and why they were even traveling in that region, known to be a center of drug violence. Supposedly, they were on their way to visit a friend in Mazatlán, farther south. The fact that they were there at all—in a dangerous area, without protection—cast suspicion over their previously unblemished careers. Whispers emerged that one or both of them were dirty. It was stated that almost 30 percent of the DEA or the Immigrations and Customs Enforcement (ICE) border guards were on the payroll of the cartels, paid hundreds of thousands to look the other way when shipments crossed the border. But Sabrina Stein, then head of the DEA's office in El Paso, ground zero in the war against drugs along the Mexican border, called both agents "exemplary," and their job reviews were filled with commendations and praise.

Still, the fact that they were there and the targets of a Los Zetas death squad raised concerns that the Bienvienes were not as lily white as once believed. Their personal bank accounts were delved into, as were the couple's purchase of a condominium in the Bahamas and expensive jewelry Rita was photographed wearing. But nothing questionable was found. Four months after the shootings, Eduardo Cano was apprehended by the FBI while in the United States, the result of a tip from one of his lieutenants, Oscar Velez, who had defected.

*Lauritzia's father.* My eyes grew wide.

But apparently no trial ever came about. Sources at the DOJ were tight-lipped on exactly why, pointing to problems in Oscar Velez's testimony. But the whisper mill suggested the decision not to prosecute was more due to troublesome things that began to emerge about Rita and Dean Bienvienes. Things which, if revealed at trial, would embarrass the U.S. government. Ultimately, Eduardo Cano was released and deported back to Mexico. Oscar Velez was granted asylum in the United States. Sabrina Stein was now working in Washington for the Justice Department as assistant attorney general for drug enforcement policy.

The same Sabrina Stein, I suddenly realized, Harold Bachman had used at the hearing as a witness against Cano.

I still had no idea who Gillian was. Or how this all led back to Curtis's death.

But a bloody ambush in Mexico; two DEA agents killed; a vendetta of blood against Lauritzia Velez's father, who had turned against his boss; the shocking decision

252

by the U.S. government to drop the prosecution—all culminated in the bombing at Westchester airport meant to kill the informant's daughter.

Who Curtis had been to visit only days earlier, and which I was now damn sure had gotten him killed.

By U.S. government agents.

The byline on the article was Curtis Kitchner.

# CHAPTER THIRTY-EIGHT

I lifted my head from the screen. An hour had passed since I had come in. Several more customers, mostly students, I guessed, were in the café. Two of them sat directly across from me, laughing at some YouTube videos. I began to think it was time to leave.

But first I put Ray Hruseff's name into Google Search.

Several responses came back, mostly newspaper articles chronicling his history of military and government service, as someone who had always put his country first throughout his career.

First in combat. He had served two tours in Desert Storm. Then in various law enforcement posts for the government. He'd only been at Homeland Security for the past year. Before that, according to what I found, he'd been assigned to Immigration and Customs Enforcement (ICE) for three years as a supervising field agent. He distinguished himself overseeing a raid that netted a group of cartel members who were running guns across the border.

"Prior to that . . ." I continued scanning his bio.

My heart came to a halt.

". . . between 2006 and 2010" Hruseff served as a field agent in the DEA out of the agency's El Paso office.

I fixed on it. Those were the same years when Sabrina Stein was in charge of that office.

I leaned in closer to the screen, my eyes wide, and read it again. The pieces were starting to fit together.

Hruseff must have worked for Sabrina Stein.

It still wasn't all fitting together. I realized I needed to find Lauritzia Velez. Ultimately she led back to Curtis. To what he was looking for. She was the one link that could get me to what I needed to know.

I didn't have a clue in the world how to find her now. But as I looked back through my notes, and clicked back on the articles I had opened, I came across the name of one person I thought would have a pretty good idea.

The person who had chartered that jet and represented her.

As I got my notes together and was about to leave, I plugged one final name into the computer.

Alton Dokes.

I stared at what came back, and suddenly everything—Hruseff, Dokes, Cano, why they were trying to keep me quiet—became clear to me.

# CHAPTER THIRTY-NINE

The modern six-story brick-and-glass office building was on Atlantic and Summers Streets in downtown Stamford.

I got there at 7:30 A.M. and waited in the garage.

I had looked up the address for Sifton, Sloan and Rubin, where the article I'd read the day before said Harold Bachman was a partner. The underground garage had two floors. I asked the attendant at the entrance if there was any designated parking for the law firm, and he directed me down to the lower floor.

I just didn't go in.

I positioned myself near the elevator, where I could get a decent look at anybody going in, and watched the procession of office workers and businesspeople arrive at work. None of them resembled Bachman.

The first hour felt like three. Worried that he might

be away or still on leave and not even coming in, I called the firm from inside the garage and asked to speak with him. The receptionist who answered put me on hold and then told me he hadn't come in yet. So I was pretty sure he'd be here at some point.

All I could do was pray he'd listen to me and wouldn't alert the police.

At ten of nine, a white Mercedes 350 drove in and rounded my corner. Through the glass I saw the driver's curly gray hair and wire-rim glasses. I checked the photo I had printed at the café.

It was him.

Bachman parked on the lower ramp, took out a leather briefcase from the backseat, locked the car with his remote, and made his way over to the elevator. I stepped out from between a couple of cars, my heart beating nervously.

"Mr. Bachman?"

He squinted back through his glasses, clearly taken by surprise. "Do I know you?"

"No. No you don't," I said. There was no one else around. "Can I talk with you just for a moment?"

I knew he wouldn't recognize me. He had no reason in the world to suspect who I was, nor that I would be here looking for him. He glanced around; I figured I looked harmless enough, or desperate. He nodded and stepped away from the elevator to a spot near a handicapped parking space and shrugged. "All right. Sure."

On the ride down from Boston I'd gone over at least a dozen times what I would say. But my blood was racing and I was nervous and scared, and there was no chance it would come out the way I planned. "Mr. Bachman, I've got something to tell you that will take you by surprise . . . and maybe bring up some things that I know are still painful . . . things you may not want to talk about. But I need you to just hear me out—"

"Who are you?" he asked me, his brow wrinkling.

I didn't know how else to say it. I just handed him a copy of the *New York Times*. There was a photo of me, one taken with Dave at an advertising industry function we had attended a few months back. It didn't exactly look like I did now. I lifted my sunglasses. But the headline said it all: WESTCHESTER WOMAN SOUGHT IN CONNECTION TO HOTEL SHOOTINGS.

Bachman looked back up at me and his eyes grew wide.

His gaze darted around again, trepidation coming onto his face, and if a security guard had come by at that particular moment, I don't know what he would have done.

"Mr. Bachman, there's no reason for you to be alarmed. I know what you've recently been through, and if there was anyone else in the world I could talk to, I would—I swear!—and not put you in this position . . ."

He looked at me and then glanced back down at the article. "You're Wendy Gould?"

259

"Yes." I nodded.

"Ms. Gould, if you have any thoughts of me representing you, I'm afraid you've sought me out for the wrong reason. First, it's not what I do; it's not my specialty. I don't do criminal work. And anyway, I'm not doing this kind of thing right now."

"No, that's not why I'm here," I said. "I don't need you to represent me—"

"You're a federal fugitive, Ms. Gould." He handed me back the paper. "I can't talk to you. You're wanted in connection with the murder of a government agent. Not to mention, if I remember correctly, the murder of your husband . . ."

"None of which is true." If I could have shown him the truth with a single, steadfast look, my eyes as solid and steady as they'd ever been, I gave it to him now. "None. I swear. At least, not the way it's being portrayed."

"Then let me say, as a lawyer, Ms. Gould, someone's doing an awfully good job of making you look bad."

I swallowed, and nodded back with a resigned smile. "That's the only part that *is* true. Mr. Bachman. Look, you can look around, but I'm the one who's risking everything just being here with you now. You can see I've changed my appearance. What would it take for you to call for security or even the police and let them know? In an hour, everyone would know."

"I appreciate the trust, Ms. Gould, and I'm truly sorry for your predicament, but unless you're looking for someone to mediate the terms of handing yourself over to the police—"

"*I can't hand myself over to the police!*" I shook my head defiantly. "I can't. I'm not here because I found your name on some lawyer's website. I'm here because you're the only person I know who can help me prove that I'm being framed. Trust me. Otherwise I'd be as far away from here as I could. Please, just hear me out. Two minutes is all I'm asking. I'm begging you, Mr. Bachman . . . I don't have anywhere else to turn."

"Why me? You said you're aware I've been through a situation of my own . . ."

"And that's exactly why I'm here."

Maybe it was the utter desperation on my face. Or that I had sought him out, the one person who could prove my innocence. But Bachman put down his bag. He nodded reluctantly. "You have two minutes. Make it good, Ms. Gould."

# CHAPTER FORTY

"Do you know the name Curtis Kitchner?" I asked him.

"Kitchner? If I recall, he was the guy who was killed in New York up in that room?"

"That's correct."

He shrugged. "Then only what I've heard on the news."

"Mr. Bachman, I did an incredibly foolish thing. I ended up in someone's hotel room I had no right being in. I'd never done anything like that before in my life. But nothing happened up there . . . and I've had nothing to do with the murders I'm being implicated in. I was actually in the bathroom, preparing to leave, when I heard someone else come into the room."

Bachman said, "I'm listening . . ."

Harried, I explained the whole thing to him. Hruseff. Curtis. How the agent killed him right in front of my eyes, and the second gun fell across the bed to me. "This person was a Homeland Security agent, Mr. Bachman. And I watched him kill Curtis. Not in a shoot-out. Not under any threat, or in self-defense as it's been alleged. But in cold blood. Right in front of my eyes. Right there on the bed."

Bachman shook his head in puzzlement at me. "Why?"

"That I don't know. That's what I'm trying to find out. Curtis was a journalist. He was working on something that implicated the U.S. government in a shooting in Mexico. Look, I found something he wrote on the subject . . ." I reached inside my pocket and took out a copy of the article. "I'm certain he found out something to do with the Mexican drug trade. Something he shouldn't have."

"You said this other person in the room was a Homeland Security agent. He identified himself?"

"No. Afterward, I looked through his pockets and found his ID. And if he was an agent, he damn well wasn't up there for any good. He was only there to kill Curtis, Mr. Bachman."

The lawyer nodded, taking it in. We heard a car door slam, and a man who had parked nearby walked up to the elevator. Bachman smiled briefly, uttering, "Morning," as I looked away. The elevator opened and the man stepped in. Then Bachman turned back to me. "The problem is, Ms. Gould, two other people ended up dead."

263

I told him the rest. How I picked up the gun, knowing that the killer would come for me in the bathroom. How I identified myself and still the guy just raised his weapon. "Yes, I shot him. He was preparing to shoot me."

"And then you just ran?"

I told him how I ran from the room and how the guy's partner tried to silence me too. Then I told him how Dave died as well. I went through the whole thing. "Not in the kitchen. Not by *my* hand. They shot him! I left that gun on the bed back in that hotel room, Mr. Bachman. I swear!"

He kept looking at me with this lawyerly, evaluating stare. I had no idea if he actually believed me. But I kept going.

"I tried to turn myself in. You heard what happened at Grand Central the other day. I wasn't trying to run away. They're trying to silence me, Mr. Bachman. For what I saw. A close friend was trying to work out my arrest, and he ended up being shot too. That's why I can't turn myself in. Not until I find out why they're trying to kill me."

"So how do I fit in?" he asked. "Assuming I even believe all this. You said I was the only person who could help you."

I reached inside my jeans and pulled out Curtis's BlackBerry.

"I took this from Curtis's hotel room when I ran. It belonged to him." I pushed the power button and then

264

scrolled through Curtis's pictures. "This is the last one he took. Just a couple of days before he died."

I held it out and watched Bachman's eyes go wide. He stared at the photo of Lauritzia Velez.

# CHAPTER FORTY-ONE

The picture hit home. Harold Bachman's face went ashen.

"Curtis visited her," I said. "Just before he died. She knew something he needed to find out. I'm sure it was connected to Cano. To the killing of those two DEA agents down in Mexico, which he thought was connected to the airport bombing that took your wife. Maybe he was trying to get to her father. Maybe *he* suspected something else about why those agents were killed."

Bachman shook his head. "This just isn't something I can get involved in, Ms. Gould."

"Mr. Bachman, this is the second time I've had to say this in the past two days, but we've both lost people we loved." I put my hand on his arm. "Whether you believe me or not, I loved my husband every bit as much as you did your wife. The difference is, I can't even grieve for him. I've got half of the United States government out looking for me. And I'm being framed for a horrible murder I didn't do.

"And the thing is, their deaths are connected, Mr. Bachman. Your wife's and my husband's—whether you can see that or not. I need to find out why Curtis Kitchner was killed. It's the only way I can clear myself and get my life back. Mourn who I've lost. And whatever that reason is"—I looked in his eyes—"I'm absolutely certain it leads through Lauritzia Velez. I'm here because I need to find her, Mr. Bachman."

"I'm afraid that's impossible, Ms. Gould."

"Why? Why is it impossible? You and your wife were her protectors. You represented her. You have to know where she is! I have to find out what she knows. Why Curtis needed to find her. What there was about the killing of those drug enforcement agents in Mexico that every one's trying to keep quiet."

"You don't understand . . ." His voice lowered, but it was still firm. "This girl's been the target of some very dangerous people, and I'm not about to put her in any more danger. Any more than I would put my own kids in danger. Besides, I'm quite sure she doesn't know anything that can help you. She wasn't a part of any of this."

"Maybe what Curtis needed to know was how to find her father? He was a part of it."

267

"I assure you she doesn't know where her father is." Bachman reached down and picked up his briefcase. "Look, I understand your predicament, Ms. Gould, and I'm sorry. I truly am. If you want, I'll recommend someone who can represent what you've told me to the proper authorities. This is the United States, for God's sake; they can't just put you in a cell and make you disappear."

"They damn well can, Mr. Bachman. They've already tried."

"But I hope you understand it's best if we don't have any further direct contact. I can't allow my name to be connected with this Cano person in any other way. I have my kids. My only goal is to protect them now. We've already seen what this man will do . . ."

He was slipping away from me, and without Lauritzia Velez I had nothing. Only possibilities. Suppositions. No proof on anyone. He made a move to leave, but I grabbed his arm. "You looked into those DEA murders yourself, Mr. Bachman. For Lauritzia's trial. Did you ever come across someone named Gillian?"

"Gillian?" He shook his head. "I'm sorry, no . . ." He moved toward the elevator.

"The agent who killed Curtis said that name. 'This is for Gillian,' he said, before he pulled the trigger and killed him. Maybe Ms. Velez would know who he meant." My voice took on a tone of desperation. "Just let me speak with her once. That's all I ask. Please . . ."

"I'm sorry," he said, "I have to go." He pushed past me and pressed the elevator button several times. "I wish I could help you, Ms. Gould. You see the position I'm in."

"Here . . ." I tried to force the article Curtis had written into his hand, but it fell to the floor. "Curtis wrote about all this. It's what got him killed."

"And that's precisely why I can no longer afford to get involved. Don't you understand?"

The elevator opened. Bachman stepped in.

I stood there looking back at him, my last chance to prove myself dissolving away. "Look up the agent I shot. Hruseff. You'll see, he wasn't always Homeland Security. He was in the DEA. He was reassigned. You'll see."

"I'm really sorry, Ms. Gould—"

"Look them all up," I said as the doors began to close. "They're all connected."

Harold Bachman's face disappeared, and I kneeled down to pick up Curtis's article, sure my last chance to prove I was innocent was now gone.

# CHAPTER FORTY-TWO

Harold sat in his corner office on the sixth floor, a view of the Long Island Sound in its large picture window. He'd gotten his coffee, checked his schedule for the day. He started to prepare for his ten thirty meeting on the *Lefco vs. Connecticut* case, but his mind kept drifting back to Wendy Gould.

He thought he'd mishandled the situation. What he should have done, he decided, was gotten on his phone as soon as that elevator door closed and called 911. He was a lawyer. He was sworn to uphold the law. Whatever her guilt or innocence, she was a fugitive, wanted for her involvement in two capital crimes. He'd lost his wife a few months ago in such a crime. If true, Wendy's story was a rough one, and he was sorry for that. He actually did believe her. But that was for the authorities

270

to figure out, not him. He had his kids. He couldn't get involved.

Putting down his brief, Harold had to admit he was nervous now. He wanted nothing to do with Eduardo Cano again. Since he first heard his name, it had caused him nothing but heartbreak and ruin. He still had Jamie and Taylor. Keeping them safe was the only thing that mattered now. Yet no matter how he tried to block him out of his mind, this Cano kept knifing his way back in. Back into his life. Someone he had never met but who had caused him the most pain he had ever known.

He glanced at his watch. He could still call 911. He could merely say that he had hesitated for an hour, that the whole thing had simply taken him by surprise. Surely the FBI would want to know her whereabouts. That she was around there.

*So why haven't I dialed?*

He leaned back in his chair and swiveled to face the window. On the credenza in front of him were several photos of Roxanne, whom he missed more than anything in the world. Whom he still couldn't contemplate having to spend the rest of his life without—who would not just call up, at any second, and ask him what he was doing for lunch or if he'd ever heard of this Off-Broadway play or this dance company that was performing in the city. Death was always something abstract and far away until it hit home; and then it became a black, bottomless pit you could never crawl your way out of. He picked up the photo of his wedding day, and then next to it one of them sailing off Nantucket, where Roxanne's eyes shone as blue and brightly as the sea. And he remembered his thoughts as he looked at her that day from the tiller, thinking that he was the luckiest man in the world to have someone of such vitality and beauty. And courage. Roxie never backed down from anything she truly believed in. Look at what that had done to her now. He missed her more and more every day.

But today those eyes seemed disappointed in him. They seemed to contain a form of accusation. For him having backed down when someone needed him so much.

To have given in to the fear when inwardly he really wanted to stand up. Stand up and say, *Yes, I believe you. I will help you.* In his heart he knew what Wendy said was true. He felt she was innocent. He could hear it in her story; he saw it in her eyes.

*Look what it has gotten you, Roxie . . .* He put down his wife's photo and looked away. All the "standing up" in the world. He put his hands over his eyes and felt like weeping.

*Look what it has gotten you.*

Was it such a crime, wanting to keep Jamie and Taylor safe? To keep this evil away from their already damaged lives? He wanted that more than anything. Except for maybe one thing . . . one thing that did burn deeply inside him. A flame he could not put out. And that was to see the person responsible for Roxie's death brought to justice.

Made to pay.

To know he wasn't out there, living in some lavish home. Basking in the rewards of his evil, gloating, never knowing the pain he'd caused and the beautiful life he'd extinguished.

*Both their deaths are tied together,* Wendy Gould had said. *Whether you accept it or not.* And as much as he wanted to deny that, the throbbing in his soul told him she was right. They are connected.

He looked at the phone. *Why haven't you made that call?*

*Look them all up,* she had said, the desperation clear in her eyes as the elevator door closed. *They're all connected.*

*Connected to whom?*

Harold logged on to his computer. He went into Google and typed in the name she'd told him to look up, Hruseff. The agent she had shot.

He paged through several articles, finally finding one that gave his personal bio. Growing up in Roanoke, Virginia. His two tours in Iraq. His short tenure at Homeland Security. Before that at ICE. There was a shooting incident the agent was involved in on the border, in which he was cleared of any guilt. "After earning his release from the army, Hruseff spent four years as an agent for the DEA . . ."

Was that what Wendy Gould was referring to? Harold took note of the years: 2006–10. He read on:

". . . rising to the rank of Senior Field Agent, based out of the agency's regional headquarters in El Paso, Texas."

That's what stopped him. The dates. El Paso.

Harold minimized his search on Hruseff and typed a new subject into the search box.

Sabrina Stein.

He dug up a government press release announcing her appointment to the DOJ, which also contained her past history. It credited her success in running the El Paso DEA office, and the Intelligence Center there, in what they called "Ground Zero in the government's war against narco-terrorism . . ."

Her tenure coincided with Hruseff's. *Hruseff worked for her.*

The killings of the DEA agents in Culiacán took place in 2009, when both of them were there.

Harold felt the blood seep out of his face. He knew anyone who stepped into his room at this very moment would be facing a ghost.

*Look them all up. They're all connected.* Was this what she meant?

He took another look back at his wife, then picked up his phone.

But instead of calling 911, he paged his secretary. "Janice, I need a favor. See if Sabrina Stein can see me tomorrow in DC."

# CHAPTER FORTY-THREE

Joe Esterhaus pointed to the tree-shaded Tudor at the end of the cul-de-sac. "That's the one." Only three days out of the hospital, he still had his arm in a sling. "Pull up over there."

His daughter, Robin, drove the car over to the curb and turned it off. There was a double line of yellow police tape still blocking both entrances of the semicircular driveway. She stared at the pretty house, thinking that only a week before this was the scene of a creepy murder. "That tape's up there for a reason, Dad. You sure you should be doing this?"

"I'm just gonna walk around a little and see what gives. You just stay in the car."

He pulled himself out, grimacing at the pain that still stabbed at his shoulder. Besides the yellow tape, a crime lock barred the front door. "This shouldn't take too long."

"I'd say, 'Don't do anything I wouldn't do,'" Robin called after him, "but I know there's not much chance of that."

"Not much chance at all." Esterhaus laughed, ducking under the tape line leading to the bricked, half-circle driveway. He winced. He still had to wear the sling, at least for another week. Then came weeks and weeks of physio. All trying to get mobility back for a guy who for the past two years could no longer put peas into his mouth with a fork. What the hell was it all for anyway?

He went down to the house and tried the front door. He knew it was a waste of time. He stared in through a frosted-glass window. The crime boys had already done their work. Been through the kitchen on their hands and knees. He had no clue what he would possibly find. Still, it was worth a look. Wendy needed anything that could drive a hole in their story.

He waved to his daughter, who was watching him while on her cell phone. Then he headed around the back. Wendy's lot was a wooded, three-quarter acre bordering a golf club. Through the gaps in the tall oaks and pines, he could see a fairway. There was a pool in the back that was covered up, and a hot tub a few steps away. Nice. He tried the French doors off the patio outside the living room. They wouldn't budge. Maybe he wouldn't be able to get in after all.

Continuing around, he followed the property's slope down to the side of the house. Under what appeared to be the kitchen was a rear basement door. Eight glass panels, not too thick. Esterhaus had no idea if the place was alarmed.

Only one way to find out.

He bent his good arm and gave a short, hard thrust into the window, smashing through one of the panels. The glass cracked and fell back into the basement.

Nothing sounded.

*So far so good.* Reassured, he cleared the glass edges still remaining in the door, then reached his hand through and unlocked it from the inside. The door opened, leading to a darkened basement. He stepped in and closed the door behind him. There was a large TV on the wall, a bunch of sofas and chairs. A primo Brunswick pool table. He had always wanted one of those. He found the stairs, which led upstairs to a mudroom off the kitchen.

*Bingo.*

*Don't do anything I wouldn't do, right, doll?* Esterhaus looked around. The kitchen had been redone. A polished marble island, a fancy farmhouse sink, antiqued wooden cabinets. There were beams above the island with a hanging iron rack with lots of copper pots.

A ton of evidence tape all around.

One taped area marked the outline where Dave's body had been found. There were numbered flags that indicated shell casings, bloodstains, some marking the wooden stool above the body. He examined it closely, admiring the work the way a craftsman might admire a well-built table. Whoever had manufactured the scene had done a nice job. They'd even created their own spatter.

Anyone would have bought into it. Why the hell not?

A cooking pot was still on the floor, and a glass was still turned on its side. Wendy's friend had already confirmed that Wendy and Dave had had a spat the night before. The gun that came from the hotel room where the government agent was shot. Everything seemed to back up what they were saying: that Dave was killed here. That maybe Wendy had told him what had happened in New York and he wasn't so sympathetic. Then she panicked, shot him, and was about to flee when the lights went on behind her . . .

Esterhaus knew this would be hard to overturn on the basis of the evidence, but he continued to look around. It was so elaborately laid out. He went back down the stairs and left by the same door he'd come in through. He wiped down the doorknob with his sleeve.

Then he squeezed through a wooden fence on the side of the house and came back around the front.

The thought started to worm even in him: What if Wendy hadn't been telling him the whole truth? What if she was up in that hotel room and panicked? And what if she did tell Dave, and he reacted. The way any husband might react. What if he threatened to tell the police and she shot him?

But he reminded himself that that hole in his shoulder was the best evidence he had that she was telling the truth.

He went back up the drive, then stopped before he got to the car, rerunning in his mind how Wendy had said it all took place. They'd been backing out of the garage. Lights flashed on from behind them. Esterhaus saw the outline of tire rubber still visible on the blacktop, where Wendy had said she floored it past the first agent. There were shots. Which didn't prove anything in itself—she was trying to escape! She drove onto the front island. He went over and saw tire marks still in the soil. Dave's door had opened. Wendy sped past the agent, and Dave was shot as they drove by.

"Dad, c'mon!" he heard Robin call from the car. "I gotta pick up Eddie."

"In a minute . . ." He walked to the top of the drive and saw where Wendy's car had bounced off the island and back onto the street. She said she stopped, looking on in horror as Dave fell out of the car. *I stared at my husband lying in the street.* Then a shot slammed into her car and she hit the gas.

Esterhaus went out onto the street. Bending, he looked over the area where he was sure the car had stopped. That's when he noticed something.

Specks.

Specks of a dark, congealed substance that had hardened into the pavement.

He kneeled. The whole thing had happened at night. Even someone looking for it afterward, in order to cover it up, would likely never have spotted it in the dark.

He reached inside his pants pocket and pulled out his key chain, which had a Swiss Army knife on it. Opening the knife, he scraped at the specks, which were hard, dried, more black than crimson.

"Son of a bitch," he muttered to himself.

How the hell had it gotten all the way out here, on the street, and not in the kitchen, unless it happened just as Wendy said?

From the car Robin came over, leaning over him. "Find something, Dad?"

"Could be . . ." Esterhaus got back up to his feet. "Run and get me the camera," he told his daughter. "It's in the backseat."

He *had* found something.

He was sure he was staring at David Gould's blood.

# CHAPTER FORTY-FOUR

Harold wasn't sure why he was doing it. He didn't know what he hoped to find out, or what he would do, if something turned up. He was a real estate lawyer, not an investigator. He specialized in REITs, not crime solving.

But waiting outside Sabrina Stein's office at the DOJ, watching the flow of staffers going in and out, he did know that he'd never ever be able to look at his wife's photo again without averting his eyes, never be able to hug his kids without the suspicion that their mother's death could possibly have been solved and he hadn't followed it up.

Much of what Wendy Gould was saying did have the ring of truth to it. And was backed up by the facts. And if there was one thing that did burn in his heart, drove him, almost as much as the vow he made to protect Jamie and Taylor and that he couldn't put away, it was that he wanted to see the people who had committed this horrible act brought to justice.

Wherever it led.

"Mr. Bachman." The twenty-something staffer stepped out from behind her desk. "The secretary can see you now."

She opened the office door as a young shirtsleeved staffer stepped out, carrying a large stack of files and giving Harold a polite but harried nod. Harold could recognize the crazed look of someone a year or two out of law school anywhere.

Sabrina Stein's office was spacious, official-looking. An American flag, photographs on the wall of the president and the attorney general. She stood up from behind her large desk, piled high with multicolored folders. "Mr. Bachman."

Sabrina Stein was in her forties, attractive, with short, dark hair and vibrant brown eyes—eyes that were both intelligent and welcoming, yet at the same time bright with ambition. She hadn't hesitated when Harold contacted her to testify on Lauritzia's behalf. She had put her own life on the line both as an agent and then as head of EPIC, the DEA's El Paso Intelligence Center fighting narco-terrorism. She'd been shot; she'd been bludgeoned with a bat in a sting in Juárez that went horribly wrong. She still walked with a slight limp. She'd spent a good part of her career inhabiting the murky area between police work and covert action. For twenty years she'd been trying to put killers like Eduardo Cano out of business or take them down.

"It's good to see you again," she said, coming around with a mug of coffee. She was dressed in a stylish short jacket and pants, a blue crepe blouse, a pretty pin on her lapel. She was from Arkansas and spoke with a slight drawl. "It goes without saying, how shocked and saddened I was to hear about your wife."

"Thank you." Harold smiled appreciatively. "I received your note."

"I know she was an extremely determined woman. With a huge heart. I can promise you that everyone in this building is doing whatever they can to see the person behind what happened brought to justice. Please, take a seat over here."

She motioned to the couch in front of the large window that had an impressive view of the Capitol dome. "I'm sorry we didn't have better luck with that court ruling down in Dallas. I've been through this situation a number of times. Once it gets in the hands of the courts, you can never tell what's in the heads of those judges. The ability to protect confidential informants and their families is one of the lynchpins of the federal justice system. Take that away, we're no better than special-ops guys without weapons. Anyway, I'm afraid I only have a handful of minutes to spend with you. I'm expected over at State . . ."

"I appreciate you carving out some time on such short notice." Harold opened his briefcase.

"Alicia said this is about Ms. Velez? I expect you're deciding whether to continue the case to a higher level? How is she doing?"

"Recovering. She's obviously been through a lot. And not just the physical trauma, of course. She was also very fond of my wife."

"Of course. Poor girl. I'm assuming you have her in a very safe place."

Though Stein certainly seemed like a person who could be trusted with the highest levels of confidence, Harold found himself hesitating. "We have her tucked away" was all he said.

"Well, you've certainly gone above and beyond for her. She's truly fortunate to have someone like you in her corner." She took a sip of coffee and faced him, indicating that the small talk was over.

"I was hoping you could answer a few questions for me," Harold said, taking out a yellow legal pad from his briefcase. "Should we go forward, as you say, I think there are some things I'll need to know, specifically about Mr. Cano and his dealings. I think I underplayed his direct connection to the deaths of Ms. Velez's siblings. So to start, can I ask your view on why the case against Cano was dropped by the DOJ?"

"I assume you're speaking of his involvement in the murders of Agents Dean and Rita Bienvienes?" Sabrina Stein replied.

Harold nodded.

She inhaled before speaking. "I don't truthfully know. The party line, as I'm sure you're aware, is that problems sprang up with Oscar Velez's testimony."

"Problems?"

"Matters of memory." Stein shrugged officiously. "It seems to happen in certain cases, when CIs come face-to-face in court with the persons they're testifying against. They get second thoughts."

"Or when their children are ruthlessly butchered," Harold felt compelled to add.

"That too, of course." Sabrina took a sip of coffee and offered a philosophical smile.

"But if that were the case," Harold said, flipping a page of his notes, "the question I would ask is why Mr. Velez wouldn't have just simply been deported? If his use to the government was negated, that would seem to have been the perfect leverage against him. Threaten to send him back to what would clearly have been certain death. To the very person who had vowed revenge against him."

"A fair question." Sabrina Stein exhaled. "And one I'm afraid I don't have a very good answer for."

"Rumors were going around . . . I'm merely echoing what's already been written," Harold said, "that Dean

285

and Rita Bienvienes were less than one hundred percent Ivory Snow clean. And that the Department of Justice grew to feel that a public trial would potentially air a series of allegations that might embarrass them."

Stein put down her coffee. "Dean and Rita Beinvienes were among the best agents I had, Mr. Bachman. What you're alluding to is what we in the trade refer to as 'back draft.' One government agency sees a firestorm rising around them, so they spread the flames somewhere else. In this case, back at the DEA. The Bienvieneses were turned upside down by our own internal investigative teams. Not a thing was ever found that would give any credence to those rumors. Zero."

"It's also possible that Eduardo Cano had some ability to influence the government's decision, isn't that right?"

*"Influence?"* The Justice Department official's eyes seemed to harden at the word.

"Affect the outcome," Harold said bluntly.

"If I follow . . . you're suggesting he was able to buy someone off?"

"Or possibly have information that might discredit people higher up, that the government might have wanted to keep secret. Cano was trained here, and he is alleged to still have high-level friends in the government. The cartels have millions and millions to spread around, correct? This is still a world fraught with corruption, is it not?"

Stein nodded stiffly, the pleasant veneer of a moment

before replaced by something guarded and professional. "Mexico is an excellent place to commit murder, Mr. Bachman, because you will almost certainly get away with it. That said, I'd still like to think that no amount of money would derail the prosecution for the assassination of two people who so selflessly put their lives at risk for the country. Not to mention the three other completely innocent individuals who tragically were caught in the crossfire."

She uncrossed her legs. "No litigator likes to take on a case they can't win, Mr. Bachman. I'm sure you're familiar with that. Especially one that can make or break one's career. For several reasons, Oscar Velez's testimony was a matter of concern from the moment he chose to defect. I think the answer to your question lies much more with the witness, Mr. Bachman, than with the United States government." She glanced at her watch, reflecting surprise at the time. "Now, if you have no more questions, I'm sorry but I have to cut this short."

"I understand." Harold closed his pad and began to pack his briefcase. Then he stopped. "Just one more. There's an addendum to this case that I found a little curious."

"Which case are we speaking of, Mr. Bachman? Cano's or Lauritzia Velez's?"

"I'm sorry, but to me, Ms. Stein, they are becoming pretty much the same."

"Well, as a representative of the United States government, I'm sorry that you feel that way."

"The Homeland Security agent," Harold said, "who was shot and killed in that hotel room in New York City a week ago . . . I think his name was Hruseff?"

Stein nodded. "That's correct."

"I was surprised to discover that he once worked for the DEA. Out of the El Paso office, as it turns out; coincidentally at the same time as the Bienvieneses' killings . . . I guess that also means he worked under you . . ."

"And your guess would be correct, Mr. Bachman." Stein stood up. "Ray was a good man. Very sad, what happened. And if I recall, there was a third person in that room. I'm pretty certain that when she's found—and she will be, soon, I promise you—and all the facts come out, it will show that Ray was simply doing his job."

"I'm sure you're right," Harold said, and stood up too.

"Only I don't see what that particular incident has to do with Eduardo Cano." Sabrina Stein cocked her head. "Ray was working for a completely different government agency at the time he was killed. On matters totally unconnected with his past role—"

"The other person in the room . . . who Hruseff allegedly shot," Harold said. "I think his name was *Kitchner* . . ."

"Curtis Kitchner." Sabrina Stein nodded.

"He was a journalist. As it happens, he was looking into Eduardo Cano at the time of his death."

"Into Cano?" She began to walk him to the door. "How would you possibly know that, Mr. Bachman? I never saw that come out anywhere."

"Because he visited Lauritzia Velez. In the hospital, just a few days before his death." Harold picked up his briefcase. "I was merely pointing out how this Cano seems to have his imprint everywhere. And how the two cases might be related."

There was a moment of silence between them. Drawn out long enough to take on a shape, hard and stony, and even a pro like Sabrina Stein couldn't hide how she was working to put it all together.

That was the moment Harold first thought she might be lying.

"Eduardo Cano continues to be a dangerous man, Mr. Bachman. A fact that I think you found out for yourself, firsthand. But to your point on Agent Hruseff, we all seem to cross paths in this business if we stay in long enough. Scratch any of us, and I suspect that's what you'll find. And now I'm afraid I have to move on . . ." She stopped at the door. "Once again, I feel like I haven't been altogether helpful."

"No, you have. I want to thank you for your time. But if you don't mind, just one more quick thing. Any chance you ever come across someone named Gillian who was connected with this case?"

"Gillian?" Stein blinked at the name.

"Maybe someone connected to Hruseff? Or possibly another agent?"

"Gillian. No, I'm sorry. Where did *that* name happen to come up?"

"No matter." Harold shrugged. "Just something this Curtis Kitchner seemed to have on his mind."

"I see. Once again, I feel I haven't been very helpful to you. Anyway, it's been a pleasure meeting with you again, Mr. Bachman. Please keep me informed of what you find."

She opened the door and they shook hands.

"I like your pin," Harold said, noticing her lapel. "Looks Aztec."

"Yes, it is," Sabrina Stein said. "I actually got it while down there."

Almost involuntarily she seemed to adjust it on her lapel—a turquoise and silver grasshopper.

# CHAPTER FORTY-FIVE

The Amtrak express train rocked gently back and forth, speeding to New York City.

Harold sat in the quiet car and took a sip of his vodka.

*Mexico is an excellent place to commit murder.* He thought of what Sabrina Stein had said. *Because you will surely get away with it.*

He had no proof, nothing he could share with anyone. Nothing that would make someone think he was doing more than just grasping at straws.

Just that Hruseff was part of Stein's DEA team back in El Paso. And that it was *he* who killed Curtis at the hotel. Curtis, who was looking into the deaths of Dean and Rita Bienvienes, who were in El Paso at the very same time, and who was sure he had found something. Something that led him to Lauritzia Velez.

Which may well have been that the Bienvienes were murdered in Culiacán by Eduardo Cano—and with the complicity of the U.S. government.

*Why?*

*Look them up,* Wendy Gould had begged him. Harold recalled her pretty but desperate face disappearing behind the closing elevator door.

*They're all connected. All of them.*

That phrase kept on coming back.

*All* of them.

As soon as the train pulled out of Union Station in DC, Harold had googled the other agent who was with Hruseff at the hotel.

Alton Dokes. The agent Wendy claimed was framing her for her husband's death.

He couldn't find much of a history on him, only a ton of recent articles that quoted him as lead investigator on the manhunt for Wendy Gould. But he did find one linking him to an article from the *San Antonio Express-News*, from back in 2008, a year before the Bienvienes were killed.

As a DEA agent, Dokes had been implicated in the shooting of a seventeen-year-old Mexican crossing the border from Juárez. The boy ended up being a drug mule, and the shooting was ultimately ruled justifiable. Dokes was fully cleared.

"Sabrina Stein, Senior Agent in Charge of Operations out of the DEA's El Paso office, commented, 'We are glad this episode is behind us and a dedicated agent is able to resume his duties . . . ' "

Harold took a sip of his vodka. So Dokes was there too.

*All of them.*

He was sure Sabrina was hiding something. But what could he possibly prove? This wasn't enough to cast even the slightest suspicion off of Wendy. Even if he handed what he had over to the authorities, he knew it wouldn't go further than the person he told. That two government agents had been in the same place years ago at the same time two fellow agents were murdered in Mexico? That, years later, they'd both had some connection to a journalist who had been killed? A journalist who was looking into that very story.

*Scratch any of us,* Sabrina Stein had told him, *you never know what you will find . . .*

The train's rattling brought him back from his thoughts.

*You're crazy to get involved,* Harold told himself. *Look what it's already cost you. You made a vow. To protect your kids. You're all they have now.* This was over. He'd already seen what could happen. His wife's desire to protect Lauritzia had cost them everything. They had nothing now, except themselves . . .

Harold finished his drink and gave the woman sitting across from him a pleasant smile. As he went to shut the lid on his laptop, he fixed on his screen saver, a photo of Roxanne. Her arms around Jamie and Taylor in their backyard, their sunny faces promising everything beautiful in life.

He could shut the computer a thousand times, but it wouldn't shut it out.

Not completely.

There was one person who would know all this, Harold realized. Who might hold all the secrets.

Curtis had gone to see Lauritzia in the days before he died. It was time to know what he had told her.

# CHAPTER FORTY-SIX

I was down to my last few dollars. Hiding out in parking lots and business parks after dark, catching bites to eat at drive-thru windows. I realized that the first time I hit up an ATM, my location would be given away. Not to mention a photograph taken of how I looked.

But I was getting to the point where I really didn't care.

I'd been in the same clothes for five days now. I also knew Jim and Cindy were probably up in Vermont by now, and there might well be a national APB out on the Explorer at this very moment. Every time I saw a flashing light, or a police car randomly drove by, my blood froze and I came to a standstill, sure that it was the one car that had closed in on me.

So far one hadn't. But I knew I was on borrowed time.

Driving out of Stamford, I passed a tiny lodging on Route 172 in Pound Ridge, just across the New York border, called the Three Pony Inn. It looked quiet and empty. Just what I needed. I just said the hell with it and pulled in. I desperately needed a shower and to wash my clothes. And to sleep in a bed. The place was a family-run B and B, and the proprietors' teenage son was manning the front desk when I came in, doing his math homework. I paid for a night at $109 with a Bon Voyage gift card I found in my wallet—one of Dave's advertising accounts, which I knew to be completely untraceable. But my funds were running out.

The first thing I did in the small but cozy room was run the shower. It was amazing how just letting the warm spray stream down my body revived me with the feeling that I could get through this and that everything would somehow be okay.

I washed out my T-shirt and underwear and spread them on the towel bar to dry. I laughed to myself that if the police barged in right then, they'd have to arrest me in my towel—I didn't have anything dry to wear. I looked at my face in the mirror. I hardly recognized what I saw. I put on the TV and curled up to the news, ecstatic to be in a bed for the first time in days and stretch my legs on the cool linens. There had been another massacre in a village in Syria. A New York City assemblyman was being sentenced on corruption charges. There was nothing on me. I was exhausted. I closed my eyes and fell asleep to the news.

I woke around three in the afternoon and called to the front desk to ask if there was a computer I could use. I was told there was an Internet setup for guests in the sunroom off the main lobby. When my clothes dried I cautiously made my way down. A woman was at the desk now, and she asked genially if I wanted a cup of coffee and I gratefully said that I would. I sat at the desk in the sunroom, decorated with a patterned couch, English roll-leg chairs, and equestrian prints.

There was an old HP computer there, and the first thing I did after logging on with the hotel code was to check Google News to see if there was anything new on me. There wasn't, but I did spot a headline on Curtis: HOTEL SHOOT-OUT VICTIM HAD TIES TO KNOWN DRUG TRAFFICKERS.

I clicked on the link.

FBI sources say that Curtis Kitchner, the journalist who was shot dead in his New York hotel room after a confrontation with a federal law enforcement agent, had maintained contacts and carried on conversations with drug traffickers familiar to law enforcement agencies, some high on the DEA's most wanted list, leading investigators to speculate that was the reason he was under surveillance by federal authorities.

Investigators now seem certain it was not Mr. Kitchner who fired the shots that killed Agent Raymond

Hruseff of the Department of Homeland Security, and are still searching for Wendy Stansi Gould of Pelham, New York, who was believed to be in the hotel room at the time. Ms. Stansi is also being sought in connection to the shooting death of her husband at their home in Pelham later that night, but her whereabouts remain unknown.

*So here it is*, I said to myself, the stream of misinformation that would make it seem as if Curtis was the bad guy and had instigated things and that Hruseff was merely doing his job. The article was from Reuters, without a byline. Otherwise I might have contacted the author to tell my side of the story.

I was growing more and more certain this all had something to do with the two rogue government agents covering up the murder of two DEA agents four years ago.

Hruseff and Dokes had both been at DEA in El Paso at the time of the Bienvienes killings. Four years later, in completely different jobs, they were both at the hotel with Curtis. It seemed certain they wanted something covered up. Something from their past, that Curtis had found out and had linked to Lauritzia Velez. Why else would he go to find her? Perhaps to find her father, who was connected to the Culiacán killings too.

Which was also connected to a person whose name

had yet to come up in anything I had read or anyone I had talked to: Gillian.

I knew that until I uncovered who that was, all I had was just supposition. They'd sink their teeth into me the second they had me in cuffs. I had nothing, nothing except suspicion in the face of overwhelming evidence that I'd shot Hruseff in panic and killed Dave to cover up what I'd done . . .

Hell, I couldn't even convince Harold.

Before closing the computer, I went back one more time to that article Curtis had written about the Culiacán ambush. Maybe if I just read it one last time, I might see what it was Curtis knew. I had to be missing something.

I looked at that shooting from every aspect I could find online. The newspaper coverage. The *Dallas Morning News* did a series of articles on it, first casting suspicion on the Bienvienes. Then the DEA's own internal investigation that cleared them fully, which was published eight months later. I looked at whatever I could find on Eduardo Cano and why his trial never took place.

It all still led nowhere.

I even found an article in the *Greenwich Time* about Sam Orthwein, one of the college students killed in the ambush, and another in the *Denver Post*: LOCAL UNIVERSITY MOURNS THREE OF ITS OWN.

In frustration, having read through everything else I could find on the subject, I clicked on it.

The article began, "They were three about to embark on the road where life would take them in just a couple of months, but where it led in the hills of central Mexico was to a tragic end for three promising University of Denver students, as well as grief and heartbreak for their families and friends who loved them."

I looked at pictures of Sam, Ned Taylor, and Ned's girlfriend, Ana Lasser.

I'd already read about Sam; he was described in Curtis's article. Ned Taylor came from Reston, Virginia. He was a soccer player and a sociology major. Ana Lasser was pretty, with shoulder-length blonde hair, high cheekbones dotted with a few freckles. The article said she was a photography major at Denver. It said some of her photographs were currently part of an exhibition at the Arts Center. There was even a link to them. A follow-up note said the collection had been expanded to include some of her final shots, taken moments before her death.

I clicked on them, not even sure why.

I scrolled through Ana Lasser's photographs of old-woman fruit vendors in their stalls by the road—sharp-cheeked, sun-hardened faces. I saw Culiacán, with its white stucco houses and church towers. I looked in the deep-set eyes of a young boy in a narrow doorway staring back at the camera. I realized this would have been just moments before the shooting. Was he one of them? One of those child killers enlisted by the cartels who a second later would have pulled out an automatic weapon like a toy and sprayed death on them? Or was he just staring back at Ana, the killers scrambling in doorways and on rooftops, knowing what, seconds later, was about to take place? His look held a kind of fascination for me.

"Ana Lasser," I read in the bio accompanying her photographs, "who was tragically shot and killed along with two other DU students in Culiacán, Mexico, moments after taking these shots, was a senior at DU majoring in photography. She came from . . ."

Suddenly it was like the off switch in my body turned on.

I stared at the words that followed, my brain sorting through what it meant. My eyes doubling in size.

"She came from Gillian, Colorado . . ."

I read it again, the truth slamming me in the face that I'd been looking at it all wrong.

*This is for Gillian, asshole. . . .*

All wrong.

Suddenly the whole thing seemed to just fall into place. What Curtis had to have known that led him to Lauritzia. What *she* had to have known.

And more important, what Hruseff would have killed for in order to keep secret.

*You have no idea what you've stepped into,* he'd said as he raised his gun at me.

Now I did. Now I did know.

That that ambush was somehow not related to the Bienvienes at all. But to this girl . . .

301

Ana. Lasser.

*"A photography major . . . from Gillian, Colorado . . ."*

I read it again and again, unable to lift my eyes. This murdered girl, this seemingly random victim, who, I now knew, hadn't stumbled into tragedy after all. But was at the very heart of it.

Who, I now realized, was *Gillian*.

# CHAPTER FORTY-SEVEN

I pulled out the throwaway phone from my bag and rushed outside. My hands shook, not from the late-October chill but from the sudden realization that Ana Lasser was Gillian. That the Bienvieneses hadn't been the intended targets of that ambush at all.

*She was.*

I hid myself against the far side of the Explorer and pressed the number I had already loaded in. I was just praying he hadn't already called the police on me.

It started ringing. The receptionist answered. "Harold Bachman," I said, as soon as I heard her voice.

"Who should I say is calling?"

Who should I say? My name was on every newscast in the country. "Wendy" was all I came up with. "Just tell him it's incredibly urgent. *Please.*"

My head spun in circles while I waited for him to come on the line. I tried to figure out just what this meant. The world had shifted. Curtis had to have found this out as well. That was why he had to find Lauritzia. To see if she knew too. Or maybe to get to her father.

In any case, he was trying to find out who the real target was that day.

*This is for Gillian, asshole.*

"Hello." Harold Bachman's voice came on. He didn't sound so excited to hear from me.

*"Please, don't hang up!"* I begged, desperation resonating in my tone. "I've found out something I need to show you. I know you said not to contact you again. I understand. I just don't have anyone else to turn to, Mr. Bachman. Please, just hear me out . . ."

I was sure he was about to cut me off. I was already on the verge of tears.

Instead, he said something that lifted the weight off my shoulders and almost knocked me off my feet.

"I have something too."

I stood there, dumbfounded, grasping the phone with two hands. "You said you never wanted to hear from me again . . ."

"I looked them up. Like you said—Hruseff. Dokes. You knew about him as well, didn't you?"

Even in my elation, my eyes were filling with tears. "Yes."

"I've been down in DC. I went to see Sabrina Stein. Do you know who she is?"

304

"She was head of the El Paso DEA office. Hruseff and Dokes both worked for her," I said.

"That's right. I know they're covering something up, Wendy."

"I know that too. And I think I know what that is."

"Look, this isn't a good place to talk," Bachman said. "Are you local?"

"I could probably be there in about half an hour."

"Not here. You can't come anywhere around here. Somewhere public. Crowded." He paused a second. "Do you know the Stamford Town Center mall?"

"I know it." I'd been there from time to time.

"There's a Starbucks and a bunch of fast-food places on the main floor. I sometimes take the kids. There are lots of tables and usually a crowd."

"I can get there."

"Grab yourself a coffee and take a seat outside."

The patter of my heart wouldn't stop. "This isn't a trap, is it? Promise me you're not going to lure me there into a bunch of cops . . ."

"Not unless they're there for me, Wendy. I give you my word."

Then my heart began to soar, with the spontaneous, grateful exhilaration of someone who felt the weight of grief and wrongful accusation tumbling off her shoulders.

"It's just after five," Bachman said. "I'll be there in half an hour."

# CHAPTER FORTY-EIGHT

Thirty minutes later, I parked the Explorer on the second level of the mall's garage and went inside.

I was sure there were security cameras everywhere. But there was also no reason for anyone to think I'd be here, and even if they did, they wouldn't be looking for someone who looked how I looked now. The mall was pretty busy, going on six on a Wednesday afternoon. Teenagers milling around after school. Families already out for the evening, heading to P.F. Chang's or the California Pizza Kitchen or the movies.

I went down the escalator and found the Starbucks on the first floor.

There was an amphitheater-style seating area with dozens of people on the steps. I ordered a latte and took a seat at an open table.

My heart wouldn't sit still. I hadn't been out in public this way since Grand Central, and I knew what had happened there. I looked at the crowd milling around me. I averted my face as a female security guard went by, talking into a radio. I wondered if she knew who I was or was just making her rounds.

Then I heard her laugh into the radio and my nerves subsided.

It was 5:45, and the later it got, the more I worried I became that Bachman wasn't coming. Or that this was some kind of trap.

It wasn't until I saw him at the top of the escalator that my fears began to subside.

He took it down, avoiding direct eye contact with me, looking randomly around. Finally our eyes met and he gave me the slightest smile of recognition. For a paranoid moment it rippled through me that this was only a scheme and that in seconds the police and the FBI were going to be all around me. But he stepped up to my table, took one last glance at the crowd, and sat down. He was in a gray suit with his tie loosened. His eyes were hooded but honest and his face pallid and drawn, his expression exhausted.

I grinned. "You look like you could use a coffee even more than me."

"Don't drink it any more. Reflux," he said, shrugging his shoulders. "Too much acid."

"In that case I'm pretty sure dragging you into this

307

mess isn't helping any either," I said with a hesitant smile. "Mr. Bachman, I appreciate you being here more than you know. I know you're taking a big risk."

"You might put it that way. Anyway, if anything happens, I'm just your lawyer and you were coming to me in order to turn yourself in—"

"I thought you said you didn't want to be my lawyer . . ."

"I'm not sure that I do. But something changed."

"You went to DC?"

He nodded. "I looked them up. Hruseff and Alton Dokes. I saw they were both there. At the DEA. In El Paso. At the same time as the Bienvieneses were killed. I wanted to hear what Sabrina Stein had to say. And to find out why Eduardo Cano wasn't ever tried."

"And what did you find?"

"That I think she's lying. Or at the minimum, covering something up."

"Which would be . . . ? "

He adjusted his wire-rim glasses. Bachman had bushy, gray-flecked eyebrows that made him resemble a professor. Right now I couldn't have cared less if he looked like Joe the Plumber. "That the government may have had a hand in the Bienvienes murders. And might even have deliberately let Eduardo Cano get away."

"What if it wasn't the *Bienvieneses*' murders?"

308

He blinked and furrowed his brow at me. "I'm not sure I understand?"

"I mean, they were killed. But what if they weren't the intended target that day? What if it was someone else?"

"Okay, I'm listening."

I looked at him closely. "Why are you even doing this for me? You said you couldn't get involved."

He shrugged and took in a long breath. "It isn't just for you . . . Don't take that the wrong way. I believed you when you first came to me. I just couldn't . . ." He took off his glasses and rubbed his brow. "They took my wife's life. For no other reason than because she was a good person, who acted from the heart. We all know who was behind this. I want him brought to justice. I want to know why. If she stepped into the middle of some kind of drug retaliation . . . or, God forbid, some kind of government cover-up . . ."

I reached over and took hold of Harold Bachman's arm. "I'm not sure that's what it was."

"Not sure it was *what*?"

"A drug retaliation. I'm not a hundred percent sure that it was even connected to the drug trade at all. Or to anything I might have been thinking a day ago."

"Ms. Gould, I'm here . . . I'm breaking every vow I made to myself. And to my kids." His eyes locked on me. "What did you find?"

"You remember I asked you if you had ever heard anyone connected to this with the name Gillian?"

He nodded.

My eyes lit up with vindication. "Well, I know who it was."

# CHAPTER FORTY-NINE

Javier Perez had worked security at the Stamford Town Center mall for two years now after dropping out of Southern Connecticut State University. Weekdays, he did the ten-to-six shift; two nights a week he was a gate guard at this ritzy residential community in Greenwich. What he really wanted to do was take the test for the Stamford police academy. He wanted to wear a real badge, not this useless steel-plated one. He wanted to trade in the radio holstered to his side for a gun. He had an uncle who worked on the force who he was pretty sure could get him in.

Driving around in a cart, keeping an eye out for shoplifters or teens huddled in a corner smoking weed, pretending he was some big-time authority figure, just didn't cut it anymore.

Javier was making the rounds in the garage, checking the plates of those who were parked in the handicapped spaces or had pulled into unauthorized spots. The only reason he'd even slap a ticket on their windshield was that if his boss came around and found he hadn't, Javier knew he could kiss that recommendation to the Stamford PD good-bye.

He wound the cart up to the second floor, stopping for a couple of sweet-looking mamas who walked by him in the crosswalk; he nodded with an admiring smile. Then his eye went to a black Mercedes 550 parked in a space blocked off with yellow lines.

Probably some hedge-fund honcho's wife who thought the world owed her special treatment, just run into Saks to pick up some outfit that probably cost as much as his car.

Javier stopped and shook his head at the hundred-thousand-dollar car parked smack in the yellow lines. It was time to take out his ticket pad.

But somehow his eye was drawn to the vehicle parked next to it. A big, blue GMC Explorer. He recalled that an APB had been tacked onto the bulletin board in the office for a dark blue Explorer. A 2004. With Vermont plates. Didn't say why they were looking for it. Just that they were.

This one had Connecticut plates.

At least *one* of them, Javier noted, checking the front. The front plate was suspiciously missing. And he knew his cars: the squared-off grill and rear lights were particular to how Explorers were made six or seven years ago.

Something about this sucker didn't seem right.

A tingling danced across Javier's skin, not far from what he imagined he'd be feeling when he stood in that starched blue uniform one day when they presented him his badge. He took his radio and called Victor in the office.

"Hey, bro, you know that APB we received yesterday . . ."

Javier was thinking that application to the Stamford police academy might've just moved to the top of the pile.

# CHAPTER FIFTY

I told Harold what I'd found. That Gillian was never a person. It never had been.

It was a town. The hometown in Colorado of Ana Lasser, the girl who had been killed in the second car along with the two other University of Denver students.

I told him how I was looking through the photos she had taken just before she was killed when I just happened on it.

"Hruseff told Curtis just before he shot him, 'This is for Gillian.' It was never about the Bienvienes. *They* were the ones who just happened in. It was always about this girl. Ana. On spring break with her friends. They were in similar cars. Maybe that was it."

"But Curtis went to see Lauritzia in the hospital," Harold said, cocking his head, "and Lauritzia doesn't

314

have anything to do with that girl. And you were sure that's what got him killed."

"No. Something to do with this girl Ana Lasser got him killed. I think the reason he needed to see Lauritzia was to confirm this. Her father carried out the hit. He needed to know if Ana was the intended target. Or the Bienvienes. That's why he needed to die."

My eyes went wide and fixed on Harold. "Eduardo Cano wanted to get back at Oscar Velez, and he wiped out his entire family. But not just for revenge. What if it was also to keep him silent? To keep him from ever divulging what he knew? That this was never, ever about those DEA agents. That they just happened in, just as randomly and tragically as we thought the three students had. But because they were DEA agents everyone assumed they were the targets. But they never were. It was always about this girl . . ."

"*Why?*" Harold said, shaking his head. He was a lawyer, clearly a person who operated in logic, and this wasn't making sense.

"I don't that know yet. I—"

My gaze was suddenly drawn to the sight of two uniformed police officers coming down the escalator.

"Maybe she photographed something?" Harold postulated. "Maybe she saw something at the hit she should never have seen and got it on film?"

"I don't know . . ." I kept watching the police. "That ambush was set up in advance. No one had a clue she'd

315

be taking photos. Anyway, it's not *her* family that was being targeted in revenge. It was Oscar Velez's. To keep him from telling the truth to the feds. About what he knows . . .

"I've been approaching this all wrong," I said. It was like some Mensa puzzle that was making my brain ache. "I've been focused on the Bienvienes and Lauritzia, when it's about this girl. Eduardo Cano has been trying to kill Lauritzia, not because of her but because of her father. Maybe it's the same thing here. Hruseff said, 'This is for Gillian, asshole,' when he shot Curtis, not 'This is for Ana.' Because it's not about her literally, but where she's from. Gillian. It's about what's there. She was just the person who was killed."

Harold nodded. "It never made sense to me that Eduardo Cano was let go simply because of holes in Oscar Velez's testimony. The man murdered five U.S. citizens. He knew something no one wanted to come out." He gave me the look of a man who was no longer fighting the truth. "Okay, I think there's someone you ought to meet."

"Thank you," I said, and grasped his arm.

Just as quickly my gaze became diverted by the sight of two more policemen. They seemed to be making their way through the crowd, checking faces against some kind of sheet.

A knot tightened in my stomach. *"Shit."*

316

# CHAPTER FIFTY-ONE

"I don't like how this is feeling," I said to Harold, drawing his eye to the cops, my heart starting to race. "I think I ought to get out of here."

Maybe the people at the inn where I was staying had somehow recognized me. I was going over what I may have left in my room—some toiletries and whatever extra clothes I had.

I realized I wasn't going back to get them.

Harold said, "I want you to talk with Lauritzia. But I'm going to need some time to make sure I'm covered with my kids. Can you meet me in the garage in my office? In about an hour?"

I nodded. The cops seemed headed our way. "Stand up and give me a hug," I said.

Harold looked at me curiously.

317

"Just give me a hug. Like you know me and we're saying good-bye. These officers are looking for someone. There's no reason they should be here for me, but . . ."

We stood up and Harold awkwardly put his arms around me and gave me a squeeze. I looked at them over his shoulder. I knew my newly clipped blonde hair and sunglasses would conceal me. And even if they were somehow on my trail, there was absolutely no reason to think I'd be at the mall.

But somehow they were on to me.

"I'll leave first," I said, pulling away. "Here's my number. If you see them come after me, I'd really appreciate a heads-up."

He glanced at them with concern and nodded.

"You are my lawyer, right?" I said, holding on his gaze with a reluctant smile.

"I guess I am. Now. If it comes to that."

"Good." I gave him an upbeat look. "I'll see you in an hour."

# CHAPTER FIFTY-TWO

I made my way to the exit without even a look behind. I found the fire staircase next to the elevators and headed to the second floor. Before the door fully closed I glanced around. The officers seemed to have moved on. No one was coming my way. I let out a sigh of relief, and my nerves began to calm.

I went up to the second floor and headed down the first row in the garage to where I'd left the Explorer, two aisles over. I took out the electronic key and was about to press the Unlock button.

I stopped.

I saw the Explorer—and realized in an instant just why all the police were at the mall. There were three or four of them—maybe a detective or two as well—hell, for all I knew they could've been the FBI!—huddled around it.

The bottom fell out of my stomach.

It took about one more second for my throat to go dry and for me to become completely encased in sweat. I turned around, pretending I'd arrived at a completely different car two rows over, and I held there like a plank, not knowing what to do. Jim and Cindy's car must have been on alert. I'd been discovered.

I was sure I was about to hear a command to stop, to get down on the ground, the authorities rushing over me. The next thirty seconds went by as slowly as any in my life. I stood in front of some strange sedan, glancing back to see if they knew I was there.

Somehow they didn't. But there wasn't any doubt that I had to get out of there. I had to get to Harold. I was close to finding out what I needed to know, what I needed to save myself, and if I waited there too long, if they had my car, the entire mall might be put on lockdown. The detectives were on their radios. All the exits were probably covered.

*How the hell are you going to get out of here, Wendy?*

I drew in a deep breath and made my way back in the direction of the mall. My legs were so rubbery, they would barely move. I didn't look behind. I just kept on walking, waiting to be ordered to stop.

As I neared the elevator suddenly a policeman stepped out of the stairwell. My heart beat so loudly I thought it would give me away. It took everything I had to hold it together. I just looked him in the face, praying, and nodded. "Hello."

"Ma'am." He nodded back and passed me by without stopping.

I exhaled.

I was about to go into the staircase when the elevator doors opened and a mother and her ten- or eleven-year-old daughter stepped out, so I ducked inside. The doors closed and I almost fainted with relief. I pushed the button for 3, not knowing what I would do there, also knowing that there was probably a security camera trained on me now, and at some point, when no one had come back to the Explorer, they would review it and know it was me.

The elevator opened on the third floor. I didn't see any police around. I did see a security cart driving up the ramp, so I went the other way, out to the atrium balcony, and peered over the railing into the mall. I thought that maybe I could get out through one of the restaurants. The Capital Grille. Mitchell's Fish Market. P.F. Chang's. They all had both mall entrances and ones that led to the outside. A couple of cops stood in front of the entrance to P.F. Chang's, eyeing whoever was going in.

*You can't risk it.* My chest filled up with fear. But in a few more minutes, the entire mall might be locked down.

I went back into the garage and headed down a row of cars, trying to think of my best way out. Steal a car? I didn't know how. Hijack one? A couple of women passed me, deep in conversation. "Then you know what she did?" A young mother dragged her whining five- or six-year-old daughter, who was carrying on about some toy. Another woman was carrying a bunch of bags from Pottery Barn and Williams-Sonoma. Not knowing what else to do, I followed her from a distance. Arriving at her car, a tan Acura SUV, she reached into her purse and took out her key. She opened the rear hatch and loaded in her bags.

I don't even know what made me watch her. She had a kindly face—I was so desperate and mixed up, I thought about just jumping in next to her and begging her to drive me out. But instead of getting in her car, the woman fumbled around in her bag and brought out her parking ticket.

I suddenly knew what to do.

She headed over to the payment machine at the top of the ramp, five or six cars away.

I hurried over to her car. I saw her trying to figure out the machine, and as she inserted her credit card I pulled open the rear driver's side door, completely hidden from her view, and threw myself in. I climbed over the backseat and fell into the cargo bay, wedging myself tightly against the seat back, hoping it hid me from view. I pulled her shopping bags around me and curled into a ball.

*This just might work.*

I pressed my face into the carpet, praying when she came back she wouldn't need to get into the cargo area again. Thank God, she didn't. The wait was agonizing, but I finally heard the lock beep again, and the woman opened the driver's door and climbed in.

My heart was going crazy. I lay there, making myself as tiny as I could, eyes closed, begging her to start the fucking car and get us out of there. I heard her arrange her bag for a minute, barely four feet away. Finally I heard the ignition and the car started up. The engine rattled—almost the same vibration as my pulse. I couldn't tell which was shaking more.

We started to back out. Suddenly I heard the woman grunt, "Shit," and hit the brakes. I was thrown against the backseat. She went, "C'mon, buddy," and I felt as if she was looking directly over me out the rear window.

I was afraid to even breathe.

Finally the car went forward. We drove down the incline and turned sharply, coming to another stop, seeming to inch along, then turned sharply again. I heard the radio go on. "New York Minute" by Don Henley. I was sure we were approaching the ticket counter on the ground floor.

Then we stopped.

"Grrrr, what is this now?" The woman let out a frustrated sigh.

What if the police were searching all vehicles? The

windows were tinted. I was pretty sure no one could easily see in. Unless they were specifically looking for me. I crunched into a ball. My limbs started to physically shake. I was on the verge of finding out what I needed. What could prove my innocence. *Please don't let them take me in now.*

We inched along to the ticket booth. I pulled the shopping bags tighter around me. I raised up slightly and saw the rate sign on the cashier's booth, the window above me. I tensed, prepared for someone to ask to open the hatch and peer in.

To my elation, all I heard was the woman ask, "Insert it in here?" I realized she was putting in the parking ticket. The next couple of seconds I just lay there with my eyes closed, sure that someone was about to pull open the hatch.

But no one did. Instead, I heard the attendant say in an accent, "Have a nice day!"

We pulled out of the garage. It was at least thirty seconds before I allowed myself to actually believe we were free. I rolled over and blew out a triumphant gasp of air.

*Now, how the hell would I get out of here?*

# CHAPTER FIFTY-THREE

Back in his office, Harold called Roxanne's mom, who'd been staying with him since the disaster, helping out with the kids. He told her he had a business thing and wouldn't be back that night until late, and that he'd call in from the road and say good night to the kids. Then he got on the computer and put in the name of the college student Wendy had told him about.

Ana Lasser.

Immediately the article from the *Denver Post* came up. Harold quickly went over it, finding the link to the photography exhibit Wendy had mentioned. He clicked on it, and looked at the black-and-white photos there, the studies of the villagers, their brown, smiling faces. He shook his head in resignation—such a shame that the life of a girl with such talent and promise had been cut short like that.

But that wasn't what he was looking for.

He scrolled down, bypassing pages of articles connected to the Culiacán ambush, until he came across something from what appeared to be the local newspaper where Ana Lasser was from.

The Alamosa *County Courier*.

STAND-OUT LOCAL STUDENT AMONG FIVE KILLED IN MEXICAN
AMBUSH

Harold clicked on the link and read how Lasser, an honors graduate of William Payne High School and the former photography editor on the school newspaper, "was listed among the victims of what appeared to be a drug-motivated shooting in a remote Mexican town." The article described how she was traveling by car through the Sinaloa region on spring break with two other University of Denver students, one of them, Ned Taylor, described as her boyfriend.

There was no mention of the Bienvienes or any details on the shooting. The article said that she was survived by her brothers Ryan and Beau, both still at the high school. And her parents, Robert and Blair Lasser, of Gillian.

Harold pulled himself away from the screen. If Ana Lasser had indeed been the target of this shooting, it surely wasn't because she was dealing dime bags of marijuana out of her college dorm room. It was clearly intended as a message to someone important, a devastating payback. Just as the vendetta against Lauritzia's family had been a payback.

And if it was, it only made sense that the person it was most likely aimed at would have been her father.

Harold checked the name again. Robert Lasser.

With time, Harold knew he could find out virtually anything he needed to about the man. Background checks, LexisNexis, D and B reports, private investigation services—the firm had the means. He knew he could uncover every bad check the guy had ever written. Every traffic ticket he'd received. Every phone call he'd made in the past few months; whether his business was healthy or in trouble. Whether he'd been screwing his secretary.

But that would take time and leave a trail of money, and Harold knew it was vital for him to be 100 percent confidential about why he would be looking into him.

The last thing he could do was risk having it coming out that *he* was the person behind the search. If it got back to the wrong people, he'd be putting everyone in jeopardy, including Jamie and Taylor. He'd already seen what these people do when they feel threatened.

He checked his watch. He still had about a half hour until Wendy was supposed to meet him. Since the police never went after her, he assumed she'd gotten out of the mall safely.

He punched *Robert Lasser, Gillian, Colorado,* into Google Search.

Dozens of hits came back—most having to do with the death of his daughter, almost four years ago, which had been picked up by newspapers around the country. Harold kept scrolling down. There were two other Robert Lassers who were on the web—a financial advisor in the Twin Cities and a personal liabilities lawyer in Boynton Beach, Florida.

Then an item caught his eye. Harold stopped on it.

### LOCAL BUSINESSMAN MAKES
### GENEROUS GIFT TO SAVE PUBLIC PARK

Gillian businessman Robert P. Lasser has donated seventy-five thousand dollars to the town's landmark preservation board to preserve Francis A. Dellinger Park, to fend off interest from an out-of-state real estate development group that had submitted plans to buy the park from the cash-strapped town and convert it into a business park. Lasser, a longtime resident of Gillian and president of Apache Sales and Marketing, and whose daughter, Ana, was tragically killed in Mexico three years ago, the victim of a drug-related shooting, said he donated the money "to preserve the integrity of our town and because it was one of his daughter's favorite spots to photograph . . ."

*Nice gesture*, Harold remarked to himself. He exited out of the article and typed in *Apache Sales and Marketing*. The company had a website. It said, "The finest in TV's and home consumer brands . . ." It looked like some kind of consumer distribution company. Harold noticed they had warehouses in Colorado, Kansas, and Texas. It appeared they distributed products to Indian reservations. The home page was decorated with the logos of several recognizable brands: Sony. Panasonic. Samsung. HP. Norelco.

Colt.

Then he saw a promotional tagline that hit him like a blunt instrument to the face: *Direct sales solutions in the U.S. and Mexico*.

He also noticed an official-looking crest with a U.S. Government "Approved Vendor" logo on the bottom of the page.

Did Apache sell to the U.S. government? Maybe to military bases? Were Indian reservations still on government land? He'd have to check that. Then there was that "in the U.S. and Mexico." He'd have to check that too.

But the connection to the Culiacán murders had just narrowed a little.

He jotted all this down, then glanced at his watch and saw the time. He picked up his phone and punched in a number only he knew. On the third ring, a woman's voice answered.

"I'm going to be coming up," he said. "I'm bringing someone. Someone needs to talk with you."

"Okay," Lauritzia said haltingly. "If you think it's wise.

"Just trust me on this. We'll be there in a couple of hours."

# CHAPTER FIFTY-FOUR

We made a right turn out of the garage onto what had to be Summer Street and pulled up at a light.

I raised myself up and peered out the window at the tops of buildings in downtown Stamford. Somehow I had to get to Harold's office in half an hour—and that was in the completely opposite direction.

And every second it was becoming farther.

We continued through the light, and I recognized the library and an Italian restaurant Dave and I used to eat at sometimes. Then we drove for a while down a long straightaway in the direction of Long Ridge Road without stopping. What began to throb in my mind like some silent alarm was what if the woman was heading back home and upon arriving went to take out her bags—she was about to get the scare of her life! In seconds she'd be on the phone to 911. Who even knew where she lived? I could be out in the middle of back-country Stamford or New Canaan with no way to get back.

I'd be dead meat for the first cop who came on the scene.

The next time we stopped, I lifted my head and saw we had merged onto Long Ridge Road. Long Ridge was a highly trafficked, commercial boulevard, fast-food places and big box stores on both sides. Suddenly I heard the woman get on her phone. It connected over the speaker.

A man's voice answered. "Hey . . ."

"Hey, hon," the woman said brightly. "Just wondering what time you'd be home for dinner?"

I lowered myself back into the rear.

"Not sure . . . should be finishing up here no later than six. Maybe around seven."

"I've got some sauce in the fridge. We could do a pasta. I could also pick up a pork chop and maybe do a baked potato?"

"Pork chop sounds good."

"Okay . . . I'm passing the Stop and Shop in a second anyway. I've got to pick up some stuff for the kids."

I figured that was my way out, as soon as she parked at the supermarket and went in. I'd just have to work out a way back downtown.

"I was at the mall," the woman said. "I picked up a few things for the house. Frames for those pictures of the kids. Then I went into Williams-Sonoma. I was looking at those Japanese knives we were talking about—"

"Okay . . ." I heard her husband sigh, beginning to lose interest. If I wasn't so damn scared, I might have laughed out loud—it sounded a lot like Dave and me.

"Anyway, I'm pulling in now. See you home."

"Love you."

The SUV turned to the right. I rolled against the shopping bags, knocking one over, a bubble-wrapped vase or something tumbling out. Did she hear? When she parked at the store, would she come around and check the back to make sure everything was all right?

I raised myself to see where we were and, to my alarm, saw that it wasn't the Stop & Shop after all, but an Exxon station.

A wave of panic sheared through me—not knowing which side of the vehicle the gas tank was on, I envisioned the woman getting out and standing virtually inches from me as she filled up the tank. Her eyes becoming twice their size at what she saw curled up inside her car . . .

She pulled up at a tank. The driver's door opened and the woman stepped out and went around the car, passing right above me. I held my breath. Thank God, the windows were tinted and I had her shopping bags pulled all around me. She crossed to the other side of the vehicle and went over to a pump.

Through the darkened glass I watched her put in her credit card and unscrew the fuel cap. My heart stood still as I realized what would happen if she merely looked up and let her eyes wander inside her car.

I froze.

Suddenly she put the pump on automatic and headed away. I lifted myself just enough to watch her go around the car and inside the market.

*This is my chance.*

I pushed aside the bags and rolled myself over the backseat. I opened the door on the gas tank side, away from the market, and slid out, shutting the door behind me. Immediately I was face-to-face with a man at the pump directly across from me. Inside I froze, but on the outside I got my wits together just enough to give him an innocent smile; to him it would just seem like anyone climbing out of the backseat. I doubted if he'd even still be there when the woman came back.

Hastily, I hurried away from the car, expecting any second to hear a shout from behind me. *Hey, you, what are you doing? Stop!*

But I didn't. Ahead of me, there was a Bed, Bath & Beyond and a Burger King across the street. I hurried to Burger King and ran around the corner, out of sight. For the first time, I exhaled in relief. I checked the time. I was two miles away from where I had to meet Harold and had no way to get there. I had only ten minutes. I did the only thing I could think of.

I called Harold on his cell.

"Yes," he answered hesitantly. I could hear he didn't want to take the call. "You made it out okay?"

"Little wrinkle," I said with a chuckle. "But doing better now."

# CHAPTER FIFTY-FIVE

In the makeshift Homeland Security–FBI Command Center at Federal Plaza in lower Manhattan, Alton Dokes looked through a series of photos that had just come in.

The first was of a navy GMC Explorer parked at the Town Center mall in Stamford, Connecticut. It had New York license plates that had been stolen off of a 2008 Honda Civic in Bridgeport four days before. The Explorer matched the one that had been reported missing from a private home in Vermont yesterday morning.

A home directly across from one owned by David and Wendy Gould.

The next photo was of that same vehicle going through the ticketing gate at the Town Center mall in Stamford an hour earlier.

Dokes focused on the driver behind the wheel and

smiled. Her shortened and newly dyed hair, the partially hidden face. *Gotcha, darling.* He chuckled to himself.

*But what was she doing here?*

A team of agents was already on their way. As well as additional surveillance photos requested from office buildings surrounding the mall. It was just a stroke of luck as it turned out, *his* luck actually, that she had managed to avoid being captured there.

He had to hand it to the gal—she had shown herself a remarkably difficult target to kill.

Still, one thing did concern him as he leafed through the photos. One of the suspect as she made her way through the mall, another of her sitting at a table having coffee in the first-floor atrium. She was huddled in conversation with a man. A man whose face might not be known to most, but it was to him. Someone connected to her in ways beyond what she likely knew.

Dokes paused on the photo. He knew what had to be done. His own survival depended on it. The survival of a host of people depended on it. That was what they did—warriors. They did the work that had to be done. The work that no one ever saw, through the muddy troughs of what ended up as history and what would never be fully known.

But that wasn't the only reason he would make sure she never got to tell her tale.

He had spent too many years getting his hands dirty in holes like El Paso and Mexicali to see it all washed away now. And Harold Bachman . . . he had gotten his nose in it. He'd been asking about Gillian in DC. Hadn't he learned?

He was another one to deal with.

One of the young agents came over, Holmes, who had been the trigger man at Grand Central, and asked, "You want me to get this out to the press?" He pointed to the close-up taken of Wendy Gould driving into the garage. "We can have her face across the country in minutes."

Dokes looked at the grainy security photograph of her behind the wheel. *You've been more trouble than you're worth,* he said to himself, *but that's about to come to an end.*

"Thanks," he said, picking up his cell phone, motioning for the agent to leave. "I'll handle it from here."

The number appeared on the screen. KVC Consulting.

On the fourth ring a woman answered. "Sabrina Stein."

# CHAPTER FIFTY-SIX

We drove for an hour and turned off Route 15 in Hamden. We wound through the quiet streets of small apartment buildings and attached houses until we were near New Haven. A sign pointed straight ahead to Quinnipiac University.

Harold pulled in front of a five-story redbrick apartment building that had probably looked modern back in the sixties. He turned off the car. It was dark and cold. A few flurries were blowing around. We both agreed that someone must have recognized the Explorer—which meant the police now knew I'd taken it. Along with Jim and Cindy, who I figured could now be put in a room with just about everyone else I knew, who now assumed that whatever was being said about me had to be true.

"Wait here," Harold said, opening the door. "I'll be back in a minute."

He got out and went around the back of the apartment building. My anticipation started to rise. I finally was about to come face-to-face with the one person who might be able to corroborate my story. Who could take me a step closer to the truth—a truth that several people had now died for. On the street, a young couple passed by the car walking their dog.

A short while later Harold came back and waved me out of the car. I crossed the street and he took me through the rear entrance, facing the parking lot, and down the narrow lobby hallway to the elevator.

"No one knows about this place," he said. We stepped inside and he pressed the button for the fourth floor. "Not the government. Though they've tried to. Not any of my colleagues. Just me and you. And just so you also know, while I value everything you've told me, Wendy, I value the person you're about to meet a whole lot more."

"I understand." I nodded. "Though it's not like there's much of anyone I could possibly tell these days," I said with a smile.

"Just so you understand," Harold said as he closed the door.

The elevator was tiny and cramped, a diamond-shaped window on the door, and it slowly clattered up to the fourth floor, where Harold pushed open the door and we went down a dark hallway. He stopped and knocked on Apartment 4C.

The door opened slightly. A woman peeked out. Adrenaline started to surge in me. She unlatched the chain.

I stared into the pretty, dark-complexioned face of Lauritzia Velez. "Please come in," she said, looking at me haltingly, opening the door.

Harold gave her a hug. "Lauritzia . . ."

She squeezed him back, appreciatively and gratefully, and led us into the small, sparsely furnished apartment. She was tiny, dressed in jeans and an orange sweater tied over a white tee. Her face was almond-shaped and pretty, just like in the photo, with narrow cheekbones and shy, mysterious eyes that in another time, if things were different, might have sparkled with joy.

"It's still a mess," she said to me apologetically. "I've only been here a couple of weeks."

"It's nice," I said, looking at the modern IKEA-style furnishings, bookshelves stacked with what looked like textbooks.

"The furniture came with it," she said. "Mr. Bachman has been very generous to me."

"Lauritzia, this is Wendy Gould," Harold said.

"I know who you are," Lauritzia said to me with trusting eyes. "Mr. Bachman explained . . ."

"And I know who you are," I said. "I have for a while."

"In a minute, maybe you can tell me how. In the meantime, can I get you some tea? A glass of water?"

"A cup of tea would be terrific." It had been a week since I'd had one. A week from hell.

"I'm good," Harold said, shaking his head slightly.

The water took a couple of minutes to boil, and I spent it looking around the living room. It was neat and barely looked lived in. I picked up a photo of what I took to be her and her brother and sisters, the girls dressed in light-blue dresses and beaming with joy, at what I figured was a family wedding. A sadness came over me. The happy faces of those who I knew were dead now. Knowing the tragic fate that awaited them all.

It was hard to look at. That was how it would be to look at my husband now . . .

I put it down.

"I keep it out because there are days that it somehow fills me with hope," Lauritzia said, bringing a tray to the small, round dining table. "And then there are days I cannot look at it. Because it makes me ashamed to be alive."

"I know exactly how you feel, Lauritzia," I said. "And how does it make you feel today?"

"I kept it out," she said with a shrug, and shifted a stack of books from the table. "So I guess hopeful. Please sit down."

The tea was hot and steamy and just what I needed. "Thank you."

"Mr. Bachman told me what has happened. I don't read the newspapers much or listen to the news. He said you came to him a few days ago to find me. How did you know about me?"

I dug into my bag and took out Curtis's phone. I scrolled to the last photo and pushed it across to her.

As she stared at it, she brightened slightly, her face coming alive in a hesitant smile.

I explained, "I went to see Curtis's mother. In Boston. I found her number in there. She told me what he was looking into at the end . . . about what happened at the Westchester airport. I looked into it, and when I read about you, I knew it was you in the photo. I had no idea who you were, of course, but I traced it back to your trial. I know why he was trying to find you, Lauritzia. Why he needed to see you. It was the last photo he took. Just before he died. You said you know who I am, right?"

"Yes. Mr. Bachman has explained to me."

"Then you also know that I was with him when he was killed."

This time she stopped, and nodded slightly, averting her eyes.

"So you know that finding out why is the only way I can get to the truth behind what happened."

"The truth . . ." Lauritzia seemed to be measuring me. "To prove why he died?"

"To prove my innocence, Lauritzia." I cupped my hands around the mug. "I had no business being up

343

there. I can't take that back. But I didn't kill those people. Though I suspect that's something you probably already know. You've been living with this kind of sentence over you for a long time."

She nodded again, this time putting her hand along her face and rubbing her cheek. "I was very sad to hear what happened to him. I knew it was not how they said. He was a nice man. I could feel that as soon as he came into my room at the hospital. I could see he only wanted the truth, not to hurt anyone. I told him he shouldn't get involved in this. That this wasn't his fight. I told him what would happen. How it would end. But he wanted to know . . .

"As soon as I heard what happened, I knew it was not as they said. You are right—I have lived with that sort of knowledge a long time. Just as I knew, as soon as I looked in his eyes and spoke with him, that he would have the same fate. The truth you call it . . . The truth for you is how you get yourself out of this, Ms. Wendy, but truth only deepens the darkness for me."

"The person who killed him"—I put down my mug and looked at her—"was a government agent, Lauritzia. He said, 'This is for Gillian,' and then he shot him. Point-blank. There was nothing I could do. I believe he was trying to stop Curtis from ever divulging what he knew. I now know the person he was referring to. It wasn't so much a person as a place. And I know what happened down there, in Culiacán . . ."

A paleness crept across Lauritzia. She brushed the hair from her eyes and looked away.

"Lauritzia," Harold said, reaching across the table, "I brought Wendy here because there are things she needs to know . . . things you might know. Things you've never told me, but I think it is safe to tell her if there are. She's been harmed in all this, just like the two of us have been harmed. You more than anyone. It's not just that she's trying to clear herself . . . It's that she's lost people close to her too. Just like us. People who she loved. And those people deserve a voice too. To make it clear who bears the guilt. Who did these terrible things and what's behind them. Just like your brother and sisters should have a voice. So it's okay—"

"My brother and sisters do have a voice. The problem is not giving them a voice but finding anyone who will listen. Who will do anything . . ."

I reached across to her and touched her arm. "I want to be that person, Lauritzia."

She stood up, away from my grasp, holding back tears. "What can you possibly do? When I look at you I see the same thing I saw in Curtis. The killing will just continue. No matter what you want to do about it. No matter who you think you can tell." She looked at Harold, fear coming from her. "Now, even you cannot back out of it!"

She went over to the window. The blinds were down and she peeked through them, to see the street below;

345

as if she could see far beyond it. To a different world maybe. To her home. My heart ached for her, with what she'd been through. When she turned around, all she did was nod. "I know what you want to know. You want to know what Curtis told me, sí? In the hospital?"

"Yes." I nodded.

Her voice grew resigned, but I heard something else in it. Sadness. And her face contained a kind of sadness too. As if she was talking to people who were now alive, who would soon become ghosts. As they all had become ghosts for her. She sat back down, put her hands on the table, and nodded. "I know exactly what you've come to hear."

# CHAPTER FIFTY-SEVEN

"He said he knew why Eduardo Cano wanted me dead. That it wasn't just revenge, revenge for what my father had done. For his betrayal. But for what he *knew*. What he had to protect against my father saying. It was why my father was driven from his family and agreed to testify against him."

I pressed. "It was that the Bienvieneses weren't the actual targets of that shooting, wasn't it? In Culiacán."

*"The Bienvienes?"*

"The government agents, in the first car. It was the girl. In the car behind them. Ana Lasser. She was the target. Yes?"

Lauritzia's face remained still for a moment, in a last defense. Then she simply looked at me and nodded. "Sí."

Suddenly it all made sense to me. Things I hadn't

347

realized before. "That's why there was a year's gap between the first and second killings. Your brother was killed a year before the others. That one was a warning. But then it turned into something different. The rest was a punishment. Your father talked."

Lauritzia put her hands in front of her face, and tears came into her eyes. "I am not saying my father is a good man . . . I know what he has done, and he will have to answer in his own way to God. The choices in life are different for us down there. He started as a worker in a kitchen. My mother died when I was four; it was a struggle just to keep us fed. My sisters had to work at an early age. I lived with my aunts and uncles. One of them knew someone who was part of *la familia*. One day my father came home with money. He no longer worked in the kitchen. Who here can judge him? Soon we were all living together again in a house. He never wanted it for any of us. He always kept it separate from us. He sent us to school. He pushed us, in the other direction . . ."

"Lauritzia, no one's judging him," I said. "We just want—"

"I am not saying the murder of three American students is somehow more forgivable than the murder of two government agents . . . but he knew, when it came out that the two *federales* were killed in that first car, that the *nortes* would never rest until they found out who had done this. Everything changed for him then. It was to save us that he did this thing. He was able to put Eduardo Cano in a U.S. prison. The Untouchable One. If he was put away, it would have only been my father who had to suffer. Then they let him go, and my family's life turned to hell."

She stood up. This time there was something deeper and more resolute carved into her face. Not fear; it seemed almost freeing. As if she was finally letting go everything she had been holding back and that had been boxed inside her for such a long time.

"Yes, that girl who was in the second car was the one they were sent to kill. My father confessed this to me the day he left. In tears. He confessed this to all of us. An innocent girl, just like me. He intended to salvage some honor in doing what he did. But all it ended up bringing him was hell."

"Why did Cano want this girl dead?" I asked. "What had she done?"

"The same thing I had done!" Lauritzia said in tears. "Or my brother had done. Or any of my sisters. *Nothing!* Only that the sins of the father are passed to the son. To the children. This is what Curtis told me. That my father had stepped into a web of lies and secrets . . . With a spider far more venomous than the one he already knew. Why is it that Eduardo Cano never went to trial? Why do you think he was able to disappear, and leave your country, after murdering five of your own citizens?"

Harold said, "Lauritzia, you said it was because of what he knew. What Eduardo Cano needed to protect."

"No, not Cano." She turned and looked away.

"Then who? Your father was already in the custody of the U.S government. Who did he need to protect?"

"Do you not see it? Do you believe the Mexican government speaks with one voice? When they promise to rid the world of these savages? When the *federales* come around and take pictures of the dead and count the bullet casings and ask for names, but nothing is ever looked into? Nothing is ever done. Does any government ever speak with one voice? Does yours, Mr. Bachman?"

He shook his head. "Lauritzia, I don't understand."

"It was about the guns! That is what Curtis told me."

*"Guns?"*

"What do you think it is that backs up their terror? They rain death upon us, but where does it come from? We sell you the drugs, you sell us the guns. In Mexico it is a crime to even sell one. They come from you. It is in your newspapers. It is on your TV. But no one intervenes. The sins of the father are passed to the son. Find Eduardo Cano—ask him! Or ask this girl's father what they have done. They can tell you what was behind it, not me."

Harold turned to me. "Lauritzia's father was in the hands of the FBI and U.S. Justice Department. But Cano was trying to protect himself from him telling someone else. *Who?*"

350

I saw that he formed the answer in his eyes.

Lauritzia started to weep. I moved over and brought her face to my chest and put my arm around her. I let her cry. She deserved to cry. Forever, if that's what it took.

*The sins of the father are passed to the son.*

*Find Eduardo Cano—ask him! Or ask the girl's father.*

"I looked into Ana Lasser's father," Harold said. "He has a trading company that does business across the border in Mexico . . . electronic equipment. Samsung. Sony. All very legit. But he also sells firearms. Colt. Remington. It's right there on his website."

I stared back at him. "He was selling illegal guns to the cartels?"

"I don't know. But there's more. There's something else there . . . a seal. From the U.S. government. He's an approved vendor to the United States of America."

My pulse started to accelerate. "That's what they were protecting. They're selling arms illegally to the Mexican cartels . . ."

"Yes, but there's got to be something more. This has all come out. You've heard of this program, on the news. What's it called, Fast and Furious. The government was selling arms to cartels, hoping to be able to trace them back when they were used in crimes and then have them as evidence. That's all public. They've testified before Congress. It has to be something deeper than that."

"He could have been trafficking himself by bringing something back," I said. "Receiving product in return for arms. What if he went around the cartels and they killed his daughter?"

"I don't know," Harold said. He took off his glasses and rubbed his forehead.

Lauritzia pulled away from me and dabbed her eyes.

"I can turn myself in," I said to Harold. "You find someone to represent me. I can show them: Hruseff and Dokes are somehow both tied in. And maybe that woman you went to see, Sabrina Stein. We can show them how Ana Lasser was the actual target of the hit. This will all come out."

"*What* will come out?" Harold shook his head cynically. "That this whole thing is just an elaborate scheme to cover up a secret government arms sale? And tell them what? That Dokes and Hruseff once worked together? Years ago? That Hruseff said to Curtis, 'This is for Gillian,' before he killed him? And that you traced it back to mean the victim's hometown? Tell them how Curtis followed it all back to that ambush in Culiacán? Do you have any documentation? His notes?"

"His computer was taken from the hotel room. By Dokes. I'm sure."

"You think any of this overrides the fact that you shot that agent? Or that it's any stronger than the evidence that you killed your husband? Assuming we can even protect you from Dokes. Or that you even

352

made it to trial. Are you planning on asking Lauritzia to testify in your behalf? And as to what? Hearsay, that her father may have told her? Which doesn't actually prove a thing. Are you going to put *me* on the stand? That I thought Sabrina Stein might have been holding something back? Well, I can't do it, Wendy. I'm already putting my family at risk as it is. I can't go into hiding like Lauritzia's father. What we need to know is what was behind this? Lauritzia, you say it was the guns. *What guns?* Guns to whom? How did it connect illicitly to the U.S. government? Do we have anything tying anything to this Lasser except the name of his hometown? *What* are they trying to hide, and who would have a motive to do so? And why?"

"There's only one way to find those things out." I let out a resolute breath. "Lauritzia said ask Cano—or ask the girl's father. So that's what I'll do."

Harold looked at me, incredulous.

"What choice do I have? You said yourself, if I turn myself in or if I'm caught, I'll be convicted. I'll be painted like some lunatic. I'm as good as Lauritzia. Put me back out on that street, and I'm dead."

"You're talking about the Zeta drug cartel, Wendy. These men are hardened killers. You don't have a fucking clue what they have to hide. You think he's just going to open up to you?"

"Then I'll have to find a way."

"*How?*"

"I don't know. I'll find one! He's lost a daughter. We've both lost someone we loved to Eduardo Cano. Grief is just as strong a motive as survival. Lauritzia knows that. And so do you. You brought me here."

"You can't just go out there alone! If you're wrong about any of this, you'll never be heard from again."

"She won't go out there alone," came Lauritzia's voice, and we both turned, surprised.

She looked at us both with resolve. "She won't be going alone. I will go too."

"Lauritzia, that's crazy. These people want to kill you . . ."

"Tell me what is my life worth here? Hiding . . . haunted by these ghosts."

"I'm sorry." Harold shook his head. "But not after what's happened. I can't allow that. Not now . . ."

She came across the table and placed her hand on his shoulder. "There is no person on this earth who has given more to me than you and your wife. You have given up everything because of me. And it is precisely because of that that I have to do this. I can't live in hiding for the rest of my life. Not if there's a chance that this can end. Even if it only ends for Wendy. Or for you."

"Lauritzia, you'll be risking everything we fought for."

"No, we fought for the end of Eduardo Cano, and that did not come. I am risking nothing now. What do I have?" She took Harold's hands and cupped them in her own. "There is a saying where I am from." She spoke in Spanish, then translated: " 'In life you have many keys, but only one opens the lock to your own story.' " Lauritzia turned to me. "You are right. You and me, we are the same. It is clear, your key is out there. But I have run and hid and cried and mourned, let myself feel anger and without hope, and what do I have? I need the truth too. I think it was fate that you came to find me. I think my key is out there too."

*"Your* key . . ." Harold pushed back his chair, like a helpless father no longer able to control his rebelling child. "What do you think you're going to find there?"

Whatever tears had burned in Lauritzia's eyes a moment earlier had dried, and in their place now there seemed to glisten a new understanding. A new resolve. "Eduardo Cano."

# CHAPTER FIFTY-EIGHT

Outside, the beat-up Toyota Corolla pulled to a stop about thirty feet behind the white Mercedes and cut the engine on the other side of the street.

Inside, a man with dark eyes and a narrow, pock-marked face watched as Harold went into the building. It took everything he had not to do it then. But he waited. A few minutes later Harold came back out and waved in the direction of his car. Then the woman went in too.

The man in the Toyota turned off the car lights.

He knew why the two were here and where they had gone. It made him feel good that he had finally found her. He would wait. He realized he'd learned nothing in his line of work if not patience. Ahead of him, a couple were walking their dog and crossed to his side of the street. There would be the right time to strike, and this wasn't it. But that time was almost upon them.

*La cuota*—it had to be paid. His. Hers. It was all of their fates. No one escaped it. It was all he knew.

He shifted the Spanish newspaper next to him on the passenger seat and checked on his gun. If he needed it, this was where the answer was.

The streetlights lit up with the blowing snowflakes. The couple who were walking their dog came back, this time on his side of the street. The man in the car placed his hand over his face as they passed by. Another car drove by, the tires crunching on the freshly spread sand. He hated the cold here. It was time to go back home. To the mountains and the endless stretching blue sky. The friendly jacaranda trees. Maybe when this was all done.

He had long covered over the line between virtue and wrong. It was a footprint washed away in the sand, the tide of his deeds making it invisible. His face and hands bore the marks of his trade—knife scars and fingers broken many times. Swollen like grotesque, disfigured things. He was a *sicario*, a killer. He had killed so many men—women, children too—he could no longer remember the faces or even bring them back in his dreams. He knew on the Day of the Dead they would all come back to him. Wearing their masks of life, they would dance around him, drag him off to hell, for there was no doubt that that's what his fate would be. He wondered, in that moment, when it was his time—when he saw the spark from the barrel aimed at him, because he knew that's how it would end for him—would it matter, that he knew he had wronged so many? That he attempted to right it?

This once.

To pay down his *cuota*.

The people with their dog were well past now, and he removed his hand from his face. The lamplight shone on him, exposing his pain for all to see, revealing one of the many tattoos etched on his neck.

The numbers 12 and 26 with a flower separating them. As if they were numbers from a death camp. But in this case they simply stood for letters of the alphabet.

Letters that had made him who he was. That had brought the dance of masks that haunted him in his sleep. Both his penance and his curse.

12. 26. The twelfth letter and the last.

*L* and *Z*.

Los Zetas.

# GILLIAN

# CHAPTER FIFTY-NINE

Joe Esterhaus waved to the man with the wiry dark hair as he came into the bar. With his broad shoulders and slick gray suit, the man might have fit the image of a mobster more than a senior agent with the FBI.

"Been a while, huh, Joe?" Bruce Paul smiled broadly and stepped up to him. His gaze landed on Esterhaus's wounded shoulder.

"Shower accident," Esterhaus said, and shrugged.

"Teach you not to do your showering at Grand Central," Paul said with a chuckle. "Club soda and lime," he said to the bartender.

Esterhaus shot him a look of surprise.

"Three years. Clean and sober." The FBI man shrugged. "Don't know what the hell took me so long."

"Arnold Palmer." Esterhaus raised his own glass. Iced tea and lemonade. "Guess it's been a while, huh?"

Bruce took his drink and they clinked glasses. "Yeah, guess it has."

They chatted for a while about some old buddies Esterhaus had lost touch with. He and Bruce had said hi a couple of times, at weddings and a funeral or two since Esterhaus left the force, but they hadn't really sat down together in more than six years.

At a lull, the FBI man turned to him. "So what's the occasion, Joe?"

Esterhaus put down his glass. "I need some help, Brucie. I need to get something passed to someone on the inside. Someone who isn't in anyone's lap."

"You mean someone completely marginalized." Bruce laughed. "It's not like the old days, Joseph. Shuffling paperwork in Nassau County is pretty much the end of the line for me. I got, what, maybe another year? Tommy Mara is already asking if I'd be interested in joining up with his security outfit."

"Someone *independent* is more what I was thinking." Esterhaus swiveled around and faced him.

"Okay, I'm listening." Bruce placed his drink down on the counter. "I'm the only one here."

"I went through her house." Esterhaus leveled his gaze on his old friend's eyes. He didn't need to spell out whose.

"That house is still a federal crime scene, isn't it, Joe?

362

Considering that shoulder, I thought you would have learned your lesson by now."

"She's innocent, Bruce. She's being set up."

"For God's sakes, Joe, the woman killed a government agent. One of us. She shot her own husband. And fled the scene . . . Look, I know you were tight with her dad—"

"She didn't kill her husband, Bruce."

"She shot him! In their own kitchen, for Christ's sake! With a gun that matched the one that killed that Homeland Security guy back at the hotel. The same hotel, I'm sure I don't have to remind you, from which she took off and ran."

"So if he was killed in the kitchen, as everyone says"— Esterhaus opened the envelope he had with him and took out a plastic baggie—"be a genius, Brucie, and tell me just what the guy's blood was doing out on the street, thirty yards away?"

Bruce Paul wrinkled his mouth without answering.

Esterhaus handed him the baggie containing the several clumps of dried blood he had taken from Wendy Gould's driveway. "I already got them checked out. I ran them against traces of the husband's blood I took out of the kitchen."

*"You took out of the kitchen?* What the hell is going on here, Joe?"

"We can talk about that later, Brucie. All that matters now is that David Gould wasn't shot in his kitchen like the investigators have said. He was shot on the street. Someone moved that body."

Esterhaus took out a pen and sketched on the manila envelope. "Look, they have this U-shaped driveway . . . The kitchen's here . . . Wendy claims she and her husband were in the garage, in their car about to leave, when lights flashed on behind them."

"*About to leave*? Jesus, Joe, it was in the middle of the fucking night!"

"I know it was in the middle of the night. She said she realized she'd left something behind at the hotel, some conference program or something. But something that could lead back to her. And she was right. So she freaked out and convinced him they had to get out of there. They were in the process of backing out of the garage when the authorities showed up. Not the police, Bruce. And this is important. The same Homeland Security guy from the hotel. She hit the gas and slammed into his car and started to drive away."

"Call me crazy, Joe, but doesn't that kind of thing usually fall under the heading of *escaping*?"

"The woman had just witnessed a man being killed! And it was the shooter's partner who was there for her at her house." Esterhaus circled a spot at the top of the driveway. "She said she stopped the car and her husband's body fell out about *here* . . . not in the kitchen. On the street." Esterhaus jabbed at the spot. "Which is where I found *this*." He tapped his finger on the dried blood.

364

Bruce wiped his hand across his face, starting to take in what Esterhaus was suggesting.

"They moved that body, Bruce. The very same people who tried to kill her at that hotel . . ."

"Where she had no right being, Joe. Unless she was up to no good."

"Where she had no right being, Bruce, I totally agree. But that doesn't mean it didn't happen just like she said. That doesn't mean she didn't stumble into some kind of a government kill squad with something important they wanted to keep quiet. This Curtis dude, the one who was killed in there, he was a journalist. Maybe he stumbled onto something he shouldn't have. Wouldn't be the first time. We go back over twenty years, Brucie. Why would the husband's blood be out on that street? She wasn't trying to run away, at Grand Central. She was turning herself in." He lifted his arm. "You honestly think this friggin' hole in my shoulder was actually intended for *me*?"

"Could have been anyone, then." Bruce chuckled amiably. "The list of suspects would be endless." He picked up the evidence baggie. "How do I know this is actually from where you say? Anything can be altered. You've already snuck into a federal crime scene. You more than anyone have a reason to want to see her cleared."

"The lab report's in there. And here's a series of photographs I took out on that street. You can see how things match up—the electrical box here . . . It's a frame-up, Brucie. What's behind it, I don't know. Only that it is."

Bruce leafed quickly through the report. When he looked back up, his lips twisted and his face resembled that of a person who had just taken a swallow of bad milk. "What exactly do you want me to do with this, Joe?"

"Someone needs to see it. Someone who won't just feed it into the shredder. Trust me, I wish I had someone else to bring it to."

"I'm a year away from retirement. You don't just drop this on someone's desk and go, 'Sorry to bother you, sir, but you know that case that's been the lead-in on every fucking newscast in the country? Well, the government's actually orchestrating this elaborate murder-cover-up scheme. And, oh, where'd I get this from? Some ex-detective pal of mine who was booted off the Nassau County force ten years ago' . . . It's like Fukushima, Joe. It's radioactive. At the end of the day, the only seat that's gonna be empty at the bureau is gonna be mine!"

"The people who want her dead, Bruce, are the same people who are in charge of bringing her in. We both know that's never going to happen."

The FBI man stared at Joe awhile, then stood up and put the evidence envelope under his arm. "And I thought you had tickets to a Rangers game or something . . ."

"You know how much I appreciate this, buddy."

"If you get an invitation to that early-retirement party, you'll know it didn't go over so well."

"I'll bring the club soda and lime."

"Always the life of the party." Bruce swallowed the rest of his drink and headed out of the bar.

# CHAPTER SIXTY

The trip out west took three days.

We took Lauritzia's Toyota, which Harold had rented for her back in Connecticut. The first night we made it all the way to Columbus, Ohio. We got a room at an Embassy Suites along the highway and basically just crashed.

The second night we got all the way to Kansas City.

That's where the reality of what we were actually doing hit me—and began to fill me with fear. And the nervousness that I was getting into something that was way, way over my head and that I had no idea how to control. That Robert Lasser was not the tragic victim of bloodshed he had no hand in, like Harold, Lauritzia, and me. But of bloodshed that he was a part of. Harold's warning kept ringing in my head: *These men are hardened killers. You don't have a clue what they have to hide.*

And now Lauritzia was on my shoulders too. We didn't talk much on the way out. If we had, we probably would have come to our senses and turned the car around. We shared much of the driving. When we did talk, I asked about her life back in Mexico, her brother and sisters. I admired a necklace she was wearing—a butterfly with a tiny diamond chip on a thin gold chain.

It made her smile with affection. "Miss Roxanne gave it to me. Before my trial. She said it stood for second chances. That we all could have them, no matter how lost it might seem."

I asked her what a second chance would look like for her, and she said being with her father again. Going back home.

"Maybe you should let me wear it sometime." I looked over and smiled. A sign told us that Missouri was a hundred miles ahead. "I could use one too."

We spent the second night at a motel outside Kansas City. It was the last day of October. There was a chill in the air. The star-rich midwestern sky stretched above.

I left Lauritzia sleeping and went outside, my blood racing with trepidation, cars on the highway whooshing by.

I felt about as alone as I have ever felt. I missed Dave so much. His strength. His humor. How he always had the skill of making something very complex seem simple. *I could use that about now!* I stood there with my back against a car, huddled in my fleece and a blanket, and I realized so painfully that I would never see him again. That whatever I was doing here, whatever I was trying to prove, it would not bring him back. That no matter how tightly I squeezed my fist, I would never wrap it around his hand again. My eyes filled up with tears. And once it started, I couldn't stop it. *Second chances,* I was thinking. I wanted my son and daughter back too. I hadn't even been able to be with them at their own father's funeral. I needed to feel them by me. I hadn't been able to grieve.

Everything I loved had been taken from me too.

I took out my iPhone. I knew everyone would be watching for it, waiting for a call. Just turning it on was dangerous; there was probably some built-in GPS they could use to find me there.

Suddenly I didn't fucking care. I just needed to feel close to my kids. To my old life. Just for one second. To turn everything back and have it be like it was before.

I thought about where they were. Maybe up at David's father's place in Madison, Connecticut. It was Halloween. Neil had always loved it. But no one would be partying now. I pictured their clapboard house near the Sound and the smoky, pipe-tobacco smell in the den. I didn't care about the danger. I began to text:

Neil, Amy,

I know you both judge me harshly, and that you think I did things that are unforgivable. And if I knew

370

only what people are alleging, and not the truth, I guess I might too.

I can't tell u where I am. Only that you will see in the end that I didn't do the things they say. I didn't shoot that agent to cover up that I was there. It happened in self-defense.

And I damn well didn't kill your dad.

Though I did betray him, or came close to, which is something no words can describe how much I regret. I miss him so much. I miss you all. When I wish I could turn back the clock, it's only our family that I long for. You, Amy-kins, and you, Neil, my handsome young man. But I can't turn it back. Whatever happens, life will never be the same. And that breaks my heart. I'm crying now.

And I'm scared.

My beautiful kids, I beg, beg, beg you to somehow hold back your scorn until you know the truth. And to remember that I love you both as deeply as if you came from my own womb. I always have. And I always will.

My deepest, deepest love,
Wendy

I looked up at the sky and thought how if I just pressed Send, it would take a second until they read this. Until they felt what was in my heart. I placed my finger on the key . . .

I stopped. I knew I couldn't press it. The police would be on us in minutes. At the very least they would know where we were.

It wasn't just for me; I had Lauritzia now.

I read what I'd written one more time, and it made me smile. *I love you, babies . . .*

Then I pressed Delete and shut down my phone.

# CHAPTER SIXTY-ONE

The next day we crossed into Colorado.

We got off I-70 in Denver and headed south toward Albuquerque on I-25. In an hour or so we passed by Colorado Springs, signs for the Air Force Academy and Pikes Peak. In another hour, Pueblo.

Forty minutes later we exited the highway on Route 160.

It was a two-lane road, and we climbed through the front range of the snowcapped Rockies. At eight thousand feet we entered the vast San Luis Valley, an endless, barren plain of sand and tundra that stretched out on both sides along the black outline of the Sangre de Cristo Mountains.

I saw a sign for Gillian, 30 miles.

My adrenaline started to rise.

I could see a huge white expanse tucked into the

foothills of the 14,000-foot mountains, and we passed a turnoff for something called the Great Sand Dunes National Park. It turned out to be sand—30,000 square miles of dunes, the highest in the United States, some rising 750 feet. Blown there over thousands of years by the winds whipping across the valley floor. The sight of the Sahara-like dunes against the dark mountains was both beautiful and foreboding in the melting afternoon light, but it wasn't why we were there.

GILLIAN. 10 MILES

There was nothing for a long time, not even a building in the vast, barren wasteland. Then we began to see auto parts warehouses and fast-food outlets. The Rio Grande railroad yards. Signs for a college.

We passed a rundown main street of old brick bank buildings and dingy 1960s storefronts—a once-thriving western town decades had passed by.

"Let's find a motel," I said. "We'll figure out what to do tomorrow."

Something called the Inn of the Rio Grande appeared on the right, with a large, white stucco façade. It looked clean, and we were exhausted. I turned in to the driveway, pulling to a stop in a vacant parking space.

I just looked at Lauritzia. She nodded back. There wasn't much to say.

We were here.

# CHAPTER SIXTY-TWO

The man with the pockmarked face drove past the white stucco motel.

He'd been following the blue Toyota for three days now. He continued on, turning into a Conoco station a hundred yards down. He was exhausted, but patience had rewarded him again.

In a few days, he could sleep for a month if he wanted.

Once they got off I-70 in Denver and headed south, he knew where they were heading. He'd known that all along.

He also knew why they were there.

The man pulled up to a vacant pump and began to fill his car. Then he went inside to pee. It felt like he hadn't relieved himself in a year. Tonight he would think of how the next days would go. How he would get it done. He had removed some cash from his leather satchel under the seat across from him, wrapping a newspaper around his gun.

Outside, he watched as the sun slid over the mountains into the horizon. He took out his phone. He removed a piece of paper from his jeans and punched in the number on it, and spoke in his best English when an operator answered.

"Homeland Security Tip Line."

"Senior Agent Alton Dokes, please."

"Agent Dokes is unavailable right now. I can assist you if you have information on the Wendy Gould case you'd like to pass on."

"I do have information." The man took off his sunglasses. "I want you to tell him I also have information about the tenth of March in Culiacán."

The operator hesitated. "Can I have your name, please, sir? I'll need to tell him who this is."

"Just tell him it's about Culiacán. He'll come to the phone."

He waited; the operator placed him on hold. He figured they had already begun a trace, but he had planned this out very carefully over the long ride out and a trace didn't bother him now. Finally he was patched through to another line. The voice that answered sounded officious and not happy to be summoned. "This is Special Agent Dokes."

"I know where she's headed," the man said, squinting into the setting sun.

"Who?" the Homeland Security agent answered, pretending surprise.

"You know who I'm talking about."

"If you have information you'd like to share concerning a federal investigation, I can certainly pass you back to the tip-line operator . . ."

"If that's what you want. I just thought this was something you were far better off knowing yourself."

"Who is this?" Dokes lowered his voice, his tone still commanding.

"The better question would be *where* . . . where I am. And the answer would be Route One-Six-Oh in Colorado. I think you know that road, don't you, *agente*? The town it goes through?"

There was a silence on the other end.

"She's in Gillian," the pockmarked man said. "And guess who she's brought with her. Someone else you may be interested in. Someone Eduardo Cano would wet his panties to find." He laughed. "You know why they've come here. So that ought to make you sleep like a baby tonight, right, huh *agente*?"

The man hung up and smiled, knowing where the next call would go.

And the call after that.

*See you soon, amigo,* the man said, chuckling, as he got back into his car.

It felt like he hadn't smiled in years.

# CHAPTER SIXTY-THREE

The next morning we waited outside Lasser's company's headquarters.

Apache Sales and Marketing was situated in a modern, one-story brick-and-glass building attached to a large warehouse in a business park on Route 17, five miles outside town. I had no idea how I'd go about convincing him to tell us what we were there for. "I'm Wendy Gould. I'm on the run for the murder of my husband and for shooting a Homeland Security agent. I know you've been secretly selling weapons to the Mexican drug cartels. And knowing why your daughter was killed is the only way I can clear my name and show I'm innocent . . ."

*That would sell.*

He'd call the cops on us immediately. There had to

be some kind of security department in a business this size; they wouldn't even let me leave. No, I had to talk to him when he was alone. At home, or on his way back from lunch maybe. Not to mention that he wasn't exactly an innocent victim in all this and had likely done things that had gotten his daughter killed. Things, like Harold said, he would absolutely want to protect.

We drove into the parking lot at 8:30 A.M. and noticed an empty space marked LASSER next to the building's entrance. He wasn't there. We parked our Toyota in a visitor's space nearby. An hour passed. A couple of dozen employees arrived and went inside. No Lasser. The longer he didn't show up, the more worried I became. What if the guy wasn't even around? What if he was on a business trip, visiting his other locations? Or on holiday? We could wait another day for him, maybe two. But not indefinitely. We'd stick out pretty good.

Around 10:00 A.M., I was set to do the same thing I'd done while I was waiting for Harold at his office, call in and ask for him, when a white Audi A6 pulled into the driveway and parked in Lasser's spot.

A decal on the back windshield read UNIVERSITY OF DENVER.

"That's him!"

He stepped out of the car, and I recognized him immediately from the photos on Apache's website. He was medium height and solidly built, wearing a blue North Face nylon jacket, plaid shirt, no tie. Fancy boots.

He had close-cropped light hair and a sharp, chiseled face. He seemed around fifty.

He was on his cell phone, a leather satchel slung over his shoulder. He went behind his car and passed about ten feet from us. Lauritzia gave me a nod of good luck. I opened the door, but something held me back.

He was occupied. I knew it wouldn't work, just running up and starting in. This guy had dealt with the cartels. His daughter had been killed four years earlier in some kind of retaliation. Harold's voice echoed again: *You don't have a clue what they have to hide.*

I hesitated, watching Lasser end his phone call and head up to the entrance. He opened the glass doors and went inside.

"I'm sorry." I turned to Lauritzia. "I couldn't do it now."

"It's okay."

"No, it's not." I noticed my hands were shaking. I was afraid.

I suddenly realized how crazy it was to try and do this at his office. I suggested we could follow him when he went to lunch. But as we sat, people going in and out, large delivery trucks heading around to the loading gates, another hour going by, I just said the hell with it and took out my phone. "I can't wait any longer."

I called the number I had for Lasser's company. An operator answered. "Apache Sales and Marketing."

"Mr. Lasser, please."

"One moment, please."

I was patched through to a secretary. An accommodating voice came on. "Mr. Lasser's office."

"Is Mr. Lasser there?"

"May I say who's calling?"

I took a breath. I hadn't rehearsed this. I wasn't sure what to say. "This may seem a bit out of the blue . . . but it relates to his daughter . . . Ana." I shut my eyes. But what else was there to say?

If pauses could kill, this one was lethal. The voice on the other end grew guarded. "Can I ask you to be more specific, please?"

"I can't . . . It'll only take a minute of his time . . ." I was pretty much stammering. *"Please."*

My heart started to race as she paused an awkward moment more and then told me to hold on. I wasn't sure that Lasser would even take the call. His daughter had been dead for close to four years now, so while the pain of it might have receded some, someone calling like this from out of nowhere, bringing it up again, might only hurtle him back to a place he did not want to be.

Then I heard someone pick up. "This is Bob Lasser."

My heart went completely still. My throat dry. His voice was clipped and not particularly friendly. A knot formed in my throat. "Mr. Lasser, thank you for taking the call. I know I made that sound a bit vague . . ."

"I'm on the line," he answered, "at least for about as long as it takes to tell you I'm not in the habit of discussing personal matters with someone I don't know. Just what is it about my daughter, Ms. . . . ?"

"I was hoping I could get some time with you, Mr. Lasser. Alone. Maybe outside the office. Today, if that would work out for you. I have something I need to go over with you, and you're the only person who can help me. I've come a long way."

"Help *you*? You're here? In Gillian?" He sounded surprised.

"Yes. I am."

"Then in the ten seconds I'm going to allot you to explain why you've contacted me, just exactly what does this have to do with Ana?"

"I'm sorry, I just can't tell you over the phone. But I know about the circumstances of her death. Including why . . . I also know how hard it is to lose someone. *I've* lost someone . . ."

"Listen, whoever the hell you are, I'm sorry, but I don't really have the time or the inclination to go through this with you. I'm going to hang up now and ask you not to ever—"

"Do you know the name Curtis Kitchner?" I interrupted him.

This time there was only silence. A silence that strongly suggested that he did. Or that his secretary was dialing the police on the other phone at this very second.

"Are you a reporter? Because if you are, I'm sure you've been told, I don't speak to them. At least, not

382

about this . . . not to mention, you're also a little late to the party. This all happened years ago. Now I'm going to hang up, so thank you very much for respecting the privacy of my family—"

"I'm not a reporter," I said. I waited for the *click*, but there was none. "Curtis was. And now he's dead. He was killed. Ten days ago in New York. I don't know if you know. In a hotel room. By—"

"I watch the news." He cut me off. "I know what happened. And what happened ought to make it pretty clear to you, you shouldn't go around asking similar types of questions. Now this conversation is over, whoever you are. Do not bother me again. Don't call me here. Don't call me at home. Don't bother my family. If you do, I'll be calling the police. This is a small town, and I'm very well connected in it. Just get yourself out of town. Do you understand?"

This time I did hear the *click*, my heart plummeting with it. I turned to Lauritzia.

"I could hear the whole thing," she said. "He sounds like a dangerous man. Maybe he's right. Maybe we should go back."

"To what, jail? And what for you—hiding?"

"If you call again, he could get the police on you as he said, and then what happens? Even worse . . ."

"We've come this far. I need to talk to him. Besides," I said, putting the car in gear, "next time I'm not going to call."

383

# CHAPTER SIXTY-FOUR

The heavyset man with the goatee in the poplin suit and white linen shirt stepped up to the passport control booth at the Denver International Airport. He nodded politely to the blue-shirted officer there and put his Guatemalan passport through the glass.

José Maria Rivera.

"How long do you plan to spend in the United States, Mr. Rivera?" the immigration officer inquired, looking up and eyeing him through the glass.

"Around ten days. I'm doing some business in Colorado," the portly man said.

"What kind of business?" The immigration official flipped through the green passport, which indicated that the person in front of him was a very worldly man. There were stamps from Germany and the United

Kingdom. Honduras, Argentina, and Brazil. Even from the United States several times.

"I'm in real estate. I represent a buyer in Central America who is looking at an investment here."

"Yet you came in from Mexico?"

"My son is studying medicine there. In Mexico City. I try to visit when I can."

The officer nodded and ran the document through the scanner, tapping into the shared databases of Homeland Security, the FBI, and Interpol. Not a single bead of sweat ran down the traveler's face. Why should it? He had been through these interviews routinely under a number of different aliases. *And they say that the U.S. border with Mexico is porous,* he said to himself, chuckling. The easiest way to get in was to go right through the front door.

"My neighbor's son is studying to be a doctor," the immigration officer said with a sigh. "*Mine* . . . can't figure out what he wants to be." He leafed to an open page in the passport and gave it a stamp. "I hope your business goes well," the official said, and pushed it back through the glass.

Eduardo Cano smiled and tucked it into his jacket pocket.

"And welcome to the United States."

# CHAPTER SIXTY-FIVE

We couldn't hang around Lasser's place forever without attracting attention. So we crossed the road to another company's parking lot that gave us a view of the road.

I was hoping Lasser would come out to lunch. He never did.

Around 3:00 P.M., Lauritzia began to complain about feeling weak. Maybe from the drive out or the altitude—we were at eight thousand feet. So I ran her back to the motel to lie down. When I got back, Lasser's Audi was still in its space. Around five, it began to get dark. Employees started to leave. I was still annoyed and frustrated that my call had gone so poorly.

My prepaid cell phone rang. Other than Lauritzia, there was only one person who had the number. It was almost seven back home.

"How's it going?" Harold asked.

"It's going," I replied halfheartedly. I told him about my botched call. "You find out anything I should know?"

He was continuing to look into Lasser's affairs, trying to confirm the gun transactions to Mexico.

"I have someone digging into the General Accounting Office records in Washington. According to what he's found, Apache Sales and Marketing has been an approved government vendor for some twelve years. It was started by his father, selling to Indian reservations. He died in 1995. Then they opened up on the border and began doing consumer goods sales to wealthy Mexicans who came across the border. It was like a boom town back then. They would come over for the day and pay cash for Sonys, Samsung. Washers and dryers. Brands that were three times as expensive down there. They would literally back up trucks. It was a gray-market kind of thing, and both governments just looked the other way. Then in 1994 the North American Free Trade Agreement was enacted and that was the end of all that. These brands could now all sell direct without the punishing tariffs. Apache is a private firm, so actual numbers aren't available, but in 2008 and 2009, the GAO lists several million dollars a year done in business with the U.S. government."

"How many millions?"

"Two point five in '08. Three point seven in '09."

"That is a lot. Any chance you happened to find invoices that list the items sold?"

"That's the thing . . . They were transacted as business loans. To build trade with what they called 'enterprise zones.' Which would likely be Indian reservations . . ."

"But you're thinking those were black-market guns that illegally crossed the border?"

"Could be. Transshipped from companies like Remington and Colt. Apache also lists some European manufacturers who make these high-velocity pistols they call cop killers."

"Over six million dollars is an awful lot of weapons," I said.

"And that's at wholesale. Double that to get the retail value. And it's only the tip. There's also something called 'ghost inventory.' "

"*Ghost* inventory?"

"Since 2008, the government figures some sixty-two thousand firearms have gone missing from U.S. gun retailers. They just fall off the books, but it's obvious where they go. According to my source, it's estimated that some two thousand guns, from AR-15 submachine guns to Barrett fifty-caliber rifles to these five-by-seven-millimeter pistols they call 'cop killers,' are smuggled across the border to Mexico literally every day."

"I thought these things all fell under some kind of government scrutiny?"

"On the contrary," Harold said, "this is all happening with tacit government approval. We already spoke about Fast and Furious, which was this program that put U.S. guns in the hands of Mexican cartels in order to trace them if they were later used in crimes. Lasser might well have had a hand in that . . ."

"But Harold, what I don't understand is, if Lasser was secretly shipping arms to Mexican cartels *with* U.S. government approval, both Washington and the cartels were his partners. What could he have done to Cano that warranted getting his daughter killed?"

"I thought that's what you were there to find out," he said with a grim chortle.

"Hold it a minute!" My blood snapped to attention as the door to Lassiter's building opened and Lasser finally came out. He stood at the entrance, chatting for a while with two other men, who looked to be employees. They walked Lasser to his car, continuing the conversation. "Our boy's about to leave. I'm going to follow him."

"Just be careful, Wendy. The more I find out on this, the more anxious I am that you're there. These people have a lot to hide."

"I promise. I'm not trying to be a hero," I told him. "More later." I hung up.

The three kept talking around Lasser's Audi. Nothing suspicious. It was probably nothing more than a billing thing, or how to speed up shipments out the warehouse.

Finally Lasser opened the door. There was no chance to get him alone. The two others waved good-bye, and Lasser climbed into his car. He turned on the ignition and started to back out.

I started up the Toyota and put it into gear.

The Audi pulled out of the lot and onto the main road that wound through the large office park. I waited until he went by, then pulled out of the lot across the street and blended in, several car lengths behind. I knew I had to keep my distance. A few other vehicles from Apache's lot had pulled out after me. I let a Jetta get in between us. Lasser's white Audi was hard to miss.

I had no idea where he was heading, but I decided to follow. If he was heading home, I resolved to find the courage to knock on his front door. I wondered if his wife knew the truth about their daughter. Why she'd been killed. I wondered if she even knew Lasser was involved in shipping guns down to Mexico.

Eventually Route 17 fed back into 160, the main thoroughfare that led into town. Traffic was steady, even all the way out there, with the afternoon rush. Lasser headed toward town. I had to speed up at a light or two just to keep up—I wasn't exactly a pro at this—or else I would have fallen too far behind and lost him.

He drove back into central Gillian, with its dark main boulevard and closed-up movie theater and empty storefronts. Three cars ahead, Lasser pulled into a turn lane, signaling left. The traffic arrow was already green; I'd let a couple of cars get in between us, and one of them drove at a snail's pace. Lasser's Audi sped away. Finally I swerved around just in front of a large truck as the light turned yellow. All I needed was to get stopped by a cop here. It would be over! But if I missed the light, I might well lose him. I held my breath and glanced around as I sped up after him. No flashing lights. I was okay.

Continuing on 160, I picked him up again, a hundred yards ahead. The light had thinned, and it was hard to make vehicles out. Finally he pulled down a road and I saw him make a right into a restaurant parking lot. The Sandy Dunes Brew Tap. I let a few seconds pass and turned in after him. Lasser parked quickly and literally went right past me on his way in, not even giving me a glance as I drove by.

I parked in a corner of the lot and waited a couple of minutes, steeling my courage. I finally said the hell with it, and got out of the car and went into the bar. It was a large, barnlike structure, and it was clear this was *the* after-work meeting place for people in town.

The place was crowded. I hung on the landing, trying to pick out Lasser in the crowd. The pretty hostess smiled at me. "Dining with us tonight?"

"No." I shook my head. "Waiting for someone. I think I'll just head up to the bar."

"Margaritas are two for one tonight."

"Thanks." Just what I needed. The last margarita I'd had had gotten me into all this!

The bar area was crowded and filled with smoke; clearly the antismoking laws hadn't made it out this way. I squeezed through a few groups and managed to find an opening amid the crowd: mostly people in T-shirts and jeans, the occasional cowboy hat. I found a spot at the frosted-glass partition separating the bar from the dining area. There were a few TVs with sporting events on over the bar. I looked around for Lasser.

I didn't see him at first. The place was large, with several different levels. A massive copper brew tank and other equipment glistened behind a glass wall. For a moment I felt the sensation that I'd been duped, that Lasser had merely gone in and slipped out a rear entrance, knowing he was being followed. Or that he was staring at me from somewhere.

But then I spotted him in the crowd. With another guy—prematurely gray, in a blazer and jeans. They'd pulled up a couple of beers and found a table away from the bar. At some point, through the maze of faces, his gaze seemed to center on me.

I shifted out of his angle of sight.

It looked like any normal conversation. The guy could have been a business contact or a contractor looking to do a project, or even some golfing buddy from his club. I squeezed my way up to the bar and caught the eye of the bartender, a good-looking guy in a white polo shirt with the restaurant logo embroidered on it. He definitely looked like he was in training for something.

"What's on tap?" I asked above the noise. A lemon-drop martini would have been nice—it had been ten days since I'd had as much as a glass of wine. But I wanted to stay on my game.

He listed the beers—there were a lot of them. I went for something called Fat Tire out of Aspen, and when it came, it was a deep amber and frosty and cold. "Start a tab?"

"Not tonight." I pulled out a few bills and left them on the bar.

He waved thanks.

I took another sip and went back to my spot, one eye on Lasser, who shifted in and out of view, blocked by the people at the bar. A chubby guy in a sport jacket and cowboy hat swiveled around and raised his glass to me. "Evening . . ."

I smiled.

If the situation wasn't so nerve-racking, I might've laughed over it being an almost identical situation that had put me in this mess, but with a decidedly different-looking guy. I lifted my drink in return, just enough to thank him, and to indicate I wasn't interested. I only imagined how I looked, in my blue pullover fleece and my hair pulled back, and not having primped myself in ten days.

I shifted back and tried to relocate Lasser, hoping that when he left, I might be able to find him alone.

But he seemed to have found me.

393

Our eyes connected—just for an instant. Just enough to tell me he was aware he was being watched. I pulled away, my heart picking up crazily.

He got on the phone.

# CHAPTER SIXTY-SIX

I suddenly felt a rush of nerves all over me. Like I was no longer in control. Like I'd been discovered and had to get out of there now.

I took a last swig of beer and edged my way through the crowd toward the entrance, pushing back the feeling that Lasser had gotten up as well and was about to tap me on the back at any second and send my heart through my throat. I stepped up onto the landing and allowed myself a quick glance around. But he wasn't there.

I went past two new people coming in and found my way outside. The film of sweat that had built up on my neck began to recede. Maybe I was just a little jumpy, but I still hadn't accomplished what I came here to do. I looked around for his Audi, deciding I'd wait and catch him at his car. I blew out a breath and fanned myself with my hand.

It was one of those crisp Colorado nights with a million stars. It reminded me of all the times Dave and I had spent out there skiing at Snowmass or Beaver Creek. I heard the sound of rushing water nearby and went to the wooden railing at the edge of the lot to take a look. It turned out to be about ten feet or so above a river, probably the Rio Grande. I felt cold spray on my face as I leaned over.

Suddenly someone grabbed me from behind.

Whoever it was took my arm and wrenched it around my back. My heart almost shot up my throat. I was certain it was Lasser—that my fears hadn't been as crazy as I thought—but it wasn't. It was an older guy, a rolled-up ponytail, a white western shirt and jeans. Tobacco on his breath.

I felt the chilling sensation of something cold and metallic pressed into my neck.

"Don't you scream, honey. Don't you even make a sound. I'll break your neck right here and toss your body into that river there, and, I promise, no one'll have as much as a thought you were even here until they find you next spring."

He turned me around and dug those gray, metallic eyes deep into me, and I didn't doubt for a second he'd do exactly what he said.

My heart thumping, I just nodded. "Okay."

"Good. You're quite the ticket, aren't you, darlin'? Which would make it all the harder what I'd have to do. But I will. Be sure of that. The problem is, some of us don't know what a fine-looking specimen like you is up to all alone in town here. But you're gonna tell me, aren't you?" He still had the gun dug under my jaw. "You're gonna tell me or I'm gonna do something I'm not inclined to do. You're understanding me, aren't you, darlin'?"

"I'm here to see someone," I said, my nerves akimbo. "They'll be here at any second. Put a hand on me, and I'll scream."

"Scream all you like." He grinned, two wide gaps in his smile. He forced me to the far side of a red pickup truck, blocking us from view. "Go on, but the first sound you make that isn't what I'm hoping to hear, there'll be a bullet through the top of your pretty little brain, and the poor fella who owns this Ford here ain't gonna like what it looks like when he comes back from his meal."

I nodded, trembling. "What do you want?"

"What I want, darlin', is to turn you right around and show you how the deer and the buffalo roam. But what I'll settle for is what is it you want here from Mr. Lasser? And what is it you claim to know 'bout his little girl? And mostly, just why the fuck is any of it your business in the first place?"

My hands braced up against the cool side of the truck

he had me up against. "I need to speak with him," I said. "Lasser."

"Mister Lasser, I believe you're meaning. Say it again, but right this time. We pay attention to our manners out here."

"*Mr. Lasser,*" I said, staring into his hard, cold eyes.

"You a reporter? Some kind of investigator maybe?"

I was so scared I could barely answer. Just shook my head.

"*Police?* Maybe the feds? C'mon, honey, I know you're not out here to see the dunes."

"If I was with the feds, don't you think you'd be facedown eating dirt in the parking lot by now with a gun against your head?"

He dug the gun deeper under my chin. Terrifying me. "God help me, lady, it's gonna take just one second for me to take you out of this world, and it won't even be on the list of the worst things I done today . . . No, by the way you're shaking, I suspect you're not a cop. But I am gonna have to check it out anyway, you understand? Just to be sure . . ."

He put his hand on my butt, groping the pocket of my jeans as if he was looking for some kind of ID. If this bastard's name wasn't Clem or Earl or whatever, his folks had missed a world-class naming opportunity. He brought his hand to my front, letting his arm brush palpably against my chest, all the while just smirking with his bright eyes to let me know he was enjoying it. He dug under my top, looking for a wire or maybe for some ID. I was too scared to even flinch. I just looked back in his eyes in helpless anger, breathing heavily, his fingers lingering on my bra. Even in the dark, his eyes had the gleam of a coyote and his dead smile convinced me he'd do what he said.

"Well, what do you know." He chuckled. "Not a thing."

When I didn't say anything again he just let his rough, calloused hand drift down my skin, until it found my belt, and he just kind of flicked his thumb against the edge of my jeans, three or four times, just to let me know it was there, all the while leering that creepy, I'm-in-control-here smile at me.

I stayed frozen.

I said, "I know how his daughter died. Mr. Lasser's. I know she was killed by the Zeta drug cartel, who made it seem like it was a hit on two DEA agents. But I know she was the actual target there. I also know he was shipping guns to the Juarte cartel. For the U.S. government . . ."

"Keep it going, sweetheart." Clem or Earl smiled his gap-toothed smile. "I'm liking how you're sounding now."

"I know there was a reporter who came to talk to him a couple of months back. His name was Kitchner. Who probably knew the same things too. And that whatever he was doing continued on up in the U.S.

government." He moved the gun straight into my face and put the muzzle against my forehead. "All I know is that it's high enough that people are willing to kill to keep it a secret, which is exactly how this Kitchner died, by the hands of a government agent . . ."

Suddenly I heard the sound of pebbles being crunched nearby. Boots walking on gravel.

My head jerked to the side, my heart pounding so loudly, I couldn't hear the sound of the river anymore.

Lasser came into view.

"You seem to know quite a lot, Ms. Gould," he said, taking off his glasses. "So I guess my next question is . . . other than whether I should let Emmit here go to work on you for good . . . if you know all you say you do, just why the hell are you here?"

*Emmit.* I pulled myself out of his grip. *How did I miss that one?* I looked at Lasser, knowing that what I said next would either save me or cost me my life.

"I need to know why your daughter died."

# CHAPTER SIXTY-SEVEN

"Emmit, do me a favor and grab a smoke over there and let the two of us have a word." Lasser nodded toward a spot about ten feet away. "You've been very persuasive, as usual."

"Yes, sir, Mr. Lasser." Emmit removed his hand with a kind of you're-one-*lucky-girl* snicker and went over to a Jeep just out of earshot and leaned against the hood.

"I could easily let him kill you, Ms. Gould, and maybe I still will. I might well be doing a lot of people a very large favor."

I took a deep breath and tried to regain my composure. "How did you know who I was?"

"You think we're just a bunch of cow chips out here? Me, I'm just a country businessman trying to live a private life. Privacy is very important to me. And I don't like it when people stick their noses into things they shouldn't be and scratch the scab off old wounds."

"You can be sure," I said to him, "I'd rather be anywhere else in the world."

He chuckled and pulled out a cigarette, lit it with a flashy lighter with a turquoise stone, blew out a plume of smoke. "I suspect you would. So why did you come here, then? Why have you tried to contact me?"

"Your daughter was killed by Eduardo Cano . . ."

"My daughter was shot in Mexico with two of her friends from college. She was caught in an ambush that was aimed at two corrupt DEA agents, who happened to be stopped at the same place . . ."

I looked at him. "Mr. Lasser, we both know that's not true."

"*Why?*" He took another drag, his measuring gaze drilled into my eyes. "Why would the details of Ana's death be of any matter to you? I'm long out of the game. I'm not some big prize. No one cares about me. The U.S. government. The narco boys. You ever heard the term *la cuota*, Ms. Gould? That which is owed. Well, I've paid that debt. A lot dearer than most. I'm out. I'm just a private guy trying to remain so. There aren't any big stories here."

"I've paid too." I nodded.

"Yes, I suspect you have. Much in the same way you seem to have your doubts about Ana, I figure it's likely the same about you. Your husband. I know how these things work. And I'm truly sorry, Ms. Gould. But not so sorry that I'm going to let you come around here and tear my life apart again and reopen old wounds. I earned my out. And I intend to keep it that way. So I ask you again, Emmit and I here are just itching to hear it from you. *Why?*"

"Curtis Kitchner came to see you, didn't he? He knew about all this. The same things I know. That you were selling guns to the cartels. As a middleman for the U.S. government. Cano."

Lasser nodded, just a twitch of his chin. "Go on."

"The man who killed him in New York. He was a government agent. He said, 'This is for Gillian,' just before he pulled the trigger. I think you know the rest of the story. I was there."

Lasser sniffed amusedly. "Seems like Door Number Three was definitely the wrong choice that day, wasn't it?"

"Yes. It was. At first I thought it was a person, of course. This Gillian. Everyone was trying to pin it on me—that I had killed the man in some kind of panic. And then killed my husband. So I had to prove I'd stumbled into something a whole lot more secret than just a roll in the hay. Like a hit. So I followed what Curtis had been working on. I came across the Culiacán shootings, then, virtually by accident, your daughter's photos at her school, and then I read where she was

403

from. Then it all kind of came together: That she had been the actual target of what happened down there, not the Bienvienes. Now the only question is why?"

"Ana's photos." Lasser smiled wistfully. "Least they came to *some* use."

"Mr. Lasser, I made a big mistake being in a place I should never have been. I've lost my husband. My family. My freedom. *My* life's been taken too. I think we both know, the people charged with bringing me in would rather see me dead than in jail. We also both know why. Well, I want out too. And I've damn well earned it as well. I can show that the man who killed Curtis in that hotel room was with the DEA in El Paso at the same time as the agent currently heading the federal task force charged with bringing me in.

"And that they were both there, at the Kitano Hotel, that night. And that they both worked for the same person in El Paso, who is now running the DOJ's department on narco-terrorism. I have every reason to believe they were all somehow connected to Cano, and that they were part of the plot to kill your daughter. What I don't know is why. What was behind Curtis Kitchner's death? What did he know that I still don't? I was a witness to his murder, and now they're trying to cover that up. They don't want to capture me, Mr. Lasser. They want to silence me."

Lasser took a last drag on his cigarette. "You *have* had your hands full, haven't you, now? And you think by knowing why my daughter died you can get your life back?"

I shook my head. "I'll never have my life back, any more than you. That's gone. But maybe, just maybe, I can get back my children's trust. You have other kids, Mr. Lasser? I know you do."

He hesitated before answering and finally just shrugged. "Yes."

"Do they know? Do they know why their sister died? Does your wife know?" Lasser's look hardened, but he seemed to get what I was saying. "So how did you earn it, Mr. Lasser? Your *cuota*. Tell me: Why did Ana have to die?"

He tossed down his cigarette butt and stamped it into the gravel with the heel of his boot. I couldn't tell if he was weighing my nerve at asking him the question I just had and was about to call ol' Emmit back over. Or if something else was brewing in him. The feeling like, *what the hell. None of it matters now.*

I kept on him. "You were selling arms to the Mexico cartels, weren't you?"

"Nothing illegal in that. They were businessmen too. I've sold merchandise across the border for twenty years. Big-screen TVs, VCRs. Levi's. Ralph Lauren. How they got them home was their business."

"AR-15 semiautomatics? Cop-killer pistols?"

"Guns are simply product to me. It rubs you the wrong way, write your congressman. That's what I do."

"Then, *what*? The government approached you to act as an intermediary to the cartels?'

A couple walked by us to their car. They seemed to have had a few too many.

"NAFTA turned my world upside down," Lasser said, turning away from the noise. "We went from a thriving business, people coming across the border in droves, backing trucks up to our warehouse. Wads of cash you'd only see in a casino. Then, *poof* . . ." He snapped his fingers. "Gone! In a year there were Apple showrooms on the Plaza San Jacinto in Mexico City. Costcos in Guadalajara. So you figure, how can something be illegal if it comes from the U.S. government?"

I let him go on.

"Don't you get it . . . some twenty-five billion dollars a year finds its way into the Mexican economy from the narco trade. Some forty-odd banks there show assets of over ten billion that no one can explain or trace where they come from. And it's not just the Mexican economy. You've got narco tycoons buying up real estate in Miami and Southern California. Half the hedge funds on Wall Street wouldn't divulge where half their money comes from. And of course the gun trade here. You think I wanted in on this? I was just riding a wave. My Ana was pretty as a rose in springtime. And talented."

I nodded. "I saw her photos."

"You walked into that hotel room . . ." He drew in a breath and shook his head. "And I—"

"You were selling guns directly to the Mexican cartels." I cut him off. "Guns that were purchased by the U.S. government with money that was repaid to you as interest-free loans. More than six million dollars in just two years. But you're not telling me it all . . . Everyone already knows about the gun trade to the drug cartels. This Fast and Furious program. That's all come out. Eduardo Cano sided with the Juartes. So what did you do to incur their wrath? And the wrath of the U.S. government?"

"What no one will ever tell you, Ms. Gould . . ." Lasser leaned back against the truck. "Several years back the Mexican government came to the conclusion this was a war they couldn't win. But that in order to regain control of their country, to stop the killings—judges, reporters, regional politicians—to get people back out on the streets, the war had to end. There had to be a winner. You cannot have a civilized country in the Western Hemisphere where over seventy newspaper and TV journalists, two dozen elected judges, hundreds of policemen and elected officials, are brutally killed."

"I understand."

"So the only way out was to take sides. Go with the strongest player. So the Calderón government made its peace with the Juartes against their rivals. And it got its big brother to the north to agree. At least, certain factions within it . . ."

407

"So all these millions you sold for the U.S. government were sent to the Juarte cartel?" I furrowed my brow. "That seems madness."

"The U.S. government wasn't trying to curb the drug trade, Ms. Gould . . ." Lasser shrugged. "Only trying to end the violence. The trade itself, it's a boon. It's good times for everybody. That's why this war had to be put to an end. It was interfering in the commerce. In everything. So they took sides."

"And you were the delivery pipeline? And Curtis found this out?"

"He came around here asking the same questions. I told him he didn't have long to live if he kept asking around."

But it still didn't answer *my* question. Why had Cano turned on him? What had Lasser done to deserve his wrath?

Suddenly it came clear.

What everyone was trying to keep buried. Why Oscar Velez had to be silenced—if it ever came out just who the real, intended target was. Why Curtis was killed, his computer files destroyed.

It wasn't just the illegal selling of guns to the cartels. That was just the first course.

The main event was that they had taken sides. That the United States government was secretly arming a cadre of murdering thugs and abetting drug traffickers across the border. That they were spilling blood and had their own hands in dozens of hooded assassinations and bodies left headless on the road. All in the hope that one billion-dollar narco conglomerate would destroy their rivals, and there would be stability there.

One winner.

And least, as Lasser had said, certain factions within it.

"How high did this go?" I asked, glancing at Emmit, who was catching a chew, wondering if I was ever going to get the chance to tell this story.

"I don't know how high. To me it was all simply merchandise. They were customers. I received instructions from one particular person. I never knew the person's name. Only their code name. The operation's name."

"And what was that?" I pressed.

Lasser chuckled. "You must be joking."

"You haven't given me a single name. You haven't given me anything that can be traced back to anyone. Or back to you."

"Damn right. That kind of information could get me killed."

"No one even knows I'm here, Mr. Lasser. Or where it would've come from. That name is my way out. It's the way to get *my* life back. I'll never bring you into it. I swear."

Lasser spread dirt over his dead butt with the toe of his boot. Then he turned away from Emmit and said a word in Spanish, barely louder than a whisper, almost under his breath. "Saltamontes."

"Saltamontes?" I stared back at him, the lamplight making his face appear white.

"Grasshopper."

# CHAPTER SIXTY-EIGHT

A couple came out of the restaurant, walking past us on their way back to their car. Lasser's man stood up and blocked any sight of us with his body.

"I think you've had your questions answered," Lasser said. "It's getting cold, and my boy Emmit here, tough as he acts, has a low tolerance for a chill. Which wouldn't be good for you."

"What's going to happen to me?" I asked.

I expected him to nod toward the suddenly weather-afflicted Emmit and that was going to be it for me. Instead Lasser rubbed his jaw with his hand, two fingers across his nose. "You're going to get yourself out of town, Ms. Gould. Consider it your lucky day. You got what you came for. Now you're going back to wherever it is you're from. Tonight. Now. You tell this story to a single soul, you implicate my name in any way, I promise on the soul of my daughter, what happened to her will be a romp in the hay compared to what your kids will go through."

"I have to tell it," I said to him. "It's the only way to save my life."

"Sorry, but that's not my concern. I think it's yours. Emmit . . ."

The grizzled cowboy came toward me. I grabbed hold of Lasser's arm. "You still didn't tell me why she was killed. Why was she targeted? The Zetas were aligned with the Juartes. Making Juarte a winner was good for them as well."

"What does that matter now? I told you what you wanted. Now it's up to you how you choose to use it." He nodded to Emmit and headed toward his car.

I grabbed his arm. "It matters because I'm not out here alone. It matters because the person who's with me, Eduardo Cano has murdered her entire family to keep what you just told me quiet. What did you do that caused your daughter to be murdered by the same people you were selling to, along with four other innocent people?"

I looked at his face and saw it. In the pale, questioning cast of guilt that came over it; he was barely able to look me in the eyes. What had he said a few minutes before: *You walked into that hotel room. And I—*

He'd been about to tell me, and now I saw it.

412

He'd walked through the wrong door too.

"You didn't just sell to them, did you? You were diverting arms. To other buyers. The Gulf cartel? Or the Jaliscos? You were selling to other buyers, and the Juartes found out. But they needed you for the arms, so they couldn't just kill you as they would normally do. So they punished you with your daughter. I'm right, aren't I, Mr. Lasser? That's what caused it. Your beautiful Ana . . ."

He pulled his arm away, but his look of shame and pain gave it all away. "It was how I stayed alive. The only way I stayed alive. Mexico is a complicated place, Ms. Gould, even with the United States as your protector. You think I had a choice? You don't think the others came to me and threatened me with far worse? But yes, they needed me. Now get in your car and drive out of town, before the situation changes."

"What situation?" I asked. His look seemed to shift.

"My largess," he said. He tapped his palms against the truck and shrugged. "I'm afraid the friend you mentioned won't be quite as lucky."

Those words were like the blade of a sharp knife curling the peel off an orange. Except the orange was in my gut. And it was throbbing. "What do you mean about my friend? Lauritzia?"

"You were wrong," Lasser sniffed grimly, "about no one knowing you were here . . . Just drive out of here, Ms. Gould. Don't even go back to your motel, if you want to remain alive. This one's not your fight."

413

My heart grew tight in terror. "Who knows we're here?"

"He only wants her. He doesn't care about you."

I saw the answer to my question reflected in his own fear that rose up in his eyes.

Cano.

Lasser dug his dead cigarette butt further into the dirt with his boot. "You didn't think you were the only ones who ended up in Gillian tonight?"

# CHAPTER SIXTY-NINE

*Lauritzia!*

A car came down our row, its headlights momentarily blinding us, and I took the chance to break free of Emmit's grasp and took off down the row of parked cars to where I'd left the Toyota. Behind me, I thought I heard the cowboy ask if he should go after me, and Lasser simply mutter, "Let her go if she wants to die so bad."

The panic and dread that was suddenly suffocating me made me realize how fondly I'd grown to think of her, and that I'd left her alone back at the motel in danger. And that I wasn't going to let someone who had suffered so much, who had lost everything in life, die now, in a place I had brought her. And at the hands of that monster.

There wasn't a doubt in my mind who Lasser meant. But who could have alerted him? How could he have known we were there? And Lasser had never told me how he knew who I was. I suddenly felt both incredibly stupid and completely in over my head, a pawn in someone else's game. Which had become my nightmare! And we'd played right into it, in our stupid search for the truth. Lauritzia was the last of her brother and sisters. And now I'd left her in danger. She might already be dead.

*Please God*, I begged. I wasn't a religious person, but I heard myself praying as I ran. *Don't let any harm come to her. Please.*

I got to the car and turned on the ignition. I threw it into reverse and did a frantic three-point U-turn to get out of the lot. Our motel was only about a mile or so away. I had no idea what I might be heading into. I didn't have a gun. I didn't have anything to protect her with. If I even got there in time. I drove onto River Street, which led back to the main drag. I took out my phone and pressed Lauritzia's number. It took a few seconds to connect. I felt my heartbeat bursting through my skin. It started ringing. Once. Twice. *Please, Lauritzia, answer.* Three times.

Her voice mail came on. *"This is Lauritzia. If you've reached this, you know that—"*

I cut it off. No point to leaving a message. She had called me only an hour before to check where I was. I pulled around cars and sped up through a yellow light, unable to stop my heart from lurching. *How could I have left her there alone?*

I thought about dialing the police and ending the whole thing there.

Two blocks from the motel, I was forced to pull up at a light, stuck behind a huge eighteen-wheel diesel. I pounded the steering wheel. *"C'mon!"* I shouted, my foot twitching on the accelerator. *I could run there from here!* I thought about jumping out and making the dash.

The light finally changed. I sped up alongside the truck and veered into the turn lane. The motel was just there on the left. I didn't know what I could do, but if she was in danger . . . I was living this nightmare all over again, just like with Dave.

I turned sharply in to the motel drive and screeched to a stop in front of our wing of the building. Our room was number 304, accessible from an outside staircase. I sprinted to it, leaving the car door open, bolting up the stairs—up two flights to the third floor—in a white stucco stairwell made to look like a church bell tower. I made it up and dashed down the long hall toward our room, praying I wasn't too late.

*"Lauritzia!"* I shouted.

I swung around the corner and, to my shock, slammed headfirst into someone. Someone large and immovable, who had clearly been waiting for me there. Almost knocking me to the ground.

I screamed. The person put his arms around me, and I shouted, *"Get off! Get off me!"* needing to get by, my arms flailing to get away from him. Crying. I knew this was bad. Lauritzia might already be dead. I knew I'd failed her.

*"No, no, no!"* I yelled. "I have to get to her. Let me by . . ."

And then finally I looked into the face of my captor and my heart fell off a cliff. I knew it was even worse.

Worse for me.

"Good to run into you again, Ms. Gould." Alton Dokes pinned my arms and smiled.

I never saw what happened next, only felt the hard blow against my chin, likely with the butt of his gun. My legs giving way.

And the sinking feeling that I'd failed her. Lauritzia. That she was dead. As he held me to keep me from crumpling to the floor, the darkness swarmed over my brain.

# CHAPTER SEVENTY

When Lauritzia got back to the room, she was hardly able to keep her eyes open at first, thinking that it might be the long drive they'd just completed; or the endless wait for Lasser; or maybe even the altitude. They were at eight thousand feet.

She napped for a while, then she came to, looking around the small room: at the printed, western-themed curtains that led out to the small balcony; the cowboy prints on the wall; their clothes folded neatly on the one chair. Why was she there?

She was there to find the answer to the one thing that had held her prisoner.

And when she found it, she would be free. She would be able to go about life like any person. Go to school. Maybe meet a boy. Get married. Have kids of her own.

Leave behind the darkness that had followed her. Rid her mind of the terrible pictures that always came to her like a horror film she would look away from.

No, she knew, this thing would never make her free.

That was what she realized in the car that had made her so distressed. Because the answer to her problems was far different from Wendy's. Wendy's would allow her to prove that she had not done these things she was accused of. To show clearly that she was caught up in someone else's evil. Not hers. It would come out, the people who had done these things. She would go back to her life. Not with her husband, but maybe with her kids. Who would one day forgive. Life didn't give you all of its blessings, only some . . . Gillian was indeed Wendy's key.

Just not hers. She had been wrong; their stories did not lead to the same place.

It would never let her go.

This man they sought, Lasser . . . he held no answers for her.

She sat up in bed. It was after 6:00 P.M. It had grown dark outside. She went to the balcony and opened the door. The cool night air hit her. She was dying for something to eat. They had not eaten any lunch.

Where was Wendy?

At first, the thought came with a shudder that something was wrong. But it was always that way with Lauritzia. A missed call, one of the kids not exactly

420

where they were supposed to be, always came with the premonition of danger.

Maybe there was a call?

She found her phone and was relieved to see a message from her. She listened, "Hey, you must be napping. I'm at a restaurant. Lasser is here. Wish me luck. I'm going to do this now . . ."

That was forty minutes ago. Lauritzia thought about calling her back but then decided she would wait. Instead, she took the phone and called down to the restaurant. Asked for some toast and tea. They said it would be twenty minutes. She went in and washed her face.

Maybe Wendy had met with him. She knew she would find the courage. Maybe she was with him now.

She went back out and threw a sweater over her shoulders against the night chill. She flicked on the TV. The local news. She found an old episode of *The King of Queens* and sat on the bed. That always made her laugh.

After about ten minutes there was a knock. "Room service. You ordered tea."

"Sí." Lauritzia went to the door and opened the latch just a crack. It was a blond young man in a red waiter's vest. She opened the door and he came in, with an amiable "Evening" and a cute smile, and set out the tray on the small table, clearing all the magazines. "There's milk in the container. Butter and jelly for the toast. Need anything else?"

"No, that will be fine," Lauritzia said. She signed the bill, leaving him a couple of dollars as a tip.

"Call down when you need it picked up."

"I will." He was cute, Lauritzia thought. He was probably in the local college here. She let him out, closing the latch on the door again. She poured herself some tea, which felt good going down and made her feel stronger. She took a couple of bites of toast and watched the end of the show, giggling amusedly at the father-in-law, who had spent the last of his money on some get-rich scheme.

She glanced at her watch. It was now 7:15 P.M.

She picked up her phone again. It had been an hour since her message. This time she would call. The room suddenly seemed to have a stillness to it. And a chill. She got up to fully shut the outside door, pressing Wendy's number on the phone.

There was another knock on the door. *She's here!*

"Room service again," the voice from outside said. "Forgot something."

Lauritzia went to the door, this time opening it without hesitation, and there was the same cute boy. "What did you forget?"

Except this time his smile was more like a deadened slate and his eyes contained an empty, blank glaze.

She gasped. "Oh God . . ." She tried to jam the door shut.

The door flew open, nearly clipping her face, and the

422

boy in the red vest seemed to crumple right on top of her, like some gangly, red spider, his legs buckling to the floor. His eyes—those cute boyish Colorado eyes—now staring at her like motionless pools.

Behind him, someone pushed into the room. Lauritzia stepped back and went to scream. But she couldn't scream—her voice was trapped; and by that time it was too late. She stared in horror at the person who had come in, as if he was the Devil himself.

Because he was the Devil to her.

"Buenas noches, Lauritzia Serafina Velez." Eduardo Cano smiled. "I am very sad to disturb you in this way," he continued in Spanish, pushing the waiter's body farther into the room and kicking the door closed behind him. "But I think we have an appointment, no? And I have waited a very long time to make your acquaintance face-to-face."

# CHAPTER SEVENTY-ONE

She would not allow herself to show him fear. *Please, Lauritzia, be strong.* She steeled herself. For Eustavio and Nina and Rosa and Maria. Though her body shuddered like an earthquake, her heart felt three times its size.

She stood straight up to him, this Satan she reviled, who had taken everything from her. Small as she was, she stood up tall. She would show no fear. She held back tears, tears of anger and of acceptance, knowing her time had come, her gaze darting to the body of the boy crumpled on the floor. Another innocent victim.

"Why?"

"I'm sorry, my dear, but it had to be done." Cano wiped the short blade of blood on the side of his pants, then slipped the blade into its sheath hanging from his belt. "Would you have actually opened up for me? That makes me feel so nice. Anyway, what is one more? So many have already died. But you know that so well, don't you? I just couldn't hold back when I heard you were here. To come and have the pleasure of finally meeting you myself. In person. You have shown a lot of guile, girl. Twice, I had the hangman ready to take you in his cart, and twice fate intervened." He scanned the room, checking the bathroom, the windows. "But I'm afraid that will not happen again."

"Do what you have to do." Lauritzia glared at him with spite. "I'm not afraid. I am only ashamed I cannot kill you myself. With my own hands. You are a monster."

"A monster, huh? You think so?" Cano stepped around the room. "You think this is all just some spectacle to me? A spectacle of blood. Like in the arena. You have no idea. Your father understood what he would bring on the moment he did what he did. It is *he* who has brought this fate on you and your family. Not me. I am only the person who carries it out. Someone has to. Look to your own father when you see him in the afterlife. Though I doubt the two of you will ever meet, unless God grants you a day trip into hell."

He took the gun from his belt. A small-caliber pistol equipped with a silencer.

"Do not insult my father. My father would only say one thing to you. To your face, El Pirate."

"And what would that be, Lauritzia?" Cano tapped the

gun against his side and came closer. "Your dick-sucking coward of a father. Tell me, what would that be?"

"*This.*" Lauritzia stood on her toes and spit in his face, the hatred burning through her eyes like an X-ray.

Cano wiped off the spit with the back of his hand and smiled. "Now I see why it's been so tough to kill you. It is hard to kill anything that has so little regard for its own life."

"*Then do it!*" Lauritzia exhorted him. She thought of Wendy, who might be returning at any second, and glared back at him with burning, ready eyes. "Do it now. I am not afraid. You have already killed the fear in me a hundred times. A little more with each of my brother and sisters. So there is nothing left, only my heart, which curses your soul for the people who can no longer speak. Go on, shoot me!" She pushed out her chest. "Your power is weakened to me. There is nothing you can take from me any longer, but my spite. The rest is gone."

"*Shoot* you?" Cano rubbed his mouth, unable to conceal his snicker. "Who said anything about shooting you, my darling." He slowly unscrewed the silencer from the gun and put it back in his jacket pocket. "No one who escapes El Pirate twice dies so easily, especially one who holds such an illustrious status as you. The last of your line. No . . ." He pushed open his jacket and showed the knife he had killed the waiter with. A short, two-inch, military-looking blade with a curl at the edge. "I think for you there is only the blade. And you should know, Lauritzia"—Cano thumbed its edge to show its sharpness—"that this is something I do very, very well. And anything done that well takes time. Lots and lots of time. Don't you agree?"

# CHAPTER SEVENTY-TWO

In the chill of the Colorado night, outside the motel room, the pockmarked man climbed across to the third-floor balcony.

It was not difficult, once he saw that Cano had arrived at the motel. His work was almost done. Patience had always been his trait, and now the bear had set foot in the trap.

And now he would cut it off.

It was not hard to hoist his way up there. The small terraces were only eight feet apart in height, so he easily pulled himself up. And in the darkness no one would see. This time he was careful not to make a sound and carefully moved the balcony door ajar, enough to hear what was going on inside, keeping himself concealed behind the heavy drapes.

After so long, his heart accelerated to be so close.

"Do it now," he heard the woman say. "I am not afraid." He smiled. Lauritzia had always been the brave one. Even as a child she would dive into the swimming hole from thirty feet.

"Who said anything about shooting you?" Eduardo Cano said. The man watched through the curtains as the killer took out his knife.

The man carefully removed the gun that he had tucked into his belt. He had waited a long time for this moment, and of all the things he thought might go through his mind as he was about to do the one thing he had dreamed of for many years, he never imagined it would be this: That, in the place of his home, people would be parading through the streets, dancing and wearing masks, this very night. The churches would be open for business deep into the night. All the undertakers would stay up late too.

He slid the door open and could not hold back his smile. Today was the Day of the Dead. November 2.

What a day to die.

# CHAPTER SEVENTY-THREE

This time Lauritzia did show fear. She could not help it. She had made her peace with God many times, and in ways, longed to be with her brother and sisters, who she believed with everything in her soul were in heaven now.

*But this* . . . Her eyes shot fearfully to the knife. Since she was a child that had been her one fear. To be cut. Even the slice from a thorn unnerved her. So now it was this.

"You say you no longer have any fear for me," Cano said with a shrug, circling the room. "So we will see. We will see just what you have left. I suspect I will find something. Are you still a virgin? You're a sweet piece of pie, Lauritzia. I can see that. Do you really want to die without ever feeling how a man feels inside you?

Even one you despise. You might not hate me as much as you think! I could make that happen, Lauritzia. Give you a little thrill before you go. What do you say?"

"I say the only way you will ever put yourself inside me is if I'm dead." Lauritzia tightened her fists. "And even then, I would not let you—"

"*Ha!*" Cano laughed greasily. "I'm not so bad." He stepped closer. "You smell nice. The smell of someone who wants exactly what she thinks she doesn't. What she doesn't know. I bet you're wet down there, my little *niña*. Wet for it with a man who represents everything you revile, right? Who has taken everything you love from you. Wet and juicy. What do you say?" He tapped the blade against his cheek. "If I cut off a nipple, you may beg me to do it. Or beg me to kill you, I think. You say I am powerless, eh? So we'll see. We'll see just how powerless I am."

Cano circled, the burning eyes of a wolf hunting its prey. He unbuckled his belt. "So tell me, my brave Lauritzia, what would you say to me, now that I am here? To the one who has slaughtered your brother and sisters, with as little thought to it as if I were ordering a beer? You must have dreamed of this moment. So here's the chance. It's just me. The famous El Pirate. See, I'll even put this away."

He placed the knife back in its small sheath hanging from his belt. "It's just you and me. Tell me what words you have for the killer of your entire family? I am yours.

431

Nothing to say?" He laughed. "What do you think your dog piss of a father would have said?"

"He would say, in the name of God, Eduardo Cano, prepare to meet your judgment."

A voice rang out from behind Cano, and a man stepped out from behind the curtains holding a gun. Cano spun around in surprise.

"And I hope that judgment is painful and endless, El Pirate, and I pray with all my heart, for that reason only, that there is indeed a hell."

*"Papa!"* Lauritzia exclaimed, her eyes as wide as if Saint Anselmo himself had appeared in the room.

It had been more than three years.

"So," Cano said, chortling with a look between bewilderment and amusement, "the fisherman has finally reeled in his big catch. The one who's been eluding him all these years. So was it you, Oscar, my old right arm, who lured me out here? Was this your plan all along? How very, very shrewd. You deserve big applause, Oscar. I mean this. You do."

"Get away from him, Lauritzia. This man is about to die, and I do not want him to soil you one more second. It's over for him. In this world. The rest, I can only hope, is only just beginning . . ."

"Papa," she uttered again, still in shock, and moved away.

"So this is the big finale?" Eduardo Cano showed his teeth and laughed. "You sound like a fucking priest,

Oscar. This is your big revenge? The afterlife? Eternal damnation. As if I need you to consign me to hell. Well, I hope it tastes sweet. Very sweet. You look a little thin, Oscar. Have you been eating your own cooking?"

"I've been living on the dream of one day holding this gun at you, Eduardo, and now I feel pretty full. You asked what I would say . . . well, I too have dreamed of this. And what I ask you is, *why*? Why, Eduardo? Was it that I betrayed you? The one you took up from nothing. Because of what I knew. Who we were meant to kill that day . . . You could have taken any of my children, and it would have kept me in anguish for the rest of my life. But *all*? Even their unborn children. Even unfed dogs do not act like this. *Why?*"

Cano wiped his face and looked into Oscar's eyes; even holding the gun, Oscar seemed to shrink from his presence. "You think it was to protect myself, eh, Oscar? Or my friends up north who let us battle to the death in our own country? You are a fool. It was because I thought it would bring you out from under a rock, you cowardly cur. It was because each one, I thought, *Now, this will bring him back. To face me*. So that I could kill you myself. So I could strangle the life out of you with my own hands. No man could sit by and watch his family slaughtered one by one. But you didn't come. Each one, you still chose to hide, while I took the things you loved. What of *that*, Oscar? Even the most cowering lizard in the desert does not behave like that."

"I was in U.S. custody, you bastard. I could not come."

"Well, now the coward has his revenge. Go on, get it over." Cano turned his back to him. "I'll make it easy for you. See if you have the guts. Go on. Right in the back of the head. Isn't that want you want, Oscar? You can brag about it. The killer of El Pirate. Do it now. Take your big revenge."

Oscar moved up behind him and placed his gun to the back of Cano's head. "Do you know what day it is, Eduardo?'

"The day the worm catches a cow and has his banquet."

"It is November second."

"Ha, the Day of the Dead! What a fucking joke! Now go on. Before it becomes November third. I'm sure your daughter can't wait to see my brains sprayed all over her pretty outfit."

"No more talk, Eduardo. Your time has come. See you in hell."

Oscar stiffened to shoot, but in the same instant, Cano's hand darted toward his belt and came out with the blade sheathed there, and as if in the same motion, he thrust it downward and spun away from the gun and dug it into Oscar's knee.

Oscar yelped, buckling, the gun firing wildly, the bullet missing Cano's head and shattering a lamp by the bed.

Cano pivoted and came upward with the blade, slashing Oscar across the forearm, tearing the gun from his grip and sending it rattling across the floor.

Lauritzia screamed.

"I told you to shoot me, Oscar, didn't I?" Cano said, his eyes now ablaze with a coyote's gleam, and he kicked Oscar's legs out from under him, toppling him to the floor, and reached into his belt and took out his own gun. He thrust his knee onto Oscar's chest and pushed his gun into Oscar's mouth. "I gave you the chance, didn't I? What a pair you are. One is a coward and the other one only talks of heaven. You know what day it is? Of course I do, Oscar, this is the day *you* die. Not me."

Oscar looked up, his eyes darting in futility, his thoughts rushing to Lauritzia. His arm flailed, seeking to locate his gun on the floor, his fingers grasping. Cano raised the muzzle to the roof of Oscar's mouth. "You were a cook when I found you, and you will always be just a cook. I am El Pirate. No one tells me when I die. I tell *you*! Now, eat this, asshole—"

"No—you are wrong, El Pirate!" It was Lauritzia who spoke, who now pressed her father's gun to the back of Cano's skull. "Just this once we do."

She squeezed.

Cano spun, his eyes wide in terror, as the side of his face caved in, like a building imploding. He rolled off Lauritzia's father and landed face first on the floor. Even dying, his hands kept grasping and twitching, like an animal moving around without its head, trying to locate his gun. His eyes rolled up, but they still had that arrogant laughter in them. *I decide who lives and dies. I do*. His chest still rising and falling with his breath, as if he were some vampire Lauritzia had seen on TV, who would not die.

He would never die.

She went up and put the gun against his temple. "For me, heaven will have to wait, but for you, hell is ready, El Pirate."

She pulled the trigger again. This time he didn't move.

"Just this once, we do."

# CHAPTER SEVENTY-FOUR

Deputy Director Carol Sinclair, third in line at the Department of Homeland Security, stepped into the make-shift offices of the joint task force investigating the deaths of Agent Raymond Hruseff and David Gould.

With her was Richard Sparks, who headed up the FBI's New York office, along with three military-looking men in suits.

The dozen or so agents manning phones or sitting behind computers sat up or hastily threw their jackets on.

"Where is Senior Agent Dokes ?" the deputy director asked them.

At first, no one spoke up. Not that anyone actually knew his whereabouts. Only that he was in the field. Following up on a lead. Dokes was their senior officer

437

in the investigation. You didn't rat out your superior, even when your superior's superior came into the room. Even with a good chunk of the U.S. military police standing behind her.

At least for about five seconds.

"He's not around, sir," a nervous agent said, standing up. "Agent Holmes may be able to help you. I know they've been in touch."

"Thank you," the deputy director said, her tone clipped and about as frigid as a glacier.

Sinclair continued down the hall, stopping at the glass-enclosed workspace that was home to the task force's senior leadership. It took about a second for the redheaded agent at the desk to see who stood at his door. He jumped up, throwing on his jacket and straightening his tie, his mind doing eighty to figure out just why they were here. "Ma'am!"

"I'm looking for Senior Agent Dokes." The deputy director stepped into his office.

The Homeland Security agent cleared his throat, the first time he'd been addressed directly by someone of this rank. "I'm afraid he's not here, ma'am."

"And where might I find him?" She had a handful of files in her hands. "There are some questions he needs to answer."

Questions that had landed on her desk about how David Gould's blood had shown up in a completely different place from where Dokes claimed he was killed.

Questions relating to certain government postings throughout his career. That coincided with other events that now had come to light.

"He's out." The young agent cleared his throat, thinking he may have backed the wrong horse in this race, the race of his once promising career. "He's in the field."

"The *field*?" The deputy director looked at him skeptically.

"Yes, sir." The agent swallowed. "The field."

"You were with him, at the Goulds' house, the night David Gould was shot, weren't you, Agent Holmes?"

"Yes, ma'am." Holmes felt his stomach plummeting. "I was."

"So why don't we have ourselves a little discussion . . ." The deputy director dropped the files on his desk. "And then you can tell me just where we can find Senior Agent Dokes." Her gaze had the firmness of concrete. "In the field."

# CHAPTER SEVENTY-FIVE

When I finally came to, everything was bumpy; I had the sensation of being tossed around. I found myself in a car—a Range Rover or Jeep, actually—my wrists bound in front of me and clasped to a handle bar on the dash-board. I yanked them toward me, and they didn't move.

Next to me, Dokes was driving. I blinked several times, trying to clear the fuzziness from my head. Along with the throbbing ache. We were on a dark road, no longer in town. And this didn't have the feel of an official trip. I was pretty certain that ache was about to become the least of my worries.

"Where are you taking me?" I turned to Dokes.

"It doesn't matter where I'm taking you. How about we say the beach." There was a tiny chuckle in his reply. "Do you like the beach, Wendy?"

I looked around and recognized the main road, 160, that led in and out of Gillian. "There's no beach around here."

"Don't be so sure. Just sit back and enjoy the ride."

I didn't like that no one else was in the vehicle. If Dokes was arresting me, he'd certainly have a support team along with him. My mind flashed to Lauritzia. I didn't know if she was dead or alive. Dead, I figured. I'd gotten there too late. We went over a bump, and I lurched forward, held back by the handle bar.

"You should've just stopped," Dokes said with an air of resignation. "Back in that hotel when I told you to."

"If I had, I'd be dead," I replied. "We both know that."

"Maybe. But you surely would have saved us both a lot of trouble. There must be a lesson in there somewhere though."

"I'm waiting . . ."

Dokes shrugged, slowing the vehicle. He put on his turn signal. Left. "Beware the piano player." He chuckled as he turned the car. "Next time someone asks you up to his hotel room . . ."

He pulled onto another road, and it was only then that I saw where we were heading.

The beach.

The Great Sand Dunes National Park.

And that's when I understood just what we were doing here. We weren't heading to any place. But to the middle of nowhere. *The beach* . . . And this would be my last ride. I jerked on my cuffs. It only made them tighter. I jerked them again in anger and desperation, trying to rip the handle bar off the dashboard.

It didn't budge. Just dug the cuffs deeper into my wrists until they hurt.

"You know it's true, what they say about them," Dokes remarked at my frustration. "I could have told you that."

We drove into the dark park. We approached the front gate. It was unmanned. Dokes drove around it anyway, bouncing onto the tundra. This was one of those open natural sites. No fences or manmade barriers to keep it in. You could get at it from probably a hundred directions, especially in the right vehicle.

"Isn't this a bit after hours, Dokes?"

He smiled and shook his head. "Not my hours."

I was growing scared. My heart started to beat faster. I knew he was taking me up there, deep into the acres and acres of desolate, barren dunes, to kill me. I jerked at the bar again. It was only tiring me out.

"You think that's really gonna make a difference." Dokes grinned at my desperation.

I said, "I know why you're doing this. I know what this is all about. I know what Curtis found out about Culiacán. That the DEA agents killed there weren't

442

the intended targets that day. That it was Lasser's daughter."

"I know you know." Dokes shrugged dismissively. "What else would you be doing here?"

"And I also know where it leads," I said, my tone growing harder and more frantic. "I know you all used to work in El Paso in the DEA. For Sabrina Stein. I know the Mexican government came up with the idea to let one cartel win, as their way to stop the violence. I know the U.S.'s role in that was to procure the arms. Lasser's job. Just the Juarte cartel. That's why you're doing this to me. So that it doesn't come out that the U.S. government was arming drug traffickers and took sides in the war between narco-terrorists. That it basically allied itself with the Juarte cartel."

"All very interesting." Dokes nodded. We left the paved road and began to bounce over the sand. "Too bad you won't be able to tell anyone."

"I'm not the only one who knows this. Others do too, and when I disappear, they'll bring it all out. We have the proof."

"You really think that's what this is all about?" We started to climb. I saw a sign: MEDANO CREEK. An arrow pointing. Another sign read: DUNES.

That was what we took.

"Trust me," he said, "it's a whole lot larger than that."

"What could be larger than the U.S. government taking sides in the drug wars? Arming killers and drug

443

cartels?" I racked my brain for what I had missed, for what was still out there.

Dokes merely laughed at me. "My career."

"Your *career*? Are you insane? Your career is more important than the United States supplying millions of dollars in illegal arms to drug cartels?"

This time he wasn't laughing. "It is to me."

He drove down the long main roadway toward the shapeless, dark mountains. Thousands of acres of them. I remembered looking it up. Whatever he had in store for me, by morning there would be no trace. It was pitch dark. The winds were whipping. The moon shed some light on the crests of the dunes, rolling like huge black waves in a turbulent sea. Soon we began to bounce. I had to cling helplessly to the handle bar to keep from being thrown out of my seat. The vehicle climbed a steep, dark incline, Dokes downshifting and powering through. The headlights cut through the darkness, flashing a widening cone of light ahead. Then the car pitched forward, like we were surfing a giant wave, traversing the backside of the dune and heading out into virtually nowhere.

"*Please*, please," I begged him, becoming really scared now. He just kept his gaze on the road, focused intently ahead.

"You don't have to do this. You're a government agent, for God's sakes. Do you have kids? I do. Two. You know that. They don't have a father now. Please, please, Dokes, don't do this." He ignored my pleas. "Say something to me, goddamn it. Dokes. Please . . ."

He didn't answer, just continued to drive. As if I wasn't even in the car. The moon lit a trail over the dunes, and it was like in *Lawrence of Arabia*, shimmering against the darkness. I knew precisely why he was taking me out there. By morning, the shifting sand would cover me completely. No one, no one would ever find me.

Not a grave. Not even a trace.

Nothing.

He drove about ten minutes longer, the wind now snapping at the windows, the temperature starting to drop. I figured he didn't have a specific destination in mind. He was just heading as deep as he could into the void. It was November. Who would ever know?

My heart felt like it might crash through my chest.

Then suddenly he stopped. Completely terrifying me. We were on the upside of a massive dune. Rising above us in the night like that giant wave in *The Perfect Storm*.

The one that drove them under.

"Please, no," I begged him.

Dokes put the vehicle into park, leaving the lights on. "This is as far as we go." He got out and came around to my side of the vehicle, but before he did, he opened the back and came out with a shovel. My heart started to beat wildly. He came around to my door and opened it, took out a key, and took off the cuffs that had bound me to the handle bar. "Let's go."

"No, no, no, no, no," I murmured.

"You shouldn't have been up there," he said. "You crazy, stupid bitch. Don't look at me. You got what you asked for. You should have just gotten on that train and gone home."

For a moment I thought I saw the slightest weakening in him—realizing he was putting an end to the life of an innocent person—but it was quickly covered up by all he was bent on protecting: his stupid rank, his pension, his career. The counterfeit notion that he was preserving the security of the United States. It had all hardened around him in this fake, inpenetrable veneer. And it wasn't going to crack. No matter what I said.

What gnawed at me most was that the bastard was going to win.

"Get out," he said, grabbing me by the chain linking my cuffs and dragging me out of the vehicle. I fell into the sand. "Get up."

I didn't get up. I just looked up at him, tears forming in my eyes. "Fuck you," I said. "Fuck you to hell. You're nothing but a piece-of-shit murderer hiding behind his badge. You're scum, Dokes. The slimiest form of it. You're going to rot in hell, and for what? To protect your fucking pension. Even the cartels are higher than

446

you. You're zero, Dokes. Pretending you're saving the country . . ."

He raised the shovel and I was sure he was about to bring it down on me and end it all right there.

I turned away.

"I said, *get up*!" he shouted at me. He hurled the shovel at me and took out a gun.

"Okay, okay," I said, and pulled myself to my feet. I started to cry.

"Start walking."

I started to walk, trudge really, stumbling into the massive dune in the dark, the only thing illuminating us the beam from the vehicle's headlights.

I thought of Neil and Amy, that they'd never, ever find out a thing behind what had happened to me. I would just disappear. That they'd never know I wasn't guilty of the things they said I was. They'd grow old despising me for murdering their father. And never fucking know.

I fell, tears and mucus covering my face. Dokes kicked me forward and ordered me to go on. I thought of Dave. *I love you, honey*, I said inwardly. *I'm so sorry for what happened. Maybe I'll see you soon. Maybe . . .*

Dokes pushed me from behind with his foot. I fell face first into the sand. I was miles from anywhere, in an unmarked grave that by morning would be invisible, swept over with sand. I would probably never be found.

447

ood over me. This was it. He brought out his
pulled back the action.

idn't want to give him the satisfaction of seeing
e cower. I wanted to look him firmly in the eyes. I
wanted to say *Fuck you* in the last, willful breath that I
would breathe. I wanted to tell him I'd meet him in
hell.

But I couldn't. I didn't do any of these things. I was
scared. I was trembling in the cold, the wind blowing
sand in my face. I looked at him, and all I could do
was turn away. Away from the gun as he pointed it
at me. *I love you, Dave* . . . I waited for what would
happen.

I centered on something, high above the dunes, in
the far-off sky. A star or a planet. A bright light flickering
amid the stars. I wasn't religious. But it brought me
some peace. I thought maybe it was Lauritzia. Pretty,
brave Lauritzia, who had come along with me to who
knew what fate? And who was with me now. I actually
felt sad.

Then I heard something . . . not the wail of the wind
across the dunes, but a whirring. In the sky. *Thwack,
thwack, thwack, thwack* . . .

The far-off star I was focused on was getting larger.

Not some glowing, spiritual light like they say happens
when you die. But like a beam, coming toward us at a
fast pace above the dunes. With an approaching hum.
The winds picking up, sand whirling all over us.

I didn't know if I was hallucinating or already dead. *An engine?*

Dokes shielded his eyes and looked up. *"What the fuck?"*

My heart began to rise.

And then the noise grew louder, until it became almost deafening in my ears. A roar. And the light glared in my eyes, blinding me, wind whipping the sand in all directions. I realized what it was, and stared up at it with my hand over my eyes.

I heard a voice over a speaker: "This is the Department of Homeland Security. Put the gun down and raise your hands in the air!" The copter hovering over us, like some angel God had sent.

Suddenly Dokes ran toward me, darting from the beam of light, his gun still trained on me. I could see in his eyes what he was calculating to do. "You may think you're going to get away, but you're not. You're still the only one who knows."

"There's no point, Dokes. It's over."

The voice bellowed from the copter again, "Agent Dokes, put your gun down now!"

"*It's not over!* I'll claim it's a matter of national security. They won't want what happened to come out any more than I do. Say good-bye." He shot out his arm to shoot. "I'm not done. You are."

"No." The noise of the copter was unbearable, and the whipping sand almost blinded me. "Please . . ."

I never heard the shot. I only saw the gun fly out of Dokes's hand and a spatter of red explode on his shoulder. He staggered back and fell to his knees.

The copter started coming down.

*Oh God. Oh God. Can I believe this?*

I couldn't help it—I started to cry. Jubilant tears at first, then they turned into deep, convulsive sobs. Maybe it was just everything I had been through pouring out of me. I realized I no longer had to be afraid. Or be brave. Or prove anything.

It was over.

I crawled up the sand and looked at Dokes, illuminated by the searchlight's beam. His left hand covered his right shoulder. Somehow he still had that smug, unworried expression; he even smiled at me like everything was going to be okay. He would roll. There were people much higher than him who would end up taking the fall. He looked up at the copter as it began to come down.

I picked up the shovel, the one he intended to use to bury me in an anonymous grave. To eliminate the final trace that I ever existed.

"This is for my husband," I said, and swung with all my might, catching him on his back and sending him face first onto the sand. I was sure I heard a few ribs crack in there too. He pushed himself back up to his knees, looking as helpless and dazed as I had felt just moments before.

"It was just business," he said. "You shouldn't have been in that room."

I raised the shovel over him one more time. "And this one's for me."

# CHAPTER SEVENTY-SIX

Dokes was put in cuffs and taken away in the copter. The last I saw of him was his glowering glare through the open cargo door as the aircraft whipped up the sand and sped off to I don't know where.

I begged them not to make me go along—rambling pretty much incoherently how I had to get back to the motel in town, how Lauritzia was in danger. How she might already be dead. They put me in the custody of two federal agents, and we jumped into Dokes's vehicle.

As we rode at eighty on the dark road back into town, I was certain that the elation I was feeling at coming out of this alive would soon turn to anguish as we got there and found her dead. Lasser's warning echoed over and over in my mind. *I'm afraid the friend you mentioned won't be quite as lucky.*

We got to town and sped up to the motel, which was now ablaze in flashing lights and emergency vehicles. Every cop in Gillian was likely there. I flung the Jeep's door open and sprinted up the stairs, ahead of the two agents who were trying to keep up with me. A throng of local cops were blocking the hallway. They stopped me before I got within fifty feet of our room.

*"Let me in! I have to get in!"* I said to two gray-uniformed cops standing guard at the door. "This is my room!" My heart was beating just as riotously as when Dokes was dragging me out into the dunes.

One of the agents accompanying me flashed his badge, and they apologetically let us through.

I steeled myself for the worst: To see Lauritzia sprawled there, her bloody body—that would have sent me over the edge.

She wasn't there.

Instead, I almost tripped over the red-vested body of what appeared to be a waiter from the motel crumpled near the door. His open eyes and blond hair leaking blood made me almost scream. A medical tech was kneeling over him.

Farther in, I fixed on the facedown body of a heavyset Hispanic man in a white shirt and jacket, the back of his head virtually caved in in a red mash, his arms splayed wide.

I was certain who it was even without anyone telling me.

Where was Lauritzia?

"Lauritzia!" I called out worriedly. I looked around for her belongings. The small traveling case she had brought with her and—I rushed into the bathroom—her toiletries were all gone.

"Save your breath," a female detective in a navy windbreaker marked GPD said to me. "There's no one here."

"She has to be here," I said, barely coherently, gazing at the two bodies and Lauritzia nowhere to be found.

"This is your room?" a second detective, a man with thinning hair and a heavy mustache, asked me.

"Yes. Yes it is." I nodded.

"Any idea who this is?" He pointed to the guy on the floor with the bullet in his head. "His ID says José Rivera. From *where*, Karen?"

The female detective checked her notes. "Guatemala."

"He's not from Guatemala," I said. "He's from Mexico. I think you'll find his name is Eduardo Cano. He's an enforcer with the Los Zetas drug cartel. He also has extensive contacts in the United States government."

The words "drug cartel" got the detectives' attention big-time. They probably hadn't had a crime bigger than drunk driving here for years.

"We have to find Lauritzia!" I turned to the federal agents with me. "I was traveling with her. She came back here ahead of me. This man has been trying to kill her. He's killed her whole family." I realized I was

454

rambling. I ran over to the window to check for her car. It was still there in the lot in the back. That wasn't a good sign. I looked back around, stunned. How she could have possibly killed Cano? Or this other guy. She had no weapon. There was only Cano's, and that was lying next to his body on the floor.

She also had no idea he was here and coming after her.

"This Lauritzia have a gun?" the female detective asked me.

I shook my head. "No."

"Then it makes me wonder just who this one belonged to . . ." She pointed to the table. There was a handgun lying there. The only other was inches from Cano's outstretched hand.

"Seems like there was a third person up here," the male detective said.

"A third person?" I asked.

"Fourth, I suppose, if you count the guy over there . . ." He motioned to the waiter. "Couple parking their car saw someone climbing up the balcony. They reported it to the manager, but by the time anyone came up, with the police, this was what they found."

Who would have climbed up here and killed Cano? Then taken off with her? It hadn't been forced. She'd even taken her things.

*Who would have even known we were here?*

Then I saw something. Over on the bed. On my pillow. I went over and picked it up.

455

A flower. A dried hydrangea from an arrangement in the room. And I thought back to something she had told me on the trip out. That when she'd had to leave Roxanne's children back in Greenwich, she'd placed a flower on each of their pillows. That it was supposed to protect them. So that the saints would watch over them.

And then, like a beam of light shot through a dark tunnel, I realized who that third person was.

Who had done these things and left with her. And I suddenly realized she wasn't in any danger.

No danger at all!

A second chance? I thought of her butterfly necklace. Were there any two people on this earth who deserved one more?

"That hers?" the female detective asked, pointing to the flower.

"No." I shook my head. "Mine."

"Well, everything's gonna have to stay as it is until we sort things out. And you're going to have to answer some questions. We have a double homicide here. And the only witness to it seems to be gone."

"Of course," I said, inwardly hiding a smile. In a day or two maybe. Enough time to let them reach where I knew they would be heading. When I was sure no one could ever find them again.

"But first I want to talk to my lawyer. Harold Bachman."

# CHAPTER SEVENTY-SEVEN

It took three more days for me to be fully released. They transferred me back east, to a secure location at Fort Dix in New Jersey. They interrogated me about everything that had happened. From the time I first laid eyes on Curtis Kitchner. To Dokes dragging me out in the dunes.

This time they called it a debriefing.

Harold was allowed to be present. When he first stepped into my tiny room, the first time since leaving for Colorado that he'd set eyes on me, the strain of our collective losses seemed to rise to the surface, and he came over and hugged me as deeply and tearfully as if it were his wife standing before him.

And in my mind as if it were Dave.

It was hard to let go.

"This isn't very lawyerly," I said, sniffing back the tears. "You're sure you want to represent me?"

He pulled away, giving me that studious smile from behind his wire rims. "Well, this is surely a lot more interesting than real estate trusts. And my principal reason not to seems to have changed."

Cano.

We sat down. "Tell me about Lauritzia," he said. He'd never heard the full story of what happened at the motel, so I told him what I thought had taken place.

"I'm sure it was her father."

"Her father?' He scrunched his eyebrows.

"Who else? Someone else was up there. Cano was dead. Her things were gone. They found a second gun."

I told him about the flower. He took off his glasses. That seemed to bring a tear to his eye.

"She'll be in touch," I said.

"No. She won't." His face was drawn, but he was trying to be upbeat. It was clear he loved her as a daughter.

"She will," I took his hand. "One day."

I asked how they had known to find me out there. So far no one had said. Not the agents who had saved me, who were out of Denver. Nor the ones who escorted me back.

And just as important, how they had come to believe I was innocent.

"Your friend," Harold told me. "Esterhaus."

"*Joe!*" My heart almost exploded with joy. "He's okay?"

"Apparently more than okay." He told me how Joe had found Dave's blood outside my house on the street. Precisely where I said he was shot. It proved the body had been moved. "He gave it to an old FBI crony of his. Apparently, it got as high as the deputy director of Homeland Security. Dokes's official vehicle had some kind of tracking mechanism in it."

"Joe always did have clout," I said, laughing. "I want to see him." I couldn't contain how warm that made me feel inside.

"Soon as we get you out of here," Harold said. "Thought that might make you smile. Here . . ." He opened his briefcase and took out a copy of the *New York Times* and tossed it onto the interview table. "This might too."

The headline read:

ROGUE HOMELAND SECURITY AGENT IMPLICATES HIGHER-UPS IN CARTEL CONSPIRACY.

EX-DEA OFFICIAL, SABRINA STEIN, NOW DRUG POLICY CHIEF, RESIGNS PENDING ARREST.

"You're right," I said, beaming. "It does."

"Next time I'm gonna choose my defense witnesses a lot more carefully."

I thought of Curtis—and Elaine Kitchner, who would now know the truth. I also thought of Dave. The people who knew and loved him. Who would now know he'd died for something.

They all had.

The third day I was told I could go home. I was a free woman. The attorney general's office said there would be no charges pending against me. A government representative came and said they hoped to give me back what I'd lost.

My freedom. My reputation.

The only thing they couldn't give me back were the people I loved.

Harold had arranged an apartment for me in New York City. I couldn't go back to the house right now. Not with what had happened there. Not yet. I had no idea how to resume my life.

"How do you just pick up and go on?" I asked Harold, as I picked up the bag with the few things I had on me at the time of my rescue. "I lost my husband. I lost who I was." I realized I was petrified to leave. Scared of the attention that I knew was in front of me. The judgment I would face.

"You have your kids," I said resignedly, as we went through a secure door leading to the barracks' entrance. I hesitated before heading outside.

"And you have your kids too." Harold pointed in front of me.

Waiting outside the entrance were Amy and Neil.

\* \* \*

I lost it there. I couldn't hold back. Everything I'd bottled up inside. About losing Dave. About thinking I was dead. What I'd gone through.

Neil came up to me, Dave's face so visible in his, and I latched onto him and just started to sob. I was afraid to let go. Afraid I'd lose them all over again. I hugged Amy too, though she was a bit more hesitant. I knew I'd done wrong and that I'd have to earn her trust back over time.

The apartment Harold set up for us was on Riverside Drive with a view of the river. I was just so grateful not to have to go back home. Not that day anyway.

That first afternoon we all sat around, just learning to trust one another again. If that would ever fully happen.

Neil asked if I wanted to talk about what I'd gone through. And I did. I wanted to tell them everything. The good and the bad. Hruseff. Dave. Dokes. Lasser.

And Curtis too.

"I'm so sorry I didn't believe you, Wendy," Neil said, hearing everything I'd gone through. How close I'd come to dying several times. How I'd watched their father being killed. How I'd lived on the run. He said, "I was just so angry about Dad, I had to blame someone. I know you tried to tell me. I just blamed you."

"It's okay." I squeezed his hand. "No more blame. I just want to be your mom again. I need you so much. Both of you. You're all I have."

Neil nodded. I wiped a tear or two off his cheek. I couldn't describe how good it felt to have them back.

"But you still went up there," Amy said. "You went up to that room. Even if you didn't sleep with him, you cheated. You cheated on Dad. You can't take that back."

"No, I can't." I nodded. "And Amy, I'm so sorry for that."

"So I can't just forgive you," she continued, hurt and some anger in her voice, "because you killed that man in self-defense. You still betrayed Dad. And it got him killed. So what I need to hear from you is *why*. Why you went up there, Wendy? Why you went up to that room? You had a good life. You had someone who loved you. You had us . . . That's all I want you to tell me. *Why?*"

I nodded. Over the past two weeks, I'd asked myself the same question a thousand times.

In the bar, when Curtis was at the piano. Our eyes casually falling on each other's a couple of times. After I'd heard him play, when everything inside told me to leave. I could have at any time.

Why I stayed?

And a thousand times the answer came back the same.

"I don't know."

We had tears in both of our eyes. Hers of accusation, mine of shame.

I knew I'd be trying to answer it for the rest of my life.

462

# *Epilogue*

Four months later . . .

We're all back together again now. We're kind of a family again. In a way. Neil, Amy, and I. I know Amy can't completely forgive me. And I don't expect her to.

I don't expect her to until I can forgive myself.

And both will take time.

I did a few TV morning shows, but that's all calmed down now. Neil is back at Bates. Amy never returned to Spain; she's back at NYU. I go into the city once a week or so, and we have dinner at some new spot she's discovered in lower Manhattan. We talk a lot—about her classes, the new yoga class I've found. I still haven't answered her question.

I'm not sure I'll ever be able to.

Harold and I see each other from time to time. We

have coffee in Greenwich. Once I went with him to a street fair there, and he brought along his kids. We're kind of tied together, he and I. I think one day he's actually going to ask me out.

And you know, I might just say yes.

I mean, he is kind of cute—in a lawyerly sort of way.

And in a strange way, like I tried to tell Amy, we're all we have.

I'm back in the house, of course. But I have it up for sale. That's one decision I've made.

From time to time, when I hear someone drive up to the top of the drive, I have this urge to run to the door, sure that it's Dave coming back from the train. Or from playing golf . . .

With his crooked, Woody Harrelson smile.

But it's always only the UPS guy dropping off a package. Or the mailman.

Which is who it was today.

It always hurts a little to walk up there, to the mailbox. Knowing it was there I saw Dave roll out of the car . . .

So I try and do it quickly, and replace the image with one I like a whole lot better. Like him prancing around after the Giants won the Super Bowl. Or snoozing on the beach in Anguilla while I built a sand castle on his belly. Or the morning that we climbed Masada at sunrise and, reaching into his pocket, he said to me . . .

"Wendy, I know we've both tried this once before,

but hell, I think we're both a little smarter the second time around . . ."

But today there were only the usual bills and catalogues, and back inside, I went to toss them onto the kitchen island when I noticed something else.

A plain white envelope, sandwiched between a West Elm and a Brookstone catalogue. Stark, handwritten on the front. Addressed to me. No return address.

It was the postal stamp that caught my eye.

Navolato. Mexico.

My heartbeat stopped as if it hit a wall. *Oh my God* . . .

I ripped it open eagerly, searching for the letter inside. But there was none.

Only a single photograph. The kind you might take in a booth at a CVS or somewhere. Except this one was taken outside.

It had a beautiful blue sky and dark hills in the background. There was a tree I couldn't identify, but that I knew had to be a jacaranda.

And in the foreground, as alive as if she were standing before me, was Lauritzia. My heart nearly exploded with joy.

And for the first time I saw that beautiful smile.

And there was someone next to her. A man. Older. His leathery, rough face in a hard, proud smile. His eyes somehow reflected both joy and sadness at the same time.

I knew exactly who he was and how he was with her.

I always knew.

And she was holding something up to the camera—the gold necklace that Roxanne had given her. She held up the little charm at the bottom, held it up as if for me to see.

*The butterfly.*

For the second chances in life. *We all deserve them.*

And I started to laugh, partly from joy and partly from sorrow. I started to laugh and shout and then cry, unable to hold it back, my cheeks slick with tears.

*Second chances.* Hers was to go back home again one day. With her father.

Mine was to regain the trust of my kids.

*We'd both found them*, I said. *We did.*

I sat down at the counter and stared at her dark eyes and that beautiful smile that could finally, unrestrainedly shine.

Then I ran to the phone and called Harold.

# *Acknowledgments*

My books always seem to start out as simply a story line and then grow into something far more personal. In this one, the transformation came about through the character of Lauritzia Velez, and the divulging of her tragic past. Lauritzia was loosely based on a newspaper editorial I came across about the travails of Edmond Demiraj, an Albanian immigrant who agreed to testify against a ruthless Albanian killer, who then suffered a bloody and terrible revenge enacted against him and his family. Cast aside by the U.S. government and denied asylum, the case went before the U.S. Supreme Court, where rightly, during the actual writing of this book, the wrong was righted, and Demiraj was finally granted asylum in the United States. I've taken some liberties with his personal story and adapting it into Lauritzia's.

But to me it became an anthem of not only the innocent victims of narco-terror, but of the horrors of a worldwide criminal enterprise that is out of control.

Several published works were truly helpful in writing this book, and I name them with appreciation: *To Die in Mexico, Dispatches from Inside the Drug War* by John Gibler (City Lights Books, 2011); *Down by the River: Drugs, Money, Murder and Family* by Charles Bowden (Simon & Schuster, 2003); "The Kingpins" by William Finnegan, published in *The New Yorker Magazine*, July 2, 2012; and "Narco Americano" by T. J. English, published in *Playboy* magazine. All the writings graphically portray the tragedies of drug violence in Mexico and our own country's ambivalent policies that have not curtailed the problem.

I'd also like to thank my dedicated team at William Morrow: Henry Ferris, Lynn Grady, Danielle Barrett, Cole Hager, and Liate Stehlik, along with Julia Wisdom in the U.K., not only for their wisdom in improving what is between the covers, but for their commitment and energies in advancing this, and all my books, to market. And to Roy Grossman for his perception in the early drafts. And to Simon Lipskar and Joe Volpe at Writers House for continuing to make me feel like the most important person in the room.

. And to my wife, Lynn, who daily makes me feel like the most important person in the room, though I am usually the only one in it.

# THE BLUE ZONE

## THERE ARE NO RULES IN THE BLUE ZONE.

They were the perfect family. And he was the perfect family man.
One day changed it all.

Arrested for racketeering, Ben Raab must take his family into
America's Witness Protection Programme. Only his eldest daughter,
Kate, chooses to stay on the outside. But the Programme's perfect
success rate is about to come to a shocking end. A case agent is
tortured to death and Ben vanishes. The one person who
might be able to find him is Kate.

Pursued by killers, forced to question everything she knows about
her life so far, Kate is plunged into a terrifying existence
for which nothing has prepared her.

Most people would call it certain death.

The FBI calls it The Blue Zone.

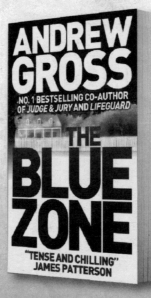

# KILLING HOUR

**A YOUNG MAN'S SUICIDE.**

**AN ELDERLY WOMAN'S MURDER.**

**A CONSPIRACY STRETCHING BACK DECADES.**

Dr. Jay Erlich's life is perfect: a wife and children he loves; a successful career. But a call comes that changes everything. His troubled nephew, Evan, has killed himself and Jay's brother is in despair.

Jay flies to California to help out, and is soon convinced Evan's death was no suicide. The police want him to leave the matter alone but he is determined to dig deeper. When his investigation takes him on a journey into his brother's shady past, Jay finds himself caught up in a world of dangerous secrets and ruthless killers…

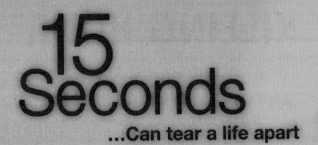

# 15 Seconds

### ...Can tear a life apart

'A TOTAL
WHITE KNUCKLE,
STAY-UP-ALL-NIGHT
THRILL RIDE'
**Harlan Coben**

## OUT OF TOWN

Dr Henry Steadman has it all: a booming practice, a daughter he loves, and plenty of time to enjoy life. But while visiting north Florida, a police-stop ends in the shooting of a local cop – with Henry as the prime suspect.

## OUT OF LUCK

Framed for a second murder, this time of a close friend, Henry goes on the run. His only lifeline is community outreach worker Carrie Holmes, no stranger to tragedy herself, who slowly begins to believe in Henry's innocence. But without evidence they are in a dead-end – the police are closing in, with no idea that the real killer is still out there.

## OUT OF TIME

But this is not just a set-up, it's far more personal. Henry's nightmare is complete when his family is targeted, and he realizes just surviving will not be enough to protect them. Everything has been taken away from him – but now, Henry has nothing left to lose...

# ✿ INTRODUCING EM ✿

I'm Em – I love when Dad pretends that it's
short for Emerald, which is much better than
boring old Emily. I was so sure this was going
to be the best Christmas ever, but something
has gone horribly wrong. Now all I want is for
things to go back to how they were. I wish that
Mum and Dad would stop shouting and love
each other again. Dad would say he'd been mad
to think of leaving us, and Mum would stop
talking about making a clean break. We'd all
be together and live happily ever after . . .

# HAVE YOU READ THEM ALL?

## WHERE TO START
THE DINOSAUR'S PACKED LUNCH
THE MONSTER STORY-TELLER

## FOR YOUNGER READERS
BURIED ALIVE!
THE CAT MUMMY
CLIFFHANGER
GLUBBSLYME
LIZZIE ZIPMOUTH
THE MUM-MINDER
SLEEPOVERS
THE WORRY WEBSITE

## FIRST CLASS FRIENDS
BAD GIRLS
BEST FRIENDS
RENT A BRIDESMAID
SECRETS
VICKY ANGEL

## HISTORICAL ADVENTURES
THE LOTTIE PROJECT
OPAL PLUMSTEAD
QUEENIE

## ALL ABOUT JACQUELINE WILSON
JACKY DAYDREAM
MY SECRET DIARY

## FAMILY DRAMAS
THE BED AND BREAKFAST STAR
CANDYFLOSS
CLEAN BREAK
COOKIE
FOUR CHILDREN AND IT
THE ILLUSTRATED MUM
KATY
LILY ALONE
LITTLE DARLINGS
LOLA ROSE
THE LONGEST WHALE SONG
MIDNIGHT
THE SUITCASE KID

## MOST POPULAR CHARACTERS
HETTY FEATHER
SAPPHIRE BATTERSEA
EMERALD STAR
DIAMOND
LITTLE STARS
THE STORY OF TRACY BEAKER
THE DARE GAME
STARRING TRACY BEAKER

## STORIES ABOUT SISTERS
THE BUTTERFLY CLUB
THE DIAMOND GIRLS
DOUBLE ACT
THE WORST THING ABOUT MY SISTER

## FOR OLDER READERS
DUSTBIN BABY
GIRLS IN LOVE
GIRLS IN TEARS
GIRLS OUT LATE
GIRLS UNDER PRESSURE
KISS
LOVE LESSONS
MY SISTER JODIE

## ALSO AVAILABLE
PAWS AND WHISKERS
THE JACQUELINE WILSON CHRISTMAS CRACKER
THE JACQUELINE WILSON TREASURY

# ✩ ABOUT THE AUTHOR ✩

Jacqueline Wilson is one of Britain's bestselling authors, with more than 38 million books sold in the UK alone. She has been honoured with many prizes for her work, including the Guardian Children's Fiction Award and the Children's Book of the Year. Jacqueline is a former Children's Laureate, a professor of children's literature, and in 2008 she was appointed a Dame for services to children's literature.

Visit Jacqueline's fantastic website at
www.jacquelinewilson.co.uk

CORGI YEARLING

UK | USA | Canada | Ireland | Australia
India | New Zealand | South Africa

Corgi Yearling is part of the Penguin Random House group of companies
whose addresses can be found at global.penguinrandomhouse.com.

www.penguin.co.uk
www.puffin.co.uk
www.ladybird.co.uk

Penguin
Random House
UK

First Doubleday edition published 2005
First Corgi Yearling edition published 2006
This edition published 2017

002

Text copyright © Jacqueline Wilson, 2005
Illustrations copyright © Nick Sharratt, 2005

The moral right of the author and illustrator has been asserted

Typeset in Century Schoolbook
Printed in Great Britain by Clays Ltd, Elcograf S.p.A.

A CIP catalogue record for this book is available from the British Library

ISBN: 978–0–440–87170–5

All correspondence to:
Corgi Yearling
Penguin Random House Children's
80 Strand, London WC2R 0RL

*For Molly Lajtha*
*(plus a big thank you to*
*Emma Chadwick-Booth)*

I thought it was going to be the best Christmas ever. I woke up very very early and sat up as slowly as I could, trying not to shake the bed. I didn't want to wake Vita or Maxie. I wanted to have this moment all to myself.

I wriggled down to the end of the bed, carefully edging round Vita. She always curled up like a little monkey, knees right under her pointed chin, so the hump that was her stopped halfway down the duvet. It was so dark I couldn't see at all, but I could feel.

My hand stroked three little woolly socks stretched to bursting point. They were tiny stripy socks, too small even for Vita. The joke was to see how many weeny presents could be stuffed inside.

Vita and Maxie appreciated Santa's sense of humour and left him a minute mince pie on a doll's

1

tea-set plate and a thimbleful of wine, and wrote him teeny thank-you letters on pieces of paper no bigger than a postage stamp. Well, Vita couldn't fit her shaky pencil printing on such a tiny scrap but she wrote *'Dear Santa I love you and pleese leeve me lots and lots of little pressents from your speshal frend Vita'* on a big piece of paper and then folded it up again and again. Maxie simply wrote a letter 'M' and a lot of wonky kisses.

I wrote a letter too, even though I was only pretending for Vita and Maxie's sake. I knew who filled the Christmas socks. I thought he was much more magical than any bearded old gent in a red gown.

I felt past the socks to the space underneath. My hand brushed three parcels wrapped in crackly paper and tied with silk ribbon. I felt their shapes, wondering which one was for me. There was a very small square hard parcel, a flat oblong package and a large unwieldy squashy one, very wide at one end. I hung further out of bed, trying to work out the peculiar shape. I wriggled a little too far and went scooting right over the end, landing on my head.

Maxie woke up and started shrieking.

'Ssh! Shut up, Maxie! It's OK, don't cry,' I said, crawling past the presents to Maxie's little mattress.

He doesn't want to sleep in a proper bed. He

likes to set up a camp with lots of blankets and cushions and all his cuddly toys. Sometimes it's hard to spot Maxie himself under all his droopy old teddies.

I wrestled my way through a lot of fur and found Maxie, quivering in his going-to-bed jersey and underpants. That's another weird thing about Maxie, he hates pyjamas. There are a *lot* of weird things about my little brother.

I crawled onto his mattress and cuddled him close. 'It's me, silly.'

'I thought you were a Wild Thing coming to get me,' Maxie sobbed.

*Where the Wild Things Are* was Dad's favourite book. The little boy in it is called Max, and he tames all these Wild Thing monsters. That's where our Maxie got his name. Reading the book to him was a *big* mistake. Our Maxie couldn't ever tame Wild Thing scary monsters. He wouldn't be up to taming wild fluffy baby bunnies.

'The Wild Things are all shut up in their book, Maxie,' I whispered. 'Stop crying, you'll make my nightie all wet. Cheer up, it's Christmas!'

'Is Father Christmas here?' Vita shouted, jumping out from under the duvet.

'Ssh! It's only six o'clock. But he's been, he's left us presents.'

'Has he left any presents for me?' said Maxie.

3

'No, none whatsoever,' said Vita, jumping down the bed and pouncing on the presents. 'Yay! *For dear Vita, love from Santa*. And here we are again – *To darling Vita, even more love from Santa*. And there's this one too, *To my special sweetheart Vita, lots and lots and lots of love from Santa*. Nothing for you two at all.'

Maxie started sobbing again.

'She's just teasing, Maxie. Don't let her wind you up. Shut *up*, Vita. Be nice, it's Christmas. Leave the presents *alone*. We open them in Mum and Dad's bed, you know we do.'

'Let's go to their room now!' said Vita, scrabbling at the bottom of the bed, scooping up all three parcels and clutching them to her chest.

'No, no, it's not time yet. Mum will be cross,' I said, unpeeling Maxie and jumping up to restrain Vita.

'My daddy won't be cross with me,' said Vita.

I always hated it when she said *my* daddy. It was a mean Vita trick to remind me that he wasn't really *my* dad.

He always said he loved me just as much as Vita and Maxie. I hoped hoped hoped it was true, because I loved him more than anyone else in the whole world, even a tiny bit more than Mum. More than Vita and Maxie. Much more than Gran.

'We'd better wait until seven, Vita,' I said.

'No!'

'Half past six then. Mum and Dad were out till late last night, they'll be tired.'

'They won't be tired, it's Christmas! Stop being so boring, Em. You just want to boss me about all the time.'

It's almost impossible to boss Vita even though she's years younger than me and literally half my size. She's the one who's done the bossing, ever since she could sit up in her buggy and shriek. It is a royal pain having a little sister like Vita. You have to learn to be dead crafty if you want to manage her.

'If you come and cuddle back into bed I'll tell you another Princess Vita story,' I said. 'A special *Christmas* Princess Vita story where she gets to fly to Santa's workshop and has the pick of all his presents. And she meets Mrs Christmas and all the little children Christmases – Clara Christmas, Caroline Christmas and little Charlie Christmas.'

'Can Prince Maxie play with Charlie Christmas?' said Maxie.

'No, he can't. This is *my* Princess Vita story,' said Vita.

I had her hooked. She got back into bed. Maxie grabbed an armful of teddies and climbed into our bed too. I lay between them, making up the story. Princess Vita stories were very *boring* because they

5

always had to be about sweetly pretty show-off Princess Vita. Everyone adored her and wanted to be her friend and gave her elaborate presents. I had to go into extreme detail describing each designer princess gown with matching wings, her jewelled ten-league trainers, and the golden crown the exact shade of Princess Vita's long long curls.

*Our* Vita wriggled and squirmed excitedly, and when I started describing the golden crown (and the pink diamond tiara and the ruby slides and the amethyst hair bobbles) she tossed her head around as if she was adorning her own long long curls. She hasn't really got any. Vita has very thin, fine, straight baby hair like beige cotton. She's been growing it for several years but it still hasn't reached her shoulders.

My hair is straw rather than mouse, and thick and strong. When I undo my plaits it very nearly reaches my waist (if I tilt my head right back).

'*Please* put Prince Maxie into the story,' Maxie begged, nuzzling his head against my neck. His hair is the same length as Vita's, coal-black with a long fringe. If he's wriggled around a lot in the night it sticks straight out like a chimney brush.

'Princess Vita has a brother called Prince Maxie, the boldest biggest boy in the whole kingdom,' I said.

Maxie sucked in his breath with pleasure.

'As if!' said Vita. 'Bother Prince Maxie. Tell about Princess Vita's trip to see Santa.'

I ended up telling *two* stories, swerving from one to the other, five minutes of Princess Vita, a quick diversion to see Prince Maxie defeating the seven-headed dragon spouting scarlet flames, and then back to Princess Vita's sortie in Santa's sleigh.

'There aren't *really* seven-headed dragons, are there?' said Maxie.

'No, you've killed the very last one,' I said.

'How do you know there aren't any more hiding in their caves?' Maxie asked.

'Oh yes, there are lots and lots, all huddled down in the dark so you can't see them, but they come creeping out at night all ready to *get* you,' Vita said gleefully.

'Will you stop being so mean to him, you bad girl!' I said. 'I'll torture you!' I got hold of her stick wrist and gave her a tiny Chinese burn.

'Didn't hurt,' Vita laughed. 'No one can hurt me. I'm Princess Vita. If any monsters come bothering me I'll give them one kick with my ten-league trainers and they'll beg for mercy.'

'OK, let's get *you* begging for mercy. I'm going to tickle you,' I said, scrabbling under her chin, in her armpit, on her tummy.

Vita giggled and kicked and squirmed, trying to burrow under the duvet away from me.

'Come on, Maxie, let's get her,' I said.

'Tickle tickle tickle,' said Maxie, his hands shaped into little claws. He stabbed at Vita ineffectively. She was in such a giggly heap she squealed anyway.

'I'm tickling Vita!' Maxie said proudly.

'Yeah, look, she's cowering away from you,' I said. 'But there's no escape, little Vita, the tickle torturers are relentless.'

I reached right under the duvet and found her feet. I held one captive with one hand and tickled the other.

'No, no, stop it, you beast!' Vita screamed, threshing and kicking.

'Hey, hey, who's being murdered?' Dad came into the room, hands on his hips, just wearing his jeans.

'*Dad!*' We all three yelled his name and jumped at him for a big hug. 'Merry Christmas, Dad!'

'Santa's been, Dad, look!'

'He left lots of presents – all for *me*!' said Vita.

'You wish, little Vita,' said Dad. He caught her up and whirled her round and round.

'Me too, me too,' Maxie begged.

'No, little Maxie, we're going to toss you like a pancake,' said Dad, picking Maxie up and hurling him high in the air. Maxie shrieked in terror, but bore it because he didn't want to be left out.

I didn't want to be left out either but I knew

there was no way Dad could whirl or toss me. I sat back on the bed feeling larger and lumpier than ever. Dad pretended to take a bite out of Maxie pancake and then set him free. Dad smiled at me. He bowed formally.

'Would you care to dance, Princess Glittering Green Emerald?'

I jumped up and Dad started doing this crazy jive with me, singing a rock 'n' roll version of 'Rudolph the Red-Nosed Reindeer'. Vita and Maxie started jumping around too, Vita light as a feather, Maxie thumping.

'Hey, hey, calm down now, kids, we'll wake Mum.'

'We *want* to wake Mum,' said Vita. 'We want our presents!'

'OK, let's go and wish her happy Christmas,' said Dad. 'Bring the presents into our room.'

'They aren't really all for Vita, are they, Dad?' said Maxie.

'There's one each for all of you,' said Dad. '*That* one is for my number one son.'

'I'm your number one daughter, aren't I, Dad?' said Vita, elbowing me out of the way.

'You're my special *little* daughter,' said Dad.

I waited. I didn't want to be his *big* daughter.

'You're my special grown-up daughter, Emerald,' said Dad.

My name isn't *really* Emerald, it's plain Emily.

All the rest of the family called me Em. I *loved* it when Dad called me Emerald.

'Shall I go and make you and Mum a cup of tea?' I offered.

I loved being treated like a grown-up too. Vita and Maxie weren't allowed anywhere near the cooker and couldn't so much as switch on the kettle.

'That would be great, darling, but if you start faffing around in the kitchen your gran will wake up.'

'Ah. Right.' We certainly didn't want Gran climbing into Mum and Dad's bed with us.

'Come on then, kids. Let's get the Christmas show on the road,' said Dad. He yawned and ran his fingers through his long hair. My dad's got the most beautiful long hair in the whole world. It's thick and dark and glossy black, like Maxie's, but Dad's grown his way past his shoulders. He wears it in one tight fat plait during the day to keep it neat, and then it's all lovely and loose at night. It looks so strange and special, so perfect for Dad. He gets fed up with it sometimes, saying he looks like some silly old hippy, and he's always threatening to get it cut.

That's how Dad met Mum. He went into her hairdressing salon at the top of the Pink Palace on the spur of the moment and asked her to chop it all off. She took one look at him and said no way.

She said she didn't usually go for guys with long hair but said it really suited Dad and it would be a shame to spoil such a distinctive look. That's what she said. I knew this story off by heart. Dad liked her paying him compliments so he asked her if she'd come for a drink with him when she finished work. They ended up spending the whole evening together and falling madly in love. They've been together ever since. Just like a fairy story. They don't live in an enchanted castle because Mum doesn't earn that much money as a hairdresser and Dad earns less as an actor, though he has his fairy stall at the Pink Palace now. He works very hard, no matter what Gran says.

We tiptoed along the landing so as not to wake her. She has the biggest bedroom at the front. I suppose that's only fair as it's her house, but it means Mum and Dad are squashed up in the little bedroom, and Vita, Maxie and me are positively crammed into our room. Gran suggested one of us might like to go and sleep in her room with her but we thought that was a terrible idea.

Gran snores for a start. We could hear her snoring on Christmas morning even though her bedroom door was shut. Dad gave a very tiny piggy snore, imitating her, and we all got the giggles. We had to hold our hands over our mouths to muffle them (not easy clutching Christmas stockings and slippery parcels!). We exploded into Mum and Dad's bedroom, dropping everything, jumping on the bed, snorting with laughter.

Mum sat up, startled, her hair hanging in her eyes. 'What . . . ?' she mumbled.

'Merry Christmas, Mum!'

'Happy Christmas, babe,' said Dad, kissing her.

'Oh darling, happy happy Christmas,' said Mum, flinging her arms round him and running her fingers through his hair.

'Give *me* a Christmas kiss, Mum!' Vita demanded, pulling at her bare shoulder.

'Me too,' said Maxie.

'Me too, me too, me too!' I said, making a joke of it, sending them up.

'Happy Christmas, kids. Big big kisses for all of you in just a minute,' said Mum, wrapping her dressing gown round her and climbing out of bed.

'Hey, where are you going?' said Dad, climbing back in. 'Come back!'

'Got to take a little trip to the bathroom, darling,' said Mum.

We couldn't be mean enough to start opening our stockings without her. She kept us waiting a little while. She came back smelling of toothpaste and her special rosy soap, her face powdered, her hair teased and sprayed into her usual blonde bob.

'Come on, babe, come and cuddle up,' said Dad,

hitching Vita and Maxie along to make room for her.

He ruffled Mum's hair like she was a little kid too. Mum didn't moan, even though she'd just made it perfect. She waited until Dad was helping Maxie with his stocking and then she quickly patted her hair back into shape, smoothing down her fringe and tweaking the ends. She wasn't being vain. She was just trying extra hard to look nice for Dad.

We had this tradition of opening presents in turn, starting with the youngest, but this wasn't such a good idea with Maxie. He was so slow, delicately picking out the first tiny parcel from his stocking, prodding it warily and then cautiously shaking it, as if he thought it might be a miniature bomb. When he decided it was safe to open he spent ages nudging the edge of the sellotape with his thumbnail.

'Hurry *up*, Maxie,' Vita said impatiently. 'Just pull the paper.'

'I don't want to rip it, it looks so pretty. I want to wrap all my presents up again after I've seen what they are,' said Maxie.

'Here, son, let me help,' said Dad, and within a minute or two he'd shelled all Maxie's stocking presents out of their shiny paper.

Maxie cupped his hands to hold them all at once: his magic pencil that could draw red and green and

13

blue and yellow all in one go; a silver spiral notebook; a weeny yellow plastic duck no bigger than his thumb; a tiny toy tractor; a mini box of Smarties; a little watch on a plastic strap; a green glass marble; and a pair of his very own nail clippers (Maxie always wants to borrow Dad's).

'How does Santa know exactly what I like?' said Maxie.

'How indeed?' said Dad solemnly.

'Will you help me wrap them all up now, Dad?'

'Yeah, of course I will.'

'I'm unwrapping mine!' said Vita, spilling her goodies all over the duvet, ripping each one open with her scrabbly little fingers. She found a tiny pink lady ornament in a ballet frock; sparkly butterfly hairslides; a set of kitten and puppy stickers; a miniature red box of raisins; a weeny purple brush and comb set; a little book about a rabbit with print so tiny you could hardly read it; a bead necklace spelling I LOVE VITA; and her very own real lipstick.

'I hope Santa's given you a very pale pink lipstick,' said Mum. 'Go on then, Em, open your stocking.'

I was getting too big to believe in Santa but he still wanted to please me. I found a little orange journal with its own key; a tiny red heart soap; a purple gel pen; cherry bobbles for my hair; a tiny tin of violet sweets; a Miffy eraser; a Jenna Williams bookmark; and a small pot of silver glitter nail varnish.

'I love that colour,' said Mum. 'Santa's got good taste, Em. I wish he'd leave me a stocking.'

'You've got *our* presents, Mum,' I said.

They weren't really special enough. We always made our presents for Mum and Dad, and so they looked like rubbish. Maxie did a drawing of Mum and Dad and Vita and me, but we weren't exactly recognizable. We looked like five potatoes on toothpicks.

Vita did a family portrait too. She drew herself very big, her head touching one end of the paper and her feet the other. She embellished herself with very long thick hair and silver shoes with enormously high heels. She drew Dad one side of her, Mum the other, using up so much space she had to squash Maxie and me high up in either corner, just our heads and shoulders, looking down like gargoyles.

I felt I was too old for drawing silly pictures. I wanted to make them proper presents. Gran had recently taught me to knit, so at the beginning of December I'd started to knit a woollen patchwork quilt for Mum and Dad's bed. I knitted and knitted and knitted – in the playground, watching television, on the loo – but by Christmas Eve I had only managed eleven squares, not even enough for a newborn baby's quilt.

I sewed the prettiest pink square into a weird

pouch done up with a pearly button. It was too holey for a purse but I thought Mum could maybe keep her comb inside. I sewed the other ten squares into one long scarf for Dad. It wasn't exactly the right shape and it rolled over at the edges but I hoped he might still like it.

'I absolutely love it, Em,' he said, wrapping it round his neck. 'I've wanted a long stripy scarf ever since I watched *Dr Who* when I was a little kid. Thank you, darling.' He stroked the uneven rows. 'It's so cosy! I'll be as warm as toast all winter.'

I felt my cheeks glowing. I knew he probably hated it and didn't want to be seen dead wearing it, but he made me believe he truly loved it at the same time.

Mum gave him a V-necked soft black sweater and he put it on at once, but he kept my scarf round his neck.

'What about *my* present?' Mum asked, as eagerly as Vita.

'What present?' said Dad, teasing her. Then he reached underneath the bed and handed her an oblong package. She felt the parcel and then tore off the wrapping. A pair of silver shoes tumbled out, strappy sandals with the highest heels ever.

'Oh my God!' Mum shrieked. 'They're so beautiful. Oh darling, how wicked, how glamorous, how incredible!' She started kissing Dad rapturously.

16

'Hey, hey, they're just *shoes*,' he said. 'Come on then, kids, open your big presents.'

He helped Maxie unwrap an enormous set of expensive Caran d'Ache colouring pens and a big white pad of special artist's paper.

'But he's just a little kid, Frankie. He'll press too hard and ruin the tips,' Mum said.

'No I *won't*, Mum!' said Maxie.

'*He will*,' I mouthed at Mum. Maxie had already totally ruined the red and the sky-blue in *my* set of felt pens. I couldn't help feeling envious of Maxie's beautiful set, so superior to my own.

'My turn, my turn, my turn!' Vita shouted, tearing at her huge parcel. One weird long brown twisty thing poked through the paper as she scrabbled at it, then another.

'What *is* it?' Vita shrieked.

Then she discovered a big pink nose.

'Is it a clown?' Maxie asked fearfully.

Dad had taken us to the circus in the summer and Maxie had spent most of the evening under his seat, terrified of the clowns.

'Try pressing that nose,' said Dad.

Vita poked at it, and it played a pretty tinkly tune.

'That's "The Sugar Plum Fairy" from some ballet. We did it in music,' I said.

Vita tore the last of the paper away to reveal

17

the huge sweet head of a furry reindeer, with two twisty plush antlers sticking out at angles. She had big brown glass eyes, fantastic long eyelashes, and a smiley red-lined mouth with a soft pink tongue. She was wearing a pink ballet dress with a satin bodice and net skirt.

'I love her, I love her!' Vita declared, hugging her passionately to her chest.

The reindeer had long floppy furry legs with pink satin ballet slippers, but she couldn't stand on them. I lifted the net skirt and saw a big hole.

'Don't look up her bottom!' Vita snapped.

'Um, Em's being rude,' said Maxie.

'No, I'm not! I've just realized, she's a glove puppet!'

'You got it, Emerald,' said Dad. 'Here, Vita, let's get to know her. We'll see if she'll introduce herself.'

He pressed her pink nose again to stop the ballet music and stuck his hand up inside her.

'Hello, Princess Vita,' he made the reindeer say, in a funny fruity female voice. 'I'm Dancer. I was one of Santa's very own reindeers. Maybe you've heard of my fellow sleigh artistes, Dasher and Prancer and Vixen? Then there's the so-called superstar, Rudolph, the one with the constant cold. *Such* a show-off, especially since he got his own song. Of course *I* was always the leading runner, until I realized that all that sleigh-pulling wasn't such a

18

good idea. I have very sensitive hooves. Santa was devastated when I gave in my notice but we artistes have to consider our talent. I am now Princess Vita's dancing companion and trusty steed.'

Dad made Dancer bow low and then twirl on her floppety legs. Vita clapped her hands, bright red with excitement.

I felt envious again. Why couldn't *I* have had a puppet? Then Dad and I could have had endless games together. Vita and Maxie had such special big presents this year. Why did mine have to be so tiny? It was just like one extra stocking present.

'Aren't you going to open your present, Emerald?' said Dad. He slipped Dancer over Vita's hand, showing her how to work her. Vita waved her wildly round and round. Maxie laughed and tried to catch Dancer. One of her antlers accidently poked him in the eye.

'Hey, hey, watch out! Oh Maxie, for heaven's sake, it didn't really hurt,' said Mum, grabbing Vita's arm and pulling Maxie close for a cuddle. 'Yes, Em, open your present. Whatever can it be?'

I undid the wrapping paper, feeling foolish with them all watching me. I got my mouth all puckered up, waiting to say *Thank you* and give grateful kisses. Then I opened a little black box and stared at what was inside. I was stunned. I couldn't say anything at all.

'What is it, Em?'

'Show us!'

'Don't you like it?'

It was a little gold ring set with a deep green glowing jewel.

'I *love* it,' I whispered. 'It's an emerald!'

'Not a real emerald, darling,' said Mum.

'Yes it is,' said Dad. 'I'm not fobbing off my daughter with anything less!'

My *daughter*! I loved that almost as much as my beautiful ring.

'Don't be silly, Frankie,' Mum said. '*Real* emeralds cost hundreds and hundreds of pounds!'

'No they don't. Not if you go to antique fairs and do someone a favour and find a little emerald for a special small girl,' said Dad.

He unhooked the ring from its little velvet cushion and put it on the ring finger of my right hand.

'It fits perfectly!' I said.

'Well, I had it made specially for you, Princess Emerald,' said Dad.

'But however much have you spent on all of us?' Mum said, shaking her head as if she'd been swimming underwater.

'Never you mind,' said Dad. 'I wanted this to be a special Christmas, one the kids will remember for ever.'

'But we owe so much already—'

'Leave it, Julie,' Dad said sharply.

So Mum left it. We had a big Christmas cuddle, the five of us – six, counting Dancer – and then we heard Gran going downstairs to put the kettle on.

Vita insisted on having Dancer on her lap at breakfast time. Maxie held onto his felt tips too, balancing them across his bony knees. I stuck my hand out after every mouthful, admiring my ring.

'Haven't we got the loveliest dad ever?' said Vita.

Gran sniffed. 'What have you done now, Frankie, robbed a bank?' she said.

Dad laughed and put his arm round her. 'Now, Ellen, no po-faces, it's Christmas. Come on, you old bat, you know you love me really.' He gave her a kiss. She pushed him away, shaking her head, but she couldn't help smiling. She actually burst out laughing when she opened *her* present from Dad. It was a pair of tight designer jeans.

'For God's sake, Frankie, I'm a grandma!'

'And you've got almost as lovely a figure as your daughter, so flaunt it, eh? You'll look great in the jeans, much better than those baggy old trousers. Try them on!'

'Don't think you can get round *me*,' said Gran – but she changed into her new jeans after breakfast.

Dad was right. Gran had a really good figure, though we'd never noticed it before. From the waist down she didn't look a bit like our gran. Dad gave her a wolf whistle and she told him not to be so daft – but she blushed.

'I'm not going to wear them *out* of course,' she said. 'Still, they're fine for the house.'

She had to go and change out of them again after Christmas dinner. We normally all eat separately. Vita and Maxie and I have our tea after school. Mum just has snacks while she's waiting to have a meal later with Dad. Gran heats up her own Lean Cuisines and eats them off a tray when *EastEnders* and *Coronation Street* are on television. But Christmas is different. We all eat together with a proper tablecloth and Gran's best white-and-gold china from the cabinet where she keeps her pink crinoline lady and the balloon-seller and the little mermaid with a green scaly tail and the little girl and boy in white china nightgowns.

We had crackers so we all wore paper hats and shouted out silly mottoes. Vita snorted with laughter while she was drinking her Ribena 'wine' and it went right up her nose and then spattered the white embroidered cloth. Gran would have gone mad if Maxie or I had done it, but she just shook her head fondly at Vita and told her to calm down.

Vita made a fuss about her Christmas dinner

too. She wouldn't eat a single sprout or parsnip and only one forkful of turkey. She just wanted a plate of roast potatoes.

'Well, why shouldn't the kid have exactly what she fancies on Christmas Day?' said Dad, scraping everything off her plate and then piling it high with potatoes.

Maxie started noisily demanding a plate of roast potatoes too. Mum and Gran sighed at Dad for starting something.

'Still, at least our Em's eating her plateful,' said Mum.

'Em always eats everything. It's a wonder she doesn't gollop the plate down too,' said Gran.

She'd started to nag me about calories and carbohydrates and all that stuff, though Mum always got mad at her and said she'd turn me anorexic.

'As if!' said Gran unkindly.

I took no notice and munched my way through my turkey and chipolata sausages and roast potatoes and mashed potatoes and parsnips and every single sprout and then I had a slice of Christmas pudding with green jelly and red jelly and cream and then a mince pie and then a satsuma and *then* three chocolates out of the Christmas tin of Quality Street.

Gran slapped my hand away when I reached in

the tin for a fourth chocolate. 'For God's sake, Em, you'll burst,' she said. 'Your stomach must be made of elastic. You'll have to learn to stop shovelling your food up like that. I don't know how you *can*. I'm totally stuffed. I'm going to have to take my posh jeans off and have a little lie down.'

'Quit nagging Princess Emerald. It's great that she's got a healthy appetite,' said Dad. 'Right, ladies, us chaps will do the washing-up. You can all take a little nap. We'll do the donkey work in the kitchen, won't we, Maxie?'

Maxie took Dad seriously and started gathering Gran's best china with a bang and a clatter.

'Hey, hey, careful, you'll chip those plates!' said Gran.

'Yeah, Gran's got a point, little guy,' said Dad. 'Tell you what, you start drawing me a lovely picture with your new felt pens. Then I can get on with the washing-up in peace.'

Maxie lay on the floor, carefully colouring, his eyes screwed up and his tongue sticking out because he was concentrating so fiercely. He was *much* more careful with the points of his own felt tips than he was with mine.

Vita annoyed him for a while, running her fingers over the felt pens in the tin, playing them as if they were an instrument, but her roast potatoes took a toll on her. She lay back on the sofa, Dancer on her arm so she could use her velvety head like a cuddle blanket. Mum curled up in a corner of the sofa. She said she wanted to watch the Queen on television but her eyes started drooping and she was asleep in seconds.

I sat back, my hand stretched out in front of me, so I could admire my real emerald from every angle. I still couldn't believe how wonderful it was. Dad said he'd got it at a bargain price but I knew it still must have cost heaps. More than Mum's silver sandals or Gran's jeans or Vita's reindeer or Maxie's crayons.

It must mean that Dad loved me just as much as Vita and Maxie even though I wasn't really his daughter. I knew I loved him more than anyone. Far far far far far far far more than my own dad.

I hadn't seen him for years now. I didn't want to. We didn't want to have any more to do with him, Mum and me.

I decided to go and help Dad with the washing-up, even though he'd told us all he wanted the kitchen to himself. I crept across the living room into the hall. I waved at my ring in the mirror above the telephone table. It winked its brilliant green light back at me.

The kitchen door was shut. I could hear Dad muttering inside. I grinned. Was he singing to himself as he did the dishes? I opened the door slowly and carefully, not making a sound. Dad had his back to me.

'Oh darling, darling, darling,' he said.

I thought he was talking to me. Then I saw the hunch of his shoulders, his hand up against his ear. He was talking on his mobile.

'Yeah, yeah! Oh Sarah, I'm missing you so much too,' he said. 'Still, I can't get out of Christmas, it means so much to Julie and the kids. I'm trying to make it happy for them, though dear God it's such an effort now. Still, I'm planning on telling them soon. I can't stay much longer. I'm going crazy. I want to be with you so badly, babe. I'm leaving them, I swear I am.'

*'Don't leave us, Dad!'*

He whipped round. I waited for him to tell me I'd got it all wrong. He wasn't really talking to some girlfriend. He was acting a part, playing some stupid joke. Dad could always talk his way out of anything. I wanted him to tell me any old story, even if I knew he was lying.

He didn't say anything. He just stood staring at me, biting his lip foolishly the way Maxie does when he's been caught out. The mobile phone buzzed as someone spoke to him.

'Call you back,' Dad said and he switched the phone off. He held it warily, as if it was a hand grenade.

We stared at each other, standing freeze-framed. I wished I could rewind a minute so I could be back in the hall, happily waving my emerald ring around.

'You're not really leaving us, are you, Dad?' I whispered.

'I'm sorry, Em,' he said softly.

The room started spinning. I staggered to the sink and threw up all over the china in the washing-up bowl.

'**I**t's all right, Em, it's all right,' Dad said, holding me.

We both knew it could never be all right again. I retched and sobbed, unable to reply.

Gran came bursting into the kitchen, disturbed from her nap.

'What's going on? Oh, for God's sake, you've been sick all over my best china!'

'Who's been sick?' said Mum, coming in too. Vita and Maxie followed her.

'Em's been sick,' said Gran. 'I *told* you not to make a pig of yourself, Emily.'

'Yuck!' said Vita.

'It smells!' said Maxie.

'You two, out of here,' said Mum. 'Go into the living room with your gran. I'll clear it all up.'

'Maybe you'll listen to me when I tell you that child should stop stuffing herself. God, what a mess! It's even splashed on the curtains!' Gran was nearly in tears herself.

'I'll wash everything. Just leave us alone, please,' said Dad.

He said it very quietly, but Gran stopped fussing and dragged Vita and Maxie out of the kitchen.

'Oh, Em,' said Mum, dabbing at me with a tea towel. 'We'd better pull these things off and stick you straight in the bath. Couldn't you have run to the toilet if you were going to be so sick?'

'It wasn't her fault,' said Dad. He was so grey-white he looked like he might be sick himself.

'What do you mean? What's going on?' said Mum, trying to hitch my sweater over my head.

'Don't tell her, Dad!' I said through layers of soggy wool.

If he kept quiet then maybe it wouldn't be real.

'I was planning on telling you anyway, but I was leaving it till after Christmas. I'm so sorry. I just hate myself for doing this to you. I didn't mean it to happen.'

'What the hell are you talking about?' said Mum, letting go of me.

Dad took a deep breath. 'I've met someone else, Julie.'

Mum scarcely blinked. 'Yes. Well. That's nothing new,' she said.

'But this time, well, I love her. I'm sorry, I don't want to hurt you, but this is it, the real thing. It's never been this way before.'

'You don't want to hurt me and yet you're telling me you love someone else?' said Mum, her face crumpling.

'Oh, Mum, don't cry,' I begged. I wanted to put my arms round her but I was so wet and disgusting I couldn't touch her.

'Go and get in the bath, Em,' Dad said. 'Your mum and I need to talk.'

'*I* need to talk too,' I said. 'You love *us*, Dad – Mum and me and Vita and Maxie.'

'Of course I love you, darling. I shall come and visit you lots, but I can't help it. I have to go.'

'You can't do this to me! You can't, you can't!' Mum started sobbing, swaying on her silver sandals.

Dad tried to put his arm round her but she started hitting him.

'Don't, Mum, don't, Dad!' I shouted.

I couldn't believe this was happening. I kept shutting my eyes and opening them, hoping that I was dreaming. If only I could open my eyes determinedly enough I'd get back to our magical Christmas Day.

Gran came back in the kitchen and she started

31

shouting too. Then she was propelling me out of the room, dragging me upstairs to the bathroom, stripping the rest of my clothes off and dunking me in the bath like a baby. She soaped me so hard it felt like she was slapping me.

Vita and Maxie kept tapping on the bathroom door, crying to be let in.

'Oh, for God's sake,' said Gran, shampooing my hair because some of it had dangled in the sick. Her nails dug right into my scalp.

I didn't dare tell her she was hurting me. She seemed so terrifyingly cross with me, as if it was all my fault.

*Maybe it* was *my fault.*

Vita and Maxie seemed ready to blame me. They came hurtling into the bathroom.

'Mum's mad at Dad because you were sick everywhere, Em,' said Vita.

'She's shouting and shouting. She even shouted at me though *I* wasn't sick,' Maxie wept.

They didn't seem to understand what was really going on. They were too little. I wanted to be too little too. Gran was bathing me like a baby. I wanted to *be* a baby. I wanted her to wrap me in the towel and pick me up and hug me close. She must have made a proper fuss of me when I was a baby – all grans did.

'There, Em, get out the bath. Don't just stand

32

there looking gormless,' Gran snapped. 'Get yourself dry and then get some clean clothes on.'

She yanked at me so that I nearly overbalanced. My emerald gleamed as I waved my arms in the air.

'Oh, Gran, my ring! I've got it all wet and soapy! Oh no, what if I've spoiled it!' I gasped.

'Yes, well, it was ridiculous giving a child your age an emerald ring,' said Gran. 'Typical badword Frankie!'

It was *such* a bad word that we all stared at her. How dare she call my dad horrible names! I looked at her pale veiny legs showing through her dressing gown.

'It was ridiculous giving an old lady your age a pair of jeans,' I said.

Vita and Maxie gasped. I backed away from her rapidly because she looked like she was going to slap me. But she just sighed and shook her head at me, as if she'd simply caught me scratching or picking my nose. I realized she was too concerned with what was happening down in the kitchen to care about me cheeking her.

Mum was still screaming and sobbing, on and on and on.

When I was dry and dressed and in clean clothes Gran made Vita and Maxie and me stay shut up in the living room. She put the television volume

33

up until it buzzed whenever anyone talked but we could still hear Mum in the kitchen. I kept switching channels until Gran snatched the remote out of my hand.

'Let's watch a video. Let's watch *Thomas*. Please, please, *Thomas*!' Maxie begged.

He hadn't watched *Thomas the Tank Engine* for months and months. He still knew it by heart. We *all* knew it by heart but we tried to watch it, even Gran. Mum was still shouting. Dad was shouting back now. Vita put her thumb in her mouth and rubbed her nose on Dancer's fur. Maxie kept his eyes on *Thomas* but under his breath he muttered, 'Bad Mummy, bad Daddy.'

I wished I had a remote for Mum and Dad so I could press their mute button. I kept telling myself that it would somehow be all right. They'd stop shouting and suddenly sigh and fall into each other's arms. They'd done this enough times in the past so they could do it again. Dad would say he'd been mad to think of leaving us. He'd swear he'd never see this Sarah again. He'd stay with Mum and Vita and Maxie and me and we'd all live happily ever after. I told myself this fairy story over and over, clenching my fists, my emerald ring digging into my skin.

'For pity's sake, look at you kids! It's Christmas!' said Gran.

34

She wrapped her dressing gown right round her and marched off to the kitchen, her bedroom slippers thwacking the floor at each step.

'She's gone to tell them off,' said Maxie.

It seemed to work. The shouting stopped. There was a lot of muttering. Then Gran came back into the living room. Dad came with her. His eyes were red as if he'd been crying too, but he was smiling determinedly. He looked like his upturned lips had been stuck on his face by mistake.

'Right, my little lovelies, what do we all want to play, eh?'

'We could play Snap,' Maxie suggested.

He was useless at Snap, so slow at recognizing two identical cards that he simply screamed '*Snap!*' at the top of his voice all the time. Your ears ached when you played Snap with Maxie.

'Snap's stupid, and Maxie can't play it properly,' said Vita. 'Let's play Happy Families.'

Dad winced. Vita wasn't deliberately getting at him. She liked Happy Families because she loved the pictures of the rabbit and the squirrel and the mouse families.

'Let's play a Christmas game,' said Dad. He looked round for Dancer and put his hand up inside her.

'We'll all dance,' said Dancer. 'Let's play Musical Bumps.'

Dad shuffled through the CDs until he found an old *Children's Favourites* with silly songs about pink toothbrushes and mice with clogs and runaway trains.

'*Not* the red-nosed reindeer song!' Dancer said, jiggling about on the end of Dad's arm. 'OK, let's get jumping! Watch me pirouette, girls and boys!'

Dad played the music really loudly. Maxie and Vita started leaping around the living room. I started jumping too. Gran sighed.

'For heaven's sake, Em, do you have to thump like that? You're rattling all my china figurines in the cabinet.'

I stopped so abruptly I twisted my ankles.

'No, no, come on, Princess Emerald, you're light as a fairy,' Dad said. 'Let me sweep you up in my arms and we'll do a merry Christmas jig.'

'Yes, merry Christmas to you too, you dirty heart-breaking swine,' said Gran, and she ran out of the room.

Vita and Maxie stood still too.

'No, no, the music's not stopped yet. Don't you children know how to play Musical Bumps?' said Dancer.

So we jumped and we bumped regardless of Gran's china. Then Dancer taught us how to play all these old-fashioned party games like Squeak Piggy Squeak and Blind Man's Buff. Dad used my woollen scarf as a blindfold. Dancer admired the scarf and said she wished she'd had something similar for those cold nights pulling Santa's sleigh.

'A chic knitted scarf with matching antler-warmers – and woolly patchwork pants would be a great idea too!' she said.

We all collapsed in a heap on the carpet and Dad gave Vita and Maxie a cuddle. I wondered if I was too big for a little kid's cuddle but Dad reached out and pulled me in.

'Dad, you're not *really* going to go, are you?' I whispered right in his ear.

'Ssh, Princess Emerald! We won't discuss state secrets in front of Princess Vita and Prince Maxie,' Dad said, putting a finger to my lips.

I didn't say any more. I held it in all through tea. Gran laid out turkey sandwiches and mince pies and chocolate log.

'Now for pity's sake go easy, Em. Maybe you'd be better off with plain bread and butter,' said Gran.

I was feeling so empty I was ready to wolf everything down. The food tasted strange though, too light, like cotton wool. My head felt stuffed with cotton wool too. I couldn't think properly. It was just like a dream. Here I was, licking chocolate off my fingers, having my Christmas tea, and Vita and Maxie were pretending to feed Dancer and being all giggly and silly – but Mum was upstairs in her room, not having any tea at all.

Gran tried taking her a tray but she brought it back down untouched.

'I want Mum,' Maxie said suddenly, sliding off his chair.

'No, leave her alone, Maxie, she's got a bad headache,' said Gran.

'She gave *me* a bad headache with all that shouting,' said Vita. Then she paused. 'She is OK now though, isn't she, Dad?'

'I think she still feels a bit poorly, Princess,' said Dad.

'No wonder,' Gran spat out. 'You lying pig.'

'Now, now. Come on. You were the one who told me to think of the kids. We don't want to spoil their Christmas,' said Dad.

He tried very hard, dancing and singing and playing jokes. When Vita got over-excited and Maxie got tearful he squashed up on the sofa with them and made Dancer tell them a long story about her little reindeerhood in Lapland. Santa came on a talent-spotting visit when the reindeer school had its sports day. Dancer ran like the wind and won her race even though she was the youngest reindeer and her antlers were still as small and furry as pussy willow.

I wanted to snuggle up and listen too but I

crept out of the room, past Gran angrily washing the tea things in the kitchen, up the stairs to Mum. I listened outside her room, scared of going in, feeling weird and embarrassed. Then I heard her little sobs, just like Maxie's, and I went rushing in to her. She still had all her clothes on but she was right under the duvet, hunched up in a soggy ball.

'Oh Mum, don't cry so,' I said. I burrowed under the covers and put my arms tight round her as if she was my little girl and I was her mother.

'What am I going to do, Em?' she sobbed. 'I can't live without him.'

'It's OK, Mum, it's OK,' I said over and over, trying to soothe her.

She wriggled away from me, suddenly furious. 'It's not badword OK, you silly little girl. He's leaving us for another woman, for God's sake,' Mum hissed.

'No he's not. He's fine now, Mum. He's being really lovely to Vita and Maxie and me. He's trying to make it up to us. He won't go, not really. He *loves* us.'

'Did he say he wasn't going?'

I swallowed. 'Yes,' I said, because I so wanted it to be true.

Mum held onto me. 'You're sure?'

'Well . . .'

Mum knew I wasn't sure but she badly wanted it to be true too. She let me convince her.

'I'll find it hard to forgive him, though,' she said. 'This isn't the first time, Em. There are things you don't know about him. I don't know why I'm so desperate to hold onto him. I'd maybe be better off without him, without all this uncertainty and heartbreak.'

'But you love him, Mum.'

'Of course I love him, Em.' Mum sat up and gave me a proper hug. Then she switched on her crystal-drop lamp and looked at herself in the mirror.

'God, what a sight I look!'

Mum's very pretty but she really did look a sight, even in the soft sparkly light of the lamp. Her hair was sticking up in clumps and her eyelids were sore and swollen, like purple grapes. Her dark lipstick was smeared all round her mouth, like Vita when she's been drinking Ribena.

'No wonder he's got sick of me,' Mum moaned.

'You go and wash your face and put lots of make-up on,' I said. 'Then you'll knock him dead.'

'OK, miss, I'll do as I'm told,' said Mum.

She got herself sorted and then slipped her feet back into her new silver sandals.

'My million-dollar mum,' I said.

'Oh, Em, you're the sweetest, weirdest kid,' said Mum, her face crumpling.

'Don't cry again, you'll mess up all your make-up!'

'OK, OK, I'm not crying,' said Mum, blinking like crazy.

We walked downstairs hand in hand. Gran came out into the hall holding a tea towel.

'God, you're going to beg him to stay, aren't you?' she said. 'You'll never learn, Julie. After the way he's treated you! He needs strangling.' She twisted the tea towel violently, as if it was Dad's neck.

Mum took no notice. She took a deep breath. She held it for a long moment, her chest high, her lips clamped together. Then she breathed out and walked into the living room. Dad looked anxious as she swayed towards him in her silver sandals. Vita sat up straight, Dancer hanging limply from her arm. Maxie jammed his thumb in his mouth and hunched up very small, as if he was trying to make himself invisible.

'Hello, darlings,' Mum said, brightly and bravely. She stretched and yawned, acting like she'd just woken up. 'Mm, I had a lovely nap. Shall we see what's on telly now?'

She wasn't really kidding anyone, not even Maxie, but we all acted like we hadn't heard any of the shouting and sobbing.

Dad gently pushed Vita along the sofa and patted

the cushion. 'Come and sit down, babe,' he said gently.

Mum sat beside him. Vita, Maxie and I arranged ourselves round them. Gran sat sniffing and sighing in her chair opposite. We watched all the Christmas specials on the television and whenever there was a funny bit we all laughed a little too hilariously. Maxie snorted so much that he gave himself hiccups.

'You're getting over-tired, young man. Time you were in bed,' said Gran.

'No no no!' Maxie squealed.

'Yes yes yes!' said Dad. 'Hey, Maxie, Dancer wants to tell you about her reindeer house back in Lapland. You'll never guess what sort of bed she has.'

Maxie let Dad carry him upstairs. Vita started clamouring, so Dad carried her on his other arm. I watched, wishing I could whittle myself down to pocket size so I could cling to Dad like a little monkey too. I clumped along behind them instead.

Dad invented an entire Lapland saga, telling us about the baby reindeer nurseries with their green mossy cots with swan's-down quilts, and then describing reindeer school, where they had lessons in dancing, trotting, galloping, and special flying instruction for advanced and extra-talented reindeer.

Maxie fell asleep first. Dad tucked him under his own blankets and ruffled his dark tufty hair. Vita allowed herself to be tucked up too, but was clearly willing herself to stay awake, her forehead furrowed with the effort of keeping her eyes wide open. But eventually she gave a little sigh, clasped Dancer to her chest, and fell asleep too.

Dad wriggled his hand free of the glove puppet and patted Vita gently on her bony shoulder. She'd refused to put on her own Barbie pyjamas and was wearing one of Mum's little black nightie tops. We'd argued over which one of us would wear it when Mum broke one of the straps and donated it to our dressing-up box. I won, but when I tried it on Vita laughed cruelly and said I looked like one of the hippos in her Disney video. I shoved her hard in the chest and said she was just jealous, but I let her commandeer the little black nightie after that. Vita looked wonderful in it, like a little midnight fairy.

'My girlie,' Dad whispered, and he kissed her high forehead.

The room seemed very quiet. Dad smiled at me, not quite meeting my eyes.

'Into bed, Princess Emerald,' he said.

'Dad?'

'Now come on, darling, it's way past your bed time.'

'Dad, promise you'll stay?'

Dad screwed up his face for a moment. Then he stood up, seized my hand and kissed my ring. 'Your wish is my command, Princess Emerald,' he said. 'Now stop looking so worried and hip-hop into bed.'

Dad started a hip-hop little song about Princess Em and her magic ring, bling bling. I sang along too. I even danced round the bed, but when Dad tried to tuck the duvet under my chin I flung my arms round his neck.

'Hey, hey, you're throttling me!' Dad joked.

'Dad, you do promise, don't you?'

'Play another tune, Princess,' said Dad. 'I said that your wish is my command, don't you remember?'

'You didn't actually *say* you promised. Say it, Dad. *Please* say it.'

'OK, OK. I promise.'

'You promise you'll stay for ever?'

'I promise I'll stay for ever,' he said. 'Now give me a kiss night-night. You never know, you might just transform me from a loathsome toad into a handsome prince.'

'You're a handsome prince already, silly,' I said, kissing him.

I was wrong. He was a total toad.

I woke early, my heart beating fast. I slid out of

bed and crept across the carpet, not wanting to wake Vita or Maxie. I padded down the hall. I listened outside Mum and Dad's door. I heard muffled sobs. I ran into the bedroom. Mum was sitting on the edge of the bed, rocking backwards and forwards, her hands tugging her hair.

Dad had broken his promise. He'd gone already.

D ad left me a note. I can't quite remember what it said. Something about not wanting to upset me. He'd drawn a little toad where he signed his name. He'd even taken the trouble to colour it with Maxie's new felt tips.

I didn't want the others to see it. I smoothed it out carefully and tucked it underneath my jumper, next to my heart. The paper tickled a little but I didn't mind.

When I was helping Gran mash the potatoes for our cold turkey lunch she suddenly cocked her head on one side.

'What's that crackling, Em?' she asked.

'Nothing,' I said quickly, mashing harder.

'You've got something stuffed down your jumper! For heaven's sake, you're not padding your vest with tissues and pretending you've got breasts, are you?'

'No!' I said, folding my arms across my chest and blushing violently.

'Don't be so *daft*, Em,' said Gran, her fingers scrabbling under my jumper.

'Don't! Get off me!' I said.

I couldn't stop her. She felt the letter. It tore right across as she dragged it free.

'My letter! Now look what you've done,' I shouted. 'You've torn it.'

Gran was holding the letter at arm's length, as if it was dripping with something disgusting. 'I'm glad I've torn it!' She said. 'I'm going to tear it into tiny shreds.' She tore and tore, little particles of paper flying everywhere.

I couldn't grab it back in time. I watched, weeping.

'You can stop that silly noise too. We've had enough weeping and wailing going on, enough tears to sink the *Titanic*. If you ask me I think you should be shedding tears of joy to be rid of that two-timing conniving Mr Smoothie. I never liked him right from the day your mother brought him home. I said as much too, but she didn't listen to me. She never does. No one in this house ever listens to what I say.'

I put my hands over my ears to show her I wasn't

48

listening either. I certainly wasn't going to help her mash the potatoes. It didn't matter anyway. None of us ate much lunch. Even Vita turned up her nose at potatoes. She didn't eat anything at all. Maxie just had pudding. Mum drank a whole bottle of wine but had nothing to eat.

I said I wasn't hungry either and went without. Then halfway through the long long afternoon I crept into the kitchen and started pulling little shreds off the turkey. Once I'd started I couldn't stop. I tore at the turkey, tearing off great strips, so hungry I wanted to gnaw at it like a dog.

I heard footsteps and leaped back, guiltily wiping my greasy hands on my skirt, waiting for Gran to give me another lecture on my greediness. It wasn't Gran, thank goodness, it was Vita. She had Dancer on her hand, the brown fur reaching all the way up her bony little arm almost to her armpit.

'Hi, you,' I said, tearing off another piece of turkey.

Vita's eyes widened. 'Gran will go bananas if she sees you doing that!'

'I don't care. I hate Gran,' I said fiercely.

Vita blinked. Then she wiped her nose with one of Dancer's antlers. 'I hate her too,' she said.

'No you don't,' I said. 'You like her heaps. You're her favourite. She's always giving you treats and letting you get away with stuff, you know she is.'

'She's horrid though. She says Dad's gone away

49

with another lady and he's not ever coming back. She's telling lies, isn't she, Em?'

'What did Mum say?'

'She just cried more and said she didn't know. She told me to go away because she's got an awful headache. Maxie says he's got a headache too. He's mad, he's gone to bed and it's only the afternoon. It's gone all weird and horrid and upside down. Gran told me to play a game but I want to play games with *Dad*.' Tears started dribbling down Vita's cheeks. 'Em, *is* he coming back?'

'Of course he is. In a bit. He wouldn't go away for good without telling us. He's *got* to come back to see us. Even *my* dad came back to see me when I was little before Mum told him to get lost.'

'I can't remember your dad,' said Vita.

'I can't remember him either,' I said. It wasn't quite true. I still had nightmares about him. I shivered, and stuffed more turkey in my mouth.

Vita looked at me. 'Our dad won't go scary like yours, will he?' she asked.

'No, of course not, Vita. Dad couldn't *ever* be scary, you know that.'

'And he will come back?' Vita said, Dancer drooping down her arm.

I wiped my hands properly and then commandeered Dancer, fitting her over my fist.

'Hello, Princess Vita,' I made her say, copying

Dad's voice for her, all funny and fruity. 'Now listen here, my dear, no one knows your dad better than I do. I say he's absolutely definitely coming back.'

'Now? Today?'

'Maybe not today.'

'Tomorrow?'

'Mm, perhaps. Oooh, just look at that scrumptious plate of turkey! I'm feeling very peckish, Princess Vita. Hint hint!'

Vita laughed and pretended to feed her, but she wouldn't be distracted. 'Dad will come back *soon*, won't he?'

'Yes, yes, my dear, Dad won't let us down. He'll come back as soon as he can. Tell you what, let's use a little turkey magic.' I made Dancer circle the turkey plate, prancing round and round, while I pulled more meat off with my free hand.

'I don't want to eat any turkey,' said Vita.

'No, no, I'm just looking for— Aha!' I scrabbled away at the turkey, tugging at a little twig of bone. I wriggled it free and then gave it to Dancer. She held it out triumphantly.

'What have I found, Princess Vita?' said Dancer.

'A bone?' said Vita doubtfully.

'A *wish*bone! You take one end, hooking your little finger round it, OK? Princess Emerald will take hold of the other end. Then when I say so, you both pull, and the Princess who gets the longest piece of bone has a magic wish.'

'That's not fair!' wailed Vita, poking Dancer as if she was a real person. 'Em's bigger and stronger than me so she'll get the turkey wish.'

'What will she wish for, Princess Poke-and-Prod?' said Dancer.

Vita thought about it. 'Ah!' she said. 'But I still wish *I* could do the wishing.'

'That's one wish wasted already,' said Dancer. 'Now quit prodding me, missy, or I'll stick my antlers up your nose.'

Vita started giggling.

'Come on, Vita, pull the wishbone,' I said, thrusting it at her.

She pulled. I pulled. I twisted the wishbone a little, applying more pressure. I knew we were going to wish identical wishes but I was just like Vita. *I* wanted to make the wish.

The wishbone shattered. Vita was left holding a tiny stump. I had almost the whole V-shaped bone in my hand.

'Ooh!' said Vita. 'Go on, then, Em. Wish. Wish it *hard*.'

I hung onto the wishbone, and shut my eyes. I wished for Dad to come back. I wished it so fiercely I felt my head would burst. I wished and wished and wished.

'Em, you've gone purple,' said Vita.

I opened my eyes and breathed out, exhausted.

'Will it come true?' said Vita, glancing at the door, expecting Dad to bound in right that minute.

'It *will* come true, but maybe not for a little while,' I said.

Vita sighed. She looked at Dancer. 'Can't *you* make it come true, as quick as quick?' she said.

I found I was looking at Dancer too, even though my own hand was up inside her. She nodded her head. She shook her head. Nod, shake, nod, shake.

'Quick as quick or slow as slow,' she said enigmatically. 'Quick quick *slow slow*, quick quick *slow*, like the ballroom dance, my dear.'

I seized Vita and quick-stepped her round her kitchen, Dancer holding her round the waist.

It wasn't quick quick. We waited the day after Boxing Day. Then the day after and the day after and the day after and the day after. Mum got up off her bed and went out looking for him – all over his favourite places in town, even up to London and back. She phoned his mobile again and again but it was always switched off. She tried phoning all his mates. She went down to the Pink Palace where they both worked even though she knew it was all shut up until after the New Year. She wandered round and round all day, wearing the silver sandals, as if she thought they might walk her directly to Dad. Her feet were rubbed raw by the time she limped home and she'd lost the tip of one stiletto heel.

'Don't cry, Mum, you can take them to Mr Minit,' I said. 'They're not badly broken.'

'Yes they are,' said Vita. 'Can I have them for dressing up, Mum?'

'*I* want them, Mum,' said Maxie, sticking his fat little feet inside the sandals and shuffling across the room.

'Get them shoes off, sharpish,' said Gran. 'Boys don't wear high heels. I don't know why you're all fighting over them. They belong in the bin with all the rest of the trash.'

'They're beautiful shoes,' said Mum, snatching them from Maxie and cradling them as if they were silver dolls.

'Yes, cost a fortune, like the rest of Frankie's ridiculous Christmas presents. *Whose* fortune, Julie? I bet he paid with your joint credit card. You'll be paying off your own presents until *next* Christmas. And what about all the money I've lent him, my savings from slaving in that blooming office? What about the kids? Is he just going to walk out of their lives without paying a penny in child support? You're rubbish at choosing men – one violent nutter, one sleazy charmer—'

54

'You're rubbish at men too, Gran,' I said furiously, because she was making Mum cry. 'Grandad cleared off ages ago.'

'Good riddance! Catch me making a fool of myself a second time,' said Gran, sniffing. 'I don't know why you're in such a state, Julie. You knew what he was like. Why do you have to let him hurt you so? You need to toughen up a bit.'

Gran seized hold of Mum as if she was personally going to shake some sense into her – but then her arms went right round her. Gran held Mum and rocked her. Mum howled. Vita and Maxie went and joined in the hug too.

I stayed separate, picking up Dancer from the floor. We went out into the kitchen together and had a sneaky snack from the larder. Dancer decided to try a raisin or two out of the packet, and then she couldn't seem to stop. She liked the icing sugar too, because it reminded her of snow.

'Snow snow, thick thick snow,' I murmured, doing the wishing dance round and round the kitchen table.

Then I heard a mobile ringing. It was Mum's mobile in her handbag, where she'd dropped it in the hallway. I dashed to answer it. It could be any of Mum's mates but I knew it was Dad, I just *knew* it.

'Hello, Julie?'

'Oh, Dad, Dad, Dad!' I said.

'Em! Hello, sweetheart! How are you, babe? How's everyone? Can I speak to your mum in a minute?'

Mum was already in the hall, on her knees beside me, trying to snatch the phone away. I hung onto it.

'Dad, when are you coming back?' I asked.

'Well, I'm planning to come and see you New Year's Day. I thought we could have a fun day out, you, me, Vita and Maxie, right?'

'Oh yes, *please*!' I said.

'What? Is he really coming back? Give me my phone, Em!' Mum said. She prised my fingers off it and listened herself.

'*I* want to talk to Dad! I must talk to him. I've got heaps and heaps to tell him,' said Vita.

'And me! I want to! Let *me*!' Maxie shrieked.

Mum sat still, staring straight ahead as if she was looking right through us.

'Mum?' I whispered.

She didn't seem to hear. She didn't react to Vita's imperious commands or Maxie's whines. She just knelt there, as if she was praying. Then she suddenly pressed the little red button, cutting Dad off.

'Mum!' we wailed.

'Good for you, Julie,' said Gran, watching from the living-room doorway.

'What is it, Mum? Why won't you speak to Dad?' I asked, stunned.

'You're the meanest mum *ever*. You didn't let me even say hello!' Vita wept.

'I want Dad!' Maxie bawled. 'Make Dad come back, Mum!'

'Stop it!' said Mum. She staggered to her feet. 'I can't *make* Dad come back.'

'He said he's coming on New Year's Day. He said it, he really did. He's coming back then,' I said.

'No. He's coming to take you three out. But he's not coming back to live here. He's making that quite plain. He's still with this woman.'

'You don't *know* that, Mum.'

'Yes I do. I heard her whispering to him,' said Mum.

'He's still going to take us out though?' said Vita.

'I don't know. I suppose so,' said Mum.

'Oh whoopee!' said Vita tactlessly. She started dancing up and down the hall.

'Dad's coming, Dad's coming!' Maxie yelled, galloping after her.

Mum stared at them. I didn't know what to say, what to do. Most of me wanted to dance too, because I so wanted a day out with Dad, no matter what. But he clearly wasn't inviting Mum. It would be so awful for her stuck at home with Gran.

I knew I should tell her that I didn't want to go. He wasn't even my own dad after all. But I couldn't bear to miss seeing him.

'I'll have to go to look after Vita and Maxie,' I said. 'You know what they're like, how silly they get. Dad's not always good at getting them to behave.'

Mum looked at me. She didn't say anything. The look was enough.

Gran seized hold of Vita and Maxie, giving them both a little shake. 'Stop that silly shrieking,' she said crossly. 'Don't go getting your hopes up. I don't think your dad will even bother to turn up.'

It looked as if Gran was right.

I was up very very very early on January 1st. We hadn't stayed up on New Year's Eve. Even Mum and Gran went to bed way before twelve. *Last* New Year's Eve we'd had a little party and Dad had bought a bottle of champagne. He gave me a tiny glassful and Vita and Maxie a few sips. Maxie rolled round the carpet afterwards, playing at being drunk, while Vita and I danced with Dad.

I tossed and turned half the night, thinking about Dad drinking and dancing with this horrible Sarah instead of us. I decided that Vita and Maxie and I had to be on our very best behaviour so that Dad would realize he couldn't bear to be without us.

I had a bath and washed my hair and then brushed it all out very carefully. I hoped Mum would do plaits at the sides and tie a velvet ribbon on for me, so that Dad would call me his pretty princess. I put on my best party outfit, a tight sparkly top and velvet trousers.

Then I looked in the mirror and took them off again. The top was way too tight now and the seams of the velvet trousers were nearly splitting. I didn't look like a pretty princess, I looked more like a pot-bellied pig. I stood in my knickers, sorting through all the clothes in my wardrobe, nearly weeping. Maxie stayed huddled up in his bear cave but Vita woke up and watched me.

'Put something *on*, Em,' she said.

'I haven't *got* anything,' I snivelled. 'All my clothes look rubbish. Correction. *I* look rubbish.'

'Yeah, well, we all know that,' said Vita. She stretched smugly. '*I'm* going to wear my disco-dancing queen outfit.'

I glared at her. Dad bought Vita this ultra-tight sparkly fancy-dress outfit for her last birthday. It had a halter top and low-slung trousers. They showed off Vita's tiny waist and totally flat stomach.

Vita was obviously thinking this too. 'I'm going to draw a special tummy tattoo with felt tips.'

'Not *my* felt tips,' Maxie mumbled from under his covers. 'I'm going to wear my cowboy outfit with Dad's cowboy boots. He left them in his wardrobe – I looked.'

'You can't wear Dad's boots, you'll fall over,' I said.

'Me can, me can, me can,' Maxie insisted.

'Quit that baby talk, Maxie, you're pathetic,' I said.

I tried on every single outfit in my wardrobe but they all looked awful. I seemed to have expanded horrifically overnight. I ended up wearing my Miss Kitty nightie over my loosest jeans. I hoped it looked like a smock top. I wondered about borrowing a pair of Mum's heels seeing as Maxie was helping himself to Dad's cowboy boots.

'For pity's sake, you look like a circus,' said Gran, when we came down to the kitchen. She was making our usual holiday breakfast – boiled eggs and soldiers. 'You needn't think you're going out like that. Take those ludicrous boots back at once, Maxie. Vita, you look like a little tart, take that horrible outfit *off*. And what are you playing at, Em, wearing your *nightie*? You're old enough to know better. You should set your little brother and sister an example, not egg them on all the time.'

'Egg, egg, egg!' Maxie shouted, bashing the top of his boiled egg so hard that yolk spurted everywhere.

'I don't!' I said, taking Maxie's spoon away. 'That's so mean, Gran. I try to make Vita and Maxie behave, don't I, Mum?'

Mum was sitting at the kitchen table sipping black coffee and smoking. She'd got up even earlier than me. She was in *her* prettiest clothes, a fluffy blue sweater and her embroidered jeans. She'd even painted her toenails silver to match her sandals.

She smiled anxiously at me, flicking her ash. 'Yes, you're a good kid, Em. Quit nagging her, Mum.'

'OK, I'll start in on you, Julie. Why in God's name are you smoking again when you gave it up years ago? Are you mad? Well yes, obviously you are, because you're all dressed up like a dog's dinner to see this pig husband of yours, when I wouldn't mind betting he won't turn up. Even if he *does*, he's not taking *you* out, he's made that plain.'

'Do you ever listen to yourself, Mum? Do you get a kick out of saying hurtful things? I can't stop you saying stuff to me, but I'm certainly not going to have you being mean to the kids, especially not now their whole world's been turned upside down. Take no notice of your gran, kids, you wear what you like. I think you all look lovely.'

I nodded at Gran triumphantly but I couldn't

really enjoy the victory. I knew Maxie really did look silly in his cowboy outfit. Dad's boots were so big they came right up to his bottom. Vita looked drop-dead gorgeous but like she was part of a dancing competition, not dressed to go out for the day. And though I kept hoping my Miss Kitty top looked perfectly OK, it was starting to look more and more like my nightie.

Still, Mum styled my hair for me and gave me my velvet ribbon. She tied another in Vita's wispy locks too, and she gelled Maxie's black mop so that it stuck up and looked very cute.

Then we waited. And waited and waited and waited. Mum had endless cups of coffee and cigarettes. I started secretly chomping chocolate biscuits because I felt so empty. I tried to keep Vita and Maxie amused, making Dancer draw her Santa experiences with Maxie's felt pens, but I didn't have a clue what a sleigh looked like and I was rubbish at drawing reindeer too.

I found it hard to concentrate because I was straining to hear Dad's footsteps walking up our path. I kept thinking I heard him and went running, but each time there was no one on the doorstep.

'I told you, he's not coming,' said Gran.

I wanted to punch her. Mum looked like she did too.

'Give him a chance, Mum. He's not late. He didn't say a specific time, he just said he'd pop over to collect the kids in the morning.'

'It's quarter to twelve, Julie.'

'It's still technically morning.'

'And you're technically a gullible mug, getting yourself all worked up over that loser. Look at the state of you – *and* the kids.'

'Stop getting at our mum and being so mean about our dad!' I said fiercely. 'You're not supposed to talk like that in front of children.'

'Children aren't supposed to talk back to their grandmas like that, you cheeky little madam,' said Gran. 'Em? Em, I'm talking to you!'

I wasn't listening. I heard footsteps. I ran. This time I was right!

'Dad!'

I threw myself at him, my arms round his neck. He hadn't shaved so his chin was scratchy and his hair was tousled round his shoulders like he'd just got out of bed but I didn't care.

'Daddy, oh, my daddy!' Vita cried, copying the girl in *The Railway Children* video.

Dad scooped her up in his arms.

'D-a-d!' Maxie bellowed, butting Dad so hard with his gelled head that we nearly all toppled over.

'Hey, kids, calm down!' said Dad.

He stopped, swallowing, rubbing the space

between his eyebrows as he looked the length of the hall to where Mum was standing. 'Hi, Julie,' he said softly, as if they'd only just met.

Mum didn't say anything. She had her arms tightly folded, her hands gripping her elbows.

'It's OK for me to take the kids out?' said Dad.

'Can't Mum come too?' I begged.

Dad hesitated. 'Well . . . this is a day out just for us,' he said.

Mum turned on her heel, walked into the kitchen and shut the door.

'Oh God. Julie? Look, OK, you come too, if you really want to. We have to talk, I know that. I just didn't want any hassle, it's not fair on the kids,' said Dad.

'How dare you!' said Gran.

'Oh God, I'm not up to this,' said Dad. 'Come on, kids, let's get cracking.' He took hold of Vita's and Maxie's hands and started pulling them out the door.

'Dad! Wait! They haven't got their coats. And Maxie can't walk in your boots,' I said, scrabbling around on the pegs for our three coats and kicking my way through old wellies and slippers for Maxie's shoes.

'You're like a little mum, Em. More grown up than the lot of us,' said Dad.

My heart thumped with pride under my Miss

Kitty nightie. We followed Dad out of the house, half in and half out of our coats, Maxie scuffling in his unlaced shoes. We didn't say goodbye to Gran. We didn't even say goodbye to Mum.

Dad took us on the train up to London. He bought a takeaway cup of black coffee at the station, and a bag of doughnuts for us. He shuddered when I offered him our bag of sugary doughnuts.

'Go on, Dad, they're delicious,' I said, biting a doughnut until the scarlet jam spurted out.

'Look, I've got lipstick,' said Vita, smearing jam round her mouth.

'Me too, me too,' said Maxie.

'I'm not very hungry, Em. You guys eat them,' said Dad.

'Don't you feel well, Dad?' I asked sympathetically.

'I'm fine,' said Dad, shivering. He pulled my woolly scarf tight round his neck. 'Ooh, what a great cosy scarf this is!'

Dad had a little sleep on the train. Vita kept wanting to wake him up and Maxie started clamouring, 'Are we in London yet?' two minutes after we got on the train, but I managed to distract them. We looked out the window at people's back gardens, playing Hunt the Child, on the lookout for swings and sandpits and bikes and balls.

Vita and Maxie kept squabbling over who saw things first. I kept glancing at Dad. He was very pale, huddled over, frowning in his sleep. I wondered if he was dreaming about us. I wanted to whisper in his ear, hypnotizing him when he was unconscious. *You are going to come back home, Dad. You love Mum and Vita and Maxie and me. You can't live without us.*

I shook his arm gently when we got to Waterloo. Dad opened his eyes and looked startled, as if he'd forgotten all about us. Then he smiled. He went to the gents at the station and came back looking a bit better, his face washed, his breath minty.

'Right, my darlings, we're off to the parade,' he said.

He told us this was a special New Year's Day parade. We had to walk there because Maxie was terrified of the escalators in the tube station. Dad kept making up stories about the parade, until he had Vita and Maxie believing there would be bareback riders in sparkly bikinis on snow-white horses and painted elephants with jewelled tusks and winged monkeys flying right over people's heads and snatching their hats off.

I knew he was making it all up but I almost believed it too, so the real parade was a disappointment. We couldn't see properly for a start because there were such crowds. Dad let Vita and Maxie take turns sitting on his shoulder. I was much too big. If I stood on tiptoe I could see the heads of lots and lots of chanting girls. Every now and then they threw sticks in the air or waved feathers, but that was all. There were big floats with famous people dressed up, waving and calling, but mostly we couldn't work out who they were.

Maxie whined whenever he had to let Vita have a turn on Dad's shoulders, so I tried picking him up.

'Lift me higher, Em, *higher*!' Maxie yelled. 'I can't see a sausage.'

Then, very spookily, a giant walking sausage came bobbing along as if Maxie had rubbed a magic lamp and conjured it up. It was part of a troupe of people advertising a new breakfast show on television. Men dressed up as eggs, bacon, cups of tea and packets of cornflakes were also parading along, having to take mincing little steps because of their big polystyrene costumes. The Sausage didn't really look like an obvious sausage when it was separated from its breakfast companions. Lots of people were falling about laughing, thinking it was something very rude.

I hitched Maxie too high. He saw the Sausage. He screamed.

'A monster! A monster! A big pink monster's coming to get me!'

The crowd collapsed, not taking Maxie's terror seriously.

'Hey, Maxie, it's just a big sausage,' Dad said. 'Don't be frightened, sweetheart. The sausage should be frightened of you. You could take a big bite and eat it all up.'

Maxie was yelling too loudly to listen to Dad. He probably wouldn't have believed him anyway.

'We've got to get out of here, Dad,' I said.

'How?' said Dad, because we were all hemmed in, barely able to breathe.

Maxie showed us how. He paused in mid scream, shuddered – and then was horribly sick all over me. The crowd parted as if by magic and Dad led us through. I was weeping now as well as Maxie. Vita started crying too, so as not to be left out.

Dad stared at us helplessly. He tried dabbing at Maxie and me with a tissue but it was hopeless. The sick was even in my *hair*.

'You'll have to go into a ladies and wash it in the basin. You'll have to help her, Vita,' said Dad.

'Yuck, I'm not touching all their sick. Anyway,

I don't know *how* to wash hair, Mum does mine,' said Vita. 'You two are disgusting. *I'm* never sick.'

'*I* wasn't sick,' I sobbed.

'You were at Christmas,' said Vita.

'That's enough, Vita,' said Dad. He was starting to look very queasy himself.

'The pink monster, the pink monster, it's coming to get me!' Maxie yelled.

'For God's sake, Maxie, we're miles away from the stupid sausage. It wasn't a monster, it was just a poor out-of-work actor just like Daddy in a manky costume. Maxie, *I've* dressed up in daft costumes. I was once a chicken in a shopping centre when a new cheapo chicken restaurant opened up. All these little kids kept barging into me going *cluck cluck cluck*.'

'He's not listening, Dad,' I said, wriggling. 'Ugh, it's all soggy round my neck. I can't stand this.'

'Here, we'll take your coat off,' said Dad, helping me out of it at arm's length. 'Oh Lord, it's all on your nightie thingy too. Perhaps we could buy you a new top or jacket or something and stick these stinky ones in a carrier bag? Where does Mum buy your clothes, Em?'

'I don't know,' I said.

It was hard to find clothes that would fit me in ordinary places like Tammy or The Gap, but I didn't want Dad to know that. Gran had once sent off for a Big Kiddo catalogue and I nearly died, because they were all clothes specially for fat kids. I *knew* I was a fat kid but I didn't want the labels on my clothes reminding me all the time.

'We'll try to clean you up a bit and then take you to one of the big posh shops. They'll have a special girls' department, Em, all sorts,' said Dad.

I guessed he meant all *sizes*. I nodded at him, grateful for his tact, though I could feel myself going bright pink.

'It's not fair!' Vita wailed inevitably. '*I* want new clothes if Em's getting them. It's not my fault that Maxie wasn't sick on me! *Please* can I have new clothes, Dad? I need a new sparkly top and some of those shiny trousers with lots of pockets and there's these pink and purple trainers with glitter on the edgy bit, they're sooo cool.'

'OK, OK, little Vita Fashionista,' said Dad. 'I'll do you a deal. Get Maxie to shut up and I'll buy you *all* a new outfit.'

I stared at Dad anxiously. I knew he didn't have any money. I'd heard Gran going on about it bitterly enough times. But I couldn't stay wearing the sick-stained stuff. I badly wanted Dad to get us all new clothes. I didn't protest.

It was a waste of time anyway. All the shops we saw were shut.

'Oh God, what are we going to do now?' said Dad. 'Look at you, Em, you're shivering. You'll catch your death of cold without your coat. Maybe we'd better take you straight home.'

'No!' Vita wailed. 'No, no, no! We're having a whole day out with you, Dad. Just send Em home!'

'Yeah, just send Em,' said Maxie.

'That's so mean, Maxie! It's all your fault, not mine!' I protested.

'Ssh, ssh, OK! We won't send anybody home,' said Dad. 'I know what we'll do. We'll go to *my* home.'

We all stared at him. What did he mean, *his* home? It sounded much too permanent.

It wasn't his home. It was Sarah's.

We went on the Underground.

'You'll have to put up with it, Maxie, we've no other way of getting there,' said Dad. 'Come on, be a man.'

Maxie couldn't even manage being a little boy. He whimpered like a baby. Dad picked him up and carried him. Maxie moaned when the tube thundered into the station. He burrowed right inside Dad's jacket, using his scarf as a cuddle blanket.

I sat, stiff and sodden and smelly, while everyone kept their distance and stared. Vita was the only member of our family looking normal. She sat demurely, smiling up at strangers, while they put their heads on one side and purred at her.

I wished I was Vita. I always always always wished I was Vita.

When we were out of the Underground at last she put her hand confidently into Dad's.

'Is your house a nice house, Dad?'

'Well, it isn't exactly *my* house, Princess Vita. Now, there's a thing. If I had my magic house it would be like a fairy castle and it would have four turrets and you could have one turret all to yourself. You'd go up all these windy stairs, carpeted in deep pink, with pale-pink walls patterned with bluebirds and butterflies, and then right at the top there would be this wooden door carved with hearts and flowers and inside would be your own special room.'

'Can it be pink too?'

'The pinkest pink ever. You'd have a pink four-poster bed with rose-pink velvet curtains and a patchwork quilt in every shade of pink with little red hearts stitched into the centre of each patch.'

'Where will Dancer sleep?'

'Oh, Dancer's got her own sleigh-shaped wooden bed. We'll hang a little bell mobile above it so that as it spins it tinkles softly, so she can dream she's back with Santa.'

'Um, you said a rude word,' Maxie said, still clutching Dad about the neck, his skinny legs wound round his waist. 'They say tinkle at nursery when you need to do a wee. Dad, I need to do a wee now.'

'Well, hold it for a bit, son.'

'I can't,' said Maxie, wriggling.

'You'd better! We've had enough contact with your bodily fluids to last a lifetime,' said Dad. 'Haven't we, Princess Emerald? OK, shall we do your turret now?'

'No, me, me!' said Maxie. 'I want my own turret, for me and all my bears.'

'Indeed, you can have a veritable bear lair and we'll make sure there are pots of honey and spoons, all sizes, only *you* get a great big giant vat of honey and a ladle and you can go lick lick lick until you're sticky all over. Then you can go to your very own indoor paddling pool and splash around until you're squeaky clean and *then* . . . OK, what do you start doing then, Prince Maxie?'

'I start in again on the honey!' said Maxie, smacking his lips.

'You got it!' said Dad. He turned round awkwardly; still lumbered with Maxie. 'Oh, poor Em, you look so miserable. Don't worry, darling, we'll get you all cleaned up in just a tick, I promise. Now, let's start on your turret.'

I so wanted Dad to invent a beautiful turret for me, but I needed to ask something first.

'What about *your* turret, Dad?'

Dad missed a beat. He knew what I was getting at. Who was going to climb up to his turret and live with him? Was it going to be Mum . . . or this Sarah?

I had a picture of her in my mind. I'd watched

old movies with Mum and Gran and seen all the soaps. I knew what bad women were like who stole men away from their families. They were blonde with scarlet lipstick and they wore tight clothes that showed off their figures. They laughed a lot and licked their red lips and crossed and uncrossed their legs. I knew I would hate her.

Dad stopped at a little parade of shops and went up to a battered door beside an Indian grocery.

'That's a *shop*, Dad,' said Vita.

'I live up above it. It's handy when we run out of bread or milk,' said Dad.

'I didn't know you could live above a shop,' said Maxie. He craned his neck, looking up, as if he expected Dad's bed to be rocking on the roof and his chair topping a chimney stack.

'It's inside, little pal. Just an ordinary flat,' said Dad, getting the door open and leading us inside.

The stairs were very dark and smelled of strange food.

'I don't like it,' Maxie wailed.

'I'm afraid you're just going to have to lump it,' Dad said gently.

'This is *your* flat, Dad?' said Vita, stopping on the stairs.

'Well, technically speaking, it's Sarah's,' said Dad.

Vita said nothing, but she reached out and slid her hand into mine. I squeezed it hard and she squeezed back. Then Dad was knocking on the door, although he had the key in his hand.

'Sarah, sweetheart! I've brought the kids back,' he called.

He unlocked the door and we stepped warily inside. There wasn't a hall. We were straight away in a living room, although there was a bed in one corner with someone huddled under the purple velvet quilt.

'Sarah,' Dad said.

She stirred but didn't come out from under the quilt.

'It's not bed time,' said Maxie.

'Perhaps she's ill,' said Vita.

'She's fine, kids. She's just sleeping,' said Dad. 'Sarah, wake up. I've brought the kids to meet you.' He reached under the quilt and gave her a little shake.

'Frankie?' she mumbled. Then she sat up straight. She wasn't wearing a nightie or pyjamas, just a little stripy vest. She was almost as small and skinny as Vita, with short black hair sticking straight up and dark eye make-up rings round her eyes. She had a bluebird tattooed on her bare shoulder and matching blue varnish on her tiny bitten nails.

She blinked at us, scratching her very short hair. Then she wrinkled her nose. 'Oh dear, Frankie, did you puke?'

'It's the kids. That's why we're here. Poor Em needs a bath.'

'I wasn't the one who was sick,' I said.

'But you *are* the one who needs a clean coat. Sarah, do you have anything you could lend Em?' Dad asked.

'Oh God, Frankie, I don't know. I expect so. Look, you kids hurry up and have your bath because *I* want one too.' She smiled at Dad. 'Make me a cup of coffee, eh?'

'Sure, darling,' said Dad.

We stared at her, outraged. What was she doing, ordering our dad around? She didn't seem *that* much older than me.

'Are you a girl or a lady?' Maxie asked.

'Neither,' said Sarah, reaching for a packet of cigarettes and lighting up. She saw me staring. 'What?' she said, sounding irritated.

I looked at Dad. He's always *hated* smoking. Mum told us she used to smoke twenty a day but she had to give them up when she met Dad. I remembered her chewing gum desperately for weeks.

'Our dad doesn't like cigarettes,' said Vita.

'Well, your dad doesn't have to smoke them. All the more for me, Em,' said Sarah.

'I'm not *Em*!' said Vita, amazed. 'I'm Vita!'

'Whatever,' said Sarah.

She didn't seem to care. She was acting as if we

78

were three mangy mongrels making a mess in her flat. She couldn't be bothered working out which was which. She obviously just wanted us out again as soon as possible.

'Off you go and have your bath then, Em,' said Dad. 'Try not to use too much hot water, sweetheart, if Sarah wants a bath afterwards.'

I ran a *minute* bath, barely a couple of centimetres of hot water, peeled off my clothes and then clambered in. I felt like a big pink hippo trying to wallow in a small puddle. I washed as quickly as I could. I had to borrow a flannel. I hoped it was Dad's. It was weird seeing his toothbrush, his razor, his special black hairbrush on the windowsill. Sarah's eye make-up and black hair dye and funny cakes of soap with bits of petal stuck inside them were scattered all over the place. Her purple and black stripy tights dangled above me from a line across the bath. Her underwear hung there too, but I was trying hard not to look at the horrible wispy things.

I got out and inspected the towels dubiously. None of them looked very clean. The bathroom floor was all bitty too. It didn't look as if Sarah ever bothered to vacuum. I thought of Mum rushing around with her hoover every morning because she had to keep our part of the house pin-neat. Gran always expected everywhere to be spick and span.

I hastily rubbed myself dry and pulled on my own knickers and jeans and socks and shoes. I couldn't put my Miss Kitty nightie back on because it was all sicky round the neck. I didn't know what to do. I didn't want to go back into the main room half dressed.

Vita tapped on the door. 'Em, let me in.'

She was holding a black jumper and a denim jacket. 'They're *hers*,' she said. 'She says she needs them back again.'

'What does she think I'm going to do, keep them?' I hissed. 'I *hate* having to wear her horrid clothes.'

I pulled on the black jumper. Sarah was a grown-up and I was still a child but the jumper was skin-tight on me. I knew it showed off all my plump bits. I covered it up quickly with the denim jacket. Even that was way on the skimpy side.

I felt my eyes filling with tears. I blinked quickly, hoping Vita wouldn't see me being such a baby.

Vita did see, but she surprised me. She reached up on tiptoe and put her arms round me. 'It's all right, you look OK, Em,' she whispered.

I plucked at the tight jumper. 'How can she be so little when she's grown up? Vita, do you think she's pretty? Prettier than Mum?'

Vita shook her head so hard her neck clicked. 'No, I think she's *horrible*.'

'Ssh!'

'I don't care if she hears. What is Dad *doing* with her?'

I didn't have a clue. I went back into the main room, standing there self-consciously.

'Wow! You look fantastic, Em,' said Dad. Then he looked past me, at Sarah. 'OK, babe, your bath time now. Then we'll all go out and get a bite to eat, right?'

It wasn't right. It was horribly wrong. Vita could barely wait until Sarah was in the bathroom.

'We want it to be just *us*, Dad, you, me, Maxie and Em.'

'Oh, come on, sweetie,' Dad said.

'This is *our* day, Dad, specially for us,' said Vita.

'Can't it be for all of us?' said Dad, tickling Vita under the chin to try to make her smile.

Vita glared back at Dad, her pointy chin stuck in the air. 'No, it can't!' she said. She clenched her fists and gave him a pretend punch.

'No, it can't!' Maxie copied, hitting out at Dad too. He didn't know how to pretend and hit Dad hard.

'Hey, hey!' Dad's voice went suddenly cold and cross.

Vita and Maxie stared at him, shocked. Dad didn't ever get cross.

'Now stop behaving like silly babies, the pair of you. I've been longing for you to meet Sarah and this is the perfect opportunity. She's very special to me.'

'She can't be *that* special, Dad. You've only been with her since Christmas,' I said.

'I've known Sarah for six months, Em,' Dad said quietly.

'You've known Mum years and years and years,' I said.

Dad sighed. 'I thought you'd understand, Em. Now come on, all of you, let's lighten up. Stop pouting at me, Vita. Maxie, don't you dare cry. I know you're all going to love Sarah when you get to know her.'

We didn't get to love Sarah. We loathed her.

We didn't get to go to McDonald's. We went to this posh Italian restaurant. Dad insisted on ordering a plate of spaghetti each for Vita and Maxie though I knew they wouldn't eat it all. Sarah didn't eat much of hers either, though she messed around with it a great deal, twirling bits round and round her fork and sucking up strands like a little kid. Dad laughed at her, but when I copied he told me to stop messing around and eat properly.

'Look, you've spilled spaghetti sauce all down Sarah's black sweater!' said Dad. 'Em? I'm talking to you.'

I didn't want to talk to him. I didn't dare take my eyes off my plate in case I burst out crying. Dad didn't seem to understand how much he'd upset me. He went back to chatting with Sarah. She snuggled right up to him and whispered in his ear. They were like two hateful kids at school ganging up on us.

I stared at my spaghetti until it blurred into wriggling orange worms. I twisted my emerald ring round and round my finger under the table. I wanted to twist it right off and drop it on the dirty floor. I decided I couldn't stand Dad any more.

We went for a walk in a park afterwards. It was cold and drizzling and I shivered in Sarah's skimpy jacket.

'Oh poor Princess Emerald, you've been fated to be frozen all day,' said Dad, and he wrapped his arms round me.

I held myself stiffly but he wouldn't give up. 'Let's thaw you out, my lovely,' he said, cuddling me close. Then he put his hands under my arms and whirled me round and round. Dad's slim and I'm shamefully big but he treated me like I was as light as a feather.

Then he held my hand and started telling me about Princess Emerald in Glacier Land. It seemed so real it truly felt as if we were wrapped in rich furs, gliding over shiny white ice, with polar bears lumbering past, seals barking and waving their flippers, and penguins sliding comically on their tummies down the icy slopes into the black sea. My heart melted in this freezing fantasy land and in two minutes I loved Dad so much I was willing to forgive him anything.

I even tried to be polite to Sarah. She didn't try to be polite to any of us. She walked along hunched up, her arms wrapped tight round her chest. Maxie tried to run after some ducks and tripped and fell headlong. Sarah didn't unwrap her arms even then. She simply stood still, waiting for someone else to pick him up and comfort him.

Dad mopped him up and then gave him a piggyback. Vita stalked along by herself, muttering to Dancer.

I tried to walk in step with Sarah.

'So where did you meet my dad?' I asked.

'Oh, around,' said Sarah, infuriatingly vague.

'Do you work at the Palace?'

'No, no.'

'So what work do you do?'

'I'm an actress.'

'So what have you been in?'

'This and that.'

I nodded. Dad usually said that too. It meant nothing very much at all recently.

'Vita wants to be an actress,' I said.

Vita heard and gave a little twirl.

'Yes, she would,' said Sarah. 'Do you want to be an actress too?'

I wondered if she was mocking me. 'I don't know what I want to be,' I said.

'Well, what are you good at?' said Sarah.

I thought hard. I started to panic. I wasn't really good at anything. I could make up stories but that didn't really count. My stories weren't anywhere near as good as Dad's, anyway. I liked colouring in my books but I was rubbish at drawing my own people. I liked dancing when I was all by myself but I'd never been taught. I'd have died if I'd had to wear one of those skimpy little leotards.

'I'm not good at anything,' I said, sighing.

'Yes, you are. Em's good at looking after us,' said Vita, glancing over her shoulder.

Sarah didn't look impressed. 'Do you *like* looking after people?' she said.

I thought about it. I wasn't really that good at it. I wished I could *really* look after everyone. I'd give Vita a starring part in a TV programme. I'd stop Maxie being so scared of everything and make all the little kids who teased him want him as their best friend. I'd make Dad a Hollywood movie star, though he'd fly back home to us in his own personal jet every weekend. I'd give Mum her own hairdressing salon and she could develop her own range of Julie haircare products.

'Hello?' said Sarah rudely, waving her hand in front of my face.

'Goodbye!' I said.

I dodged past her, caught hold of Vita's hand, and we ran together. Maxie left Dad and clutched my other hand. We all three ran like crazy people, yelling at the tops of our voices.

We ran and ran and ran, along the gravel path and round the pond and right up the hill. I thought Dad would get scared and come rushing after us. I waited for him to start shouting our names.

There were no thudding footsteps, no calls.

When we were almost at the top of the hill Maxie stumbled and fell over again. He lay there, panting. Vita stopped too, clutching her side, her face scarlet. I turned round, the blood drumming so hard in my head there was a red mist in front of my eyes. I blinked. I saw Dad far away below us, a little doll's house father. He had his arms round Sarah. He was kissing her. It wasn't the sort of kiss he gave Mum. It was a real filmstar kiss.

'Yuck!' said Vita.

'Yuck yuck yuck,' said Maxie, sitting up. Then he saw what we were looking at. His bottom lip stuck out. 'Why is Dad kissing that lady?' he said.

I swallowed. 'Because he likes her.'

'Well, we *don't*,' said Vita. 'And now we don't like Dad either. We want to go home.'

'We want to go home,' Maxie echoed.

I wanted to go home too. I hated this cold bleak stupid park.

We walked back down the hill holding hands. They were *still* kissing when we got right down to the bottom.

'He looks like he's eating her, yuck yuck *yuck*,' said Vita. 'Let's creep up on them and give them a big push right into the duckpond.'

We all laughed in a weird high-pitched way.

'Let's do it now,' Vita urged.

I didn't know if she was serious or not. I didn't care. I was suddenly overwhelmed by this image of Dad and Sarah shrieking and splashing. I saw Sarah dripping with green slime, ugly and ridiculous.

'We'll run at them,' I whispered.

But at that moment Dad spotted us. They broke apart. Sarah laughed at our faces. Dad smiled anxiously.

'Hey, you three. Having fun?'

'No, we're not,' said Vita. 'We want to go home.'

'Back to Sarah's?'

'That's not *home*,' said Vita in disgust. '*Our* home.'

'Not yet, Princess Vita. Come here, darling, let me tell you all about Princess Vita's new holiday home. She has a house right on the top of the cliff made of shells, thousands and thousands of tiny shells stuck in pretty flower patterns—'

'I'm not listening! I don't care about stupid princesses. I'm not listening, not listening, not listening,' Vita chanted, her hands over her ears.

She wasn't a pushover like me. She wouldn't let Dad win her round, though he tried his best. She wouldn't even kiss Dad goodbye when he'd trailed us all the way back home. Dad tried to kiss her anyway. Vita rubbed her cheek fiercely, as if he'd smeared her face with something disgusting. Maxie held his head stiffly to one side so he couldn't be kissed either.

'Oh, kids,' Dad said sadly. He looked at me. 'You'll give me a kiss, won't you, Em?'

I wanted to kiss him, of course I did. I wanted to wind my arms round his neck and beg him to stay. But I kept thinking about the way he'd kissed Sarah. I dodged round Dad and rang our doorbell quickly, ignoring him.

'**I** can't believe he took you to that woman's flat!'
said Gran. 'Here, take those clothes *off*, Em.'

She pulled them off me so violently it's a
wonder my skin didn't come off with them. Mum
picked the black jumper up with the tips of her
fingers.

'She must be very small, very slim,' she said. 'Is
she very pretty, Em?'

'No! Not a bit. She's weird.'

'In what way weird?'

'Like she's got this tattoo on her arm. And her
hair's really really short. She looks sort of scruffy,'
I said, pulling on my pyjama top.

Vita and Maxie were already in bed, though it
had been a struggle to get them there. Vita showed
off like anything, prancing around like the dancers

91

in the New Year's Day parade, twirling two old socks above her head like streamers. Maxie got the giggles and then gave himself hiccups and couldn't stop. He kept his mouth open when he hiccuped to sound as grotesque as possible.

I couldn't get them to shut up. Mum didn't even try. She leaned against the bathroom door, staring into space. Gran had to come in and give them a telling-off, scooping them both out of the bath and shaking them hard. She had them dried and dressed in their night things and tucked firmly into bed in ten minutes, with dire warnings if she heard another peep out of them.

She let me stay up because she wanted to know every last detail about Dad and That Woman. Mum started concentrating then, asking me question after question. My head ached, trying to tell her the right answers.

'Do you think he really loves her, Em?' Mum asked, her voice a sad little whisper.

Gran sniffed. 'That's not the word I'd use. Frankie doesn't know how to love anyone, not in the real sense of the word.' Gran went off on a rant. Mum and I weren't listening. Mum was looking at me desperately.

I struggled, not knowing what to say. I kept thinking about the way Dad looked at Sarah, the way he followed her around, the way he kissed her.

That was love, wasn't it? Then I remembered a word from one of Mum's magazines.

'I think it's just infatuation, Mum.'

Gran laughed and called me a little old woman, but Mum took me totally seriously.

'So you think it's all a five-minute wonder and he'll come back to us?'

'Yes, yes, of course he's going to come back to us,' I said. How could I say anything else?

'You'll be a fool if you take him back,' Gran said.

'OK, I'm a fool. I don't care,' said Mum. 'You don't understand.'

'Too right I don't,' said Gran.

'Haven't you ever been in love, Gran?' I asked. 'You once loved my grandad, didn't you?'

'Look where it got me,' Gran snorted. 'He pushed off and left me stranded with your mum. Still, at least I learned from my mistakes.' She shook her head at Mum.

'You don't always have to be right, Gran,' I said. 'Dad *will* come back, you'll see. It will all come right and we'll be happy again.'

'What's that pink animal flapping past your nose? Whoops, it's a flying pig,' said Gran. 'If you ask me, I doubt you'll ever see him again.'

'We're not asking you. Of course we'll see him. I'll see him every day at the Palace,' said Mum.

The Pink Palace really looks like a palace. It's

a huge Victorian building with little towers and turrets. It used to be owned by a big insurance company but they sold it off in the 1960s and someone painted it bright pink all over and turned it into a gift emporium. The pink is faded and peeling now and the towers and turrets are crumbling, but the gift emporium is still there, though half the stalls have closed down.

There are still T-shirt stalls and silver jewellery stalls and second-hand CD stalls and weird stalls that sell all sorts of junk and rubbish. The best stall of all was my dad's Fairyland. It was very tiny, in its own dark little grotto, with luminous silver stars twinkling on the ceiling and a big glitter ball making sparkles all over the floor. There were fairy frocks and fairy wings and magical fairy jewellery, fairy wands and fairy figurines and entire sets of Casper Dream fairy books.

*I* was the one who gave Dad the idea for Fairyland! When I was much younger I had this embarrassing obsession with fairies. I was desperate to have a proper fairy dress. I can't help squirming now, because I've always been a great fat lump even when I was little, but I still fancied myself in a pink gauze sticking-out skirt with matching wings.

Dad searched everywhere to buy one that would fit me for my birthday. He tried to find a specialist fairy shop. Then he had this brilliant idea. He decided to open his own fairy stall and call it Fairyland.

It was a success at first, because his prices were very low and if kids came along and looked wistful he'd often bung them free fairy bubbles or pixie toffees. He even hired himself out to do themed fairy parties on Saturdays. All the little girls loved him. The mums loved him too. But whenever Dad had an acting job he shut the stall up, and even when he wasn't working he couldn't always be bothered to trail down to the Palace and sit inside his Fairyland. He started to lose customers, so Mum would attach a little card to his white security railings: IF YOU FANCY ANY OF THE FAIRIES, PLEASE APPLY TO JULIE AT THE RAINBOW HAIRDRESSING SALON ON THE THIRD FLOOR.

Mum went into work five days a week, sometimes six when they were short-staffed, and she worked right through till ten on Thursdays, when it was late-night shopping. She really did dye people's hair all colours of the rainbow. Vita and I begged her to dye *our* hair shocking pink or deep purple or bright blue but she just laughed at us.

She went back to work on 2$^{nd}$ January. I stayed at home with Vita and Maxie and Gran. I got out my brand-new journal and sat staring at the first blank page. After ten minutes I wrote: *Saw Dad*. I waited, sucking the end of my pen. Then I closed the journal with a snap. I didn't feel like writing any more.

It was a long long long day. I couldn't wait for Mum to come home. She was later than usual. I started to get excited. Maybe that meant Mum and Dad were having a drink together, talking things over. Maybe right this minute Dad was telling Mum he had made a terrible mistake. Then he'd kiss her the way he'd kissed Sarah. They'd come home together, arms wrapped round each other, our mum and dad.

I went running to the front door as soon as I heard the key in the lock. Mum was standing there all by herself. Her face was grey with the cold and there were snail-trails of mascara down her cheeks.

'It's the wind making my eyes water,' she said, wiping them.

'Did you see Dad?' I asked softly, not wanting Gran to hear.

Mum shook her head. She closed her eyes but the tears still seeped out under her lids. I put my arms round her.

'He'll go to the Palace tomorrow,' I said.

He didn't. He didn't go there the next day or the day after that. He didn't ever have his mobile phone switched on. There was no way we could get hold of him.

'I need his address. Suppose there's some terrible emergency?' said Mum. 'Can't you remember where this Sarah lived, Em? What was the name of the road?'

I thought hard but it was no use. I'd been in such a state of despair and embarrassment I hadn't taken any of it in. I couldn't even remember which station we'd got out at, though Mum made me stare at a tube map to try to jog my memory. I stared until all the coloured lines wavered and blurred. None of the names meant anything to me.

'For God's sake, Em, how could you be so useless?' Mum snapped.

I went off by myself and had a private weep in the toilet. I *felt* useless. I twirled my emerald ring round and round my finger, wishing it was magic so I could conjure Dad from thin air.

I couldn't understand how I'd been so mad with Dad on New Year's Day. Why hadn't I given him a goodbye kiss? I'd have given anything to kiss him now.

I knew Vita felt the same way. She was unusually quiet during the day, sitting curled up with Dancer. She went to bed without a fuss and seemed to go to sleep straight away but when I woke in the night I heard someone sobbing. I thought it was Maxie and stumbled out of bed to his little lair. He was huddled up with his bears, breathing heavily, fast asleep. The sobbing seemed to be coming from my own bed.

'Vita?' I whispered. 'Are you crying?'

She was howling, her head under her pillow. She was wearing Dancer like a big furry glove.

'Hey, come out, you'll suffocate.'

Vita turned away from me, hands over her face, embarrassed.

'It's OK, Vita. Here, have you got any tissues?'

'I've used them all up,' Vita gulped.

'Hang on, I'll go and get you some loo-roll.'

I slipped out of bed again, pulled off a long pink streamer of Andrex and tiptoed back to our bedroom.

'Is that you, Em? Are you all right?' Mum called from her bedroom.

'Yeah, Mum, I'm fine,' I whispered, not wanting to worry her. It sounded like Mum might have been crying too.

I got back into bed with Vita and tried to mop her face for her.

'Get off! I'll do it,' she said fiercely.

When she'd finished wiping and blowing and snuffling I tried putting my arms round her. She didn't wriggle away.

'Poor Dancer, you've made her all wet,' I said, feeling her. 'Have you stopped crying now?'

'I'm trying to. But I just keep thinking about Dad and how I wouldn't listen to him and now he's so mad at me he won't come and see me—'

'Rubbish! Dad never gets mad at anyone, especially you, Vita. You know you're his favourite.'

'I'm not!' said Vita, but she sounded hopeful.

'You're *everyone's* favourite,' I said, sighing.

Vita gave a small pleased snort.

'Blow your nose again,' I said, giving her another wad of loo-roll.

She tried to blow her nose with her Dancer hand.

'There now, Princess Vita,' I made Dancer say. 'We all come over a little weepy at times. Let me wipe your little nose for you. There now. Shall I tell you a secret?'

'What?' said Vita.

'You're *my* favourite too. You're much prettier than boring fat old Em and you're not a silly little sausage like Maxie.'

Vita giggled. 'Yes, he *is* a silly little sausage,' she said. She paused. 'Em's a *bit* pretty. She's got lovely hair.'

'She's got a lovely nature too, putting up with a sister like you,' I said.

'When Dad comes next time I'm going to be much much nicer to him,' said Vita, snuffling. 'So long as he doesn't bring that Sarah!'

'She's horrible,' I agreed. 'Dad's gone mad, liking her better than Mum.'

'When I'm married I'm not going to let my husband run off,' said Vita.

'I'm not going to get married at all,' I said. 'It's too easy to pick the wrong person. I'm going to live all by myself and I'm going to eat all my favourite things every day and stay up as late as I like, and I shall read all day and write stories and draw pictures with no one bothering me or fussing or needing to be looked after.'

'Won't you be lonely?' said Vita.

'I shall have a friendly dog and a little cat to curl up on my lap. My sister Vita will come visiting riding on Dancer the Reindeer with her good kind obedient husband and six pretty little girls, and my brother Maxie will come visiting with his big bold wife and his six silly little sausage boys and so I will have more than enough company, thank you.'

'Will Mum come visiting too?'

'Yes, of course. I'll take her on holiday and make her happy.'

'And Dad?'

'He'll come too,' I said. 'He'll have made this fantastic Hollywood movie and be ever so rich and famous so he'll have his own special holiday beach house. We'll all go and stay, and swim and laze on the beach and be happy happy happy.'

'Happy happy happy,' Vita murmured. Then she was still, suddenly asleep.

I lay awake for a long time, trying to tell stories to myself. I could make them seem real enough to comfort Vita, but it was much harder trying to convince myself. I eased Dancer off Vita's hand and made her stroke my head with her furry paws.

'Cheer up, dear old Em,' Dancer said. 'Don't you start crying now. Chin up, big smile, that's my girl. Now, close your eyes and snuggle down and go fast asleep. Fast asleep. Fast fast asleep.'

I didn't manage to go *fast* asleep. It was a very *slow* process, and even then I still woke up very early. I decided to fix myself a bowl of cornflakes and have a private early breakfast with my book. I was rereading *Elsie No-Home* by Jenna Williams. Elsie was good fun, even though she told terrible jokes. I understood exactly how she felt having to look after her little sister and brother all the time.

Mum was sitting at the kitchen table in her nightie, sipping a cup of tea. We both jumped. Mum spilled half her cupful into her black nylon lap.

'I'm sorry, Mum! I didn't mean to startle you,' I said quickly, scared she might get cross with me again.

'It's not your fault, Em,' said Mum. 'Oh come here, love. Don't look so worried. I'm sorry I've been so snappy with you.'

She dabbed at her nightie and then I climbed onto her damp lap. I must have really squashed her but she didn't complain. She held me and rocked me like a little baby.

'My Em,' she said. 'What would I do without

you, eh? We've come through thick and thin together, you and me, babe. Do you remember your real dad?'

'A bit,' I said cautiously. I didn't like remembering.

'Whenever he yelled or hit me you'd come and find me crying. You'd put your chubby little arms round me and tell me not to cry, remember? You've always looked after me, Em. And now you look after Vita and Maxie too.'

'So I'm not really useless?'

'Oh don't! I was so mean to say that. I'm sorry, love. Hey, how about coming to the Palace with me today? You be my best girl and help out, yeah?'

I was thrilled at the suggestion. I went off to work with Mum, while Vita and Maxie had to stay at home with Gran.

I loved Violet, the lady who owned the Rainbow Hair Salon. She was quite old, about Gran's age, but she dyed her own hair a crazy pink, and crammed her plump body into very small girly clothes. She always wore hugely high heels, though by the end of the day she usually kicked them off and shuffled round in her stockinged feet.

She pretended not to recognize me. 'So you're the new apprentice, are you, sweetie?' she said. 'How do you do! I'm glad you're coming to work for me. We'd better find you an overall.'

102

She wrapped a big blue robe round me. It came right down to my ankles but it didn't really matter. I rolled the sleeves up and started cleaning the washbasins and sweeping the floor. When Mum had her first client I rinsed off all the shampoo and wrapped a fresh towel round her neck and then I passed Mum the brush and comb and made the client a cup of coffee while Mum tinted her hair. It was great fun, especially when the client gave me a couple of pounds as a tip! I wasn't sure whether she was joking or not.

I showed the money to Violet, asking if I should put it in the till.

'No, darling, don't be silly! It's all yours. You've jolly well earned it too. You're a nice willing little worker. Your mum can bring you along any time you're off school.'

I grinned at Violet.

'So where's that dad of yours? His fairy shop is still shut up. Can't he get out of bed these days?'

My grin faded. I looked anxiously at Mum.

'Oh, Vi, you know what Frankie's like,' she said lightly.

'Yeah, I know all right,' said Violet, shaking her head. She was looking at Mum intently, her eyes narrowed. She took three pound coins out of the till.

'Here, Em, call these your wages. So now you've got a fiver, right? Why don't you have a little skip round the Palace and see what you want to buy with all this lovely lolly.'

I knew she wanted me out of the way so she could have a proper talk to Mum about Dad. I looked at Mum. She nodded at me. So I sloped off, clutching the five coins in the palm of my hand. I jingled them around, trying to feel pleased I had so much to spend. It was all mine. I didn't have to divide it into three to share with Vita and Maxie. They hadn't earned it, I had.

I went to the T-shirt stall and looked at the five-pound bargain rail. I liked a purple T-shirt with a little cat with diamanté eyes on the front, but it had some funny words on it too.

'Maybe your mum and dad might mind. It's a bit rude,' said Manny, the T-shirt guy. He had some very very rude words on *his* T-shirt. 'Maybe your dad could find you a fairy T-shirt,' he suggested.

'Maybe,' I said.

I spent ages at the Fruity Lips make-up booth, trying out all the nail varnish testers, purple, silver and navy blue. My nails were so bitten and stubby I could only fit a slither of colour on each finger. I smeared some sample lipsticks round my mouth and smudged mascara on my lashes experimentally.

'You look beautiful, Em,' said Stevie, the guy who owned Fruity Lips. I think he was maybe kidding me.

'Hey, is Frankie around? I just have to tell him what happened to me over Christmas. I need his advice. It's been the best Christmas ever! Did you guys have a great Christmas?'

'We had lovely presents,' I said carefully.

'Kids!' said Stevie. 'That's all you care about, your presents.'

I didn't argue with him. I wandered down the aisle to the Jewel in the Crown and gently ran my finger along the hanging bead necklaces so that they tinkled. Angelica just laughed. She was always specially friendly to me and let me try on any jewellery I fancied. I tried on every green bangle and bracelet so that they clanked right up to my elbows.

'You're going for the co-ordinated look, right?' said Angelica, flicking her long hair out of her face. She wore so many rings and bangles herself she jangled when she moved.

'Yeah, to match my emerald ring,' I said, showing it to her proudly.

'Oh wow, that's lovely,' said Angelica, holding my hand and admiring my ring from every angle. 'Is it your mum's?'

'No, it's my very own ring. Dad gave it to me for Christmas,' I boasted.

'Your dad is just so wonderful,' said Angelica, sighing. 'His stand is still shut up. Is he coming in today? I was wondering about buying a really big fairy to display some of my jewellery. Do you think he could find one for me?'

'I'm sure he could. I'll tell him when I see him,' I said, and slipped away.

I went right to the end of the aisle. I peered through the white security railings into Dad's darkened Fairyland. The luminous stars stuck on the ceiling shimmered softly. A single strand of fairy lights flicked on and off, on and off, on and off, red and deep blue and amber and glowing emerald green. I looked at the fairies inside, grey and ghostly in the half-light, wings limp, wands trailing.

'Wish for Dad to come back,' I whispered. 'Wish wish wish.'

I shut my eyes and imagined every single fairy waving her wand and wishing, all the big fairy dolls and the little fairy ornaments, all the fairies on the prints and postcards, all the carved fairies on the rosebud soap and the lavender candles, all the pouting baby fairies on the dolls' china tea sets and all the beautiful painted fairies inside all the Casper Dream books.

I was very worried about going back to school. Dad still hadn't come back. I didn't know whether to tell Jenny and Yvonne, my best friends.

We hadn't been friends for that long. I'd only been at this school since we moved in with Gran. It had been horrible trying to fit in with a new class of kids. They didn't treat me like a proper person at first. I was simply Fatty and Greedy-guts and Hippo and The Lump.

Dad heard them calling me names one time last year when he came to collect me from school. He acted like he hadn't heard a thing, but next Monday morning he dropped a handful of tiny silver glittery fairies inside my school bag.

'These aren't selling very well in Fairyland,' he

said. 'Maybe you'd like to give a few of your special friends a present?'

He knew I didn't *have* any friends, special or otherwise. The fairies were a cunning bribe. I wasn't sure they would work though. *I* thought the fairies were magical but probably the other girls would think them pathetic or babyish.

I decided I'd keep them incarcerated in my school bag along with my secret comfort Mars bars and Galaxies, but one fell out as I was taking my homework out of my bag and Jenny picked her up.

Jenny was the girl who sat in front of me. She had very glossy neat black hair, bright blue eyes and pink cheeks, just like one of those little wooden Dutch dolls. I'd always liked the look of Jenny. She liked reading and always had a spare storybook stuffed in her school bag. She sometimes read underneath her desk in maths. She wasn't too clever at maths like me, but she didn't seem to care. She wasn't that great at sporty things either. Her cheeks went even pinker when she ran, and her arms and legs stuck out stiffly as if she was really made of wood. She never joined in any games of football or rounders or skipping in the playground. She liked to go over to the brick wall by the bike shed, hitch herself up and sit swinging her legs, reading her book. I always wanted to clamber up beside her and read my book too, but there was one small problem. Yvonne.

She was Jenny's best friend. She really *was* small, only up to Jenny's shoulders, a little skinny girl with a mop of curly red hair. She didn't seem to think much of reading. She didn't sit on the wall beside Jenny, she did handstands up against it, showing us her matchstick legs and her white knickers. She was so-so at most school things but brilliant at arithmetic, so lucky Jenny got to copy off her.

Jenny and Yvonne had very little in common but they'd been best friends since their first day at nursery school together, so it didn't seem remotely possible that they'd ever split up so that *I* could be Jenny's best friend.

They weren't mean to me like some of the other kids. They were so caught up in their own happy best-friend world they barely noticed me. Until Jenny picked up my fairy.

'Oh look! She's so lovely. Where did you *get* her, Emily?' Jenny asked, balancing the fairy on the palm of her hand.

'She comes from Fairyland,' I said.

Jenny looked at me. I blushed scarlet in case she thought I meant a real fairyland.

'It's a stall in the Pink Palace; down near the market,' I said quickly. 'It's called Fairyland. My dad runs it, when he's not acting.'

'Is he that guy with the long hair?' said Yvonne.

111

'Yeah, I think I've seen him on telly. I saw him in *The Bill* once. So he's your *dad*, Emily?'

'Yes. Well. My stepdad,' I said.

Yvonne rolled her eyes. 'Uh-oh. I've got a stepdad. I can't stick him.'

'Well, my dad's lovely,' I said quickly.

'What a cool thing for your dad to do,' said Jenny, gently throwing the fairy in the air and then catching her. 'Look, she can fly!'

'You can have her if you want,' I said.

'What, just to play with for today?'

'No, to keep.'

'Oh Emily! Really? How wonderful!'

'You lucky thing,' said Yvonne enviously.

'You can have one too,' I said, digging in my school bag.

I didn't particularly want to give a fairy to Yvonne. I liked Jenny much more, but I couldn't really leave Yvonne out.

'Oh wow! Thanks. She can be my lucky mascot,' said Yvonne.

'Em, have you ever read any of Jenna Williams's books?' Jenny asked, floating her fairy through the air.

'Like she's my favourite writer ever,' I said.

'Have you read *At the Stroke of Twelve*? These fairies are just like the ones Lily makes in that book.'

'I know, that's why I like them too,' I said. I thought quickly. 'So, what's your favourite Jenna Williams book, Jenny?'

We had this wonderful long conversation about books while Yvonne sighed a bit and did cartwheels round us and told us were both boring-boring-boring old bookworms. But she was just having a little tease, she wasn't really being nasty. She kept interrupting to ask about my dad and what it was like to be the daughter – well, stepdaughter – of someone famous.

Dad wasn't really *famous*. He'd just had a few small parts on television and appeared in a couple of adverts. He hadn't had his big break yet. Still, I happily showed off about him even so.

I wondered if they'd take any notice of me the next day. I hung back a bit at play time, my heart thumping. I so badly wanted to be friends but I was scared they'd feel I was muscling in. But it was all right! It was more than all right, it was wonderful! Jenny had brought her favourite Jenna Williams book *Forever Friends* to school with her. I hadn't read it because it wasn't out in paperback yet.

'I thought you might like to borrow it, Emily,' Jenny said. 'Come and sit on the wall with Yvonne and me.'

We were all best friends after that. I knew that

Yvonne was still Jenny's best *ever* friend, but I was their second-best friend and that was still great.

They both seemed pleased to see me on the first day of term. Jenny told us all about her Christmas at her auntie's house and how her twelve-year-old cousin Mark had kissed her under the mistletoe and all her family wolf-whistled and Jenny just about died of embarrassment. Yvonne said she'd had *two* Christmases, one on the 25th when she'd stayed at home with her mum and her stepdad and her sisters and they'd had turkey and presents and watched DVDs, and then another on the 26th when she'd gone to her dad and his girlfriend and their new baby and they'd had turkey and presents and watched DVDs. It was the *same* DVD too.

Then they looked at me.

'It started off the best Christmas ever,' I said. 'Dad gave me an emerald ring, a real emerald ring, honest.'

'Oh wow! Your dad's so amazing, like the coolest dad *ever*,' said Yvonne. 'Let's see it then, Em!'

'I'm not allowed to wear it to school, of course, but you can maybe come to my house sometime soon and see it. And he bought Vita this wonderful reindeer puppet and Maxie a huge set of felt pens and Mum some silver sandals and Gran some designer jeans.'

'He bought your gran *jeans*?' said Jenny, and

started giggling. 'I can't imagine *my* nan in jeans. Still, your gran's ever so slim.'

'I know. It's not fair. So's my mum. I just get fatter and fatter,' I said, pinching my big tummy.

'No, you don't,' Jenny lied kindly. 'You're not really fat, you're just sort of comfortable.'

I wriggled. I didn't feel comfortable. They were my friends. I had to tell them.

'But then it all went wrong,' I said. 'There was this row. Then my dad . . .'

I suddenly found tears spurting down my face. I put my head in my hands, scared they'd call me a baby. But Jenny put her arm round me and Yvonne put her arm round me the other side.

'Don't cry, Em,' said Jenny. 'My mum and auntie had a row over visiting my great-grandma in her nursing home, and my dad and my uncle drank too much beer and wouldn't get up to go for a walk on Boxing Day and Mum got mad at Dad. All families have rows at Christmas.'

'Yeah, that's right, Em. My mum found out my dad let one of my sisters have a glass of wine at his house and she just about went bananas,' said Yvonne. 'My mum and dad always have rows at Christmas even though they aren't a family any more.'

'I don't think we're a family either,' I said. 'My dad's got this girlfriend. He walked out to be with her and he hasn't come back.'

I started howling. Jenny pressed closer, her cheek against mine. Yvonne found me a tissue and slipped it into my hand.

'What's up with Fatty?' someone asked, passing by in the playground.

'Don't call Em stupid names,' Jenny said fiercely.

'Yeah, just mind your own business,' said Yvonne.

They bunched up beside me protectively.

'Take no notice, Em,' said Jenny.

'You won't tell anyone?' I wept.

'It's nothing to get worried about. Heaps and heaps of families split up. Your mum and dad still love you, that's what matters,' Yvonne gabbled, like it was a nursery rhyme she'd known since she was little. Then she paused. 'But we won't tell, promise.'

They treated me with extra care and gentleness all day, as if I was an invalid. I got to choose which games we played, I got to share Jenny's lunchbreak banana and Yvonne's box of raisins, I got first go on the classroom computer and the best paintbrush, and when we had to divide up into twos in drama Jenny and Yvonne insisted we had to be a *three*.

They were so kind I found I was almost enjoying myself, though I still had an empty ache in my stomach all the time. It got worse during afternoon school. I started to worry about telling Jenny and

Yvonne. It had made it seem too real. Maybe if I'd kept quiet it would all magically come right. *Mum* hadn't told anyone. Violet at the Rainbow Salon had tried her hardest to get her to talk, I knew, but Mum hadn't said a word.

I didn't seem able to keep quiet at all. If I'd only held my tongue when I heard Dad whispering on his mobile to Sarah, then none of this might have happened.

I thought of Dad, Dad, Dad. The ache in my stomach got worse. I hunched up, clutching my front.

'What's the matter, Emily?' said Mrs Marks, our teacher.

'Nothing, Mrs Marks,' I mumbled.

'Well, sit up straight then. And don't look so tragic, dear. I know you find maths difficult, but there's no need to act as if you're being tortured.'

Most of the class laughed at me. Jenny and Yvonne gave me sad comforting looks, raising their eyebrows at Mrs Marks's attitude. Jenny passed me a hastily scribbled note: *Take no notice of mad old Marks-and-Spencer, you know what she's like. Love J xxx.*

The ache didn't go away though. I kept thinking of Dad looking so sad when I wouldn't kiss him goodbye. I tried to remember that *he'd* done the bad thing by leaving us. He'd inflicted that horrible

Sarah on us and she'd made it plain she couldn't stick us. Dad didn't seem to care. If he just wanted to be with her then why *should* we be nice to him?

I knew why. We loved him so.

'I love you, Dad,' I whispered. 'Come back. Please please please come back. I'll do anything if you come back. I'll never ever be mean to you again. I don't care what you've done. I just need to see you. We all need you so. I promise I'll always be good, I'll never ever moan about anything. Please just come *back*.'

The ache got worse and worse. I started to be scared I might throw up in class or have an even more embarrassing accident. I fidgeted around in my seat, praying for the bell to go. When it rang at long last I shot off straight away, not even waiting to say goodbye to Jenny or Yvonne.

I got to the loo in time, thank goodness. I was still ahead of most of the others when I went out into the playground.

I don't know why I looked at the gate. It wasn't as if I was all set to go home. I was ready to go next door to the Infants after-school club. I went there instead of my own Juniors club because I needed to keep an eye on Vita and Maxie. We stayed there till five thirty, when Gran or Mum came to pick us up after work.

I liked helping out with all the little ones, not

just my own sister and brother. They all liked me because I told them stories and played with them, all of us squashed up in the Wendy house, and I made them a whole Noah's ark of funny dough animals. I was thinking of making a dough reindeer for Vita to cheer her up. Maybe I could do one for Maxie too. I was working out how to manage clay antlers in my head when I saw the figure standing by the gate. It was a man with a plait.

**7**

'**D**ad!' I shouted. '*Dad!*'

He turned and waved. It really *was* him. I hadn't made him up. He was there!

I went flying across the playground, through the gate, and then I hurled myself at Dad so hard he staggered and we both nearly toppled over. We clung to each other, swaying and laughing. I dug my fingers into his denim jacket, making quite sure he was real, that I wasn't just imagining him.

'Oh Dad,' I said. 'I was wishing and wishing and wishing you'd come back.'

'And here I am, Princess Emerald. Oh God, I've missed you.'

He gave me another hug. I saw Jenny and Yvonne standing still in the playground, staring dumbfounded at Dad and me, but for once I couldn't be bothered about them.

'I went to pick up Vita and Maxie first but they didn't come out with the other kids. Where are they?'

'They'll be in the after-school club, Dad.'

'Oh, right. Well, let's go and collect them, eh? I'm taking you kids out for tea. We'll find somewhere really special.'

I wanted to go *home* for tea but I knew that wasn't an option.

'Where are we going then, Dad?'

'Wait for the magical mystery tour, Princess. But I promise your royal highness there'll be chips and candyfloss and ice cream and doughnuts and chocolate – everything you love and you're not normally allowed.'

'Are you kidding me, Dad?'

'I'm deadly serious, sweetheart. Your wish is my command.'

I hung onto his arm proudly, never wanting to let him go. I didn't want to share him with Vita and Maxie. I wanted to keep him just for me for five minutes, but I knew it wasn't fair, so I took him to the after-school club. The moment Maxie saw him he came running across the classroom, scattering crayons and bricks in his wake. Vita hesitated a moment, but then she came running too, bright pink in the face.

'Dad! Dad!'

'Hi, darlings,' said Dad, letting us all hang onto him, giving us a great big hug.

'Well, there's a fine welcome!' said Miss Piper, who runs the after-school club.

'It's cupboard love, because I'm taking them out for a treat tea,' said Dad. 'Come on then, kids.'

We skipped off with Dad without a second thought.

'Your carriage awaits,' he said, leading us to a shiny silver car parked down the road.

We stared, open-mouthed. Our last car had been an old banger that had given up the ghost last year.

'You've got a brand-new car, Dad?' I asked shakily.

'You bet,' said Dad, clicking the doors open with his keys. Then he laughed at us. 'Just for today. I've hired it so we can go for a little spin.'

I wasn't sure who Dad meant by 'we'. There was no one waiting in the car, but I wondered if we'd drive straight to Sarah's flat and pick her up too.

'Is it going to be just us?' I said delicately.

'Just us, Princess.'

For one magical moment I wondered if Sarah was already history. Then Dad said, 'Sarah's had to go for an audition. It's such a shame, she really wanted to be in on this little trip. She wants to get to know you all properly.'

We stared at Dad pityingly. Vita rolled her eyes at me. We knew perfectly well Sarah didn't want to get to know us at all. Who did Dad think he was kidding?

'Have you got any auditions lined up, Dad?' I asked, as we set off in the super shiny car. I was allowed to sit in front like a grown-up. I didn't have to cram in the back with Vita and Maxie.

'Oh, I've got all sorts of stuff lined up, Em,' Dad said vaguely.

'It's just I wondered if you had an acting job or an advert or something, seeing as you haven't been at the Palace the last few days,' I said, trying to sound very casual.

'Well, there hasn't been much point. Folk don't hot-foot it to Fairyland at this time of year, right after Christmas. In fact I was wondering about jacking it in altogether.'

'You can't close down Fairyland!' I said.

'Well, maybe that's a bit drastic. I'll think about it. And meanwhile I'm sure your mum won't mind keeping an eye on it for me.'

'Everyone misses you so at the Palace, Dad. Violet, Manny, Stevie, Angelica . . . and Mum.'

'Well, I miss them all too,' said Dad, staring straight ahead. 'Especially your mum,' he added softly.

'So why won't you come *home*, Dad?' Vita said,

leaning forward and poking her face between us in the front.

Dad didn't answer straight away.

'*Dad!*' Vita said sharply, right in his ear.

'Hey, darling, ssh! Now sit back and put your seat belt back on. I've got to concentrate on my driving for a little bit, OK?' said Dad.

'Where are we driving *to*, Dad?' I asked.

'Come on, Em, you're meant to be my bright girl. Where do you get ice cream and chips and candyfloss? We're off to the seaside!'

I stared at Dad. It was a raw dark January afternoon. It didn't seem like a very practical idea. But Dad started talking about paddling and donkey rides and sandcastles so that I almost believed he was talking us to a magic seaside where it was warm and sunny and golden and we'd play on the sands together for endless happy hours. Vita believed it too, and started planning a new bucket and spade and a bag to collect pretty shells. Maxie went very quiet. I worried he might be feeling sick again.

'Are you feeling all right, Maxie?' I asked, craning round.

Maxie ducked his head.

'Dad, we might have to stop, I think Maxie feels sick.'

'Oh God, Maxie, little man, every time I see you

now you start projectile vomiting,' said Dad. 'You can't feel carsick, I've only been driving two minutes.'

'I'm *not* feeling sick,' Maxie mumbled.

'So what's bugging you then, Maxie?' I asked.

'I don't want to paddle. The fish will chew my toes,' Maxie said, drawing his feet up onto the car seat and shuddering, as if giant piranha fish were nibbling at him there and then.

Dad roared with laughter. So did Vita.

'Don't laugh!' Maxie said crossly.

'Well, you're so stupid!' said Vita. '*I'm* going paddling, Dad. If I had my costume with me I'd go right in swimming. I'm not afraid of fish, I *like* them. Dad, will you take me to swim with dolphins one day? That would be *so* cool.'

'We'll put that idea on hold for a little while, Princess Vita, but you can paddle with cod and haddock and plaice to your heart's content today.'

We didn't do any paddling though. It was dark by the time we got to the seaside. It was colder than ever, with an icy wind blowing right off the sea.

'Mmm! Breathe in that fresh air,' said Dad, but he was shivering inside his thin jacket.

Maxie's sticking-out ears were painfully crimson, so Dad wrapped my stripy wool scarf round them, tying it in a knot on top of Maxie's head.

'You look like a silly girl with a hair ribbon,'

Vita teased. She insisted she wasn't cold but her teeth were chattering, and when I held her hand her fingers were like little icicles.

'Let's run along the sands,' said Dad.

We couldn't find any sand – there were just hard pebbles. We held hands and tried running, making a great crunching din. Maxie kept whining and tripping.

'Ye gods, you're a fusspot, little guy,' said Dad. He picked Maxie up and sat him on his shoulders.

'Pick me up too, Dad!' said Vita.

'Have a heart, darling, I'll keel right over,' said Dad. 'Come on, blow the beach walk. We'll go up on the prom and make for the pier.'

It glittered in the dark, fairy lights outlining the silver domes.

'Is that a palace?' Maxie asked.

'It's the Palace Pier, clever guy. See that stripy tower? That's your very own tower, Prince Maxie, where you can sit on your golden throne and command your magic kingdom.'

Dad bought us food from every single stall on the pier – lemon pancakes and doughnuts oozing jam and salty chips and fluffy candyfloss and 99 ice creams, just as he promised. Vita and Maxie licked and nibbled and slurped until they had food stains all down their school uniform and pink candyfloss scarring their cheeks.

Their hands were too sticky to hold comfortably, so I had to steer them by the shoulders. I ate every scrap of all my takeaways, munching great mouthfuls until my school skirt strained at its zip, but I still didn't feel full enough. The empty ache was there even though I kept telling myself I was having a wonderful day out with Dad and I should be happy happy happy. I'd conjured him up and here he was, all ours.

I started walking very carefully down the pier, trying hard not to step on any cracks whatsoever so that my luck would last and Dad would come back home with us and see Mum and stay for ever. I tried my best, but the pier planks were gnarled and twisted with age and it was hard placing my feet dead centre every single step. I could see through the planks to the dark sea hissing below. It made me dizzy and I had to look up. When I looked down again my shoes were spread all over the place, going over line after line.

Dad saw me looking dismayed. 'What's up, Em? Want another ice cream?'

'Dad, I'm meant to be on a *diet*.'

'Don't you take any notice of your gran. You eat all you want, darling. Come on, let's go in the amusement arcade. I'll see if I can win you all a present.'

There were huge stuffed animals bigger than

Maxie decorating the rifle stalls: cream camels with lolling pink tongues; fat elephants with huge flapping ears and tiny twinkly eyes; stripy zebras with stiff black-and-white manes and thick black eyelashes; spotted amber giraffes with long swaying necks and short tufty tails.

Vita and Maxie and I gazed at these luxury animals in awe. Then we looked hopefully at Dad.

'No way, kids. It's all a con. I'd never win enough points,' Dad said.

He tried all the same, changing a ten-pound note into coins, shooting over and over again.

'Tough luck, sir,' the young girl stallholder kept saying, eyeing Dad up and down.

'It *is* tough, darling, when my kids have set their hearts on one of your lovely animals and I haven't got a hope in hell of winning one,' said Dad, giving her his special smile. 'Hey, you've already had one tenner off me. How about I give you another and you make my kids deliriously happy with a camel?'

'I wish I could,' said the girl, sidling up close to Dad and giving him a little smirk. 'But the camels are all counted.'

'An elephant? A zebra? What about that giraffe over in the corner with a wonky neck?'

'My boss would go bananas,' said the girl. 'I can't, I truly can't, not unless you win fair and square.'

'But you know and I know there's no way you

can win,' said Dad. 'It's not fair and it's not square.'

'That's life,' said the girl, shrugging. 'Here, your kids can have these as a little consolation prize, eh?' She threw us a packet of jellybeans each. 'Maybe you can come back later . . . without the kids?'

Dad laughed and whispered something in her ear.

Vita glared and tugged at his arm. 'Come *on*, Dad,' she said crossly.

Dad pulled a funny face. 'Sorry, Princess Vita. I'm simply trying to sweet-talk that girl into letting you have a special camel. Still, never mind, let's win you a teddy instead,' he said, stopping at one of those crane machines. Rainbow-coloured teddies were stuffed against the glass, squashed in so tightly their snouts twisted sideways and their beady eyes bulged.

'Uh-oh! They're so crammed in I'll never be able to pull them out,' said Dad.

'But I *want* one,' said Maxie, standing on tiptoe so that he was eye to eye with the huddle of bears.

'You've got hundreds of bears at home, little guy,' said Dad.

'But I haven't got a stripy one. I want *this* one, Mr Stripy,' said Maxie, stabbing the glass with his sticky finger.

'I want a bright pink one. It's exactly the colour

of Dancer's nose. They can be best friends. Please please please win me the pink one, Dad,' said Vita pleadingly, jumping up and down.

Dad rolled his eyes and then looked at me. 'OK, Princess Emerald, I suppose you want an emerald-green teddy,' he said.

'It's OK, Dad,' I said, though I *did* want one badly. I wanted a very small green bear with bright blue eyes and an anxious expression.

'It's that one, isn't it?' said Dad, pointing to my blue-eyed bear.

'You're magic, Dad,' I said semi-seriously.

'I'll do my best to win you your teddies, but it's not going to be easy,' said Dad.

He changed another ten-pound note and then started manoeuvring the crane. It was the most unwieldy thing ever, the metal claws brushing past each bear uselessly. Sometimes it held onto a paw or an ear or a little snout but after a tug or two it swung away again, empty.

We watched goggle-eyed, holding our breath each time the crane hovered. All four of us went 'Ooooh' at each failure.

On the very last go Dad managed to capture a little lopsided yellow bear that clung onto the crane grimly with one paw.

'Is he mine, Dad?' asked Vita.

'I really wanted Mr Stripy, but the yellow one

131

might do instead,' said Maxie, though he didn't sound sure.

'The yellow ted isn't for you, Maxie. He isn't for you either, little Vita.'

'Is he for *me*, Dad?' I asked.

'Sorry, sweetheart, he's already taken,' said Dad. 'He's *mine*.'

'Are you going to call him Mr Yellow?' asked Maxie.

'No, my little bear's called Ray.'

'That isn't a very special name,' said Vita.

'Yes it is, darling. He's my little Ray of Sunshine. He's going to remind me of our happy day together.'

We had one last longing look at Mr Stripy, Pinky and little Blue-Eyes. Then we went out of the amusement arcade, gripping hands and shivering all the way down to the end of the windy pier where the rides were. Maxie cowered away from the dodgem cars and squealed in horror at the great waltzer hurtling round and round.

'You're such a pain, Maxie,' Vita grumbled. 'You're always too scared to go on anything.'

'No I'm not,' Maxie insisted. 'I do want to go on one of the rides. I want to go right up in my tower.'

We looked at the pink-and-red-striped helter-skelter tower.

'I don't think it's *really* got a golden throne inside, Maxie,' I whispered.

'I know,' said Maxie. 'That was just a story, wasn't it, Dad? But it can still be *my* tower, can't it?'

'Of course it's your tower, Maxie. You're very generous and you're happy to share it with Vita and Em and me and all these other people too. But it's going to be dark inside – is that OK?'

'Of course it's OK,' said Maxie bravely.

Dad paid for us all to go into the helter-skelter and climb up and up and up the steps to the top.

'See, Vita, I'm not the slightest bit scared,' said Maxie, his voice just a little squeak.

Vita didn't argue. She didn't like it much herself. Halfway up she hung onto my hand and wouldn't let go. When we got to the top at last a man was handing out coconut mats.

'Can I share your golden throne, Maxie?' said Dad, sitting on the mat and pulling Maxie onto his lap.

The man pushed them out onto the slide and they vanished into thin air. We heard Maxie shrieking.

'I don't think I want to,' said Vita. 'Let's go back down the stairs.'

'We can't, Vita, there are people coming up behind us.'

'I don't care.'

'*They* will. Come on. We'll go on a mat together. It'll be OK, you'll see,' I said.

'Aren't you scared, Em?' said Vita.

'No,' I said.

'You're shaking.'

'I'm *cold*. Now come on, get on the mat with me.'

I sat on the mat and Vita perched on my lap, hanging onto my legs tightly with her little pincer fingers. The man gave us a big push and then we were off, out into the dark night, flying round and round and round, the wind in our face and the sea swooshing far below and the lights twinkling all along the promenade. It was as if we'd stepped straight into one of Dad's magic stories. I never ever wanted it to end. It was a shock shooting abruptly right off the slide and landing on the ground, though Dad was there, picking us both up.

'Can we do it again?' we all begged.

Dad gave us another go. This time I took charge of Maxie and Vita flew with Dad. I wished I could have one go on Dad's mat, but Vita was too little to manage Maxie and I knew I was way too big to share with Dad.

I wondered if I should really try sticking to my diet and cutting out all my secret snacks – but when Dad suggested fish and chips for supper I didn't object.

I got frightened when I saw the clock in the fish restaurant. Dad saw me looking.

'Don't worry, Em, it's not twelve o'clock yet.

We're not going to turn into pumpkins.'

Vita and Maxie giggled. I waited, eating chip after chip. I ate half of their chips too, trying to get up the courage to ask Dad something.

'You did tell Mum and Gran you were taking us out, didn't you, Dad?'

He shook his head at me. 'You're such an old fusspot, Em. You're my kids. I don't have to ask permission to take you for a fun time.'

I loved it that Dad included me as his kid. But the little worry inside me was getting bigger and bigger.

'But Dad, if you *didn't* tell them, won't they be wondering where we are?'

'Just leave it, Em. Don't spoil things,' said Dad.

'Yes, shut up, Em,' said Vita. 'And stop eating my chips. I want to make a little log-cabin house with them.'

'Yes, shut up, shut up, shut up,' Maxie chanted.

Gran always tells us off it we say shut up. Maxie said it over and over again, showing off.

They were both starting to be silly because they were tired out. I was tired too. I felt my eyes pricking with baby tears because Dad had been sharp with me. It wasn't fair. I didn't want to spoil things. But I couldn't help thinking about Mum and Gran and how worried they would be.

'Maybe we could ring Mum?' I mumbled.

135

'There's no point. We're going to go home now – if that's what you want,' said Dad.

'No, it's *not* what we want,' said Vita. 'We want to stay out with you, Dad. We want to stay out all night.'

'Yes, *all night*,' said Maxie, though his eyes kept drooping and his chin was on a level with his cluttered plate.

I bit my lip. I didn't say any more. Dad paid the bill and picked up Maxie.

'Me too,' Vita wailed, holding her arms up like a toddler.

Dad did his best to carry her as well. I stumped along behind.

'Tell you what, Em,' said Dad, struggling to turn round to me. 'We could all check into a little hotel as the kids are so tired. Then we can drive back tomorrow.'

'But . . . but we haven't got our pyjamas or our washing things,' I said anxiously. 'And we wouldn't be back in time for school tomorrow.'

'Oh, for God's sake, don't be so boring. You sound more middle-aged than your grandmother,' Dad snapped.

I couldn't keep back the tears this time. Dad saw. He stopped. He knelt down with difficulty, Vita and Maxie hanging from either shoulder like rucksacks.

'Em. Em, I'm so sorry. I didn't mean that. I

wasn't being serious. I was just playing with the idea. I don't want tonight to end, darling.'

'I don't either, Dad,' I sobbed. 'I don't mean to be boring. We can manage without night things – Maxie doesn't even *wear* pyjamas. It would be great to miss school. It's just . . . Mum might think we're never coming back.' I thought of Mum worrying so and I cried harder.

'Don't cry, Em. Please. I can't cuddle you properly with these two. Come nearer, sweetheart. There now. Dry those tears, Princess Emerald. You're the brave little girl who looks after us all and never cries, right? Don't, darling, you're breaking my heart.'

'I've stopped now, Dad,' I sniffed.

'It's OK, baby. I'm going to take you home now. It's going to be all right, Princess Emerald. I'm ordering up your silver carriage right this minute.'

Dad and I settled Vita and Maxie on the back seat.

'Do you want to curl up in the back too, Em? You look exhausted.'

'No, I want to sit with you, Dad.'

I was too anxious to go to sleep. Dad tried telling me elaborate Princess Emerald stories all the way home but I couldn't concentrate properly. He kept losing the thread himself, so that it all started to sound like a dream. We jumped from the princess's palace to her marble swimming pool, but then we were swimming with dolphins way out in the ocean. I started to wonder if it was *all* a dream and I'd wake up all over again on Christmas morning. It would really be the best Christmas ever and Dad wouldn't walk out.

Then we drew up outside our house. The lights were all on. The front door opened and Mum and Gran came running down the front path. They were both crying.

Mum gave me a huge hug and then delved in the back of the car for Vita and Maxie. They were so fast asleep she couldn't wake them up. She started shaking them frantically.

'Vita! Maxie!'

'Hey, hey, they're fine. Don't worry,' Dad said gently.

'Don't *worry*?' said Mum.

She pulled Vita and Maxie out of the car and tried to carry them both, though their weight made her buckle.

'Let me carry them, darling,' said Dad.

'Darling?' said Mum. 'For God's sake, Frankie, stop torturing me. Are you coming back to us now, is that it?'

Dad hesitated. 'Oh, Julie. I still care for you so much. But I've got to be honest. I'm not coming back, my life is with Sarah now.'

Mum's chin shook. She pressed her lips together. Tears slid down her cheeks.

'I wish I could be here. I wish I had the kids around me, I miss them so,' said Dad. 'I love them, Julie.'

'How dare you!' said Gran. She slapped Dad hard across his cheek, her bracelets jangling. 'Do you have any idea how frantic we've been? We thought you'd abducted them. Did you know the police are out looking for you?'

'For God's sake, did you have to bring the police into it? I'm not a kidnapper, I'm their dad.'

'What sort of a dad are you, walking off at Christmas, leaving them desperate, crying their little eyes out.'

'Now come on, I didn't do that, you know I didn't. I tried hard to make it easy for everyone.'

'This is *easy*?' said Mum.

'It's not easy for me either,' said Dad. 'Can't you quit shouting and slapping and making things so horrible and heavy. I wanted today to be lovely for the kids, a treat they'd remember for ever.'

'Why?' said Mum. 'Are you clearing off for good, is that it?'

'Well, Sarah's had this offer with a Scottish theatre. I thought I'd go with her, see if I can maybe get work up there too. But don't worry, babe, I'll come back and see you and the kids as often as I can, even though the fare down is pretty huge.'

'You save your money,' said Gran. 'Though most of it is *my* money that I was fool enough to lend you. We don't want to see you ever again. Push off with your stupid little girlfriend and never ever come back.'

'You don't mean that,' said Dad. He looked at Mum. '*You* don't mean that, do you, Julie?'

'Yes I do,' said Mum. 'Get lost, Frankie. I'm over you already. Let's go for a clean break. I never want to see you ever again, do you hear me? Leave me and my kids *alone*.'

Dad stared at her. One of his cheeks was still scarlet where Gran had slapped him. He rubbed it, looking dazed. Then he took a deep breath.

'OK. If that's the way you want it,' he said. He looked at Vita and Maxie and me. 'What do you want, kids?'

I didn't know what to say, what to do.

I wanted to tell Dad I wanted to see him all the time.

I wanted to tell Mum I didn't ever want to see Dad ever again.

I wanted and wanted, torn in two.

Vita was sobbing now, exhausted.

'What do you want, Princess Vita?' Dad asked softly.

'I want to go to *bed*,' Vita wailed.

Maxie was past saying anything. He was crumpled in a heap in the hallway, whimpering.

'Look at the state you've got them in,' said Mum. 'What sort of a dad are you?'

'OK, OK. I'm a lousy dad, a useless husband, a hopeless provider,' Dad shouted. 'Right then, I'll make everybody happy. I'll clear off out of your lives. We'll go for a clean break.'

He jumped back in his silver car, started the engine and zoomed off into the night.

$D$ad didn't come back. It looked as if he meant it.

A clean break.

He sent Mum a cheque with a Scottish postmark on the envelope. He didn't put his address. He didn't write a letter either. He just scribbled on the back of the cheque, *Love from Frankie and xxx to the kids.*

'That's not a proper letter we can keep,' I said sadly.

'It's not a proper cheque either,' Gran sneered. 'He still owes me thousands and yet he's acting like Lord Bountiful sending your mum a cheque for a hundred pounds. As if that's proper maintenance!'

A hundred pounds seemed a huge amount to me. I thought of running round the Flowerfields shopping centre with a hundred gold coins in my school bag. I could go to the Bear Factory and buy a cuddly black cat with his own cute pyjamas; go to the bookshop and buy an entire set of Jenna Williams stories; go to Claire's Accessories and buy all sorts of slides and scrunchies and glittery make-up; go to the Pick 'n' Mix Sweetstore and choose a whole sackful of sweets . . . and I'd *still* have heaps left to buy presents for Vita and Maxie.

Then I thought of all the boring stuff like bills in brown envelopes and cornflakes and loo-rolls and spaghetti and milk and Maxie's new school shoes and Vita's leotard for ballet and my new winter coat. Maybe a hundred pounds wasn't very much after all.

I put Dancer on my hand and made her talk to me.

'Cheer up, Princess Emerald,' she said. 'Your dad won't let you down. He's the most wonderful man in the world, you know he is. I'm sure he'll send another cheque soon. This time there'll be a proper letter you can keep, just you wait and see.'

I waited. Dad didn't send anything. He didn't pay his rent to the Pink Palace either. The fairies grew dusty behind their bars.

'I don't know what to do,' Mum said. 'I can't keep it on. I can't be in two places at once. It never brought in much money even when Frankie was around. We'll have to let it go.'

'You can't let them close Fairyland!' I said, appalled. 'What will Dad do when he comes back?'

'Get this into your head once and for all, Em. He's not coming back,' said Mum, taking hold of me by the shoulders and speaking to me practically nose to nose.

'Yes he is, yes he is, yes he is!' I said inside my head.

I made Dancer whisper it to Vita and Maxie and me every night when we went to bed. We all believed her. Maybe Mum did too, in spite of what she said. She paid the Fairyland rent herself right up until Easter.

We'd all started hoping that Dad would come back then, even if it was just for a visit. He always made such a special day of Easter. I remembered one Easter, when Vita was very little and Maxie was just a baby, Dad hired a huge rabbit costume from a fancy-dress store and pretended to be the Easter Bunny, crouching down and hopping, flicking his floppy ears from side to side.

Another year he hid hundreds of tiny wrapped chocolate eggs in every room of the house and all over the garden, and we spent all Easter morning running round like crazy, seeing who could find the most (me!).

Last year Dad gave us all different eggs. Maxie got a big chocolate egg wrapped in yellow cellophane with a toy mother hen and three fluffy chicks tucked into the ribbon fastening. Vita got a pink Angelina Ballerina egg with a tiny storybook attached. I got a Casper Dream fairy egg with a set of Casper Dream flower fairy postcards. He gave Mum a special agate egg, with whirls of green and grey and pink, very smooth and cool to touch.

'It's called a peace egg,' Dad told her. 'You hold it in your hand and it calms you down when you're feeling stressed.'

Mum held her agate egg a lot through January and February and March. Sometimes she rolled it over her forehead as if she was trying to soothe all the worries inside her head. She held onto it most of this new Easter Day.

Mum tried her hardest to make it a special day. She made us our favourite boiled eggs for breakfast and she even drew smiley faces on each one.

We had chocolate eggs too, big luxury eggs with bright satin ribbons. When we bit into them, teeth clunking against the hard chocolate, we found little wrapped truffles inside. Mum said we could eat as much chocolate as we wanted just this once – but we were all keyed up waiting for Dad to come with *his* Easter surprises.

We waited all morning. Gran cooked a chicken for lunch. We waited all afternoon. Gran suggested we all went for a walk in the park but we stared at her as if she was mad. We didn't want to risk missing Dad.

'He's not going to come,' Gran said to Mum. 'You *know* he's not. You haven't seen sight or sound of him since that dreadful day when he ran off with the kids.'

'He didn't run off with us, Gran. It was just a day out,' I said heavily.

'A day and half the night, with the police out searching,' Gran sniffed.

'I *have* heard from him,' Mum said. 'You know he sent another cheque last week. And he put *Happy Easter* to all of us. So I thought . . .' Mum's hand tightened on her peace egg.

'You thought he'd come running back with his silly fancy presents, getting the kids all over-excited and driving you mental,' Gran said.

'Shut *up!*' Mum shouted. She suddenly flexed her arm and hurled her peace egg to the other side of the room. It landed with such a clunk we all jumped. The peace egg stayed smoothly intact, but it dented Gran's video recorder and chipped a big lump out of Gran's skirting board.

'Oh God, I'm sorry!' Mum said, starting to sob.

We thought Gran would be furious. Her eyes

147

filled with tears too. She went to Mum and put her arms round her.

'You poor silly girl,' Gran said. 'I can't bear to see you sitting all tense and desperate, longing for him. You're making yourself ill. Look how thin you've got.'

I looked at Mum properly. I hadn't noticed. She really had got thin. Her eyes were too big in her bony face, her wrists looked as if they would snap, and her jeans were really baggy on her now, so that she had to keep them up with a tight belt.

It wasn't fair. I missed Dad every bit as much as Mum and yet I hadn't got thin, I'd got fatter and fatter and fatter.

It didn't stop me creeping away and eating my entire Easter egg all in one go. I licked and nibbled and gnawed until every last crumb was gone. My mouth was a mush of chocolate, pink tongue covered, my teeth milky brown. I imagined my chocolate throat and chocolate stomach. Yet I *still* felt empty. I was like an enormous hollow chocolate girl. If anyone held me too hard I'd shatter into a thousand chocolate shards.

I felt so lonely during the Easter holidays. Whenever we went out to the shops or the park or the swimming baths there were fathers everywhere. They were making the teddies talk to the little kids in the Bear Factory; they were helping their kids feed the ducks and pushing swings and kicking footballs; they were jumping up and down playing Ring-a-Ring o' Roses in the water.

There were dads in every television programme, making a fuss of their kids. One time we even spotted *our* dad in an old film. It was just a glimpse, in a crowd, but the plait was easy to spot.

'It's Dad, it's Dad!' I said.

'*Dad!*' Vita screamed, as if he could hear her.

Maxie didn't say anything. He turned his back to the television. He'd stopped talking about Dad the last few weeks. He just looked blank when Vita and I said his name.

'Maybe he's forgotten him,' said Vita, when we were getting ready for bed. Gran was in the bathroom with Maxie, washing his hair. He'd poured concentrated Ribena over his head because he said he wanted to dye his hair purple.

'Don't be silly, Vita, he can't possibly have forgotten Dad already.'

'Well, he's such a baby. And totally weird,' said Vita.

'I know, but it's only three months since we saw Dad.'

'Three months two weeks and four days,' said Vita.

I stared at her. Vita could barely add two and two.

'How do you know so exactly?'

'Because I've been marking it off on my calendar,' said Vita.

'What calendar?'

'I made it at school just before Christmas. We had to stick it on an old card and do glitter and I got bored and did a red-glitter bikini on Jesus' mummy and my teacher got cross with me and said I'd spoiled my calendar and couldn't send it to anyone. So I put it in my desk and now I mark off the days,' said Vita.

'You could have given the calendar to Mum or Dad. Dad would have found it ever so funny,' I said.

'Well, I could give it to him when he comes back. I could do red-glitter hearts all round the edge of the dates,' said Vita.

I thought of her own little red heart thumping with love for Dad underneath the fluffy kitten jumper Gran had knitted for her. I didn't always *like* Vita but I loved her a lot. I wanted to give her a big hug but I knew she'd wriggle and fuss and say I was squashing her. I put Dancer on instead and she gently hugged Vita's little stalk neck and blew breathy kisses into her ear.

'Make Dancer kiss *me*,' Maxie said, running into our room stark naked. His newly washed hair stuck up in black spikes.

'Dancer doesn't want to kiss silly little bare baby boys,' said Vita primly. 'Put something on, Maxie.

We don't want to see your woggly bits. I'm so so glad I'm a girl, aren't you, Em? Dad always said I was his favourite little girl.'

'He said I was his favourite grown-up girl,' I said.

I wondered if he said that to Sarah now.

Maxie didn't join in. He gathered up all his bears, a great tatty furry bundle. 'We're all bears,' he shouted. 'I'm bare and they're bear! We're all bears.' He shrieked with laughter and yelled it over and over again, in case we hadn't got it the first time. We did our best to ignore him, so he started nudging us with his teddies. He got wilder, bludgeoning us with bear limbs. One paw went right in my eye and hurt a lot. I *frequently* didn't like Maxie and recently it was very hard to remember that I loved him.

He'd always been silly but now he acted positively demented, running around all over the place, yelling his head off, throwing baby tantrums in the supermarket and the street. Mum worried he might have some serious problem and thought she should take him to the doctor.

'That child doesn't need a doctor, he needs an old-fashioned smacked bottom,' said Gran. 'Plus a daily dose of syrup of figs to keep him regular. He spends hours in that toilet! Still, I'm not surprised – all his finicky ways with his food: won't eat this, won't eat that, and fuss fuss fuss if his beans touch his egg or his chips aren't in straight lines, for pity's sake. I'd never have let you play me up like that, Julie.'

'Maxie's traumatized, Mum,' our mum protested.

'Nonsense, he's simply spoiled rotten. I've always thought you were an idiot pandering to him the way you do, giving in to every little fear and fancy. You've got to help him toughen up. After all, Maxie's going to have to be the man of the family now.'

Vita and I collapsed into helpless laughter at the idea of Maxie the Man protecting us in any way whatsoever. Mum was near tears but she started snorting with laughter. Even Gran couldn't help smiling. Maxie himself ran amok, laughing like a hyena though he didn't understand the joke.

We called him Maxie the Man after that. For a couple of days he strutted around, growling in as deep a voice as he could manage, calling Vita and me his 'little girlies'. He did his best to boss us about. We put up with it for a while because it was quite funny at times. Mum and Gran joined in, letting Maxie order them around. He took to calling Mum 'Woman!' and it always made her laugh.

'Don't you go calling *me* Woman, you saucebox,' said Gran, shaking her finger at Maxie.

'Gran's *Old* Woman!' I whispered to Vita.

'I heard that!' Gran said sharply. 'I don't think we should encourage Maxie. He'll carry on in the same manner when he's back at school, trying to tell all the teachers what to do.'

Gran had a point. I tried to get this across to Maxie but he just stood shaking his head at me, hands on his funny little hips.

'Don't take that tone of voice with me, Little Girlie,' he said, coming out with one of Gran's favourite phrases. 'Kindly remember, I'm the Man of the House.'

'No, you're not, you silly little squirt,' said Vita irritably. '*Dad's* the Man of the House.'

Maxie didn't react.

'Maxie, you do remember Dad, don't you?' I asked.

Maxie shrugged. He tried to tell us off again, his hands clutching his sides so tightly that his shorts rose comically up each leg.

'You look so stupid,' said Vita. 'No wonder they call you names at school.'

'What names do they call him?' I asked. They called *me* names and it was horrible. I couldn't stand it if little Maxie was being teased like that too.

'They call him *heaps* of different names,' said Vita.

'No they don't!' said Maxie.

'Yes they do. All the Infants call him stuff.'

153

'Like *what*?'

'Maxie wee-wee, Maxie pee-pee, Maxie widdle—Oooh!'

Maxie leaped up at Vita and yanked her wispy hair so hard he pulled out a whole hank. Vita shoved Maxie violently. He toppled and banged his head, hard. Vita jumped on top of him and banged his head again, harder.

Mum and Gran came rushing. They had to prise them apart, both scarlet and screaming.

'For pity's sake, what's the matter with you both? Are you trying to kill each other?' said Gran, shaking them.

'Yes!' they both roared.

'Come on, I'm not having children behaving like little devils in my house. Up to bed this minute, both of you.' Gran seized hold of them by the wrists and started hauling them upstairs.

'Mum, stop it, they're *upset*,' said our mum. 'Leave them be. Come on, Maxie, Vita, stop crying. Come and I'll read you both a story.'

Gran shook her head. 'That's plain silly, rewarding them for temper tantrums.' She glared at me. 'Why are you standing there so gormlessly, Em? Can't you keep your little brother and sister out of mischief for two minutes?'

This was so horribly unfair I couldn't bear it.

'Why should I always have to sort them out just

because I'm the eldest? I'm not their mother!' I said.

'Now stop that! You should be glad to help out. Your own mum is doing her best but she can't cope.'

'I *can* cope! You mind your own business, Mum!' our mum shouted. 'I know you mean well but I'm sick of you bossing the kids around and being so strict with them all the time. They're not being deliberately naughty. They're *unhappy*. We're all bloody miserable.'

'For pity's sake, I'm only trying to help,' said Gran. 'It's time you got a grip. It's been months since that idiot walked out. Can't you get over him?'

'No I can't,' said Mum. 'Come on, kids. We'll go upstairs and leave Gran in peace.'

'Are we still being sent to bed?' said Vita, as we went upstairs.

'Well, how about if we all come and cuddle up in my bed?' said Mum.

'Just Vita and Maxie?' I said.

'No, no, you too, Em darling. All of us. We'll read stories and play games and I've got some chocolate tucked away somewhere.'

We all got into our night things and crammed in Mum's bed, though it wasn't as much of a squash now. Vita stroked Dad's pillow.

'Is it lonely not having Dad to cuddle up with?' she said.

'Of course it's lonely, Vita,' I said. I still often heard Mum crying if I had to get up in the night to go to the loo.

'Yes, it's very lonely,' Mum said. 'I sometimes take Dad's pillow and tuck it in beside me and then in the middle of the night when I'm asleep it's as if he's there.'

'You can borrow Dancer sometimes if you like,' said Vita, making Dancer stroke Mum with her velvety paw.

'You can have one of my teddies,' said Maxie, patting Mum too.

Mum started talking more about Dad, telling us all the things she really missed, the way he hummed under his breath, the way he always invented some new sweet pet-name for her, the way he hugged her, the feel of his lovely long dark plait . . .

Vita and I started crying, remembering too. Maxie stayed dry-eyed, his pats changing to sharp little slaps.

'Shut up, Mum,' he said. 'Shut up, shut up, shut up.'

'Now then, Maxie, you know you're not supposed to say shut up. And I don't *want* to shut up. I want to talk about Dad and how sad I am. I want you three to talk about him too. It might help us feel a bit better if we talk about him.'

'Maxie's forgotten Dad,' Vita snuffled.

'Don't be silly, sweetheart, of course he hasn't,' said Mum.

'He *has*. Maxie, who's Dad?' said Vita.

'Don't know, don't know, shut up, shut up,' said Maxie, struggling out from under the covers.

'Ssh now, Maxie. Snuggle back in, darling,' said Mum. 'Oh dear, I know you don't want to talk about Dad and yet I think we should.'

'He's coming back soon, Mum, we know he is,' said Vita.

'Well, we *wish* he'd come back,' said Mum.

'Em wished it. It will come true,' said Vita. 'We just mustn't ever give up. That's right, isn't it, Em? Dancer says so.'

I took Dancer and made her nod her head.

'I'm magic, my dears. I've lived with Santa and he's taught me all his little tricks. He frequently confided in me. I was his right-hand reindeer.' I made Dancer wave her right paw in the air, showing off.

They all laughed. I did too. It was so weird. I was working Dancer, making it all up as I went along, and yet it was almost as if she was a real separate person saying things I'd never think of.

She told us a long story about a child who asked for her dad to come back as her Christmas present. Santa had to search for this dad all the way across the world to Australia. It was stiflingly hot and sunny so Santa went as red as his robes and the furry reindeer were all exhausted, so they cooled off on Bondi beach. Santa paddled with his robes tucked up round his waist, showing his baggy longjohn pants. Dancer and all the other reindeers swam in the surf, seaweed swinging from their antlers. Then they all renewed their search and found the dad shearing sheep. It turned out he was on such a remote farm there wasn't a postbox, so he didn't know how much his daughter was missing him. As soon as he realized he jumped onto the sleigh with Santa, and Dancer and the team of reindeers galloped all the way across the world. The dad jumped off the sleigh at dawn and went running into the house. He woke up his little daughter—

'And she cried, *Daddy, oh my daddy*,' said Vita. She frowned. 'But if Santa was dashing off to Australia and back how could he deliver all the children's presents too?'

'I don't know,' I said, irritated. 'He can manage anything. He's magic, like I said.'

'I think your story was magic, Em,' said Mum. 'You're so good at making up stories. You obviously take after Dad. He could always make up wonderful things.'

'She can't take after Dad,' said Vita. 'He's not Em's real dad. He's *my* dad.'

'He's been a lovely dad to Em too,' said Mum.

158

'I think he's helped her make up super stories. You should write them down, Em. I'd love to keep them.'

'To show Dad when he comes back?'

Mum sighed. 'Darling, we've got to start thinking he's not coming back.'

'He is coming back, Mum. He is, he is, he is,' I said.

'Oh, Em. Do you really think if we say it enough times it will come true?' said Mum.

'It will,' I said.

'Definitely,' said Vita. 'Yes yes yes.'

'Yep,' Maxie mumbled, but he was half asleep.

The next day Mum sidled up to me when she came home from work.

'Here, Em, I've got you a little present. Don't let on to Vita and Maxie or they'll feel hard done by.' She handed me a paper bag. There was a familiar rectangular shape inside.

'Oh Mum, is it the new Jenna Williams book?'

'You and that Jenna Williams! No, take a look.'

I took a shiny red book out of the bag. I tried not to feel disappointed. I opened it up and saw blank pages.

'It's for your Dancer stories.'

'Oh.' I wasn't sure this was such a good idea. It was so much easier just *telling* them. If I wrote them down I'd have to plan it all out and remember all the boring stuff about punctuation and paragraphs. And never beginning a sentence with 'And'.

Mum was looking at me anxiously.

'Great,' I said, sounding false. 'Thank you very much.'

'You don't *have* to write the stories,' said Mum. 'I just thought it might take your mind off things. But it's not meant to be hard work, it's meant to be fun.'

'Do I have to do it like at school?'

'No, you write it however you want,' said Mum. 'Draw pictures too, if you like.'

I started to get more enthusiastic. I decided I'd do lots of pictures. I'd colour them in. I'd *maybe* use a certain nearly new set of beautiful felt-tip pens.

Maxie never seemed to use them nowadays. He'd done a handful of his wonky doughnut people during the Christmas holidays, but then he scribbled over all of them with the black pen.

Gran said she'd take them away from him if he just did silly scribbling, though she said it wasn't Maxie's fault, he was far too young to own such an expensive set of pens.

Mum said Gran didn't have the right to take them away from Maxie, though she did privately beg Maxie to use them properly. She'd found a lot of black scribble on the wall beside Maxie's mattress and had spent ages scrubbing with Vim.

Maxie didn't use his pens at all after that, though he guarded the big tin carefully and shrieked if Vita or I went near them.

I waited until he was fast asleep in his bear lair and Vita was snuggled up with Dancer. Then I crept out of bed, tiptoed across the carpet and very cautiously felt under Maxie's mattress. I found the great big smooth tin of felt tips and gently eased them out, careful not to make them rattle. I took them to the bathroom with me. I put all the towels bunched up in the bath to cushion it and then hopped in with my new notebook and Maxie's pens.

I opened the red notebook up and smoothed out the first page. I selected the black pen, ready to write '*Dancer the Reindeer*' in my best swirly handwriting. The black came out as a faint grey trickle. It was all used up.

Maxie had obviously been doing a lot of secret scribbling somewhere or other. It looked like Mum was going to have to buy another can of scouring powder.

I chose the scarlet pen instead. It came out the palest pink. Maxie had used the red up too! I tried the gold, the purple, the brightest blue. They were nearly all completely used up. The only pens still working were Maxie's least favourite colours, the dark greens and all the browns.

I couldn't understand it. I'd not seen Maxie

using them. How could they possibly all be used up already?

I had to start my Dancer story using my own inferior gel pens. I didn't know how to get started properly. It sounded so silly and babyish writing Dancer the Reindeer did this, did that. It was so much more interesting when she told her own story.

I had a sudden idea. I crept back to the bedroom, eased Dancer out from under Vita, and went back to my special bath. I put Dancer on my right hand and tucked a pen between her paws.

'What's this?' she said, twiddling it around.

'You know what it is. It's my special pink gel pen, to match your pretty pink nose. I want you to write your story for me, Dancer. Tell it like an autobiography, right from the beginning, when you were born.'

'When I was a tiny fawn, all big eyes and no antlers?' said Dancer.

She breathed in deeply, wriggled the pen more comfortably in her paws, and began.

*I am Dancer, a reindeer. I was born in a blizzard, such a deeply snowy night that my poor mother could not find shelter for us. She did her best, arching her poor weary body over me, while I nuzzled up to her weakly, up to my snout in thick snow. You would think this*

162

*chilly start in life would leave me susceptible
to colds, but although I am of dainty build
even now in my middle years, I have always
prided myself on my stout constitution. I never
have a cold or a chill or any bout of flu. My
nose stays prettily pink, never ever red and
shiny. I would feel I was seriously blemished
if I was famous for being a red-nosed reindeer,
and had a popular song written about me.*

*I do not wish to boast but I am sure I am
equally famous for my dancing skills. I can
do ballroom, I can bop like a demon, I can tap
up a storm, but my speciality is ballet. I am
the Anna Pavlova of the reindeer kingdom.*

I pressed Dancer's pink nose and made the
'Sugar Plum Fairy' music tinkle. Dancer twirled
round and round, her net skirt whirling. She
pirouetted up and down the bath and then jumped
on and off the taps.

'I'm doing my tap dance now!' she announced.

We both hooted with laughter.

'Em?' Mum knocked at the bathroom door. 'Em,
what are you up to in there? What are you doing
out of bed? Who's in there with you?'

'Just Dancer, Mum,' I said. I clambered out of
the bath and let her in.

'You and Dancer! You're a daft girl,' said Mum.

'I can't get over the way you kids act like she's real. You're daft as a brush, babe. Still, you're good at making up her stories. Have you started writing them in your new book?'

'Yep!' I said, flashing a page at her.

'You've been writing in the *bath*?' said Mum, looking at the scrunched-up towels.

'It's my special writing couch, Mum,' I said.

'For goodness' sake,' she said. 'You're not meant to be writing now. You're meant to be fast asleep in bed.'

'Haven't you heard of burning the midnight oil, Mum? I'm inspired!'

'You've got an answer for everything, my Em,' said Mum, giving me a hug. 'Let's read your story then.'

'Not yet. Not till it's all finished and I've filled the book right up.'

'There, it was a good idea of mine, wasn't it? I got blank pages instead of lined so you can do as many pictures as you like. Maybe Maxie will let you borrow his fancy felt tips if you ask him really nicely.'

'Maybe,' I said.

I decided not to tell on Maxie. I needed to do my own investigating first.

I didn't tackle him directly. I simply kept an eye on him the next day. I watched him sneak the dark brown pen out of his tin and stick it down his sock when he was getting dressed.

I followed him round doggedly, though it was very tiring. Maxie dashed here, charged there, darted up and down the stairs, running riot everywhere. He jumped on Mum, he badgered Gran, he tugged my hair, he pinched Vita. He knocked the cornflakes packet over, he spilled his juice down his front, he tripped over the vacuum and screamed blue murder – but he *didn't* take the felt pen out of his sock to scribble.

I waited patiently, biding my time. Maxie went to the loo. I followed him upstairs to the bathroom and waited outside. I waited and waited and waited. Gran was right, Maxie had started to take an awfully long time in the loo.

I was needing to go myself. I got fed up waiting. I knocked on the door. 'Maxie? Come on out, you must be finished now.'

'Go away, Em,' Maxie said, the other side of the door.

'Maxie, you've been in there fifteen minutes. What's the matter? Have you got a tummy upset?'

'No! Just bog off!' Maxie yelled crossly.

He knew he wasn't meant to say this. It was an expression he'd picked up off a television programme and it drove Gran nuts.

'I'm not bogging off anywhere, Maxie. You come

*out!*' I paused. 'I know what you're up to in there!' I hissed through the keyhole.

'No you don't!' said Maxie, but he sounded panicky.

'You come out or I'll tell,' I threatened.

Maxie went quiet. Then he suddenly unlocked the bathroom door and came out.

'You're not allowed to lock yourself in, you know that,' I said. 'What if you get stuck?'

'I'd jump out the window,' said Maxie. 'Like this.' He jumped along the hallway like a giant frog. He was jumping slightly awkwardly, his hands clamped over his T-shirt chest. I knew that problem. He was hiding something.

I played along with him, jumping too, pretending to be a fellow frog. Maxie croaked delightedly, wobbled, and threw out his arms. It was my chance. I slid my hand up his T-shirt and grabbed. I came away with a giant wad of crumpled pink loo-roll.

'Yuck!' I said, dropping it immediately.

'Don't, don't, don't!' Maxie screamed, though I'd already done it.

'Maxie, what are you playing at? You throw the used loo-roll down the toilet, you don't stick it up your T-shirt!' I said. I caught hold of his wrists as he scrabbled to get hold if it.

'Give it me back!' Maxie roared.

'No, it's dirty!' I cried.

166

But when I looked properly I saw it hadn't been used in the way that I'd feared. There were at least twenty separate sheets of loo-roll. Each one had been scribbled over with Maxie's brown felt pen. Not any old angry silly scribble. This was a very careful painstaking up and down long string of nearly-letters, all the way down to the bottom of each strip. Then there was a wobbly M for Maxie and a whole line of uneven xxxx.

'These are letters, Maxie,' I said. I let him go and started smoothing them out.

'Give them *back*,' said Maxie, hitting me.

'Who are these letters to, Maxie?' I asked, although of course I knew.

'Shut *up*, Em!' Maxie wailed.

'Emily, what are you doing to your little brother?' Gran called from downstairs.

'Nothing, Gran. I'm just sticking his head down the loo and using it like a toilet brush,' I called.

'You're doing *what*?' Gran shrieked.

'Joke, Gran, just *joking*,' I said. 'I'm just sorting Maxie out, that's all.'

Then I knelt in front of Maxie on the landing, my nose nearly touching his. 'They're letters to Dad, aren't they, Maxie? You haven't forgotten him one little bit. You just don't want to talk about him because it hurts, right?'

'No no no,' said Maxie, but big fat tears were

167

starting to spurt down his cheeks.

'What are you saying in your letters? Are you asking him to come back?'

'I'm saying I'll be a big brave boy if he comes back,' Maxie wept.

'Dad doesn't mind you being little and silly,' I said. I gave him a big hug. He struggled for a bit but then relaxed against me, rubbing his thatch of black hair into my neck.

'I've written him millions and millions of letters,' he said.

'But what did you do with them all?'

'I posted them. Properly, in the postbox down the shops. Gran wasn't looking,' Maxie said proudly.

I thought of all those tattered loo-roll letters clogging up the bottom of the postbox.

I nearly cried too.

When we went back to school we had to learn how to wire up a circuit in technology.

'That's good,' said Gran. 'My entire house needs rewiring and I haven't got the money to get it sorted. Maybe you'll do it for us, Em.'

She didn't really mean it. She was being sarcastic.

Mrs Marks, our teacher, suggested we use a clown's face with a dicky bow tie and a nose that could light up if we wired the circuit properly.

'Don't let's do a boring old clown,' I begged Jenny and Yvonne. 'Let's do Dancer, and have a pink light for her nose!'

'You're obsessed by that flipping reindeer,' said Yvonne, who'd heard one too many Dancer stories.

In our art lesson I painted a portrait of Dancer

171

in the style of Picasso, with her antlers lopsided, her legs all over the place and both her eyes on one side of her head. I thought it was a very good painting. I gave it to Vita as a present but she wrinkled her nose at it.

'Dancer doesn't look a *bit* like that,' she said. 'Even Maxie knows where the eyes go on your head, one either side of the nose.'

'Well, you can stick Dancer's antlers right up *your* nose,' I said crossly.

In drama we had to act out the Seven Deadly Sins. I chose Wrath. I got very angry indeed. I had Jenny and Yvonne as my partners and they got quite scared when I screamed at them.

'I was just *acting*,' I said.

'Well, you're a bit too good at it,' said Jenny.

I wasn't good at maths at all, I was totally hopeless. We were learning about percentages and I was 100 per cent hopeless at it. Mum found me rubbing out frantically on Sunday night, unable to get the right answer to anything.

'Can't you tell the teacher you don't understand how to do them?' said Mum. She peered at my messy figures. '*I* don't have a clue. Can the other children do it? What about Jenny and Yvonne?'

'Yvonne's brilliant at maths. Jenny sits right next to her and she can copy off her. Then when we have homework Jenny gets her dad to do it.'

Mum sighed. 'Well, even if your dad was home here, he couldn't do any sums to save his life. You could try asking your gran.'

I decided I'd sooner get into trouble at school. Gran was in a really mean crabby mood a lot of the time now.

'I know she's a bit cross, Em. She's tired having to work so hard. She's paying all the bills now and she's fed up about it,' Mum whispered.

I knew money was a Big Problem. Dad hadn't sent any more cheques at all, and Mum wasn't making much money at the Rainbow Hair Salon.

'Gran thinks I should report Dad and get the courts to make him send child support regularly,' said Mum. 'I know I maybe *should*, but it seems so awful. And if he hasn't been able to get work in Scotland then he won't have any money anyway. I'm sure he'd send something if he could.'

We were learning about the Tudors in history. Henry VIII made Dad seem like a very *good* husband. I hated it when Gran went on and on about him. I was sorry her work made her tired, but at least she was just sitting in an office, not on her feet all day like Mum. We were learning about an Indian village in geography where old ladies like Gran had to trek backwards and forwards with great sticks or big water pots on their heads, and toil all day in the fields.

I had to do an awful lot of toiling at school in PE because we were practising for our sports day. It was all right for Yvonne. She came first every time we raced, she jumped the highest and the longest, she leaped the furthest in the sack race, she won the egg and spoon race *without* cheating with Blu-tack. She even won the three-legged race tied up to Jenny. Yvonne would have won a *no*-legged race.

At least Jenny was almost as slow as me when we practised. We huffed and puffed at the very end of each race. I think Jenny might have been able to run a little bit faster but she was kind enough to slow down and keep me company, so we were equal last. As Jenny and Yvonne were partners in the three-legged race Jenny suggested she and I join up for the wheelbarrow race.

We didn't do *too* terribly when I was the runner and Jenny was the wheelbarrow, but after a few minutes Mrs Marks blew her whistle and said we had to swap roles. My heart started thudding. All the wheelbarrows had to be pushers. All the pushers had to be wheelbarrows. I was more like an armoured truck than a wheelbarrow. I was much much much too heavy for Jenny to lift. She tried valiantly but couldn't haul my legs up.

'Don't, Jenny, you'll hurt yourself,' I said, lying on the ground, scarlet as a lobster because everyone was staring at us and sniggering. 'I'm far too flipping *fat*.'

'No, no, it's because my arms aren't strong enough. I haven't got any muscles,' Jenny insisted kindly.

I had another traumatic moment in English. Mrs Marks said we were going to spend the term reading and writing stories about dilemmas and issues, children going through all sorts of problems.

'What, like kids being bullied, Mrs Marks?' Yvonne asked.

'That's certainly one area for us to explore. So why do you think some children are bullied?'

'Because they're wimps?'

'Because they look weird?'

'Because they're *fat*?'

I felt the whole class looking at me. I stared straight ahead, wanting to die.

'There's a Jenna Williams book all about bullying, Mrs Marks,' Jenny said quickly. '*The Girl Gang*. Please can we all read it? It's got all sorts of dilemmas and issues in it.'

'You girls and your Jenna Williams books,' said Mrs Marks. 'Isn't it time you branched out and read something else? Still, you can choose bullying as your homework topic, Jenny, and write me a book report on *The Girl Gang*.'

'Can I do it too, Mrs Marks?' said Yvonne.

'And Emily?' said Jenny.

I smiled at her gratefully, but I wanted to do my own topic.

'The dilemma of being a girl obsessed by a glove puppet?' said Yvonne.

'Oh, ha ha,' I said.

'So what do you want to do, Em?' Jenny asked.

'Oh, just stuff about dads,' I mumbled. 'Well, what it's like when your dad isn't always there.'

Jenny patted my knee understandingly.

'I bet there's a Jenna Williams story about that,' said Yvonne.

'Yep, *Piggy in the Middle*.'

It was about a girl called Candy whose mum and dad split up and they kept arguing over who was to look after her. Candy had this cute little toy piglet called Turnip that she took everywhere with her.

I'd read it at least five times so I could write a book report straight away. I wrote four whole pages. Then I drew a picture of Candy and her mum and her new family and her dad and his new family. I even did a picture of Turnip in his own little shoebox sty.

'You're a very quick reader, Emily,' said Mrs Marks, when I handed my report in the very next day. 'I tell you what, why don't we find you a few more books about children going through the same situation as Candy in *Piggy in the Middle*.'

She started sorting through the classroom shelf of children's classics, the ones that no one ever looks at, let alone reads.

'No one ever got divorced back in olden times,' I said.

'No, they didn't get divorced, but families still split up, or children lost their fathers in some sad way,' said Mrs Marks. 'Try reading *A Little Princess*, Emily, I think you'll enjoy it. Then there's *Little Women* and *The Railway Children*.'

I brightened a little. 'I've seen the film,' I said. 'I like it a lot. But isn't the book a bit old-fashioned and hard to read?'

'Why not give it a try and find out?' said Mrs Marks.

Yvonne pulled a horrified face when she saw I'd been given three classics to read. 'You do your homework quicker than anyone and yet you get *punished* for it?' she said. 'You poor thing, Em!'

Even Jenny looked appalled. But I found I got sucked straight into the story of *The Railway Children*. After a page or two it was just as easy to read as Jenna Williams and I didn't mind a bit that it was old-fashioned. It was a bit weird knowing that Bobbie was fourteen and yet she didn't wear make-up or high heels, she dressed just like a little girl. She didn't *act* like one. Bobbie and Phyllis and Peter were allowed to wander all over the countryside by themselves and their mother didn't worry one bit.

The bits about their father interested me the most. I thought the children were a bit slow to catch on when it was obvious he'd been taken away to prison. I wondered how I'd feel if Dad was in prison. At least I'd be able to visit him once a month, and I'd be able to send him letters and phone him.

It was so awful not knowing where he was. I looked at a map of Britain in an atlas at school. Scotland didn't look very big on the page. I hoped you might be able to search all over in a week or so, but when I asked Mrs Marks she said it was hundreds of miles wide and long. Dad could be up Edinburgh Castle or wandering down Sauchiehall Street or crossing the Tay Road Bridge; he could be sailing across a loch or climbing a mountain or paddling in the sea or patting a Highland cow or playing the bagpipes or wearing a kilt . . .

The sisters in *Little Women* didn't know where their father was either. He was away for most of the book, fighting in a war. I couldn't ever imagine our dad fighting. He was a total pacifist and believed all wars were wicked. Meg, Jo, Beth and Amy were very proud of their dad though, and knitted him socks – just like me knitting Dad his stripy scarf! I wondered if he was still wearing it.

Probably not, as it was getting too hot. I hoped he wouldn't just throw it away. If he'd stuffed it in a drawer somewhere, did he take it out sometimes and hold it to his cheek and think of me? Did he ever think about Vita, his little princess? Did he ever wonder how Maxie was managing without him?

The March sisters' dad came back home after he was wounded in battle. If our dad got ill, would he come back to us? I couldn't imagine Sarah doing any nursing.

There was a lot about illness in *Little Women*. I liked the chapter where Beth nearly died. I read it over and over again. If Vita became dangerously ill I'd nurse her devotedly and spoon-feed her and comb her hair and wipe her fevered brow with a cold flannel and tell her endless Dancer stories.

Then I read *A Little Princess*. That was the best book of all, though it was so so sad. I loved the beginning when Sara's father bought her trunkfuls of beautiful clothes – silks and furs as if she really was a little princess. Then Sara's china doll – Emily! – got kitted out with little cut-down versions of each outfit. I hated it when he left Sara at the girls' school and she missed him so much, but the worst bit of all was when she found out he'd died.

I could bear it if I got so poor I had to work as

a servant or live in an attic like poor Sara, but I simply couldn't stand it if Dad ever died.

I so identified with Sara that I wore one of Mum's old black T-shirts and her black skirt (I had to use a safety pin to do the waistband up – it's terrible when you're much fatter than your own mother). I trudged about in my last year's winter boots, holding my head high, pretending to be a princess even though I looked like a ragamuffin. I wore Dancer on my hand, pretending she was a very big pet rat.

'For pity's sake, what do you look like, Em?' said Gran.

I gave her a silent look of contempt. This was the way Sara dealt with Miss Minchin and it always unsettled her. It *infuriated* Gran.

'Don't you look down your nose at me, Emily! Take those awful black clothes off. And get rid of that wretched reindeer! You're too old to go round clutching a silly soft toy all the time.'

'Dancer isn't a toy, she's a puppet,' I said.

'It isn't even *your* puppet, miss.'

'Vita doesn't mind me borrowing her. She *likes* it when I make her talk to us.'

'I haven't seen you letting Vita borrow *your* Christmas present,' said Gran.

'She'd only lose it,' said Mum. 'She's not careful like Em. Quit nagging at her.' Mum put her arm round me and whispered 'Take no notice' in my ear.

I waited until night-time and then when Mum came to tuck me up I hung onto her, pulling her down on the bed beside me.

'Hey, hey, careful, chickie!' said Mum.

'Mum, why does Gran always get at me?'

'She gets at all of us, Em. I told you, she's tired, and she's at a funny age. Try not to let it bother you. I switch off when she's having a go at me and sing a song in my head. You try it some time.'

'I know Gran gets grumpy with all of us . . . but she's meaner to me than Vita or Maxie. I just get on her nerves all the time. She acts like she can't stand me.'

'Oh, darling, don't be silly. Gran loves you, she loves all of us.'

'She doesn't love me like she loves Vita and Maxie,' I said. I pulled Mum's head close beside me on the pillow. 'Is it because I'm fat?' I whispered.

'Oh, Em!' Mum's voice cracked as if she was going to start crying. 'You're not *fat*, sweetheart. You're just going through a little podgy stage.'

'Like I've been in a podgy stage all my *life*. Look at those baby photos of me. I look like a sumo wrestler!'

'Rubbish!'

'I still look like a sumo wrestler now. It's so

181

unfair, when you're all so weeny. Especially you, Mum.' I seized hold of her bony little wrist with my big pink sausage fingers. It felt like it could snap as easily as a wishbone.

'You're so skinny now, Mum. You're not ill, are you?'

'No, of course not.'

'Are you sure? Oh, Mum, I do worry about you.'

'You're just my sweet little worrypot. You mustn't worry so, Em. You're just a little girl. I'm the mum. It's my job to worry, not yours. Here, where's Dancer?' Mum put Dancer on and made her tickle my neck with her antlers.

'Cheer up, Em! How about a smile, eh? You need a bit of *fun* in your life.'

It was May Day Monday the next week. Vita, Maxie and I were off school. Mum and Gran had a holiday from work.

'There's a Green Fair in Kingtown,' said Mum. 'Shall we go and see what it's like?'

'A *Green* Fair?' I said. I imagined emerald roundabouts and jade giant wheels and olive dodgems, peppermint candyfloss and sage chips and apple ice cream. 'Like everything's green? Wow!'

'Will you talk *English*, Em?' said Gran. 'Don't be so soft, of course it's not coloured green. More mud-brown, if you ask me.'

'It's green because it's an environmentally friendly fair,' said Mum.

'Full of hippies and gypsies and druggies and drunks,' Gran sniffed. 'You're off your head wanting to take the kids. I don't know what's the matter with you. I did my level best to bring you up decently and yet you run off with the first weirdo who comes along—'

'Mum!'

'And look where that got you – not even able to go to college, and lumbered with a baby, and *then* you fall for Frankie Fly-by-Night and land yourself with more kids, and you won't even work in a decent hairdressing salon, you end up in a crumbling dump like the Pink Palace.'

'The Palace isn't a dump, it's lovely,' I said.

'Can we dress up as hippies and gypsies?' said Vita. 'Can I wear lots of jewellery, my bead necklace and my bunny brooch and my sparkly tiara and my Indian bangles? You can wear Dancer, Em, if you let me wear your emerald ring.'

'Some nasty druggie thief will have that ring off your finger in five seconds,' said Gran.

Maxie was trying to juggle his teddy bears. He couldn't catch even one teddy but he kept throwing them in the air enthusiastically.

'I'm going on the helter-skelter,' he said, out of the blue.

'I'm not sure there'll be a helter-skelter, darling,' said Mum. 'But there'll be lots of other lovely things, food stalls and face painting and lots of music. There might even be juggling. How would you like to try a special juggling workshop?'

'I can juggle already,' said Maxie. 'I want to go on a *helter-skelter*!'

'I want this, I want that! Whatever happened to *Please may I*?' said Gran. 'It's madness taking the children to this godforsaken fair, especially with Maxie in one of his moods. We need to go shopping. All three kids could do with new shoes, though I suppose I'm the one who's got to fork out for them.'

'It's very kind of you, Mum, but I think the children can wait for their shoes,' said Mum, trying to keep her voice steady. 'You go shopping by all means, but *we're* going to the Green Fair.'

I wondered if Mum would back down at the last minute, but she organized us into getting ready, leaving the emerald ring hidden at home but letting Dancer come with us.

'She has to. She's part of the family,' said Mum. 'Say goodbye to your gran, everyone.'

We said goodbye. Gran sniffed at us. She waited until Mum was opening the front door.

'I know why you're going to this wretched fair,' she called. 'You're such a *fool*, Julie.'

Mum slammed the door behind us with a big bang.

'Interfering old biddy! Why does she have to keep bossing us about all the time?' Dancer said.

Vita and Maxie laughed. Mum tutted at me, but she couldn't help laughing too.

I worked out what Gran meant when we got to the Green Fair. It was heaving with colourful people in rainbow-coloured clothes. A lot of the guys had long hair. Some had dreadlocks, some had ponytails – and several had plaits.

Vita and Maxie clamoured to have their faces painted. Vita chose to be a lilac fairy with flowers on her cheeks. Maxie was an orange stripy tiger.

'What about you, Em?' said Mum.

'No thanks, it's just for little kids,' I said.

'You *are* my little kid,' said Mum.

'And you're my little mum,' I said, putting my arm round her tiny waist. I kept holding her. 'Mum, Dad's in Scotland now.'

'Yes. He is. Well, as far as we know,' said Mum.

'Are you hoping he might be here, even so?'

'Of course not,' said Mum, but she went pink in the face. 'For goodness' sake don't say anything to Vita or Maxie! No, Dad won't be here, that's a mad idea. Though he did always come to the Green Fair when it was on, and he even talked about trying a Fairyland stall here. You know how he loves this sort of thing.'

I tried to love the Green Fair too, but it didn't

have the right sort of fair food. It was all tofu and couscous and grated carrot with weird watery coconut milk to drink.

It didn't have the right sort of fair rides either. There was no helter-skelter. There were no dodgems or big wheels or roundabouts. There were tyres on ropes hanging from trees instead of swings, but they weren't much use to us. Vita and Maxie were so little and skinny they'd have fallen straight through the hole, and I was so big and fat I worried I'd poke my head and shoulders through and then get stuck for ever.

I liked a stall of semi-precious stones. I stayed there for ages, fingering the smooth agate and amethyst and crystal pebbles while the stallholder told me they'd bring me love and luck and happiness. I wanted them all.

'You don't need *semi*-precious stones, Em,' said Mum. 'You've got your very own emerald safe at home.'

I squeezed Mum's hand. I thought hard about my emerald. My head filled with its intense green light. 'Please please please grant me love and luck and happiness,' I wished inside my head.

I opened my eyes, almost believing I'd find Dad there in front of me. I turned my head from side to side, my eyes swivelling over the crowds, searching for him.

Mum was looking round too. Then she stood still, her eyes wide, her mouth parting.

'Mum? Mum, what is it? Have you seen Dad?' I asked, shaking her arm.

I couldn't see any sign of him. Mum seemed to be staring at a family by the children's tent. There was a massive guy in a black vest, his big jeans buckled under his beer belly. He had long coarse yellow hair past his shoulders and a face the colour of tinned ham. He was helping his tubby little toddler son to ride a trike, bent over so that you could see too much of his horrible wobbly bottom. His skinny dark-haired wife had a fat baby riding on her hip, guzzling juice from a bottle.

The big fat guy was staring back at Mum. Then he waved his big beefy arm and started striding across the grass towards us.

'Who's this man, Mum? Do you know him?' I asked.

Mum swallowed. 'Oh, Em. It's your dad.'

I looked at Mum like she'd gone crazy. How could Mum think this massive meaty man could possibly be Dad?

Then I realized. He was my *real* dad.

'Let's run, Mum, quick,' I said.

I'd been too little when we did a runner to remember what he looked like. Mum had long since torn up all the photos. But I couldn't forget the threat of his voice, the thump of his blows, the sound of Mum screaming.

I grabbed Mum's arm and pulled. She was standing as if her silver sandals had grown roots and she was planted for ever in the muddy turf.

'It's Julie! By God, it really is!' he shouted, marching over to us.

'Who's that man?' Maxie asked, biting his bottom lip.

'How does he know you, Mum?' Vita asked.

'Quick, we're all going to run for it,' I said, but it was too late.

He was standing so close we could smell him. He was grinning, hands on his hips, shaking his head so that his hair rasped on his shoulders.

'I can't believe it! Well, Julie, long time no see.' But he wasn't looking at her, he was looking at Vita, with her painted flower face and her fluffy hair and her pink and lilac little-girly clothes.

'Is this little fairy my Emily?' he said.

'I'm not Em!' Vita said indignantly. '*That's* Em.' She pointed at me.

My dad took a proper look at me and then burst out laughing. 'Of course you're Emily!' he said. 'How could I have mixed you up? Talk about a chip off the old block!'

I was appalled. I didn't really look like this big fat ugly dad, did I? Oh God, I did, I did. I shrank as his big blubbery hand reached out and squeezed my shoulder.

'My, you've grown up, kiddo. I can't believe it! So who's the fairy and the little gnome, Julie?'

'They're my other kids, Barry,' Mum said shakily.

'I'm not a gnome, I'm a tiger. I'll bite you if you don't watch out,' Maxie threatened.

I grabbed hold of him but the big guy was just laughing.

'Help! Help! Don't eat me, big tiger,' he said, in a silly squeaky voice. Then he looked at Vita. 'What are you going to do, Magic Fairy? Are you going to wave your wand and grant me a magic wish?'

'No way,' said Vita, folding her arms. 'I'm keeping all my wishes for me.'

My dad laughed again and looked at Mum. 'Well, your kids do you proud, Julie, all three of them.'

He played silly tricks with Maxie and Vita, pretending he was twisting their noses off, sticking his thumb through his fingers to make them think he'd really done it. They laughed at him scornfully, not the slightest bit frightened. Then he tried it with me, but I dodged out of his way.

'Sorry, sorry!' he said, holding his hands up. 'You're too old for larking about, I know. How did you get to be so grown up, Emily? Dear oh dear, you and me have missed out on a lot. Perhaps we could spend some time together so you can get to know your old dad?'

'I've already got a dad,' I said.

Mum tensed.

'Oh well, I'm glad to hear it,' said my dad, nicely enough. 'So things have worked out for you, Julie?'

Mum nodded, holding my hand tight.

'That's good. I know you and me – well, it didn't work, did it? Maybe I gave you a bit of a rough time.'

'Maybe,' said Mum.

'Still, I'm off the drink now. Regular family man. That's my new lady over there, and my boys, bless the little bruisers. Want to come and meet them?'

'Maybe not,' said Mum.

'Yeah, it's all a bit awkward. Oh well. It was nice seeing you. And I'd like to keep in touch, hear about my Emily. Where are you living now?'

Mum hesitated.

'At Gran's,' Maxie blurted out.

My dad pulled a silly face. 'Oh dear! Perhaps I'd better keep my distance. We were never the best of friends!'

He waved his fat fingers at us and then ambled back to his new family.

'Thank God he's gone!' Mum whispered.

'Is that man really Em's dad? I thought Em's dad was a really scary man?' said Vita.

'He is,' said Mum. 'Well, he was. I don't know. Maybe he's changed.'

'I don't like him,' said Maxie. 'He took my nose.'

'I don't like him either,' I said. 'Come on, let's all walk the other way, quick.'

'Our dad's much nicer than Em's dad,' said Vita.

'That's enough, Vita,' said Mum sharply. She put her arm round me. 'Don't worry, sweetheart,' she said. 'He's gone now. We'll never see him again. Come on, there's an ice-cream van over there. Proper Whippy ice cream. I'll treat us all to a ninety-nine.'

I had a large cone with strawberry sauce and rainbow sprinkles and two chocolate flakes. I caught sight of myself reflected in the van window as I had my first long lick. I saw my big pink face, my fat sausage fingers. I stopped licking. I let the ice cream melt until it dripped up my arm. Then I threw it down and trod it into the mud.

'**Y**ou didn't see him, did you?' Gran said, when we got home.

'We didn't see *my* dad, but we saw Em's!' said Vita.

Gran thought she was making it up at first. Then she got furious with Mum.

'You mean you didn't pin him down about making maintenance payments for Em? For pity's sake, Julie, what are you like? There was a golden opportunity. Why do you let all these awful guys in your life walk all over you? Why won't you try to screw them for everything you can get? I know that pig doesn't give a damn about his own daughter, but he's her father and he should pay for her.'

'Stop getting at Mum, Gran,' I said. 'My dad *does* give a damn, he wanted to take me out, so there! But I don't want to so I don't have to, do I, Mum?'

'That's right, darling,' said Mum.

'Oh yes, that's right, you all do what you want. What about me? When can I do what *I* want?' said Gran. 'I've worked hard all my life. I've managed on my own. I've brought you up single-handed, Julie. Just when I've got to the time of life when I thought I could ease off, have a bit of fun, take a holiday like anyone else, I'm landed with you and your three kids and I'm the muggins paying all the bills.'

'I'm trying to pay my way, Mum, you know I am. Once I get the credit cards paid off I'll be able to pay a lot more,' my mum said, her face crumpling.

'Look what you've done, Gran, you've made her cry,' I said furiously.

'Oh, it's easy to give up and burst into tears. Did you see *me* crying when that con-man Frankie stole my savings?'

'He didn't steal them, Mum, he just borrowed them,' Mum sobbed.

'Oh yes, and he'll pay it back? And pay off all your debts too?' Gran glared at Vita and Maxie and me. 'You kids think your dad's such a lovely guy for giving you all these ridiculous treats and presents – and flipping emerald rings! He didn't pay a penny for them. Your mum and I are the poor fools who've ended up forking out for the lot.'

194

'Shut up, Gran! My dad *is* lovely,' Vita yelled. 'I looked and looked and looked for him at the Green Fair and it's so mean, because Em got to see her dad and I want *mine*.' She started shouting it over and over again, almost having a Maxie-type tantrum. He was crying too, just so he wouldn't be overlooked.

'There! I told you going to the stupid Green Fair was a silly idea. The kids have got all worked up and over-excited,' said Gran.

I wondered if she knew how much she twisted things round. Did she really think she was right all the time? Did she like making us all feel bad?

I could hear Gran and Mum carrying on rowing all the time I was upstairs with Vita and Maxie. I put Dancer on my hand and told them a long story about the special Snowy White Fairs they have in Lapland. When I came downstairs at last I found Mum and Gran sitting on the sofa together. Mum was still crying but Gran had her arm round her.

'Come here, Em,' said Gran, holding out her other arm. 'Come and have a cuddle.'

'No thanks,' I said, sitting on the spare chair instead. I flipped through Gran's *Hello!* magazine as if I couldn't care less.

'Ooh, look at Little Miss Sulky,' said Gran.

I did my best to ignore her. I stared hard at *Hello!*, imagining living in a huge house with white sofas and gold chandeliers and televisions hanging on the walls like a painting. I pretended Dad was a truly famous movie star and Mum had her own chic chain of hairdressing salons and I was their thin-as-a-pin daughter, sitting at their feet and smiling sweetly at the camera.

'What are you smirking at, Em?' said Gran.

My smile soured to a scowl. I still didn't say a single word. I didn't even say goodnight when I went up to bed.

Mum waited until Vita and Maxie were asleep and then she crept in to see me. She eased Vita over to the other side of the bed and slipped under the covers with me.

'Gran's sorry, Em.'

'She didn't say so.'

'No, well, she doesn't ever *say* sorry, you know that. But she knows she went too far.'

'I hate her,' I said.

'No you don't.'

'She hates me!'

'Of course she doesn't. She loves you. She loves all of us. That's why she gets so worked up. She's not really cross with us, she's cross with your dad. *Both* your dads!' Mum gave a little sniff. 'It was so weird seeing your real dad again, Em. He seems so different now. Maybe he was just horrible with us. He looked like he was happy with that other woman and the little boys. I'm sure he doesn't batter them.'

Mum sniffed again. I felt her cheeks in the dark to see if she was crying.

'Don't be scared, Mum. If he comes round to batter us we'll call the police, quick.'

'I'm not worried about that, love. No, I'm just thinking, maybe there's something about me that makes men go funny. Maybe I'm just a useless partner.'

'You're a brilliant partner, Mum. You didn't make him horrid to us. He was just mean and he wanted to shout and scare us. He *hit* us,' I said. 'Mum, I *wish* he wasn't my real dad.'

'He wasn't all bad, pet. Maybe you'd like him if you got to know him now.'

I wanted to think he was totally bad. I didn't want to like him. I loved my *new* dad – even though he'd gone off and left us.

'I'm never ever living with any man,' I said.

'That's silly, pet. You can't say that just because things haven't worked out for me.'

'No one would have me anyway!'

'Of course they would! You're a lovely lovely girl.'

'All the boys at school think I'm rubbish. They call me Fatso and The Blob and they all puff out their cheeks, imitating me.'

'Oh darling, that's horrible.'

'It's OK. I call them names back. But I am a Fatso Blob. I take after my real dad, don't I?'

'You're not a bit like your dad. You're a sweet kind gentle caring girl.'

'I *look* like him. If I wore a black vest and jeans I'd be just like a little replica.'

'You're *nothing* like him,' Mum lied. 'You're not like him, you're not like me. You're *you*, my lovely Em. I think it's rot we're all supposed to take after our parents. I certainly don't want to be like Gran!' Mum paused. 'For pity's sake, Julie,' she said, in Gran's thin whiny voice.

We both burst out laughing. Vita woke up and sleepily complained that we were shaking the bed and would we please stop now, immediately.

'I think *Vita* takes after Gran,' I whispered to Mum. 'She's bossier than her already.'

Gran nagged just as much the next morning, when we were all rushing off to school and work, but that evening she made us spaghetti bolognese, with strawberries and ice cream for pudding. She gave me an extra scoop of ice cream *and* let me scrape round the empty carton afterwards.

'But it's back on that diet tomorrow, Em, OK?' Gran said.

I did wonder about trying harder. I still mostly chose chips instead of salad at school dinners but

198

I didn't buy secret supplies of KitKats and Mars bars and Smarties with my pocket money now. I still wanted them desperately but I wanted to save all my treat money. I wanted to save up so I could pay Gran some of the money we owed. Then she'd maybe stop moaning.

Mum was trying hard too, taking on as much extra work as she could. The Pink Palace didn't open till midday now because they got so few morning customers. Mum made herself some 'Good Fairy' cards using stationery from leftover Fairyland stock, saying she was willing to fly round to clients' houses and cut and blow-dry their hair between nine and twelve. She started to get booked up most mornings, and she had a special regular job on Wednesdays at an old people's day centre, snipping her way through silvery locks, one old lady after another at a special £5 rate.

'I have to cram as many in as possible, doing them for that rate,' said Mum. 'It's a bit like sheep-shearing. I'll be taking hold of them by their Scholl sandals, throwing them over my shoulder and clipping their perms into crewcuts soon.'

Mum got up even earlier on Saturday mornings, doing special wedding hairdos, often fitting in the bride, chief bridesmaid and the bride's mother before rushing to start her stint at the Palace.

'Imagine if I got mixed up, and dyed all the

wedding clients purple and magenta and gave twee mother-of-the-bride shampoo and sets to all the goths at the Palace,' said Mum.

She tried to make a joke of it, but she was so tired now that she fell asleep as soon as she sat down on the sofa when she got home.

'Mum's no fun now,' said Vita. 'She won't make me up like a grown-up lady or play Fairy Queens or do *anything* now, she just falls asleep.'

'Yes, I was telling her about this bad boy who pushed me and she didn't *listen*, her eyes kept closing,' Maxie said indignantly.

'Mum's tired out,' I said. 'Leave her alone. *I'll* make you up and play Fairy Queens with you, Vita. Just let me give Maxie a cuddle first and find out all about this bad boy.'

I knew I had to be very grown up and understanding but *I* wished Mum wasn't so worn out. She was skinnier than ever, with dark circles under her eyes.

Gran was worried about her too.

'You're exhausting yourself, Julie. You don't have to take on quite so many clients. Never mind the blooming money. I wanted your deadbeat missing bloke to pay his debts. I didn't mean *you* should work yourself to death on his behalf.'

'I'm fine, Mum,' Mum murmured, rubbing her forehead and yawning.

'You need a holiday. We all do,' said Gran.

'Yes, well, holidays cost money,' said Mum. 'We'll have to make do this year. Maybe I'll be able to take the kids on a day out here and there.'

I started to think and think and think about a summer holiday. Jenny was going to the seaside in France, ending up with a day in EuroDisney. Yvonne was going to Spain for a week with her mum, and CenterParcs for three days with her dad.

I couldn't help daydreaming for days about Dad inviting us on holiday with him. We didn't have to go *away* anywhere. We'd have been happy to stay in one room with him (just so long as Sarah wasn't there too).

I kept thinking of that evening at the seaside. It sparkled in my mind like the fairy lights on the end of the pier. I wondered what would have happened if we'd stayed the night like Dad suggested. Would he have kept us? Sometimes, when Mum was tired and Gran was snappy, I'd wish and wish we could live with Dad instead.

Then I'd feel desperately guilty and try harder than ever to be good to Mum. I didn't always try to be good to *Gran*.

'I *wish* I could take Mum on holiday,' I whispered to Dancer.

'Lapland's pretty in the summer,' she said.

'I'd like to take Mum somewhere really warm

and sunny so she'd lie and sunbathe and get brown and look happy again,' I said.

'You could try wishing,' said Dancer.

I took my hand out of her head and looked at my beautiful emerald ring. I held it up so that it caught the light and wished as hard as I could.

Then I looked at the ring again.

I kept on looking at it.

I wondered how much emerald rings cost. Dad said he'd bought it second hand, but Mum and Gran said they thought it was still worth hundreds of pounds.

If I had hundreds of pounds we could all go on holiday.

I thought about it day after day. I loved my emerald ring so much. It was the best present in the whole world. I wasn't allowed to wear it very often. Obviously I couldn't wear it to school, and Mum didn't like me wearing it outside just in case I lost it. I wore it at home whenever I could, but mostly it was kept in its little box, hidden in my knicker drawer in case of burglars.

I couldn't bear the thought of selling it so that I'd lost it for ever. But maybe, just maybe, I could *pawn* it?

I'd read about pawn shops in one of my favourite Jenna Williams books, *The Victorian Project*. I knew loads and loads of poor people pawned their rings and their watches and even their best Sunday suits back in olden times. I wasn't sure you could still pawn things nowadays.

There was an old jewellery shop in an alley by the market place. It had three golden balls hanging above its doorway. It *used* to be a pawn shop. Maybe it still was one. And *maybe* it might be interested in my beautiful emerald ring.

I didn't know how I would ever raise the money to get it back again, but at least it wouldn't be selling it for ever. Maybe they'd display it in the window so I could go and look at it.

I got my chance the very next Saturday, when Mum was doing a wedding and then going on to the Palace. Gran had to take Vita, Maxie and me into town to buy new sandals. We all needed them badly. I was still stomping around in my big lace-up winter shoes. They were so small for me I felt like I was lacing my toes into corsets every time I tied them up. Vita was wearing her winter buckle shoes too. My last year's sandals were still way too big for her, and she insisted she'd sooner go barefoot than wear my horrible scuffed cast-offs anyway. Maxie had Vita's old sandals and he didn't mind wearing them one bit, but they were pink jelly plastic. Maxie adored them but when he wore them to school everyone said they were girls' shoes and sniggered at him.

It was a very long and fraught morning. Gran lost her temper, Maxie howled, Vita sobbed and I despaired, because my new flat black sandals were so big they looked like flippers.

'For pity's sake, what a fuss!' said Gran. 'Let's go up to the food court and have a cup of tea. I'll treat all three of you to a cake if you'll only shut up, the lot of you.'

'Um, Gran, you said shut up!' said Maxie.

'Can't we go down to McDonald's instead? I want a McFlurry ice cream,' said Vita.

My mouth was watering at the thought of cake *or* ice cream, but this was my big chance.

'I'm not going to have anything. I want to stick to my diet,' I said.

'That's the ticket, Em,' said Gran, looking surprised.

'But it's torture watching everyone else eat, so please may I go and look at the bears being made in the Bear Factory while you're in the food court?'

Gran hesitated. 'Well, if you promise you'll go straight there and not talk to any strangers and then come right back here in fifteen minutes . . . then OK,' said Gran. 'Only take that blooming glove puppet off your hand – you look gormless, a great big girl like you.'

'No, Dancer wants to see the bears too,' I said. 'Don't you, Dancer? You want to see the special

204

bear ballet dancers with their pink satin shoes, isn't that right?'

I made Dancer nod emphatically, her antlers waving in the air.

'It's not fair, she's *my* puppet,' said Vita.

'Yes, give her back to Vita,' said Gran, but she was distracted by Maxie screaming at the escalators.

I dashed off before she could stop me. If I took Dancer off she'd see I was wearing the emerald ring on my finger. I wanted Dancer's company anyway. It felt a bit weird and scary going right out of the Flowerfields shopping centre and over to the market place. I knew Gran would kill me if she ever found out.

I ran all the way to the jewellery shop, my heart thumping. I checked on the one, two, three golden balls dangling above the door. I wasted two of my precious minutes pretending to look at the window display, too scared to step inside.

'Go *on*,' said Dancer, and she put her front hooves on the handle and pulled the door open.

I stood in the middle of the shop while fifty clocks ticked and tocked at me all around the room. An old man and a young man stood at either side, behind counters. The young man sighed at the sight of me, but the old man cocked his head on one side and looked obliging.

'Can I help you, young lady?' he said.

'I hope so.' I moved towards him, trying to tug Dancer off. My hand was so hot and sticky it was a struggle. 'Is this a pawn shop?'

'Well, we do offer a loan service. But not to children, I'm afraid,' said the old man.

I thought quickly. 'Oh, this isn't for me. This is for my mum. She's too embarrassed to come herself. She wants to know how much she'd get if she pawned this emerald ring.' I peeled the last piece of Dancer off and flapped my hot hand in the air, flourishing my beautiful emerald. Its green glow sparkled all around the room.

The young man clucked his teeth. 'Does your mum know you've got her ring?' he said.

'Of course she does. I *said*. Do you think I'm a liar?' I said, getting hotter and hotter.

'May I see the ring?' said the old man, still courteous.

I had to lick my finger until it was slippery enough to ease the ring off. The old man took hold of it gingerly. He held it to the light. Then he shook his head at me.

'Why don't you go home and stop wasting our time,' he said.

'What do you mean? Won't you take my emerald – *Mum's* emerald?'

'It isn't an emerald. It's green glass in a gilt setting. You used to be able to buy them in

206

Woolworths for a shilling. It's not worth much more now.'

'Funny joke, dear,' said the young man, poker-faced.

'It's not a joke. It *is* an emerald, I know it is. My dad got it from an antique fair. I know he paid heaps of money for it,' I gabbled.

'Then he was conned, dear,' said the old man, handing me my emerald back. My fingers closed over it protectively.

I ran out of the shop. I heard them laughing behind me.

I poked my finger into my poor ring, clutched Dancer and ran. Tears pricked my eyes. When I got to the Flowerfields shopping centre I took deep breaths, trying to stop snivelling.

'There there, sweetheart,' said Dancer, wiping my eyes tenderly. 'Take no notice of those idiots. *They're* the con men. They were probably just trying to trick you out of your emerald. Of *course* it's real.'

I looked at it on my finger. Just for a moment its green glow dulled. I saw a chip of coloured glass stuck in cheap gilt, a Christmas cracker ring.

Dancer changed her tactics. 'It's the same ring Dad gave you, so it's the most special ring in the world whether it's a real emerald or not. And I say it *is* real. As real as you and me.'

207

I hugged her and looked at the ring again. Its glow was back, glittering green.

I got back to Gran and Vita and Maxie just as Gran was looking at her watch and frowning.

'You're two minutes late,' she said. 'Come on, now, Maxie's desperate for a wee and we'll have to take him to the ladies with us.'

'You ran off with *my* Dancer,' said Vita, frowning. 'But I still saved you half my cake.'

She'd licked all the icing off, but it was still sweet of her.

'Did you *really* go to the Bear Factory?' said Vita, while Gran was mopping up Maxie and his damp dungarees. 'I peered over the balcony railings and I thought I saw you on the escalator.'

'It must have been somebody else,' I said – like there were *lots* of big fat girls in too-tight jeans and a fairy T-shirt with a reindeer glove puppet on their right hand.

I didn't want to tell Vita about the jewellery shop. It was too awful and embarrassing. There was no point anyway. I couldn't take us on holiday after all.

But Gran could. The day we all broke up from school Gran made us wait for tea till Mum came home. Then she sent out for a giant pizza, opened a bottle of wine for her and Mum, with Coke for us kids.

'What are we celebrating?' said Mum.

'The start of the summer holidays,' I said.

'I wish we were *going* on holiday,' said Vita.

'Let's go to the seaside. The seaside with the helter-skelter,' said Maxie.

'Ssh, Maxie, Vita. We can't go away on holiday, you know we can't,' I said.

'Yes we can!' said Gran. She opened up her handbag and produced a little folder of tickets. 'It's all booked up. We're going to Spain for a week, all five of us, staying in a great big hotel by the sea.'

'With a helter-skelter?' Maxie persisted.

Vita whooped with excitement. I whooped too, but I felt wrong-footed.

'But Mum, how on earth have you managed it?' said our mum, looking dazed.

'Never you mind. I just felt we all badly needed a holiday,' said Gran. 'Now simmer down, kids.'

We couldn't simmer. We were boiling over with excitement. Vita started dancing round the room, showing us her version of Spanish dancing. Dancer demonstrated too, doing a mid-air flamenco. I stamped my foot in time. Maxie gave up on the helter-skelter and jumped wildly up and down.

'For pity's sake, mind my—' said Gran. Then she stopped in mid sentence.

I looked over at the china cabinet. There was something the matter. The little pink crinoline lady was spreading her skirt in solitary splendour on the top shelf. Where was the balloon seller and the little mermaid and the children in their white china nightgowns?

'Gran, your china!' I gasped.

'Has someone stolen it?' said Vita.

'Stolen!' said Maxie fearfully.

'Don't be so silly,' Gran snapped. 'I decided to weed out a few pieces. They were just gathering dust, no use to anyone.'

'Oh, Mum, you loved your china collection!' said our mum. 'You sold it to pay for our holiday. It's so sweet of you.'

Mum gave Gran a big hug. I couldn't help feeling jealous. *I'd* so wanted to take everyone on holiday by pawning my emerald ring.

'Did you pawn your china, Gran?' I asked.

'Did I *what*?' said Gran. 'No, of course not, I sold it in the antique centre. Honestly, Em, where do you get all these silly ideas from?'

'They're not silly! If you pawn things you can get them back again when you've got enough money,' I said. 'Why do you *always* have to say I'm silly?'

'Hey, hey, that's enough, Em. Don't cheek your gran, especially when she's done such a lovely thing for us,' said Mum sharply.

I started to get seriously fed up with this holiday

as the weeks went by. I had to act eternally grateful to Gran. She traded on it too. Every time I moaned when she told me to wash up or I argued over what I wanted to watch on the television or I locked myself into the bathroom to write my Dancer story, Gran would threaten me.

'You'll do those dishes because I say so. Vita's too young, she'd only break them. Now make yourself useful or you won't go on holiday!'

'We're not watching *The Bill*, it's not suitable. Just because your dad was in it once doesn't make it compulsory viewing for the rest of us. Now take that sulky look off your face or you won't go on holiday.'

'What on earth are you up to in there, Emily? For pity's sake, come out of the bathroom at once! You watch it, young lady, or you won't go on holiday.'

I decided I didn't *want* to go on holiday. I'd stay at home by myself and eat chocolate bars all day long and watch whatever I wanted on the telly and read all my Jenna Williams books and write my Dancer story in perfect peace.

# 11

I didn't stay at home. I went on holiday with Mum and Gran and Vita and Maxie. I actually had a fabulous time! The hotel was a big white tower overlooking the sea. Our two rooms were right at the very top, which was a bit of a problem. Maxie kicked and screamed at the very idea of going in the glass lift.

Gran got cross and tried giving him a good talking to. Maxie got crosser still and screamed back. Mum tried bribing him with sweets. Maxie swallowed them quickly but still refused to step into the lift.

'So what are we going to do? March up twelve flipping flights of stairs?' Gran said.

'I'll walk up the stairs with him,' I said.

'Don't be so silly, Em. You couldn't get up *one*

213

flight without huffing and puffing,' said Gran.

'I'm not being silly,' I said, through gritted teeth. 'Come on, Maxie, I'll take you. We'll race up those stairs, won't we?'

We raced up the first flight of stairs. Then we slowed down a little. My heart was thumping a bit but I *wasn't* huffing and puffing. We went up the second flight and the third. Maxie hung on my hand, dragging his feet.

'Come on, Maxie, keep going,' I said.

'Don't want to. I'm tired,' Maxie said, flopping down on the stairs.

'Do you want to try the lift again?'

'No!'

'Then it's stairs or nothing.' I bent over him, feeling the sharp little bones sticking out at the back of his T-shirt. 'Are these wings? Yes, they are! They'll help you fly up. Come on, Maxie, we'll fly like Peter Pan. Wheeee! Wheeee!'

We 'flew' for another couple of flights. Then we both had to have a little sit down. Maxie put his head on his knees.

'It's too high up,' he moaned.

'Yes, it is, ever so high. Let's pretend it's a mountain and we're climbing way way up to the very top. When we get there we'll plant a flag on the summit and get filmed for television.'

'Like the special videos?' said Maxie.

We had three special videos of Dad. One was his proper speaking part in *The Bill*. The second was an *EastEnders* market crowd scene where Dad gets to smile and wave though he doesn't actually say anything, The third was an advert for a mobile phone. That always made me cry because I kept remembering Dad in the kitchen at Christmas. I still watched it though. When Dad first left at Christmas I watched the videos over and over, every single day. I still watched them at least once a week. So did Mum and Vita. Maxie never *seemed* to be watching, but he was often in the room.

I put my arms round him. 'I was just pretending, Maxie,' I said. 'We're not *really* going to be filmed. Gran's brought her camera though, so we'll have photos of us on holiday. We'll take a photo of you looking all cute in your new shorts and your big boy's baseball cap, yeah?'

'Mmm,' said Maxie, his chin still on his knees.

'Are you thinking about Dad, Maxie?' I whispered.

Maxie shook his head, but I knew he was.

'Dad would give you a ride on his back up the stairs, wouldn't he?' I said. 'But *I* can't, Maxie. I just can't manage to carry you. I want someone to carry *me*! But we're going to get up these stupid stairs just to show Gran, right?'

'Right,' said Maxie.

He stood up, flexing his little arms. Then he tried to take hold of me.

'What are you doing? Hey, that tickles!'

'I'm trying to carry you,' Maxie said.

'Oh Maxie, you're so sweet! You could never ever ever pick up a big fat lump like me,' I said. 'Come on, we'll hold hands and take turns helping each other, right?'

We climbed on upwards – and met Mum, rushing down to find us, worried we'd collapsed on the way.

Vita had already taken charge of the bedroom, commandeering the entire double bed, and all of the chest of drawers, spreading out her T-shirts and shorts and fairy dress and disco-dancing costume so that each drawer had one garment. She insisted that Dancer wanted the little single bed all to herself too.

There's one advantage of being the big sister – especially when you're a *very* big sister. In two minutes Vita had been thoroughly vanquished and squashed until she begged for mercy, and I had allocated the bedroom more fairly. Vita was left with half the double bed and *one* drawer. Dancer stayed in her single bed because Maxie pulled the mattress off, made a cave and huddled there quite happily with his tattered teddies. (We'd had to bring them with us, in a bulging laundry bag.)

We had our very own ensuite bathroom. We tried

the shower taps to see if they were working. They were working a little too efficiently. Mum just laughed when she saw us.

'Never mind! Let's go and check out the swimming pool, seeing as you're all soaked anyway.'

The pool was fantastic, a big turquoise rectangle with green deckchairs and sun loungers spread all around, with a little poolside café in case you got peckish. We spent day after day there, Gran and Mum lying on sun loungers and smoothing on suncream and reading their fat paperbacks, and Vita and Maxie and me having six swims a day. Well, Maxie didn't technically swim. He lay on his tummy in the paddling pool and kicked his legs and pretended he was swimming. Vita got brave enough to come in the big pool with me but she insisted on wearing her inflated armbands and a rubber ring, and she screamed if she ever went under. I was the only one who swam properly.

I'd learned to swim at school. It had been total agony having everyone staring at me in my swimming costume and making horrible comments. I was terribly shy of swimming in public in the hotel pool, even though Mum had bought me a new big blue costume and insisted I looked lovely in it.

'Yeah, like a lovely blue whale,' I said, and made mournful whale whistles.

I thought I'd stick out appallingly but there were a couple of other fat kids who were dashing about in teeny weeny costumes, not seeming at all self-conscious. I tried not to care what I looked like either. I shrugged off my big towelling dressing gown and jumped into the pool.

I discovered something extraordinary. I was good at swimming. I'd only swum widths at school. Now I swam lengths. Once I'd relaxed and got used to it I found I could swim and swim and swim up and down the pool, faster than all the other kids, even faster than a lot of grown-ups!

They'd only taught us breaststroke at school. I wished I knew how to do some other strokes. I watched this nice dad showing his little boy how to do freestyle but the kid was nearly as wimpy as Maxie and kept whining that he was getting water up his nose. I couldn't remember if our dad could swim. I wished he was with us to teach me, standing beside me, smooth and tanned with his pigtail sleek down his brown back.

I tried to copy what the dad was saying. He spotted me windmilling my arms and kicking my legs.

'That's it, love! You've got it. You're a great little swimmer. Here, curve your fingers more, like this.'

He ended up teaching me while his little boy

Edward played ball with our Maxie. Neither of them could catch but they had a lot of fun running after each ball.

Edward's dad told Mum and Gran that I was a real little water baby and ought to have proper lessons. Mum gave me a hug and said she was proud of me. Gran asked straight out if Edward had a mum. She looked disappointed when she found out she'd just gone on a shopping trip.

'That's such a shame,' said Gran. 'I thought you'd do just fine for my daughter!'

'Mum!' our mum hissed, mortified.

Mum and Gran had a little row about it later when we were all having ice creams.

'Will you please stop trying to pair me up with someone! It's dead embarrassing. I'm not *interested*.'

'It's no use wasting your life hoping Frankie will come back,' said Gran.

'He *will* come back, he *will* come back, he *will* come back,' I mouthed at Vita.

She nodded and mouthed it back to me.

I counted the cherries in my ice-cream sundae. One – he *will* come back. Two – he won't. Three – he *will* come back. Four – he won't. Five – he *WILL*! I crammed all five cherries into my mouth at once and choked, so that Mum had to thump me on the back.

'Stop being such a greedy-guts, Em. And how

many calories are in that ice cream? What about your diet?' said Gran.

'Mum, give it a rest! She's on holiday!' said my mum.

'All right, all right, it's just that it would be a shame to give up on it just as she's doing so well.'

'What do you mean, Gran?' I asked.

'You've lost a bit of weight, love,' said Mum.

'*Have* I?' I said.

I peered down at myself. I still looked horribly blue-whaleish. Maybe there was just a *little* bit less of a tummy. Was this just because I'd stopped eating my secret snacks? How could going without one little chocolate bar – or two, or maybe even three – each day make so much difference? I'd carried on saving up all the money. I hadn't been able to take Mum on holiday but I *could* take her out for a special meal.

'I'm going to take us all out for our dinner,' I announced proudly.

'We don't need to go out,' said Gran. 'We're getting dinner at the hotel. It's already paid for.'

'I want to take us *out* for dinner,' I said. 'I want to buy Mum a special meal for a holiday treat. Look, I've got money, heaps of it. I can change it into euros easy-peasy and pay for it myself.'

I delved into my school bag, scrabbled through my cardie and beach towel and flip-flops, my

Dancer notebook and my three favourite Jenna Williams books, and right at the bottom found the fat envelope chinking with gold coins. I shook it like a tambourine.

'For pity's sake, Em, have you robbed a slot machine?' said Gran.

'Oh lovie, you've saved all your treat money! *Months* of it!' said Mum, and she gave me a big hug. 'OK then, my wonderful generous girl, you take us out for a meal tonight.'

We all changed into our best things after a day's sunbathing and swimming. I wore the only dress I like, a deep green silky shirt-dress that hangs loosely. Mum plaited the top of my hair and tied it with a green velvet ribbon. My emerald sparkled on my finger. Vita sparkled all over in her favourite rainbow disco outfit, and Dancer had pink ribbons tied around her antlers. Maxie wore his baseball cap back to front and wouldn't tuck his shirt into his shorts so he looked cool (well, *he* thought so). Mum wore her white dress with a silver chain belt and her special silver sandals.

Gran scoffed at all of us and said she wasn't going to bother changing, but at the last minute she rushed up to her room. She came down wearing a pink lacy top, pink strappy sandals just as high as Mum's, and the black jeans Dad bought for her at Christmas. She hadn't worn them since. We hadn't known she'd even taken them on holiday.

'What are you all staring at?' Gran said grumpily, but she couldn't help smiling a little bit. She had pink lipstick on too.

'You look pretty, Gran!' said Vita.

'You look like a *lady*!' said Maxie.

'Oh, thanks very much, our Maxie. So I normally look like a *man*, do I?' said Gran, pretending to swat him.

'He means you look a total glamour puss,' said Mum. 'Hey, this is *my* night out. What are you doing upstaging me? You don't look like my mum any more. You look like my sister.' Then Mum smiled at me. 'And you look so gorgeous and grown up in your green dress that you look like my sister *too*, Em.'

It was so lovely to see Mum being all happy and bubbly with her white dress showing off her new tan. I felt thrilled to be giving her a real treat.

I did get a bit worried when we walked along the beach road into town and couldn't find a good place to eat. There were lots of burger and chip places with special menus in English but they were all a bit noisy and messy and Gran got sniffy about holidaymakers who didn't have the sense to sample the local cuisine.

When we got near the fish market there were lots more restaurants displaying plates of squid and octopus with wriggly slimy tentacles, and huge weird slabs of fish with scary faces. Gran shut up sharpish, because this food was a bit *too* local for any of us.

We trudged on to the posh end of town and found a proper restaurant, all white linen tablecloths and flowers on the table and waiters in evening clothes.

'This looks a lovely place, Mum!' I said, clutching her arm.

'Hang on a tick. Let's look at the menu,' said Mum.

I peered round a fat man in a blue shirt and squinted at the menu. It was all in Spanish, but I could understand the prices. My heart started thudding. I'd thought I was so rich – but I didn't have enough to pay for *one* meal, let alone five.

'I think it looks a horrible uncomfy snobby sort of place. I'd *hate* to go there,' Mum said quickly.

'Well, where *are* we going to go?' said Gran. She looked at her watch. 'We could rush back to the hotel. We've missed the starters but they'll probably still serve us the main course.'

'I don't mind just having pudding,' said Vita.

'Pudding!' said Maxie. 'I want pudding!' He rubbed his tummy emphatically.

'Ssh, kids, we're all going to have pudding, *and* a main course too – but this is my special night *out*,' said Mum, steering Vita and Maxie out of the fat man's way. He smiled at Vita and rubbed his tummy back at Maxie.

'We've just got to find somewhere nice to eat, that's all,' I said, trying to sound positive.

'Well, we've been looking long enough,' said Gran. She wiggled her foot out of her pink strappy sandal and rubbed a sore toe, wincing. 'It's obvious we're not going to stumble across somewhere cheap but decent by chance. If only we could speak a bit of Spanish, then we could ask someone.'

The fat man turned round to us and pointed at himself enquiringly. Gran was taken by surprise and wobbled on one foot. He caught her quickly by the elbow and steadied her.

'Thank you!' she said. 'Sorry – *gracias, señor*.'

'You're very welcome,' said the fat man, his blue eyes twinkling.

'You speak wonderful English,' said Gran, shoving her sandal back on.

'I should hope so. I *am* English, though I've lived here for several years now. I was eavesdropping shamelessly. I think I know the perfect place for you all to have a lovely relaxed meal. It's a real family restaurant, and they'll make a big fuss of the children. It's only down the next alleyway and round the corner. Shall I show you?'

'How very sweet of you. Yes please!' said Gran.

She started chatting away to him while we trooped

along behind. We heard Gran asking if his family all lived in Spain too. She made attentive cooing sounds of sympathy when he said his wife had died a year ago. Then she looked over her shoulder at Mum, giving her a wink. Mum looked appalled.

'Oh God! She's matchmaking again!' Mum whispered. 'What is she *like*?' She saw I was looking anxious. 'Don't worry, Em, if this place of his looks out of our league we'll just say we don't fancy it. I've been thinking, I'd rather like to get fish and chips and eat them on the beach. Wouldn't that be fun?'

I knew Mum was just saying that because she was worried this fat man's recommended restaurant was going to be too expensive. But it turned out to be the perfect place, a small friendly very cheap restaurant crammed with local families. They were sitting on wooden benches, with red candles on the tables and red-and-white place mats. A red-cheeked lady in a red-and-white checked apron greeted us as if we were long-lost relatives. She made Vita twirl round to show off her outfit, she tickled Maxie under the chin, and she stroked my long hair. She said in Spanish that she thought my hair was beautiful, definitely my crowning glory. The fat man translated for me.

'Don't you wish we could speak fluent Spanish, Julie?' said Gran. She gave the fat man a big lipsticky smile. 'You're so clever. I don't suppose you could translate the menu for us too? In fact, why don't you join us for supper? We'd love that, wouldn't we, Julie?'

'Mum!' my mum hissed.

'Now then, don't look so embarrassed. He can always say no,' said Gran.

'But I'm going to say yes please!' he said. 'I'm Eddie, by the way.'

'I'm Ellen and this is Julie, my daughter. She's separated, on her own now. Julie, make room for Eddie. Em, mind out the way. Come and sit beside me.'

I glared at Gran. I didn't want to be stuck sitting beside her. I didn't want this Eddie muscling in on *my* special meal for Mum. I sighed meaningfully and started heaving myself up off the bench.

'No, no, Em, you stay where you are. I'll sit next to your gran,' said Eddie, settling himself. 'So, Ellen, are you single now too?'

'Oh yes, I'm definitely single,' said Gran.

'I'm single too,' Vita announced, knowing it would make them all chuckle. 'I used to have this boyfriend Charlie right from when we started in Reception, but he wouldn't play in the little house with me so I chucked him, and then in Year One I had two boyfriends, Paul and Mikey, and they kept fighting each other and they wouldn't stop even though I kept telling them off, so I chucked them both and then . . .' She went on and on and on. Eddie laughed obligingly, and then turned to me.

'What about you, Em? Have you led a checkered love-life too?'

'Em doesn't like boys, she just likes her boring old books,' said Vita, sighing at her sad sister.

'I'm a total bookworm myself,' said Eddie. 'So what do you like to read then, Em?'

'I'm really into Jenna Williams,' I said.

'What sort of books does she write?' Eddie asked, unbelievably. He'd never ever heard of Jenna Williams!

Before I had a chance to tell him all about her, Gran jumped in again.

'Our Julie's a great reader too, always got her head in a book,' she said. 'Isn't that right, Julie? She reads all sorts, even classics.'

'I don't, Mum! I just had a go at *Pride and Prejudice* once, after it had been on the telly.'

'She's so modest, my Julie. She was bright at school, could have gone on to university, but – well – she had other plans,' said Gran, shaking her head at me.

'I didn't go to university myself. Left school at sixteen, did an apprenticeship, worked my way up the building trade, got my own business, did very nicely, thank you, then when the kids were off our hands I sold off the business and planned to sun myself in Spain and live happily ever after.' Eddie shook his head sadly. 'But then my wife got ill, and it didn't work out the way we wanted.'

'How sad. Still, you never know what might be in the cards for the future,' said Gran. She smiled at him and passed him the menu. 'Right, Eddie, we're in your hands. What shall we eat?'

I glared at Gran again. I'd wanted to show Mum the menu and tell her to choose whatever she fancied. Gran and this Eddie seemed to have taken over completely. Eddie felt we should sample a proper paella, all of us sharing. Gran said she thought this was a splendid idea, though she looked a little taken aback when this huge sizzling plateful arrived and she saw it was seafood and rice. It smelled marvellous but we all wondered if there were tentacles and slimy fishy bits hidden in its depths.

'Fantastic!' Gran said determinedly.

Vita and Maxie weren't convinced.

'I don't like it,' said Vita. 'Can't I have chips?'

'Chips!' said Maxie.

'Now don't play up, you two,' said Mum.

'Oh, let them have chips, if that's what they want!' said Gran, unbelievably. 'Anything to keep them quiet!'

'What about you, Em? Would you like some paella?' Mum asked. Underneath the table she reached for my hand and gave it a quick squeeze.

I ended up having a big plateful of paella *and* a huge portion of chips, and they were both delicious.

'I like to see a child with a healthy appetite,' said Eddie.

'That's our Em,' said Gran, not breathing a word about my diet.

I decided to make the most of things and ordered a big ice cream for pudding. So did Eddie. Vita and Maxie clamoured for ice cream too, but Mum asked the waitress if they could share one on two plates. Mum didn't want an ice cream herself, or any other kind of pudding, though I tried hard to persuade her.

'Surely you're not on a diet, Julie, there's nothing of you,' said Eddie.

'She's lost a little weight because life's been a bit of a struggle for her recently,' said Gran. 'But things are looking up now, aren't they, dear? Though she does work ever so hard. She runs her own hairdressing business – she's so enterprising. Tell Eddie all about the Good Fairy business, Julie.'

'Oh Mum, give it a rest!' said my mum.

Eddie excused himself tactfully and went off to the gents.

'Isn't he *gorgeous*!' said Gran, leaning forward, showing quite a lot of her chest above her pink lacy top. 'Julie, for pity's sake, *talk* more, try to impress him. He's obviously very smitten but you've got to encourage him.'

229

'I don't want to,' said Mum. 'I keep telling you, I'm not interested in any other men. And he's old, anyway.'

'He's *mature*. That's what you need, a real man who wants to settle down, not some boyish fool who'll play around and break your heart. Eddie's still in his prime.'

'And he's fat.'

'He's just well built, and he obviously likes his food. He looks a fine figure of a man. He wears his clothes well too. His cream trousers are beautifully cut and I love his shirt, don't you. Exactly the colour of his eyes.'

'You're just impressed with him because he's got money,' Mum snapped.

'Well, money's not such a bad thing, is it? Think of the difference he'd make to all our lives! And you would be giving him back a reason for living, companionship, fun, laughter. He even gets on well with the kids, so he'd be a good father to them.'

'We've *got* a father,' I said indignantly. 'Stop it, Gran. You're spoiling everything. This is meant to be *our* meal, me treating Mum and you lot. Now it looks like I've got to fork out for this Eddie too.'

'Of course you haven't, Em,' said Gran. 'As a matter of fact, I think Eddie's over there sorting out the bill himself.'

I could have burst into tears. I wanted to rush over, elbow Eddie out the way and pay myself, but Mum hung onto me.

'We'll have *your* meal tomorrow, Em,' she said quickly.

'I think Eddie might have other plans,' Gran said. 'Maybe he'll want to invite you out for a quiet meal, just the two of you. Don't worry, I'll babysit the kids. You just go for it, Julie.'

'I don't *want* to go for him, Mum! And you're wrong too, I don't think he fancies me in the slightest,' said Mum.

But after we'd all finished thanking him for the lovely meal (I said it through gritted teeth) Eddie said how very much he'd enjoyed meeting us all – and that he hoped we could all meet up again before the end of our holiday.

'What about tomorrow evening?' Gran said quickly.

'Well, that would be great,' said Eddie. 'But I was actually wondering about a quieter meal for two tomorrow?'

Gran grinned triumphantly. Mum went bright red. She looked at Eddie, agonized. But he wasn't looking at her.

He was looking at Gran.

'Would you care to come out with me tomorrow, Ellen?' he said.

# 12

I couldn't wait to go back to school to see Jenny and Yvonne.

'You'll never guess what happened!' I said.

'Your dad came back and you all went on holiday together?' said Jenny.

I swallowed. 'As if!'

'Yeah, tell me about it,' said Yvonne. 'Mind you, I'm not sure I'd *want* mine back. He kept moaning he was tired because my new little half sister keeps crying at night. He'd only come down the swirly chute and swim in the proper pool once. Most of the time we had to stay in the boring little toddler's pool with boring little Bethany.'

'I went swimming heaps of times. I can swim freestyle now – *and* dive.'

'You can do a proper dive?' said Yvonne. 'You mean just off the side?'

'And off the springboard!'

'Hey, will you teach me?'

'Sure,' I said airily. 'Let's go swimming together. You too, Jen.'

'No, catch me, I *hate* getting my head under the water. I didn't go in swimming properly all holiday, I just paddled. I suppose I'm a bit of a wimp.'

'But you've got beautifully brown,' I said. 'Honestly, Gran kept smothering me in so much sunscreen you wouldn't ever think I'd had a week in Spain. Listen, let me tell you about Gran! She's got a boyfriend!'

'She's what? But she's old!' said Yvonne.

'And she's all grumpy and bossy, if you don't mind my saying so, Em,' said Jenny.

'It's true, though! Isn't it amazing! He's five years younger than her too, so Mum and I keep kidding her that Eddie is her toy boy. You think she'd get mad but she just goes all pink and giggly. She isn't anywhere *near* as grumpy and bossy now.'

'Does she see a lot of him?' asked Jenny.

'Well, he lives in Spain, but she went out with him while she was there, and now she's home she keeps phoning. He's coming over sometime this autumn and then she's planning to stay with him sometime in the winter,' I said.

'Have you seen them snogging?' Yvonne asked, giggling.

'People their age don't *snog*!' said Jenny.

'Oh yes they do!' I said. 'You should have seen them saying goodbye at the airport! Vita and Maxie kept going yuck-yuck-yuck – you know what little kids are like – but Gran and Eddie took no notice, going slurpy slurpy like film stars.'

'Do you think they'll get *married*?' said Jenny. 'That would be cool, then you'd get to be a bridesmaid.'

'Oh ha ha, imagine me in a bridesmaid's pink satin frock. I'd look like a giant meringue,' I said.

'You can have any colour bridemaid's dress. Blue would suit you, Em. Or green.'

'OK. Think blue whale. Think jolly green giant,' I said.

'What are you on about?' said Yvonne. 'Are you fussed because you're fat?'

'You don't call people *fat*, Yvonne, it's rude. You say big or large or overweight,' said Jenny. Then she put her arm round me. 'But actually, Em, you're not *as* big as you used to be.'

'Yeah, I thought you looked a bit different,' said Yvonne. She pinged the waistband of my school skirt. 'Look, it's not tight any more. Maybe it was just puppy fat before. Or puppy *big*!'

'Woof woof!' I said, clowning about like a big puppy, making them both laugh.

I really was losing weight, even though I didn't always stick totally to any boring old diet. I just didn't fill up all the time on chocolate.

I started to go swimming regularly too. I went with Yvonne on Saturday and we had a great time. She was just as fast as me at breaststroke but I could beat her at freestyle! I taught her to dive too, though we couldn't practise much as the pool attendant said diving wasn't really allowed during public swimming sessions.

'You could join our special Earlybirds club though, and come and train before school if you wanted.'

Yvonne wasn't keen because it would mean having to get up way too early. I wondered if I wanted to go by myself. It was so great to be good at something like swimming. I got such a thrill storming past heaps of other kids in the water. I was so used to being rubbish in any race and coming last. I wondered if I could ever come *first* in a swimming race if I trained hard.

I asked Mum if I could join this Earlybirds club.

'Oh Em, it's such a rush in the morning as it is. I honestly don't see how I could manage taking you all the way to the baths and getting Vita and

Maxie ready for school and me off to my first hairdressing appointment.'

'I could take myself there, Mum, you know I could!'

'Well, I know you're more grown up than any of us, but I'm sure they wouldn't allow it.' Mum paused. 'Well, we'll find out.'

There was a notice up in the swimming baths. CHILDREN UNDER NINE YEARS OLD MUST BE ACCOMPANIED BY AN ADULT.

'It's OK, Mum! I'm over nine! I can go!' I said triumphantly.

Mum still took me the first time, while Gran took Vita and Maxie to school.

I started to get nervous as we got nearer the baths. My tummy was in a knot by the time I got in the changing rooms. I could see a whole bunch of kids under the showers. They were all much much much thinner than me. The girls all had sleek black costumes too, real serious swimmer stuff. No one else had a big blue flowery costume. I pulled it right down at the back to make sure it covered my bottom. I held in my stomach, so that the knot tightened.

Mum walked with me to the edge of the pool. There were lots of children swimming. They threshed up and down, up and down, in lane after lane. They were all so fast, so fit, so fantastic. They could all swim much much much better than me.

'I want to get out of here!' I mumbled to Mum.

I was all set to scoot straight back into the cubicle, pull my clothes on and make a run for it. But a big blonde woman in a tracksuit spotted me and came bounding over in her bouncy trainers. She beamed at me cheerily. She was surprisingly fat herself, filling her tracksuit right up so that it clung as snugly as a wetsuit.

'Hello there, chickie. I'm Maggie. Have you come for the Earlybirds session? Let's see what you can do.'

'I'm not good enough,' I said, looking at the children splashing up and down the pool. 'I can't swim as fast as that.'

'Don't worry, neither can I, not nowadays!' said Maggie. 'Come on, jump in and show me.'

I looked round at Mum. She gave me a little thumbs-up sign.

I jumped in the water. I was in such a nervous state I kept my mouth open and swallowed a bucketful. I coughed and choked, going scarlet.

Don't worry, darling,' said Maggie. 'Take a few deep breaths, that's the ticket. Now – swim!'

I swam while she watched. Then she nodded.

'I'm not as good as the others, am I?' I said.

'Not yet. But you've got potential. You wait and see. You stick at it, and you'll be swimming like a little fish by Christmas, and maybe you'll be the star of all my Earlybirds by next summer.'

I wasn't so sure, but I did stick at it. I went most days before school. A few of the prettiest, skinniest girls giggled and whispered when I was in the shower, but I did my best not to take any notice. Some of the boys were OK. I helped one very little boy sort out his locker when his key had jammed and he tagged round after me like I was his mum. He wouldn't give his own mum a look-in, it was all 'I want *Emily* to dry my hair' or 'I want *Emily* to tie my laces.' I ended up having to fuss round him just like I did with Maxie and Vita but I didn't mind. He was quite sweet. He was wicked in the pool, so fast and so strong. I knew I'd never get to be as good as him even though he was half my size. Still, after a few weeks I did get a lot quicker, and could just about beat some of the smaller girls.

'You're going great guns, chickie,' said Maggie. She tweaked my upper arms. 'Getting muscles just like Popeye too! My Emily Earlybird is getting mega fit.'

She was just joking, being sweet to me, but I really did seem to be getting a lot fitter. I was still rubbish at PE and games at school, but at least I didn't get so breathless now. I was really getting thinner too. I was still *fat*, but not ultra-wobbly-enormous.

'You're like Nellie in Jenna Williams's *Teen*

series,' said Jenny. 'She goes swimming in *Teens on a Diet*, remember? Hey, Em, did you know Jenna Williams is doing a big book-signing up in London next Saturday?'

'Really!'

'Yes, there was all this stuff on her fan club website. She's got a special new book coming out. It sounds soooo good – *The Emerald Sisters* – and there's a big new bookshop in Covent Garden called Addeyman's. Jenna Williams is going to be there all day. I'm so mad though, because we're going to stay with my gran and grandad in Devon that weekend. I've begged and pleaded with my mum but she says I've got to go with them, there's just no way I can make them see reason, so if I give you all my books, Em, will you get Jenna Williams to sign them?'

I blinked at Jenny, trying to take it all in. 'Next Saturday? Jenna Williams is really going to be there? You can actually meet her and talk to her and get her to sign books?'

'*You* can, you lucky thing. *I* can't. But you will take all my books to be signed, won't you? Please say you will, Em. Then I'll be your best friend for ever.'

'Hey, *I'm* your best friend!' said Yvonne, giving her a nudge.

'Yes, but if you read Jenna Williams like Em and me you'd find out you can have *two* best friends, like in her book *Friends Forever*, when Emma and Ali are parted but then Emma gets to be friends with Jampot as well. And threesomes work perfectly – look at Nellie and Marnie and Nadia in the *Teen* books.'

'Will you just shut *up* about boring old Jenna Williams and her silly old books,' said Yvonne, yawning hugely. 'Don't you two ever think of anything else?'

I found it very difficult to think about anything else.

I badly wanted to go up to London on Saturday and meet Jenna Williams.

I waited until Mum got home from work, and we were all having tea together. It was Spanish omelette. Gran now had this thing about all things Spanish. We were just waiting for her to scrape her hair into a bun and don a frilly flamenco frock.

'I don't like Spanish omelette. I just want chips,' said Vita.

'I want chips too,' said Maxie.

'Stop it,' said Gran. 'Eat your lovely omelette up, Vita, and set your brother a good example.'

'But it's horrible,' said Vita, poking it with her fork. 'Look at all these bits hiding inside!'

'Lovely vegetables,' said Gran.

'Yucky vegetables,' said Vita. 'It looks like someone's been secretly sick inside my omelette.'

'Vita! Stop being so naughty, especially when Gran's been kind enough to cook us all a meal,' Mum said.

'Yucky sicky yucky sicky,' Maxie chanted.

Mum pretended to swat him. She smiled wearily at me. 'Thank God I've got one sensible child. You're ever so quiet, Em. Nothing's wrong, is there?'

'No, everything's fine.'

'How are you doing at swimming?'

'Great. Maggie taught me how to do a racing dive this morning.'

'Are you in a swimming race, Em?' said Gran, scraping Vita's offending vegetables out of her omelette.

'I'm not fast enough to *enter* any races yet, but I'll know how to do the proper dive when I am,' I said.

'Yucky sicky yucky sicky,' Maxie persisted.

'Put another record on, Maxie,' said Mum, rubbing her forehead.

'Sucky yicky sucky yicky,' Maxie chanted, and then screamed with laughter.

'Mum . . .'

'Yes, love?'

'Mum, you know Jenna Williams?'

'Yes. Well?'

'She's doing this big book-signing up in London on Saturday. I so want to see her, and I've promised

242

Jenny I'll take all her books to get them signed, and I can't let her down because she's my best friend, and anyway, I'm desperate to go myself. Can I go, Mum? Please say yes. Please please please!'

'Oh, Em.' Mum leaned back in her chair, rubbing her forehead again. 'I know how much you'd like to go, pet. But it's Saturday. I can't take you on a Saturday. Especially not this week, I've got a big wedding. I have to be at the bride's house at breakfast time, and I'll be working flat out till I start at the Palace. Then I can't let Violet down, it's just the two of us now, and there's a whole disco-dancing troupe coming in to get their hair dyed violet for their Deep Purple routine.'

'I know, Mum. But you don't need to take me. I can go by myself.'

'Don't be silly, Em,' said Gran.

'I'm *not* silly! Look, I go swimming by myself, don't I, and I manage perfectly, and then I go to school by myself, I do heaps and heaps of stuff by myself, so I'll be fine going to London, it's just a simple train ride, and I promise I won't talk to any strangers. Please say yes, Mum.'

'You *are* being silly, love,' Mum said despairingly. 'I couldn't possibly let you go up to London by yourself.'

'But I have to meet Jenna Williams, Mum, I just have to!'

'Oh Em, don't.' Mum pushed her plate away and buried her head in her hands. 'If only your dad was here to take you!'

She whispered it, but we all heard.

Maxie stopped chanting his stupid nonsense and slid under the table. Vita reached for Dancer and put her thumb in her mouth. I clasped my hands so tightly my emerald ring bit hard into my finger.

'We don't need him,' said Gran. 'I'll take Em.'

We stared at her.

'Don't look so gob-smacked!' she said. 'Why shouldn't I take my grand-daughter to meet this Jenna Williams? I know she means a lot to her. So I'll take her.'

'Oh Gran!' I said, and I rushed round the table and gave her a big hug.

'Hey, hey, get off me, you daft banana, you're squashing me,' said Gran, but she gave me a quick hug back.

'But Mum, what about Vita and Maxie? I can't take them with me, not if I've got all the bridal hairdos and then all the purple tints at the Palace.'

'Oh well, in for a penny, in for a pound,' said Gran. 'I'll look after them too. We'll have a proper treat day out in London.'

'But we don't like Jenna Williams,' said Vita. 'She's not a treat for me and she's certainly not a treat for Maxie because he can't even read yet.'

'You'll have to choose your treat too,' said Gran.

'Oh wow!' said Vita. 'Then I want to go to a ballet and I want to go to a rock concert and I want to go to a big big shop and buy heaps of clothes and toys and my own television and I want to go to the zoo and ride on an elephant and feed the tigers and—'

'I'll feed *you* to the tigers, you greedy little madam,' said Gran, laughing. 'What about you, Maxie? What do you want for your treat?'

'Want to go on the helter-skelter,' said Maxie.

'The what?' said Gran. 'Oh great! Where do you think I'm going to find a helter-skelter? In the middle of Piccadilly Circus?'

'Not the circus, I don't like the clowns,' said Maxie. He looked surprised when we all laughed at him.

'I'm going to be the clown, taking you three up to London,' said Gran, sighing. 'I'm beginning to regret I ever made the offer.'

I gasped, wondering if she might go back on it altogether. She saw my face.

'Don't worry, Em. I *will* take you. You deserve a little treat.'

I fixed up my towel nest in the bath that night and did a little rewriting of my Dancer story. I tore out several pages about Dancer's mean ancient grandma reindeer who had cross-eyes and knobbly knees and a habit of giving her grandchildren a sharp thwack about the head with her gnarled antlers.

'Em? Are you writing in there?' Mum called. She slipped into the bathroom and sat on the edge of the bath. 'How's it going? Let's have a peep.'

I showed her my discarded pages. They made Mum giggle.

'I should stick them back in, they're very funny,' she said. 'You know what, Em. I should take your story with you on Saturday and show Jenna Williams.'

'Really? No, she'd think it was rubbish. It *is* rubbish, all babyish and stupid.'

'I think it's really great. Just show it to her, Em. I'm sure she'd be tickled that you like writing stories too.'

'I can't believe Gran's actually taking me! Why is she suddenly being nice to me?'

'Oh Em, work it out! If it hadn't been for you she'd never have met her Eddie. Isn't it a laugh, those two. She's so head over heels, just like a teenager. And yet she's always been so anti men. She couldn't stick my dad.'

'Or mine,' I said. I paused. 'Mum, don't you really want to meet anyone else?'

Mum reached out and twiddled with a long strand of my hair. 'I really don't, Em. I can't get interested. Not even if Robbie Williams and David Beckham came along and had a fight over who was taking me out tonight.'

'You just want Dad back?' I whispered.

'I don't even know if I *really* want Dad back either,' said Mum. 'But anyway, that's not going to happen. No matter how many times you mutter it under your breath!'

I muttered it anyway in bed afterwards, Dancer on my hand and my story clasped to my chest. I couldn't decide whether to show Jenna Williams or not. I planned in my head what I was going to wear to see her on Saturday. It had to be my green dress and my emerald ring, seeing as her new book was called *The Emerald Sisters*. My new denim jacket would detract from the all-green theme, but I could take it off inside the shop. I could ask Mum to do my hair for me, tying it with the green ribbon.

Then I had an even better idea. I couldn't wait till the morning. I slid out of bed and pattered along the landing to Mum's room. She was sitting up in bed reading a book called *How to Enjoy Being Newly Single*.

'Em? What is it, love?'

'Mum, will you dye my hair?'

'What? No, you know I won't! Not till you're sixteen.'

'I don't want it dyed *permanently*. I just want

it tinted emerald-green for Saturday! Oh please, please, please, Mum, it would look so cool and I know Jenna Williams would love it.'

'I'm not sure even your newly constructed nice gran would take a bright green grand-daughter up to London,' said Mum.

In the end she got up very early on Saturday morning and sprayed me a small emerald streak down one side. It looked sooo cool.

Vita wanted one too. And Maxie.

'No, this is just for Em. She's the one who's Princess Emerald after all,' said Mum. 'Now I want you all to be very very good for Gran, do you hear me? Don't give her any cheek, Em. Don't show off, Vita. And don't throw one of your wobblies, Maxie.'

Mum kissed us all goodbye and went off to blow-dry the bride and all her bridesmaids. I poured out cornflakes for Vita and Maxie and then made a round of toast and a pot of tea for Gran. I set it all out on a tray as prettily as possible, even cutting off the crusts and dividing the marmalade toast into neat triangles. It glowed against the best blue-and-white china. I cut one orange flower off her potted chrysanthemum and floated it in a little glass dish. Then I carried it carefully to Gran's bedroom.

She was still asleep, looking so much softer without all her make-up. She had a little smile on her face. Perhaps she was dreaming about Eddie.

She frowned when she woke up and saw her special breakfast tray. 'Why on earth have you used my willow pattern, Em? I don't want to risk getting it chipped. And you're not supposed to pick the flowers off pot plants, you silly girl.'

'I just wanted to make your breakfast look nice for you, Gran,' I said.

Gran sat up properly, smoothing her hair with her fingers. Her face smoothed out too. 'Oh, Em. Well. It *does* look nice. Almost too good to eat. Thank you, dear.' Then she blinked. 'Em? What's happened to your *hair*?'

She wasn't at all pleased about the green streak, but there was nothing she could do about it.

'Jenna Williams will like it,' I said.

'Then Jenna Williams has no taste,' said Gran. 'It's criminal to muck about dyeing your lovely hair.'

'My crowning glory! *Eddie* said so,' I said, bouncing on Gran's bed.

'Watch my tea! Keep still, Em.'

'I can't, I'm so excited! I'm going to see Jenna Williams!'

'All this fuss! You're a weird kid, our Em,' said Gran. 'Still, it's good to see you so full of beans.'

We had a little argument when we were about to leave home.

'What on earth are those huge great carrier bags?' Gran asked.

'It's all Jenny's Jenna Williams books. I promised I'd get them signed for her. Then there's *my* Jenna Williams books too,' I said. There was also my Dancer story, but I felt too shy to tell Gran that I might be going to show it to Jenna Williams. I had Dancer too, but I didn't have to carry her – she sat on my hand and helped me carry the bags.

'For pity's sake, you can't lump all that lot round London. Jenny can get her own books signed,' said Gran.

'But she *can't*, Gran, that's the whole point. I *promised*. I can't let her down, she's my friend. And I've got to get *my* books done.'

'Choose one of your books and one of Jenny's, that's more than enough. And for pity's sake take that silly puppet off, we're certainly not carting that up to London too.'

'Dancer's part of our family, Gran!'

'Don't talk so wet! She's not yours anyway, she's Vita's.'

I had done a deal with Vita (involving a big bag of fizzy cola sweets, my silver glitter nail varnish and my purple gel pen) that I got to wear Dancer. I needed to hide my emerald ring so that Gran wouldn't fuss about me losing it. I also needed Dancer's comfort and support in case I was struck dumb in front of Jenna Williams.

'I don't mind sharing Dancer with Em,' Vita said sweetly, in a goody-goody little girly lisp.

Gran patted Vita and shook her head at me. 'All right, Em, if you want to look a fool wearing that reindeer puppet, then so be it. But you really *can't* drag all those books along. I can't carry them for you, you know how my hands play me up. You'll end up with arthritis too, lumping heavy bags around like that.'

'OK, OK, I won't take the carrier bags,' I said, changing tactics. 'I'll just take a *few* books, and I'll put them in my school bag and carry them on my back.'

I rushed off to the bedroom. I managed to cram nearly *all* Jenny's and my books into my school bag, with my Dancer story squashed in at the side. I nearly fell flat on my face when I dragged the bag onto my back, but I was sure I'd get used to the weight. I pretended it was feather-light in front of Gran, and thank goodness she didn't see just how bulky the bag had become.

I was boiling hot and exhausted by the time we'd walked ten minutes to the railway station, and my long hair kept getting stuck under the bag straps so that I nearly got scalped if I bent my head.

'Are you all right, Em? Is that bag too heavy for you?' said Gran.

'I'm fine! It's not heavy at all,' I said determinedly.

It was an enormous relief to take the bag off on the train. I wriggled my sore shoulders. Vita and Maxie copied me, and we made up our own mad little sitting-down dance routine, left shoulder wriggle, right shoulder wriggle, left arm out, right arm out, hands on top of head, both hands waving in the air, repeat as often as you like.

We repeated it a great many times. Gran told us off at first, saying we were making an exhibition of ourselves, but some other children started copying us, and then their mum and dad joined in too. Gran raised her eyebrows and sighed at all of us – but she had one quick little go herself as the train drew into Waterloo Station.

'I looked up the Jenna Williams website on the computer at work,' Gran said. 'She's not signing until one o'clock, so we've got plenty of time to look around first.'

We walked along the embankment, staring up at the great Millennium Wheel.

'Oh, Gran, can we go up in it?' said Vita.

'There's a big queue already. I don't think so, pet. I can't stand hanging around in queues. It makes my back ache just standing still – and it's such a waste of time,' said Gran.

'Oh please please please, pretty please, Gran,' said Vita.

'Well . . .' said Gran, wavering.

252

Maxie stared at them as if they'd gone mad. 'No!' he said. 'No, it's too big, too high, too scary!'

'I thought you liked helter-skelters,' said Gran. 'They're big and high and scary.'

'I'm on a mat on someone's lap in a helter-skelter,' said Maxie.

'Tell you what, Maxie, we could put my jacket on the floor of the glass pod and you could sit on my lap and then you'd feel safe as safe,' I said.

We persuaded him it would work. We had to queue for tickets and then we had to join another queue to get on the wheel.

'My blooming back!' said Gran. 'I don't know about Maxie sitting down, but I'm going to have to *lie* down, stretched full out. I don't think this is a very good idea.'

Maybe Gran was right. I kept remembering a Jenna Williams story called *Flora Rose*, where little Lenny gets terribly scared on the Millennium Wheel. I was starting to get a little bit anxious myself. It did look very very high, and you were shut up in the pod a long time. What would happen if the wheel got stuck when you were right at the top, unable to get out?

'I don't want to!' Maxie whined. 'It's scary.'

'No, it's not,' I lied. I tried to pick him up but I couldn't manage to carry him *and* the book bag.

Gran had to carry Maxie, though she sighed

some more when his dusty shoes kicked at her pale pink skirt.

'Watch your feet, Maxie! And stop that whining, it's getting on my nerves.'

Maxie stopped whining and started full-bodied sobbing.

'Oh, for pity's sake!' said Gran. 'Look, this is meant to be a treat. Do stop acting as if I'm torturing you. Maybe we're just going to have to give up on this, Em.'

'No, no, *please* let's go on, I want to, don't be mean!' Vita wailed. She started sobbing too.

'Oh, dear God, stop it, both of you, or I'll knock your heads together. Why did I ever say I'd do this?' said Gran, looking at me balefully.

'You said you'd take us up to London because you're a lovely kind gran and I'm very very grateful,' I said, laying it on with a trowel – no, a huge great *spade* of praise!

'Yes, I am lovely and kind – and very very stupid,' said Gran, hanging onto Maxie and Vita. They were trying hard to outsob each other. Gran give them a little shake. They sobbed harder. People were staring.

'Stop it! Stop it at once, you're showing me up! If you don't stop this minute we'll go straight back home without any treats at all,' Gran threatened.

I panicked. 'It's OK, Gran. I'll stay on the ground with Maxie. You go on the wheel with Vita.'

Gran thought about it. 'But then you'll miss out altogether, Em, and you're the only one behaving sensibly. Won't you mind terribly if you don't get to go on the wheel?'

I didn't mind one little bit, but I didn't let on. 'Perhaps I'll get to go on the wheel another time,' I said, trying to look wistful.

'You're a good girl, Em. Here!' Gran fished in her handbag and tucked a five-pound note in my hand. 'Buy yourselves an ice cream while you're waiting for Vita and me.'

I was more than ready for something to eat. I'd been so busy fixing everyone else's breakfast I'd forgotten to eat any myself. I bought Maxie and me large 99s from a Whippy ice-cream van. Maxie had given himself hiccups after all that sobbing.

'Lick your ice cream slowly, don't make your hiccups worse,' I said. 'Look, Vita and Gran are getting into their pod. Up they go!'

Maxie shuddered. 'I'm sorry I'm not a big brave boy,' he said forlornly.

'You can't help it, Maxie. Don't worry. What would you like to do for *your* treat then? Vita's had the ride on the wheel. There she is, waving, way up high already, look!'

Maxie ducked his head. 'Don't want to look!' he said.

I waved back to Vita. I picked Maxie's limp arm

255

up and waggled it, so that he was waving too. His other arm waggled in sympathy and he dropped his ice cream on the ground.

'Oh, my ice cream!'

'Oh dear. Well. You can finish mine if you like. Or I'll get you another one. Gran's given me heaps of money.'

'Will that be my treat, another ice cream?' said Maxie.

'No, no, you can choose something else.'

'A helter-skelter?'

'Maxie! Look, there *aren't* any helter-skelters in London, trust me. They're just at funfairs and the seaside. And even if we took you all the way back to the one on the pier, I don't think you'd really like it. You could sit on my lap on the mat, but it's not me you want, is it? It's Dad.'

Maxie put his sticky hands over his ears but I knew he could still hear me.

'I miss him too, Maxie. So much. I'd give anything for him to come back. I've wished it over and over.' I took Dancer off my hand and looked at my ring. 'We could make another wish if you like, on my magic emerald.'

'Will it come true?' said Maxie, taking his hands away from his head.

'Well, it hasn't come true *yet*. But it could come true this time. Shall we try?'

Maxie clasped my hand and we wished for Dad. I muttered a whole lot of stuff. Maxie just went, '*Dad Dad Dad Dad Dad*.' Then we both looked round over our shoulders. There were dads everywhere, shouting, laughing, calling, chatting, joking, pulling funny faces. But not *our* dad.

Dancer wriggled onto my hand and stroked Maxie's cheek with her paw. He brushed her away, not in the mood for her stories. I wasn't really either. I undid my school bag and read the first page of my Dancer book. My heart started thumping. It seemed so stupid now, so totally babyish. Why on earth would Jenna Williams want to read it? She'd probably say something nice to me, but privately she'd be thinking me a totally sad idiot. I crammed my story back into my school bag, hiding it under all the books.

We sat silently on some steps, waiting. It seemed an age before Gran and Vita got out their pod and came over to us. Vita was dancing, twirling round and round. 'It was so great up on the wheel! I saw Buckingham Palace and the Queen waved to me,' she carolled in a cutesie-pie voice.

'It was amazing, you could see for miles,' said Gran, jigging around, almost breaking into a dance herself. 'Oh dear, you two, what glum faces! Maxie, you're such a prize banana. Come on then, let's go for a little walk along the embankment.'

'Hadn't we better go and find the bookshop now?' I said anxiously.

'Don't be silly, Em, your blessed Jenna Williams isn't going to be there for an hour and a half. We don't want to be hanging around waiting with nothing to do. No, I want to show you the Globe Theatre – it's only a couple of minutes away, we could see it from the pod. It's been built just like a proper Elizabethan theatre.'

'I want to go on the stage and dance!' said Vita, holding out her arms and simpering, as if she could hear tumultuous applause.

So we trudged along the embankment. My book bag got heavier and heavier and heavier, but I didn't dare complain. Maxie trailed beside me, scuffing his feet. Vita stopped prancing and started pestering for an ice cream, because Maxie and I had already had one. Gran had to stand on one foot and adjust the straps on her sandals, sighing.

'Maybe this isn't such a good idea,' she said. 'It looked so near when we were in the pod, but it's obviously miles away.'

'Miles and miles and miles,' Maxie said glumly.

'It's not fair, *I* want an ice cream,' said Vita.

'What's the time? Maybe we should start going back now,' I said. 'I want to be first in the queue at Addeyman's bookshop.'

'I told you, there's heaps of time yet. We'll just

go as far as that big chimney, see it? I think that's Tate Modern, the art gallery. I wouldn't mind getting some postcards,' said Gran.

'To send to Eddie?' I said.

'Maybe,' said Gran. 'Though I don't want to send any picture of daft scribble or dead cows or what have you.'

We didn't get to go inside the gallery. We all stared transfixed at the huge sculptures outside, on the forecourt. There were four gigantic towers, one red, one yellow, one blue and one green, with shiny silver slides spiralling round and round, down to the ground. There were doors at the bottom, and stairs leading up inside.

'Helter-skelters!' Maxie shrieked.

'Well I never! There you are, Maxie, your wish come true! They *look* like helter-skelters, certainly,' said Gran. 'But they're not real ones.'

'They look real. I want to go on the red one!' said Vita.

'You can't go *on* them, they're sculptures,' said Gran.

'No, Gran, look, people *are* going on them,' I said, pointing to heads bobbing at the top of each tower.

'So they are! Well, all right, I don't see why you can't go too,' said Gran. 'Maxie, you go on with Em.'

'No, not Em. I'm going with *Dad*!' said Maxie.

'Your dad's not here, Maxie,' said Gran, sighing.

'He will be, he will be! We wished it, and it's come true, it really has!' said Maxie, his face radiant.

'Oh Maxie,' I said, but I wondered if Dad *might* just be up at the top of these magical helter-skelters, waiting for us.

I took Maxie and Vita on all four helter-skelters. They weren't dark inside. They were lit up with a wonderful golden glow and there were pictures to look at as we climbed the steps. There were strawberries and scarlet ribbons, roses and Little Red Riding Hood in the red helter-skelter; bananas and teddy bears, sandpits and smiley suns in the yellow helter-skelter; turquoise pools and clear skies, cornflowers and little boy babies in the blue helter-skelter; Granny Smith apples and grassy meadows and an entire Emerald City of Oz in the green helter-skelter.

Everyone emerged at the top with great smiles on their faces before they spiralled all the way downwards on the shiny silver slide.

Everyone but Maxie.

We went up the red helter-skelter, the yellow helter-skelter, the blue helter-skelter, the green helter-skelter. Maxie didn't give the pictures a second glance. He was peering round, looking desperately.

'I give up!' said Gran, when he started sobbing. 'He asks for a helter-skelter in the middle of

London. One, two, three, four helter-skelters appear as if by magic. And is this child delighted? No, he bawls his blooming head off!'

'It's not really Maxie's fault, Gran. He was hoping to see . . . someone,' I said. I picked Maxie up and gave him a cuddle, though I could barely move for the big book bag on my back.

I was starting to get a bit anxious. It was twenty to one. I didn't want to be late for Jenna Williams.

I struggled with Maxie for a minute or so.

'Oh, for pity's sake, Em, put him down. Why should you have to lug him along like that?' said Gran. 'Maxie, stop that silly snivelling. Stand on your own two feet and walk properly.'

Maxie couldn't manage it. In the end Gran sighed deeply and took him from me.

'I'll carry you for one minute, that's all. You watch your feet on my skirt, and for pity's sake don't wipe your snotty little face all round my shoulders! Oh, the joys of being a grandma!' said Gran.

We trudged back along the embankment and up over Waterloo Bridge. Gran threatened to chuck Maxie over the parapet into the water. Maxie knew she was joking, but decided to clamber down from her arms and walk under his own steam, just in case.

Vita was the one whining and dragging her feet now, complaining that no one ever carried *her*. I

261

was feeling pretty exhausted myself. I seemed to be carrying at least a hundred Jenna Williams hardbacks in my bag. There was a cold wind up on the bridge but I was so hot my green dress was sticking to me.

'Is it far now, Gran?' I asked.

'Just at the end of the bridge, over the road and round to the left,' said Gran. 'Five minutes. Don't fuss, Em. We'll be there on time. You'll be one of the first to see her. Then we'll all go off and have a bite to eat. I can't wait to sit down, these flipping sandals are killing me. And my back's playing up worse than ever after hauling ten-ton Maxie all over London. I must be mad.'

We got to the end of the bridge. We could see a huge queue winding halfway down the Strand.

'Why are all those people there, Gran?' said Vita.

'Don't ask me,' said Gran. 'Hang on, there's that musical, *The Lion King*, on at the theatre up ahead. Maybe they're queuing for a show. There's lots of children, that must be it.'

My heart was starting to thump hard inside my green dress. There were lots and lots and lots of children. The girls all seemed to be clutching Jenna Williams books.

We got to the top of the street. The queue was thicker now, ringing round the Covent Garden piazza. There were crash barriers stretching all the way to the big Addeyman's bookshop over at the other side. The queue disappeared inside the door.

There was a huge book display in the window, and emerald fairy lights and a big poster of Jenna Williams and a special notice. JENNA WILLIAMS SIGNING STARTS AT 1 TODAY!

'Oh no!' said Gran. 'I don't believe it! This can't be the Jenna Williams queue!'

'I think it is, Gran,' I said. 'Shall we go back and join on the end?'

'For pity's sake, we can't hang around here all day, Em! We'll be hours and hours!' said Gran.

'Please!' I said.

'No. I'm sorry, but this is beyond a joke. We're all exhausted as it is.'

'Oh Gran, please, I've *got* to meet her.'

'She's just some boring middle-aged lady with a funny haircut,' said Gran, peering at the poster. 'What's so special about her? Look, we'll go to another bookshop and I'll buy you a copy of her new book, all right?'

'But it won't be signed! And I so so so badly want to speak to her. Oh Gran, *please*!' I could feel my face screwing up. Hot tears started dribbling down my cheeks.

'Now now! Oh dear Lord, it's bad enough Maxie and Vita bawling their heads off. Don't you start, Em. All right, all right. We'll go to the end of the queue. We'll give it an hour or so, see how we go.'

'Oh Gran, thank you, thank you!' I jumped up and down in spite of my huge bag of books.

'Steady on now! You kids. You're all mad. And so am I. Absolutely barking!'

We went all the way back to the end of the queue. There was a big smiley man at the end, with a pretty little girl about Vita's age.

'Hello!' he said. 'Join the queue! Have you brought your camp beds and your picnic?'

'I wish we had!' said Gran. 'Honestly, isn't this ridiculous! We must be mad.'

'Well, we're just fond parents,' said the man, patting his little girl's silky golden hair. 'This is my Molly. What are your three called?'

Gran simpered. 'I'm their gran, not their mum!' she said. 'This is Em, she's the number one Jenna Williams fan. Then this is Vita and this is Maxie – they're not really into the books yet.'

'I am!' said Vita. 'I like the one with all the parties and the presents where the nasty girl wets herself.'

'I like that one too,' said Molly, giggling. 'And I like *Friends Forever*. I like the funny dog in that one. I love dogs. I've got this little dog called Maisie, she sleeps on my bed at night.'

'*I've* got this great big reindeer, Dancer – she sleeps in my bed,' said Vita, snatching Dancer off my hand and making her shake paws with Molly.

Molly's dad laughed and admired Dancer. Vita made Dancer prance around, and then let Molly have a go.

'Now me, now me,' said Maxie.

'You can have a go any old time,' said Vita.

'No, let him, he's only little,' said Molly kindly. 'Here you are, Maxie, we'll all take it in turns, eh?'

I took my heavy bag off my shoulders and sighed deeply with relief. Vita and Maxie seemed happy talking to Molly. Gran seemed happy chatting to Molly's nice dad. I didn't want to talk to anyone but Jenna Williams.

# 13

We queued and we queued and we queued.

One hour went by. Vita and Molly larked around together. Vita showed Molly how to do a little modern dance routine. Maxie tried to copy them, kicking out his stick legs and nearly tripping people up. Gran seized hold of him and told him to behave. Maxie glared, determined to behave *badly*, but Molly's dad quickly distracted him, producing little sandwiches and tiny cakes and apples from his briefcase. He insisted on sharing them with all of us.

Another hour went by. Vita got fed up with working Dancer and ordered me to take a turn. I made Dancer tell them a story. Then another and another. Molly seemed to like them a lot.

'Are these stories from a book, Emily?' Molly's dad asked.

I shook my head shyly, not realizing he'd been listening too.

'You don't mean to say you make them all up yourself?'

'Well . . . my dad made up some of the stories,' I mumbled.

'Yes, he's very good at making up stories,' Gran sniffed. 'He's out of the picture now,' she mouthed to Molly's dad.

'Em's made up heaps of the Dancer stories herself though. She makes up a new one every day,' Vita said, surprisingly.

'Then you're very clever and inventive, Emily. You should write them all down,' said Molly's dad.

'She has! In a special book and she does pictures too, she showed me,' said Maxie.

'You must be very proud of your grand-daughter,' Molly's dad said to Gran.

Gran smiled and put her arm round my shoulders! 'Yes, she's a clever girl, our Em,' she said. 'Here, darling, if I give you my purse can you go to that coffee shop over there – look, on the other side of the piazza – and buy a coffee for Molly's dad and me, and some juice for all the children.'

I set off importantly, threading my way through the crowds watching the street performers. There was a guy juggling on a very elongated unicycle, a conjurer in a top hat, and a girl in a silver dance frock pointing her toe on a little platform. I thought at first she was a statue because her skin and her hair were painted silver too and she was standing stock-still, not moving a muscle. But then a man threw a coin into a saucer on the ground and the silver girl smiled and twirled round once. Another man threw two coins and she did two twirls and then stood still again, toe pointed, back in her statue position.

I wanted to make her twirl myself, but I didn't dare spend any more of Gran's money. I went and bought all the drinks, wondering how on earth I was going to carry everything. Gran wouldn't carry on calling me clever if I spilled scalding coffee everywhere. Luckily the coffee shop gave me a cardboard tray.

A *third* hour passed, much more slowly. The drinks weren't such a good idea. Gran had to take Maxie and Vita off to find a loo on the second floor of the bookshop. I wouldn't have minded going too, but I was scared that if we all left the queue Gran might give up on the whole idea and drag us home.

Molly's pretty mum turned up, with her two big sisters Jess and Phoebe. They'd all been on a clothes shopping trip. They stood with Molly while her dad went off for a little walk to stretch his legs.

'Don't be long, Dad!' Molly said anxiously.

'I'll be back in ten minutes, tops,' he said.

He came back in *exactly* ten minutes, because I counted. Molly didn't bother. She obviously trusted him.

'Dad!' she said, her blue eyes sparkling.

She leaned against him and he clasped his hands loosely round her neck, tickling her under her chin.

I wished I had a dad like that.

I wished wished wished I had a dad who would come back in ten minutes, tops.

I'm sure Vita and Maxie were wishing it too. They'd been so good for so long, but now they started whining and moaning and flinging themselves around.

'It's no good, Em, they can't hang on here much longer,' said Gran. 'I can't either, sweetheart. I'm in agony. I've got to have a sit down soon or I'll just keel over.'

'Oh, Gran. Please let's stay, especially now we've waited all this time. We *can't* give up now! We're nearly in the door.'

There was a kind curly-haired smiley man waiting there, helping everyone get their books open at the right page.

'Have you been waiting for ages?' he said sympathetically to Gran. 'I'm sorry the queue's so long.'

'Well, it's total madness, hanging around like this,' said Gran. 'Still, I suppose it's very good business for your shop.'

'Oh, I don't work for the shop,' he said. 'I'm Bob, Jenna's driver. But I like to help out with the queue if I can.'

'So you know Jenna Williams?' said Molly.

'I certainly do, young lady. Have you got a question you want to ask her?'

'Mmm . . . I know, I'm going to ask her if she's got any pets,' said Molly.

'I'm going to ask her to put a little girl called Vita in one of her books,' said Vita, smiling cutely.

'Me too. I want her to put a little girl called Maxie in one of her books,' said Maxie, getting muddled.

He went very red when we laughed at him.

'Never mind, Maxie, you're already in the Wild Things book,' I said.

'Are you a Wild Thing, Maxie?' said Bob. 'Oh dear, I hope you're not too scary.' He cowered away from him, pretending to be afraid. Maxie started giggling, delighting in the game.

Then Bob turned to me. 'Is that great big bag full of Jenna Williams books? Goodness, you're obviously a very big fan.'

'She would insist on bringing them all. Some belong to her friends. I told her to leave them behind but Emily wouldn't hear of it,' said Gran.

'What are *you* going to ask Jenna, Emily?' said Bob, helping me pull the books out of my bag.

'I don't know,' I said shyly.

'I think you should ask her to give you a few writing tips,' said Molly's dad. 'Emily's very good at making up stories. She's been keeping the children very happy with her stories while we've been waiting.'

'That's lovely,' said Bob, helping me balance all the opened books in a neat pile. 'There's one more book left in your bag, I think. Here, let me get it out for you.'

'Oh, that's nothing,' I said quickly, trying to stuff the red book back again.

'It's not the reindeer story, is it?' said Molly's dad.

'Well . . . sort of,' I said, embarrassed.

'Can we have a look?'

'Oh no, it's stupid, I don't know why I brought it,' I said.

'Can *I* see?' Molly begged, so I had to let her.

Her mum and dad read bits over her shoulder.

'Oh Emily, it's wonderful! I think you'll be a rival to Jenna Williams when you grow up!' said Molly's mum.

'You'll have to show Jenna Williams,' said Molly's dad.

'No, no, I couldn't!' I said quickly.

'She'd like to see it, I'm sure,' said Bob.

'We're moving again!' said Molly, as the queue surged forward and we were inside the shop at last. It was very hot and very noisy now, with children laughing and chattering and shouting. Some of them had been given balloon animals and they kept making horrible squeaking noises. Every now and then a child clutched one too tightly and the balloon burst with a bang.

'I don't like it here!' Maxie wailed. 'I want to go out!'

'Please, Maxie, try and be good for just a tiny bit longer,' I begged him. 'We're nearly there now.'

'I *am* trying to be good – but I still don't like it!' Maxie said desperately.

'I don't like it either. People keep pushing me and shoving me and I'm hot and I want another drink,' said Vita.

'We're nearly there, I'm sure we are. Hang on just for a bit, please, *please*,' I said.

Then the queue moved forward again and we turned a corner and we *were* nearly there.

'Look!' said Molly's dad, and he picked her up to show her. 'There's Jenna Williams, over there, in the corner.'

I stood on tiptoe, craning my neck.

I saw a big emerald banner with more fairy

lights, and a chair and a table with a shimmering green cloth, and there was this small short-haired lady smiling at everyone, signing book after book. She was wearing a top and skirt the exact same shade of green as my own dress! She was wearing a lot of rings. I wondered if any of them were real emeralds.

I took Dancer off my hand and looked at my own ring, twiddling it round and round my finger.

'My goodness, that's a lovely ring,' said Molly's dad.

'It's an emerald,' I said. 'Well, I think it is.'

'A perfect ring to wear today,' said Molly's mum. 'It won't be long now! Are you getting excited, girls?'

Molly was certainly excited, hugging her dad. Her sisters Jess and Phoebe seemed quite excited too. They'd read lots of Jenna Williams books when they were younger, and although they'd passed them all down to Molly now, they'd kept one favourite one each for Jenna to sign.

I clutched my books and Jenny's books, tucked Dancer under my arm and hooked my bag on my shoulder, in a terrible fluster. I wished I'd gone to the loo when I'd had the chance. I tried to sort out a sensible question in my head. I wanted to learn it by heart so I wouldn't make a fool of myself. It was so silly, I'd been longing to meet Jenna

Williams all my life, I'd queued for hours and hours to see her . . . and yet now I was starting to feel weirdly scared.

What if I couldn't get my words out properly? What if I just stood there blushing like an idiot? What if I dropped Jenny's books? Oh dear, what was I going to do if Jenna Williams asked my name and then started to write 'To Emily' in Jenny's books?

The little cluster of children around Jenna Williams suddenly moved away, waving and smiling, and Molly and her mum and dad and sisters went up to the signing desk. They were there a long time. Molly didn't seem a bit shy. She was saying all sorts of things, making Jenna Williams laugh, while her family looked on fondly.

Molly's dad bought a copy of *The Emerald Sisters* for Molly, a copy for Jess and a copy for Phoebe. Molly was really too young for the story and Jess and Phoebe were too old. Then he picked up a fourth copy from the big glossy green pile.

'This one's for you, Emily,' he said. 'Come and get it signed!'

I stumbled, desperately trying not to drop my pile of unwieldy books. Vita dodged round me and got to Jenna Williams first.

'Hi, Jenna, I'm Vita. I just love your books,' she said. 'Will you put a girl called Vita in one of them?'

275

'I might just do that. Vita's a lovely name,' said Jenna Williams.

'I'm Maxie. My name's already in a book about Wild Things,' said Maxie.

'I know. I like that Wild Thing book,' said Jenna Williams.

Gran was poking me in the back. 'You go and say something, Em!'

I still hung back, agonizingly shy.

'Oh, for pity's sake, don't tell me you've been struck dumb, when we've been queuing all these hours!' said Gran. She shook her head at Jenna Williams. 'Kids! And this one's your number one fan, too!'

Jenna Williams smiled at me. 'Ah, are you Emily, the one who writes reindeer stories?'

Molly's dad grinned at me. I blushed to the roots of my hair.

'Can I see your story for a minute, Emily?' Jenna Williams asked.

She helped me balance all my books and Jenny's books on the table so that I could delve into my bag. I dropped Dancer in the process.

'Oh, is this the reindeer puppet? I hear you've been doing a grand job entertaining the children in the queue. Go on, give me a demonstration.'

I put Dancer on my hand. She had more courage than I did. She didn't mind talking one bit.

'I'm delighted to meet you, Jenna Williams,' she said. 'I'm flattered that you want to look at my story. Here it is.'

She handed her book over to Jenna. She read a little bit, then flicked through the pages.

'It looks wonderful, Emily! It's such a great idea. Watch out, I might put it in one of *my* books!'

'Emily and I would be thrilled if you do!' said Dancer.

'Maybe I'd better write *"To Emily and Dancer"* in your *Emerald Sisters* book,' said Jenna Williams. 'Hey, you're wearing the perfect colour. And I love the matching green streak in your hair!'

'It's in your honour,' said Dancer. 'I wanted my antlers painted emerald-green too.'

'I'm sure they'd have looked very fetching,' said Jenna Williams.

She signed the book that lovely Molly's dad had bought for me, then my paperbacks, and then I managed to ask if she could sign all the hardbacks to Jenny. Her rings flashed and twinkled as she wrote her name over and over again. I looked at the big green ring on her little finger.

'Is that a real emerald?' I whispered.

'Well, I like to pretend it is,' she said. She smiled at me. 'Writers are good at pretending.' She gave me back my Dancer book. 'I think you're definitely going to be a writer yourself one day, Emily. It was lovely meeting you. And Vita and Maxie. And you too, Dancer.'

Dancer waved her paw while I scrabbled with the other hand to get all my signed books back in my bag.

Then Gran took me by the shoulders and steered me away. 'There, happy now? I'm not sure that was worth all that long long wait!' she said.

'Still, how lovely that Jenna thinks Emily will be a writer too,' said Molly's dad.

'You've been very kind to us all,' said Gran. 'Thank Molly's dad for getting you the new book, Em – though we must pay for it.'

'No, no, it's a little gift to you for keeping Molly so happy while we were queuing. And are *you* happy now, Emily? Have all your wishes come true?'

'Almost,' I said. I felt my ring finger through Dancer's fur, turning the emerald again.

'Don't, Em, that tickles!' Dancer nagged. 'Don't waste your time wishing. Don't you ever give up?'

'No, I don't!' I hissed into her small felt ear. 'You shut up for a minute! I'm sick of you hogging the limelight. You're just a glove puppet, OK?'

I shut my eyes and wished one more time.

'Watch where you're going, Emily, it's so crowded,' said Gran, steering me along through the crowded shop. 'Vita? Maxie? For pity's sake, why have you all got your eyes shut?'

278

'Ssh, Gran, we're all wishing,' said Vita.

'Wishing and wishing and wishing,' said Maxie.

'I give up!' said Gran. 'Now come on, open your eyes this minute and say goodbye to Molly and her family.'

I'd screwed my eyes so tightly shut that everything was blurred for a moment. I blinked, trying to focus, as we pushed our way outside Addeyman's, into the bright daylight. Vita blinked her long lashes as she gave Molly a big hug. Maxie rubbed his eyes and then opened them wide.

He should have kept them shut. The man making the balloon animals was performing for the queue. He was dressed up in baggy white trousers, great big boots and a round red nose.

'A clown!' Maxie shrieked – and started running.

'Oh Lord,' Gran groaned. 'Maxie! Come back here, you little silly! Em, go after him, quick!'

I ran across the piazza after him. Maxie only had little stick legs, but blind panic made him run like the wind.

'Stop, Maxie! Come back! You'll get lost!' I shouted.

Maxie dodged in and out of the crowds, ran even harder away from the juggler on the unicycle – but then stopped dead, staring over at the silver lady.

I rushed up to him. 'Maxie, you're so mad, you *mustn't* run away like that!' I shouted at him.

279

He didn't blink. He wasn't listening to me. He stood transfixed, eyes huge, pointing at the silver dancing lady.

'She's just a lady pretending to be a statue, Maxie,' I said. 'Come on, back to Gran.'

Maxie was so rigid I couldn't move him. He shook his head wildly and kept pointing. I stared over at the silver lady. Someone had put a whole handful of coins in her plate, so she was twirling round and round while he clapped appreciatively, looking up at her.

He had a scarf round his neck. A knitted scarf all different colours. A scarf just like the one I knitted Dad last Christmas.

Who was this strange man wearing my dad's scarf? He looked a little like Dad himself, but he was thinner, much more ordinary looking, with boring short black hair sticking straight up.

The man was saying something to the girl. She was trying to get back into her statue pose but he was making her giggle. That was so like Dad.

He put his head on one side, grinning.

It *was* Dad.

'Dad!' I yelled. 'Dad, Dad, Dad!'

I pulled Maxie's arm and we ran full tilt towards him.

'*Dad!*' Maxie shrieked.

He looked round, startled, but he didn't spot us.

He said something else to the silver dancer and then started walking away.

'Oh Dad, please, wait, *wait*!' I shouted, running round the piazza, pushing people out the way.

My eyes were fixed on Dad, terrified that he'd disappear.

I forgot all about the unicyclist. I didn't even see him. I careered straight into him, nearly knocking him flying. Maxie tumbled onto his knees, yelling. I staggered too, unbalanced by my huge bag of books. I hurtled forwards, arms out, desperate to catch my dad. I careered straight into him, sending him sideways. I reached out but I couldn't grab him. I fell flat on my face, landing heavily on my arm.

I lifted my head and screamed. '*Dad!*'

'Em! Oh my God, Em!' He was on his knees beside me, clutching me to him, cradling my head.

'Oh Dad, oh Dad, is it really you?' I sobbed. 'Where's your *plait*?'

'Oh darling, never mind my wretched plait. What are you *doing* up in London? Are you all by yourself?'

'I'm here, Dad!' Maxie shouted, limping and hopping and hurling himself onto Dad.

'My little Maxie! And you look as if you're in the wars too! So where's Vita?'

'I'm here! Oh Daddy, my daddy!' Vita yelled,

running too, with Gran right behind her, shoes in her hand, her skirt hitched right up her hips.

'Oh my Lord, it's you, Frankie! I might have known! For pity's sake, what have you done to the kids?' Gran said. 'Maxie, have you hurt yourself?'

'Yes!' said Maxie, clinging to Dad.

'Poor little guy,' said Dad. 'What about you, Em? You went down with such a wallop.'

'My arm hurts,' I said, and I burst into tears.

'I fell over too and *I'm* not crying!' Maxie boasted.

'What's happened to Dancer?' Vita wailed.

I looked at Dancer on the end of my arm. Her antlers were bent and her delicate pink nose was torn right off.

'We'll mend Dancer, Vita, don't worry. But we've got to get Em mended first. Here, let's see what damage you've done.' Dad started gently plucking at Dancer, trying to ease her off. I couldn't help crying harder.

'Stop it, you're obviously hurting her!' Gran said, kneeling down beside us. 'Let me have a look, Em. Don't cry so.'

'I'm fine, really. Dad's not hurting me a bit,' I wept.

Dad rocked me gently, peering at my arm. It was bent at a weird angle. It didn't seem to want to go straight any more.

'I think you've broken it, you poor darling,' said Dad. 'Don't worry, you can go to hospital and they'll be able to plaster it up for you.'

'Will you take me to the hospital, Dad?'

Dad hesitated.

'*I'll* take you, Em,' said Gran, trying to push Dad out the way.

'I want my dad!' I cried.

'He's *my* dad,' said Vita.

'My dad, my dad,' said Maxie.

Dad suddenly had tears in his eyes. 'Yes, you're all my lovely kids, and of course I'm taking you to the hospital, Princess Emerald. I'll make all the doctors and nurses take excellent care of you, and we'll demand an emerald-green plaster cast for your sore arm, OK?'

'Can I have a plaster too, Dad?' Maxie begged. '*I* want a broken arm!'

'This is all your fault, Frankie, she was running after you,' said Gran.

'I know,' said Dad, a tear rolling down his cheek.

'Don't cry, Dad! It's not anyone's fault. I just fell over. I'm a big fat lump.'

'You're not at all, my baby. You've changed so much. It's so awful, I hardly recognized you!'

Dad held me tightly, and Vita and Maxie. He clung to us as if he could never bear to let us go.

'It's no use just sitting there with everyone

staring! Stop play-acting with the kids and get on your mobile for an ambulance, Frankie,' said Gran. 'We've got to get Em to hospital.'

We didn't go in an ambulance. Jenna Williams's driver Bob had seen me falling. He came hurrying over to us.

'My car's just round the back of the shop in the loading bay. I'll get you to hospital in five minutes. It'll be quicker than waiting for an ambulance to get here. You're being such a brave girl,' he said to me, hauling my book bag on his back. Dad and Gran helped me up and we went round the back of the shop to the loading bay. We couldn't believe it when we saw the big shiny silver car.

'It's a Mercedes!' Gran hissed.

'I feel like a real princess!' said Vita, bouncing on the leather upholstery.

'I'm going to sit on Dad's lap in the posh car,' said Maxie.

Dad sat in the back with us, one arm round Vita, one arm round me, with Maxie on his knee. Gran sat in the front next to Bob.

'This is very kind of you,' Gran said. 'I'm so sorry to put you to all this trouble. Em, you're not bleeding, are you? Mind the upholstery!'

The hospital wasn't very far away. I wouldn't have minded if Bob had driven us to a hospital in

Timbuktu. I just wanted to stay cuddled up to Dad for ever and ever and ever.

I was very scared that Dad might go as soon as we went into the Accident and Emergency area. Gran kept *telling* him to go.

'I'm staying,' Dad said firmly.

'Let me phone Julie on your mobile. Em needs her mum, not you,' said Gran.

Dad handed it over and Gran started phoning. The second she told Mum, she said she was on her way. I was so relieved, but I still had to hang onto Dad.

'I need Mum *and* Dad,' I said.

'So do I!' said Vita.

'So do I!' said Maxie.

I twisted my emerald on my poor throbbing hand and wished again.

Dad saw what I was doing. 'Still wearing your ring, Princess Emerald?'

'Of course, Dad.'

'You'd better take it off right this minute!' said Gran.

'No!'

'You've got to. Your whole arm is starting to swell. You need to take the ring off or it'll get stuck on your finger for ever.'

'I want it to be stuck! No, Gran, please, don't take it off! *Ouch!*' I tried to jerk my hand away from her and jarred my broken arm unbearably.

'Hey, hey, leave her. Calm down, Em. Your gran's right. Come here, darling, I'll ease your ring off. Don't worry, you'll be able to wear it every day for the rest of your life, just as soon as your poor arm gets better.' Dad tenderly wriggled the ring around until he'd slipped it right off my finger. 'Have you got a pocket?'

'Can't you keep it for me in *your* pocket, Dad?'

'OK, I'll keep it safe for you, sweetheart. And I'll take Dancer to the reindeer hospital, Vita, and get her poor bent antlers fixed, and make sure she has a discreet little nose-job.' Dad looked at Maxie. 'How are your felt tips, little guy?'

Maxie wouldn't answer, just burrowing his head hard against Dad as if he wanted to bore right into him.

'They're all used up because he wrote you so many letters,' I said.

I thought Dad would be pleased but he looked as if he might start crying again.

'Yes, well might you weep,' said Gran bitterly.

The nurse came up to us and said they were ready for me to go and have an X-ray.

Gran got up and started trying to pull Vita and Maxie off Dad. 'Come along, you two, we have to go with your sister,' she said briskly.

'No, I'm afraid they're not allowed. Just Emily

– and maybe Daddy can come too?' the nurse suggested.

'Oh, yes please!'

So I got to go off with Dad. We stayed together while I had my arm X-rayed and then I was taken to a little room where we waited, just Dad and me.

'Are you too grown up a girl to sit on my lap?' said Dad.

'I'm not a bit too grown up,' I said, climbing on his knees. 'Just make sure I don't squash you.'

'There's nothing of you now, I'm telling you. Where's my little chubby-cheeks gone?' Dad gently poked my cheeks with his thumb and forefinger. 'Ah, at least you've still got your dimples!' he said.

'You've got thinner too, Dad,' I said.

'Ah. Well. It's because I've been missing you,' said Dad.

I reached round to the back of his neck with my good arm. I tentatively ruffled the back of his shorn spiky hair.

'When did you have your plait cut off, Dad?'

'The other month. Hannah kept nagging me, saying it was sad and pathetic, an old guy like me hanging on to his hair like a hippy, so I cut it off to shut her up.'

'Hannah?' I said, puzzled.

'My girlfriend.'

'She's called Sarah!'

'Oh. No, Sarah and I split up soon after I went up to Scotland. So then I came back down south and eventually fetched up with Hannah.'

I thought it all through in my head.

'What is it, Em?' said Dad.

'So you could have come to visit us all this time?' I said.

'I wanted to, darling, I wanted to so much. You've no idea just how I've missed you and Vita and Maxie – and your mum too.'

'So why didn't you?'

'I knew I wasn't wanted. It was going to be a clean break, remember? That's what your mum wanted.'

'She just said that because she was cross with you then. She didn't really *mean* it.'

'You were all pretty cross with me. I felt dreadful. I thought maybe you were better off without me. I didn't want you all getting so upset and angry. I honestly thought it was for the best.'

I looked at Dad.

'Don't look at me like that, Em, I can't bear it,' said Dad. 'All right, all right, I didn't *really* think that. I just couldn't stand all the rows and the sadness and feeling that it was all my fault. I always want everyone to be happy. Then *I'm* happy too. So I tried to put you all out of my mind, and I know I should have kept in touch, I should have sent your mum money, though I truly didn't make much. That's another reason why I went – I've been such a failure, I can't make a go of anything, I just don't seem to get the breaks. So I thought a fresh start, a new love, it would all work out for me. Only it didn't.'

'It would never work with that Sarah, she was horrible,' I said.

'Well. I'm no catch,' said Dad.

'What about Hannah?'

'I don't know. It's early days.'

'Dad. Come back to us.'

'I *want* to, Em. But it's not that simple. There's your gran for a start. We all know she can't stand me.'

'Gran's got this boyfriend though. He lives in Spain, she's talking about living over there with him. She's even spending this Christmas with him – she won't always be around.'

'Ye gods, your gran's got a *boyfriend*?' said Dad. 'I don't believe it!'

'His name's Eddie. We all thought he was after Mum at first, but it was Gran he fancied.'

'He must be mad!' Dad paused. 'What about your mum? Has she got her own boyfriend now?'

'Oh, Dad. Mum doesn't want any boyfriends. She wants you.'

'I've been such an idiot, haven't I, Princess

Emerald? How are we going to make everything end happily ever after, eh? How are we going to reunite foolish King Francesco with poor long-suffering Queen Juliana?'

He started spinning me this long fairy tale. My arm was starting to throb so painfully it was hard to concentrate. The rest of me was hurting too, my arms, my neck, my head. It was as if I'd been shaken up all over.

I tried so hard to believe what Dad was saying, but I didn't know if he meant it or whether he was just making up a fairy story. I didn't know what was real any more. When I closed my eyes all my dreams had come true and Dad had his arms round me, telling me a wonderful story and making everything better. But when I looked at him properly he seemed so different, not really like *Dad*. He was just this pale thin man with short spiky hair and a grubby denim jacket, telling me a whole lot of stories.

It was easier keeping my eyes closed. I was so worn out with all the amazing things that had happened I could feel my head nodding.

'That's it, sweetheart, have a little sleep,' Dad said softly.

I think I must have napped for a while, because I was dreaming I was running after Dad all over again, and then when I hurled myself at him he stepped sideways and I found myself tumbling down a hole in the pavement, down down down in pitch blackness, and I started screaming.

'Em, darling! It's all right, I'm here. Does your arm hurt really badly?' said Dad. 'The nurse has just come, pet, they're ready to plaster you up.'

I clung to Dad, scared that it might be very painful. It *did* hurt when they gently but firmly straightened my arm out.

'There we go. We'll have you right as rain in no time,' said the young doctor, smiling at me. 'There's no complications. It's a nice clean break.'

I winced at those two words.

'Sorry, pet, it'll all be over soon,' said the doctor, misunderstanding. 'Now, you have a very important decision to make. What colour plaster would you like? We can do you a very pretty pink, a fetching shade of blue – or what about a vivid emerald-green?'

'I told you so, Em,' said Dad triumphantly. 'There. You can truly be Princess Emerald now.'

I laughed uneasily, suddenly a little embarrassed for Dad to be talking about the whole princess thing in front of the doctor.

Dad went on and on about Princess Emerald as they wound a bandage tightly round my arm and sloshed on the plaster. I knew he was only doing it to distract me. He was being so sweet. But somehow it wasn't working.

'Em's been my Princess Emerald ever since she was little,' Dad told the nurse. 'Look, she's all dressed up in green today. She's even got wondrous emerald hair!'

'That's because I was going to see Jenna Williams, Dad, and she's got this book *The Emerald Sisters*, see?'

Dad saw. He nodded a little sadly. 'Oh well. I guess you're getting too old for my fairy stories,' he said.

'No, Dad! I didn't mean it like that. I'm sorry!' I said quickly.

'It's OK, sweetheart. You're not the one who should say sorry,' said Dad.

I wasn't sure what we were talking about again. It was so hard to make sense of anything when my arm hurt and I was so tired and my head felt so fuzzy. I hung onto Dad with my good hand, gripping him very tightly.

A nurse popped her head round the door. 'How are we getting on here? Oh good, nearly done. Emily, your mum's here.'

'Mum!'

Mum came rushing in, very pale, her make-up smudged, her hair tangled. She scarcely looked at Dad. She came over to me and put her head against mine.

'Oh Em, darling, are you all right?'

'I'm fine, Mum. I've just broken my arm, that's all,' I said.

'How did you *do* it?' Mum glanced at Dad, then back to me. 'Gran said Dad knocked you *over*!'

'God, that woman!' said Dad.

'It was me, Mum, I saw Dad and I ran after him, and then I fell. It wasn't *Dad's* fault!' I said.

'How could you ever think I'd knock her over, Julie?' said Dad.

Mum shook her head. 'I didn't really believe it. I'm not even sure Mum did either. So, Frankie, what are you doing here?'

Dad smiled weirdly at Mum. 'I suppose I've come back,' he said. 'I still love you, Julie. I want to be with you and the kids. Say you'll take me back.'

'What?' said Mum, sounding dazed. 'Look, let's just concentrate on Em and her broken arm for the moment.' She shook her head apologetically at the doctor and nurse.

'Take no notice of us,' said the nurse, smiling. 'We're used to all sorts in here. It's our very own soap opera, night after night.'

She pinned a sling on my new bright-green arm with a flourish. 'There you go, little green girl. Off you go with Mum and Dad.'

We walked down the corridor together, Mum with her arm round me, Dad still holding my good hand.

'Come on, Em, let's get you home,' Mum said wearily. 'We'd better go and find poor Gran. I think Vita and Maxie are driving her round the bend.'

'Don't go back to her, not for a few minutes,' said Dad. 'Look, let's go and have a coffee somewhere and talk.'

'Frankie, Em's exhausted, we all are. We just need to get *home*,' said Mum.

'Well, I'll come too.'

Mum paused. 'You don't really mean it. You're just feeling all shaken up because of Em.'

'Well, of course I'm shaken up, but that's a good thing, isn't it? I've missed you so, you and the kids.'

'I bet you've hardly given us a second thought,' Mum said. She didn't even sound angry, she just sounded weary.

'I think of you nearly all the time!'

'You haven't been in touch for months and months. You haven't sent a penny for the kids in ages. They could have starved for all you've cared,' said Mum.

'I know, I've got no real excuse, but I swear I've been thinking about them. That's why I was up in London today, I was going to get a signed copy of Jenna Williams's latest book for our Em and send it as a special surprise.'

'It would have been a surprise, all right,' said Mum.

'What's up with you, Julie? You seem so . . . hard.'

'I suppose I've had to toughen up a bit,' said Mum. 'Not before time. Anyway. We're going home now. If you want to stay in touch that will be wonderful, especially for the kids. But we can't just wave a magic wand and pretend all this year hasn't happened.'

'It *hasn't* happened,' Dad said urgently. 'We're rewinding right the way back to before Christmas. We're still a family, you, me and the kids, and we all love each other and it's all going to work out, you'll see. It *will* work, won't it, Em, if we wish hard enough?'

I started crying.

'Don't, Frankie. Don't do this to her. It's been hard enough on her as it is,' said Mum. 'Come on, Em, we're going home. You go now, Frankie, please.'

Dad insisted on ordering a taxi for all of us, saying we couldn't possibly make our way home on the train. We all squashed in together, Dad too.

'He's not coming back to *my* house,' said Gran. 'God, what do you look like, Frankie? Are you dossing down in the gutter nowadays? Have you run out of stupid girlfriends so you're trying to sponge off us again?'

'I'm just seeing my family back safe and sound, you mean-spirited old witch,' said Dad.

'Stop it, both of you,' said Mum fiercely. 'Think about the kids, please.'

Maxie and Vita sprawled on Dad's lap, half asleep. I curled up beside him, my head on his shoulder. I so badly wanted to believe in magic and wishes and fairy stories. I wanted the taxi to turn into an emerald chariot and whisk us off to an enchanted land where we could all live happily ever after. But we ended up at Gran's house instead, and the taxi fare was so much that Dad couldn't pay it, and Gran started goading him again, reaching for her purse.

'*I'm* paying this,' said Mum.

'I'll send you the cash tomorrow, Julie,' Dad said.

'Yes, you do that,' said Mum.

'You don't trust me, do you? I don't blame you. But you wait and see. Believe in me just this once,' said Dad.

He kissed Vita and Maxie and me goodbye. He kissed Mum too. She didn't put her arms round him. She just walked away, but when we were back in the house I saw she was crying.

I couldn't sleep much at all that night. I couldn't turn over and snuggle down because of my arm. I lay flat on my back, stiff and sore, staring into the darkness. I didn't know whether I could believe in my dad or not.

I didn't know whether he wanted to stay with

his new girlfriend or come and live with us.

I didn't know whether he really had been going to get me a Jenna Williams book.

I didn't know whether he thought my ring was a real emerald.

I didn't know whether I'd ever get it back again anyway.

I didn't know whether my wish had come true or not.

# 14

We stayed up very very late on Christmas Eve. We huddled on the sofa, Mum, Vita, Maxie and me, eating our way through the huge tin of Christmas Quality Street. I knew Mum had bought me a pair of seriously cool kids' designer jeans for my Christmas present. They were a large size, but I was still thrilled to be able to squeeze into them. It was going to be more of a squeeze tomorrow, after all the chocolate, but I didn't care. I kept shoving one sweet after another into my mouth, even though I didn't really like chocolate so much nowadays.

Vita and Maxie were half asleep, cuddled up like puppies, chocolate drool round their mouths. I'd made us all little wine glasses out of the coloured cellophane on the sweets, and they wore theirs on their fingers.

299

Mum had a real wine glass in her hand, and had got through most of a bottle by herself. 'Don't you tell your gran!' she said, as I poured her the last little slurp.

'She's probably swigging back the vino too with old Eddie,' I said. 'I don't want to be mean but it's soooo much nicer having Christmas without her.'

'Yes, it's great, just the four of us,' Mum said, though her voice wobbled a little. Maybe it was the wine.

'Not four. Five!' said Maxie. He flipped his fingers, counting. 'One, two, three, four, five.'

'Shut up, Maxie,' I said quickly. I couldn't bear him to keep on hoping.

'Four of us . . . and Father Christmas,' Mum said. 'So you kids had better go to bed in case he doesn't come in the night.'

Vita sat up, stretching. 'Is there really a Father Christmas?' she said.

'Of course there is. Who do you think leaves your presents at the end of the bed?' said Mum.

Vita's little face screwed up. 'I know who leaves the presents,' she said. 'I know who gave me Dancer.'

I put my finger to my lips and nodded at Maxie. Mum and I held our breath. Vita thought it over, and then decided she liked being one of the big girls with us. She put her own finger to her lips. She cuddled Dancer, rubbing her nose against her soft velvet.

Dancer had been posted back in a pink-tissue lined jiffy bag, as good as new, her antlers straightened, a perfect pink nose at the tip of her snout. She was wearing new pink striped pyjamas and a rose fluffy towelling dressing gown with a tiny handkerchief in the pocket. She had a little suitcase carefully packed with a party frock and a pinafore and her special pink ballet dress.

Maxie had a padded parcel too, with a brand-new set of felt pens, and a special pack of letters and envelopes and a booklet of first-class stamps.

I had a little parcel, specially registered. My emerald ring had been sent back to me in a jewellery box studded with green sparkly jewels. When I opened the lid a little ballet dancer twirled round while music played.

Dad had sent Mum a red beaded purse in the shape of a heart, stuffed full of money.

He hadn't come to see us – but he hadn't forgotten us.

It was silly to hope for anything more. These were our Christmas presents this year.

We still hoped, all the same.

We sat up until we heard midnight striking.

'Happy Christmas, darlings,' Mum said, kissing

us. 'Come on, into bed, all of you. Help me, Em, I'm all woozy. Oh dear, I'm a terrible mum.'

'No you're not, you're the best mum in the whole world,' I said, giving her a hug.

I picked Maxie up and herded Vita in front of me. We all three tumbled into bed, and Mum lay down on the covers beside us, kissing us all goodnight.

'Are the socks still empty?' Maxie mumbled.

'So far,' said Mum sleepily. 'Oh, dear Lord, Mother Christmas is going to have to get busy.'

'*Father* Christmas, silly,' said Maxie.

'Whatever,' said Mum. 'Night-night then, sweethearts. Sleep tight.'

She stood up and staggered a little.

'Are you OK, Mum? Hey, I'll put you to bed, shall I?' I said, sitting up.

'No, no, I'm fine. I'm just so stupid. I'm like you, Em, wishing and wishing. How stupid is that?'

'Wishes never come true the way you want,' I said.

Then we heard a noise downstairs. A tapping at the door. Then the letter box banging.

'Who's that?' Mum called, her voice high-pitched.

'Ho ho ho!' someone called.

We all four sat up, and then we jumped up and started running downstairs. It looked like there was a Father Christmas after all. Maybe it was going to be the best Christmas ever.

## ☆ CLEAN BREAK ☆

I feel very fond of Em, the girl who tells the story in *Clean Break*. She tries so hard to be a good big sister to irritating little Vita and Maxie and she's a true friend to her mum. She adores her dad. The story starts with a very traumatic Christmas, though Em thinks it's going to be the best Christmas ever. I do hope her next Christmas lives up to expectations.

I love writing about Christmas, especially choosing all the presents for everyone. I also liked making up the stories that Em tells Vita and Maxie. I think she's the sort of girl who might well become a writer when she grows up. She certainly loves reading. When I was writing the story I tried hard to think what sort of books Em would like reading best. I imagined this shy, sweet girl going into a bookshop and browsing in the children's section. What would she choose?

The thought popped into my head that maybe she'd choose my books. Yet I couldn't actually put that in *Clean Break*. It would sound horribly like showing off. So I decided to invent an alternative me, Jenna Williams. We'd share the same initials and write very similar books. I wrote about a child called Elsa in *The Bed and Breakfast Star*.

Jenna Williams wrote *Elsie No-Home*. I wrote *Best Friends* about Gemma and Alice who wanted to stay friends forever. Jenna Williams wrote *Forever Friends*. I wrote *The Diamond Girls* and old copycat Jenna wrote *The Emerald Sisters*.

Nick Sharratt drew a picture of Jenna Williams talking to Em at a book signing session. He drew her looking very like me, with short spiky hair, black clothes and a lot of big silver jewellery. There's only one difference between Jenna and me – she has long dangly earrings, whereas I don't ever wear earrings. I don't even have pierced ears.

There's one other character in *Clean Break* based on a real person. In chapter 13, Em falls when running to her dad and breaks her arm. She's taken to hospital by Jenna Williams' special driver Bob in his silver Mercedes.

When I'm doing book tours all over the country I have a lovely, jolly, fair-haired gentleman called Bob driving me everywhere in his Mercedes. Look out for him if you ever come to one of my book signings. He'll be very happy to say hello!

*Jacqueline Wilson*

# ✰ HOW WELL DO YOU ✰ KNOW EM?

What's the special name Dad has for Em?

✰ ✰ ✰

What are the names of Em's
little brother and sister?

✰ ✰ ✰

What present does Vita get
for Christmas from Dad?

✰ ✰ ✰

Who is Em's favourite author?

✰ ✰ ✰

Where does Dad take Em and her
brother and sister on a surprise trip?

✰ ✰ ✰

Which new talent does Em discover she
has when on holiday in Spain?

✰ ✰ ✰

What's Grandma's new boyfriend called?

What colour streak does Mum put in Em's hair?

⭐ ⭐ ⭐

What's the name of the bookshop where
Grandma takes Em to meet her favourite author?

⭐ ⭐ ⭐

What's the name of the new friend
Em makes in the queue?

**Answers: Emerald; Maxie and Vita; a reindeer ballerina puppet;
Jenna Williams; the beach; swimming; Eddie; green; Addeyman's; Molly**

★ ★ ★ ★ ★ ★ ★ ★ ★

# ☆ EM'S STORY CORNER ☆

Em is absolutely brilliant at making up
stories – maybe you like writing too?
Have a go at using the story prompts
below to start you off on some exciting
adventures of your own devising.

*What happens when . . .*

. . . the pictures you draw come to life?

☆ ☆ ☆

. . . your pet starts talking to you?

☆ ☆ ☆

. . . your best friend develops a magical ability?

☆ ☆ ☆

. . . you enter a television baking competition?

☆ ☆ ☆

. . . you see a flying reindeer?

★ ★ ★ ★ ★ ★ ★ ★ ★

# ✫ WORD SEARCH ✫

There are ten important words in
Em's life hidden in the grid below –
can you find them all?

| F | Z | O | E | C | G | H | W | K | K | E | J | C | Z | A |
|---|---|---|---|---|---|---|---|---|---|---|---|---|---|---|
| W | A | Z | K | R | M | R | Q | R | H | U | I | D | B | D |
| E | H | I | R | F | I | K | N | E | M | P | U | X | Y | J |
| B | P | Y | R | T | H | K | L | A | F | U | G | S | A | J |
| D | Y | M | I | I | O | F | Z | D | X | C | M | R | S | M |
| P | L | N | J | A | E | R | W | I | N | W | D | R | V | Z |
| X | G | J | T | Z | E | S | D | N | E | I | R | F | M | H |
| J | S | I | H | Z | A | O | J | G | H | A | Z | Z | Y | U |
| B | V | A | G | U | P | C | G | O | H | D | V | W | E | H |
| K | G | B | Z | N | N | Q | G | Y | Y | O | F | Y | N | G |
| U | D | U | I | F | G | M | P | R | F | U | G | Z | A | R |
| P | J | H | D | H | G | V | Y | Q | I | V | R | Q | R | Y |
| L | S | Z | Q | K | C | S | W | I | M | M | I | N | G | M |
| D | A | D | O | L | M | V | H | K | Q | O | O | D | X | N |
| S | C | C | B | Z | W | N | C | G | A | H | A | Z | M | A |

DAD  FAIRIES  FRIENDS  GRAN
MAXIE  MUM  READING  SWIMMING
VITA  WRITING

## ☆ VISIT THE WEBSITE ☆

There's a whole Jacqueline Wilson town to explore! You can generate your own special username, customize your online bedroom, test your knowledge of Jacqueline's books with fun quizzes and puzzles, and upload book reviews. There's lots of fun stuff to discover, including competitions, book trailers, and Jacqueline's scrapbook. And if you love writing, visit the special storytelling area!

Plus, you can hear the latest news from Jacqueline in her monthly diary, find out whether she's doing events near you, read her fan-mail replies, and chat to other fans on the message boards!

**www.jacquelinewilson.co.uk**

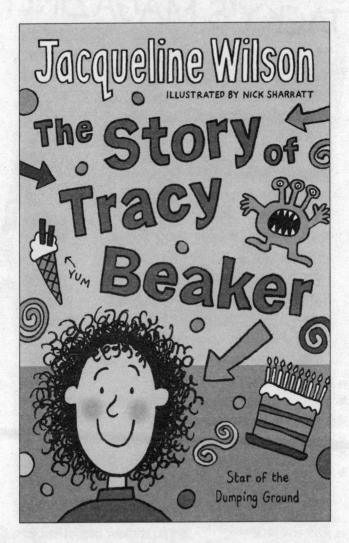